Moon Spell

~a Tale of Lunarmorte novel~

SAMANTHA YOUNG

Copyright © 2011 Samantha Young

All rights reserved.

ISBN: 1466437715
ISBN-13: 978-1466437715

All Rights Reserved. No reproduction, copy or transmission of this publication may be made without written permission. No paragraph of this publication may be reproduced, copied or transmitted save with the written permission of the author. This work is registered with and protected by Copyright House.

Other books by Samantha Young

River Cast (The Tale of Lunarmorte #2)
Blood Solstice (The Tale of Lunarmorte #3)

Slumber (The Fade #1)

Drip Drop Teardrop, a Novella

Blood Will Tell (Warriors of Ankh #1)
Blood Past (Warriors of Ankh #2)
Shades of Blood (Warriors of Ankh #3)

Smokeless Fire (Fire Spirits #1)
Scorched Skies (Fire Spirits #2)
Borrowed Ember (Fire Spirits #3)

To Mum, Dad and my brother, David.

For Always Believing.

1 – Hidden

Caia recognized his ruddy face and chocolate eyes from long ago memories, memories that poked and prodded her heart and set it racing, her ears burning hot with the sudden onslaught of blood rushing to them.

Life was going to be very different from now on.

His dark eyes settled on her only companion these last ten years, Irini, and shifted from soft concern to steely determination.

"It's finally safe for you to return her, Irini." His gaze flickered back to Caia as if trying to gauge a reaction.

Irini sagged down into the sofa beside her as her wide eyes flew to his face. "Dimitri, please promise this is for real."

"I know you have lived alone for a long time… but it's finally time to come home."

"What happened?" Irini breathed in disbelief.

Dimitri managed to fold his huge, muscular body into the small armchair before them. He looked to be somewhere in his forties but she knew he must be much older than that. He was an Elder after all.

"Lucien returned five years later to reclaim the pack."

Caia looked to Irini and then to Dimitri. She had been seven when she was taken from the pack but she still remembered Lucien, a young headstrong male who'd had a fall out with his family and ran away from the pack at fourteen years old. It was less shocking than it sounded, since a fourteen year old lykan was more than capable of taking care of himself, especially one who was bred to be an Alpha. A year after Lucien's departure, his father, Albus, the Pack Leader, had been killed by The Hunter.

Irini looked shocked at this news. "And the pack welcomed him with open arms?" She shook her head.

"After Albus' death, no one else tried to track The Hunter. With Lucien being a.w.o.l. everyone was caught up in who was going to be Pack Leader. While you were stuck in this goddess-forsaken place under Marion's protection, we were trying to reassemble our lives. Then Lucien returned. He didn't give us much of an explanation…but he told us what he had been up to." Dimitri's eyes narrowed. "He killed The Hunter, Irini."

His eyes went to Caia as did Irini's. She was puzzled by their guarded looks. Shouldn't they be happy? The Hunter had killed her father and mother and had wanted to murder her as well. If it hadn't been for Irini taking her into isolation The Hunter would have killed her. As it was, Albus, a beloved Alpha, was gone because of his determination to see herself and Irini returned to the pack. After all, her father had been Albus' greatest friend.

"I suppose that gained him his rightful place then?" Irini sneered.

Dimitri shook his head. "No. Magnus and I were willing to see him take up the mantle of Pack Leader-"

"How could you after-"

His hand came up between them shushing her accusation. "Irini, he is extraordinary. Everything his father was and more. He just … needed time."

"Time?"

"Time." He sighed and then narrowed his eyes. "Of course there were others, some of the younger males who felt the need to challenge him. We felt it only right that those who challenged him were truly willing to risk everything for the mantle …"

"A Lunarmorte?" Irini breathed.

He merely nodded.

Caia looked between the two of them again. Irini was somewhat closemouthed about the pack and their way of life, but this she had mentioned. Lunarmorte was an ancient ritual amongst their specific lykan pack, dating back to their Portuguese origins. If there was a break in the hereditary line of the pack, or a rebel rising within it, it fell to a Lunarmorte to determine the Pack Leader. It was fought during a full moon and only happened once in a blue one.

"As you can imagine, in the end only one challenged Lucien. Lucien killed him within seconds."

"Who?"

"Dermot."

Irini look unsurprised by this. "You sound impressed. I assume my brother's done well as Pack Leader these last five years?"

Dimitri stood, towering over them, stating his authority physically. "It was Lucien's idea to keep you here protected. There are still some Midnight followers of The Hunter on the loose, and we had no way of knowing if they still held plans for Caia." He nodded towards her, using her name for the first time. "Instead he wanted to wait until we had built a safe new life."

"And I'm guessing you have now that you're here."

"Yes. Lucien has managed to integrate us into a good town. All the families have good jobs. Lucien's got this furniture business going ..." he drifted off at the sour look that passed over Irini's face.

"We've been left here for ten years, Dimitri."

"I know."

Irini shook her head in anger. "No! You don't know. I have been left here with Caia while my brother gallivanted around goddess knows where - not allowed to come home for my father's funeral, not allowed to even speak one word to my mother!"

"Irini-"

"And now my brother just expects me to come home. Like nothing happened? Like he didn't abandon us? Goddess-"

"Irini!" he growled, and Caia slid back in her seat. She had lived with Irini's tantrums for ten years. Not entirely sure how to deal with the behavior she had merely listened as Irini hissed and snarled about her predicament. Apparently Dimitri didn't have the patience for it.

Irini's eyes widened and she inched closer to Caia.

"You would not even be able to return if it wasn't for Lucien. As soon as he learned of Albus' death he hunted The Hunter and he won. He didn't send for you immediately because he wanted to make sure you had somewhere safe to come home to. And now you have."

"And if we don't want to?" she whispered, although Caia was sure she didn't really mean it.

Dimitri glanced at Caia. "You must," he said, throwing Irini a meaningful look.

Irini turned to her and reached for her hand. Clasping it she nodded in agreement.

"Do we leave now?" Caia enquired.

Dimitri looked startled by her question. It was the first time she had spoken. "Yes," he eventually acknowledged. "While you pack, I'll summon Marion so she can finally drop the protection spell."

2 – THE UNKNOWN

They traveled by plane. Caia sat by Dimitri leaving Irini alone to her thoughts.

"You're apprehensive." Dimitri smiled kindly down at her. She brushed her hair behind her ears so she could look up at him. Being so close to him she could smell his own individual brand of beautiful damp earth that identified him as a lykan. It brought with it unprepared for memories. In truth, she sighed inwardly, she had been so long without the pack that if it hadn't been for her weekly runs with Irini in her true form, she would have felt almost entirely human - a socially deficient human, but one nonetheless. Looking into Dimitri's eyes she saw blurry images of a life long gone, a life where she had felt a part of something. But it no longer existed, and now they just expected her to what... be one of them again? The pack didn't know her anymore, and she didn't know them.

"Of course," she muttered in reply to his question. "I'm the returning orphan who stole away a member of their pack."

He laughed. "Irini? She'll get over it."

"Really? Because that's what lykans do, they get over it?"

"Well," he shrugged, his eyes twinkling, "True we're a temperamental bunch, but Irini has never blamed you for what happened. No one has."

Right.

"Good to know." She turned away and gazed straight ahead with her jaw set in determination. Out of the corner of her eye she felt him nod in understanding. It was irritating - she wanted to hide where he couldn't see through her false bravado.

"Well, as for having no immediate family that will change. It's only right you go back to staying with Irini and her mother Ella... and Lucien, of course."

"What about Uncle Magnus?" she tried to sound indifferent. Magnus was an Elder like Dimitri and Ella, and in truth, the lykan she remembered the most.

"He's there ... waiting for you, too."

They're all waiting for me, she sighed, trying to tamp down the butterflies in her stomach.

"You've been living a civilized life with Irini in a big town much longer than the pack has. I'm sure you fit in at high school much better than any of the pack kids."

She turned towards him at that, smiling wryly, shaking her head. "Uh well ... I wouldn't say I exactly fit in."

"What would you say then?"

"I ate lunch in my car."

"Oh."

The door was thrown open, his tall, gangly assistant, Lars, almost falling into the room in his hurry to get to him.

"The spell!" Lars heaved as he lunged at him, out of breath.

"You've been *running*?" he asked him incredulously, following the trail of sweat that trickled down his assistant's forehead.

Lars nodded, bending over, his hands braced on his knees as he tried to regain composure. "I … I … I still … haaaa … haven't … mastered the communication spell you taught me." He gulped for air again, wheezing as he flopped down beside him.

"Well obviously you rushed with a purpose, spit it out."

Lars turned to him now, his eyes bright with excitement. "The protection spell is down. She's unprotected."

He stiffened at the news "You're certain?"

"Positive. I've been on Marion duty for two years. Her protection spell on the girl has been dropped."

A tingling of anticipation and bitter hate rushed through him and he found a slow, predatory smile stretching his lips. It was his first smile in many days. "Well you know what this means…"

"It's time?"

"Activate our agent."

"They're on their way, Magnus." Lucien strolled into his sitting room. Magnus was sprawled across an armchair while his mother Ella poured them all coffee.

The Elder looked up at him and smiled brightly. "I get to see my Cy again."

"I forgot how fond you were of the little brat."

"You were too busy chasing anything in a bra at the time to notice the little blonde kid who was constantly perched on his shoulder," Ella pointed out wryly.

"I remembered her," his voice was low, tone a warning. Instantly a chill fell over the room.

Ella stood slowly, her eyes narrowed on her son. "No one would dispute that you were very aware of Caia's existence, Lucien. I meant only that you avoided her, so you knew nothing about her."

"She was a cute kid." Magnus chuckled, straightening up beside Ella, his warm teasing bending the steel of tension emanating from Lucien. His huge hand came down on Ella's shoulder. "You got any more of those cookies I like?"

Nodding stiffly she left the room, muttering under her breath about sensitive dogs.

Magnus turned to the Alpha, a young man he considered a son. "You need to ease up, Lucien. Everyone is well aware that you've fulfilled your responsibilities to this pack and that you intend to fulfill the one that's on that plane. Defenses down, please."

Lucien grunted. "Thought I was the Pack Leader?"

Magnus laughed and cuffed him across the head, pushing him into a seat. "You're still a pup."

After Ella had returned with more coffee, and it was clear the tension had eased between son and mother, talk returned to pack business.

"So when do they get here?" Magnus queried, his excitement evident. Lucien had been so wrapped up in dealing with what was to come from Caia's return that he had forgotten about the one person who was actually looking forward to it. The girl had never known anything but Albus and Ella, and in particular, Magnus.

He didn't want to burst Magnus' bubble but they needed to get serious about the situation. "Magnus-"

"Don't start with that tone... this is a happy occasion. This is what your father fought for: the safe return of Rafe's daughter."

Lucien sighed. "I know. And I am happy to finally have that realized. Goddess knows for this reason only I will have made the old man proud. But Magnus," his hard silver eyes searched Magnus' happy ones, "We have to deal with the pack."

Reluctantly, the Elder nodded in agreement. "Stupid, scared judgmental lykans."

"That may be, but they're our lykans, and we've got to make sure the pack is happy."

Ella cleared her throat from the corner of the room. "I've already made sure most of the mated females are clear that they have to welcome Cy home. It's the young I'm worried about. Most of them will see her as an outsider anyway. They still fear what they don't know, and they fear possible war ... *and* the fact that she's more competition for our males ..."

Lucien smirked. "Yeah, I see where you're going. Fine." he heaved, slapping his knees in determination and standing to his feet. "We'll gather the whole pack here. It must be made perfectly clear to them that Caia is part of this pack's future; that mention of the war is to be kept to minimum, absolutely nothing about her parents ... *and* I want a full pack welcome."

"Oh I dunno." Magnus shook his head, his forehead wrinkled with anxiety. "Full pack welcome? That could be a little overwhelming. Lucien, this girl has lived without a pack for ten years. Irini would only have been able to teach her so much."

"Irini will have taught her well," Ella replied tersely, her look defying him to speak otherwise.

The Elder looked between son and mother, their posture relaxed but their eyes determined.

He knew when he was outvoted. "Pack welcome it is then."

3 – Home?

"Have we got everything?"

The noise was overwhelming. Why were there so many people going places, and did they have to be going there today? Someone bumped into her and nudged her into someone else. Was it warm here? Jeez, they really needed more windows in this airport. She wanted to brace her hands on her knees and tuck her head between her legs in an effort to breathe but she refrained. She didn't want to look like a weak idiot who succumbed to panic attacks at the littlest things.

"Caia?"

They were here already. How did they get here so fast? She wasn't ready yet.

"Caia?"

Pain flared up her arm and she looked down to see the cause of it. Dimitri was gripping her tightly by the elbow, so tightly he was close to cutting off her circulation. She gazed up at him stupidly, her eyes clearing at his worried expression.

"You alright?"

She needed to get herself together. Lykans didn't act like this. They didn't wimp out. Nodding, she pulled from his grasp.

"You got everything, then?" he repeated, looking a little annoyed now. "We really should get going."

Oh my.

Those earlier butterflies suddenly burst into flames in her stomach, the metaphorical residue covering her lungs in an attempt to suffocate her.

"I... uh... I just need to... use the bathroom."

"Fine. Hurry up."

She slammed the door of the women's toilets behind her and stumbled over to the sinks, striving to get her breath back. *Stop thinking about it, stop thinking about it, stop thinking about it, stop thinking about it.* But the more she said that the more her head whirled. She was returning to the pack. The actual pack. *The pack.* Holy Artemis, what the hades-

Caia suddenly stilled at the beginnings of a rumbling noise.

Was that her heart?

No, she shook her head, looking around as the rumbling increased in volume. Caia exhaled, her eyes widening as she stepped back from the sinks. The entire row before her was shaking ferociously, the rumbling coming from the pipes. What the...

All the taps blasted open and water streamed out into the sinks with the power of a fireman's hose, the original rumbling now deafening. Ceramic cracked and fell away from the walls and water billowed over the sinks and onto the tiled floor.

"Caia?"

She whipped her head towards the door where Irini stood looking shocked. The water abruptly stopped.

"What the Hades?" Irini indicated the watery mess in front of her.

She gaped at her stupidly. "I have no idea."

"Well, come on, quickly, before you get the blame," she snapped, grabbing her by the wrist and dragging her outside.

"How could I get the blame?"

"Just come on."

Her breathing had regulated once they left the airport. However, her breathing was feeling a little forced again. They had traveled a good hour or so from the airport, driving down the state highway and pulling off at the sign for Woodrush Point. Woodrush Point wasn't too small a town but it was much smaller than the city she and Irini had been living in for the last ten years. They drove right on through so Caia could check it out. She was too nervous to really pay attention. Dimitri pointed out his own house but Caia could only nod numbly, a vague impression of a moderate sized white cladded home with a driveway and a huge tree out front registering with her. Over the tops of houses in the distance she could see the woodland, the woodland that followed the highway and seemed to encapsulate the whole of the town. It was easy to see why the pack had picked this place. Lots of trees to play in. With a sigh, Dimitri took a right past a car garage and they were out onto the highway again. Twenty minutes later, the Elder slowed his car, turning down onto a track in the woods that had been widened, the trees cut heavily back from it. The gravel kicked up under the tires and through the overhanging branches Caia could see flashes of white.

At last they pulled up into a huge circled clearing. In the center sat a large white home with an old-fashioned wraparound porch. She drew in a deep breath.

"The whole pack is here?"

Dimitri nodded, his kind eyes brimming with understanding. "It's the only way to really welcome you, kid."

Irini on the other hand was bubbling with excitement. Before Dimitri had even parked, she was out of the car and running for the house. He merely laughed and finally shut the engine off.

"Ready?"

"No." She shook her head nervously. "But then I'll never be ready for this moment so we might as well shove my ass out of the car, right?"

He chuckled getting out of the driver's side. "That's the spirit."

Caia had no idea how she managed it, but she got out of the car and slowly followed Dimitri up the front steps to the porch. Her lykan ears could hear the sound of Irini crying happily and people murmuring warm words of welcome to her. She could hear her growl Lucien's name, but then start crying and mumbling 'I missed you brother' over and over.

I guess all is forgiven, Caia thought wryly.

As her light foot came off the last step she was seized once more with absolute anxiety, undiluted and pure. She steadied herself, taking a deep breath. She couldn't let them see how nervous she was. Dimitri had swung open the porch door, and was now throwing open the main door with as much grace.

"Well hell!" he shouted in amusement. "Look at you all … you didn't eat everything already, did you?"

"I managed to save you some food," a laughing female voice called back to him. "I hid it from these vultures for you."

She could hear Dimitri smack a kiss on someone and the pack chuckled lightly. The sounds of familiarity between them all sent another wave through Caia's stomach, but before she could melt into an anxious puddle on the floor Dimitri's head popped back in sight around the door frame. "Come on, kid."

A sudden hush fell over the room. Slowly, she pushed her way through the porch door and stepped into a beautiful open hallway with a wide antique staircase winding up from the center of the room to the next floor. Bracing herself against her own insecurities Caia turned to the opening to the left of the hallway and took in the sight of the large pack that was to be her new family. There looked to be about thirty of them - large feral, handsome males, young and older; beautiful, athletic females; small children with enquiring eyes.

This was Pack Errante.

The whispering immediately began as all eyes drank her in from head to foot.

Lucien was stunned. Whatever he had expected it was not this. Caia stood at the front door gazing at them, her cat-like green eyes still and calm as she took in the sight of the pack staring back at her from his large living room. He could tell by her tentative step towards them that she was more nervous than her placid expression let on. He watched in satisfaction as people came forward to shake her hand politely.

They had taken his warnings to welcome her to heart.

As distracted as she was by his pack she had yet to notice him, and so he took pleasure in the moment to really look at her. Her heritage gave her away, he decided… as did her smell. She wouldn't realize it, how could she? She didn't know. She was as graceful as the lykan she was but looked more fey than wolf. Moreover, she held herself far more coolly than the rest of them. She was like water to their fire.

He was stunned by his reaction to her.

He had not expected attraction.

He watched her sleek, light eyes widen every now and then depending on what kind of welcome she was given. Her skin was pale compared to the golden glow of his and his pack's skin, her figure slight compared to the curvaceous shapes of the other women. He frowned, wondering how much of a problem this was going to be - she didn't look like one of them at all. She stopped suddenly in the middle of shaking one of the mated female's hands. Her bright gaze flew across to the other side of the room and widened.

"Uncle Magnus?" Lucien heard her whisper. In an instant Magnus had crossed the room and had the little lykan wrapped in his big arms. Lucien smiled at her surprise and then her tentative happiness. *This is a good sign*, he decided. It was a show of family, and it seemed to ease the tension radiating from his anxious pack. Magnus of course, Lucien realized wryly, seemed unaware of any tension.

"My Artemis!" Magnus exclaimed heartily, holding her slight weight away from him so he could inspect her. "Look at the size of you, Cy. I wouldn't have recognized you on a clear, full moon!"

She teased her lip shyly between her teeth. She shed no tears, Lucien realized. Not like Ella and the others who had wept at his sister's return.

He watched as Magnus lavished praise over her. She blushed prettily and kept holding onto him.

Suddenly Magnus looked up at him and turned the young lykan towards him. "Caia," Magnus' voice rumbled in the room, "I'd like to introduce you to Lucien: Pack Leader."

Before this moment she had been bemused, but happy, in the arms of Magnus, his laughing eyes and coarse voice drowning out the buzz of wariness and apprehension she felt oozing from the rest of the pack. Although some seemed genuinely glad to have her returned, excited by her presence for reasons that were not yet clear to her, others - in particular females - viewed her as a threat. She could feel it on them, see it in their eyes...

The bubble of happiness Magnus had momentarily created popped as he spun her around to introduce her to the Pack Leader.

She had vague memories of a tall, dark haired teen that was moody and forever in some kind of argument with his parents. He barely spoke to her, never looked at her, and at times she had even felt like he despised her. There had been things said, arguments started, and she had been sure they had something to do with her, but as a child she'd had no comprehension of what they meant.

That dark haired young man had turned into a powerful lykan. He towered above most of the others in the room, excluding Dimitri, Magnus, and one young male who was gazing at her with an almost cruel twist to his lips. However, it was safe to say that standing at least at six and a half feet, with broad shoulders and an intimidating musculature, there was no question as to why this man was Alpha here. His face was all sharp lines and hard angles, his eyes like liquid mercury. She couldn't believe any human would believe this man was not supernatural. His gaze bore into her, intent, watchful, waiting. His scent flooded her - an overwhelming combination of earth and rain. In fact, she decided, he smelled exactly the way the air did on the verge of a lightning storm. She held her hand out formally to him, and determined not to be intimidated by the brute, held his silver gaze with her own soft green one. He seemed to search her eyes for something and when finding nothing, clasped her small hand in his own large one. A rush of heat exploded like a million darts of fire shooting up her arm. *Damn*, she knew her eyes had widened in surprise. She was only appeased when his eyes mirrored her reaction. In reflex, she tried to pull her hand out of his, but he held firm, pressing his callused skin into her softness.

"Welcome home," his low timbre spread a second rush of heat through her body. The feeling frightened her enough to give her the strength to pull away from him.

"Thank you," she whispered. She wanted to tear her gaze away, was embarrassed even by the long look they shared, annoyed by the outrageous arrogance she felt pouring from this lykan, but she couldn't. If it hadn't been for Ella suddenly pulling her into a hug, she may have stood looking at her Pack Leader like a fool for the entire night.

"Ella." She managed a small smile, inhaling her adoptive mother's scent of earth and lavender. She remembered that smell more than the tall woman holding her. It told her of the affection this woman had once given her, and for this she hugged her more tightly.

"Now that you've met everyone," Ella gave a sweeping gesture with her arm to indicate the pack crowded around her living room, "I suggest we let you unpack and get some sleep."

The room was huge. A large four-poster bed dominated the center of the space. The grand oak of the posts was matched in the twin bed-side tables, the large wardrobe to the back of the bedroom, the cabinet facing the bed, and the chunky desk to the right of the door, not to mention the beautiful flooring that would feel cool on a warm summer's night. The walls were painted in the softest green; bedspread and curtains matching. Caia was surprised by the color choice. It was so tranquil, so her. *How did they know?* She turned questioningly to Ella, who was standing patiently at the door. "This is all for me?"

Ella chuckled and stepped inside, taking her backpack from her and dumping it pointedly on the floor next to Caia's suitcase that had been placed at the foot of the bed. She straightened, her grey eyes smiling at her. She was a slightly older version of Irini, Caia thought. An Elder also, many years older than what she looked, she was as beautiful as all the other lykans, with her svelte physique and long sable hair. "Yes. We wanted you to feel as at home as quickly as possible."

"Thank you." Caia really didn't know what else to say, her eyes widening at the laptop that was sitting on the desk for her. "I like green."

"Good."

They were quiet for a moment, just gazing at each other awkwardly. The sound of raucous laughter from downstairs seemed to shake Ella. "This will all pull together, Caia."

She merely nodded, not quite so sure. She felt so much like an outsider.

"We wanted you to have the utmost privacy. And if you can't sleep there is a television and DVD player in that cabinet." She pointed to the monstrosity facing the bed. "There should be plenty of films to choose from in there too. Laptop's yours. Internet is up and running so …"

Caia couldn't take it all in. "Thank you. You know you didn't have to do all this … I never …"

Ella shook her off uncomfortably. "Shush. It's done."

She received another hug and a motherly kiss on the cheek before the older woman gracefully slipped from the room.

Caia sighed. *Oh boy.*

She thought about unpacking for two seconds before deciding against the idea. It would just make everything that little bit more permanent. Instead she strolled to the window facing the back of the house and gazed over the small backyard with its footpath leading into the thick, dark woods surrounding the house. To anyone else, those woods encroaching so close to the home would have perhaps been off-putting. To a lykan it was a dream to have the cover of the trees at your fingertips. She thought of her and Irini having to drive to the woods in order to run. Irini was so happy to be home. She'd barely looked at Caia once since their return, and she was beginning to wonder if the woman perhaps resented her far more than she had let on. They hadn't a close relationship, but they were kind and considerate of one another. Irini had worked as a secretary during the day, a cover to fit in with the humans. The apartment was already bought for them so they had never needed to worry about rent, and the pack had set up an account for Irini to pay food and bills, and whatever else they needed.

Caia had lived her young life listening out for any small scrap of information Irini gave. She knew returning to the pack was all Irini thought about. It was how she got through her meaningless job each day. Caia was different. Irini had told her little of her parent's death despite Caia's pleas. She knew only that a member of the Midnight Coven had targeted her and her parents, and that the pack had been thrown into a miniature war with a man they called The Hunter. The reason why she and her parents had been targeted had not been explained to Caia. When she was younger she had thought her heart might break with the pain of not having known her parents, and of not knowing why she'd had them ripped from her, but as she got older she learned to stop asking, and the need had dissipated to a gentle thrum tucked somewhere under her skin. It had though left her with a desire to be free of everything; the tiny apartment they shared, the obligation she felt towards the pack for having protected her. Caia wanted to travel the world - to have tasted the full scope of moonlight.

The war, however, made leaving the pack impossible.

The pack doesn't think like that anyway.

They mated, had baby lykans, and lived their lives all together. Safety in numbers. Lucien's face suddenly appeared before her eyes and, even though there was no one there to witness her wayward thoughts, she felt her face warm. *Well that can just stop right now*, she snapped at herself. *The Alpha. Pfft!* Turning, she caught her blushing reflection in a long mirror attached to the wall. Caia frowned. She was quite small, she realized, studying her body and features. Her kinswomen seemed taller, fuller-figured, their features darkly exotic with their tanned complexions and rich-colored hair and eyes. They were all so beautiful compared to her pale scrawniness. Why didn't she look like them?

The sound of laughter from downstairs pulled her from those thoughts. She was exhausted from the upheaval of her once - yes dismal - but quiet existence, to this 'my goddess they're everywhere' existence, but *not* weary enough to sleep. She tip-toed out of the room, not wanting to alert the rest of the pack downstairs - thirty pairs of hyper sensitive ears made that a difficult task. But she managed to make no sound as she crept down the hallway, gazing at the simple black and white photos of what she could only determine was the surrounding country. She encountered a large bathroom and then a gymnasium. Why, she thought, Lucien needed a home gym when he naturally looked like one big muscle she had no idea. She was about to leave the gym and creep further on when she heard Ella and Irini in the next room, whispering to one another.

"You were lonely," Ella was stating grimly.

She received no answer, but the rustling of clothing suggested Ella and Irini were hugging.

"It was just so strange being without the pack. Not to mention frightening, being out there … alone. I felt cold all the time."

"You had Caia for company."

"I know."

There was a moment of silence and Caia's body tensed in anticipation. Maybe Irini really did hate her.

"What is she like? I mean really like, Irini?"

Why does Ella sound so worried?

"She's good, Mom."

"Good?"

"Yes. Good. Kind, I mean. Gentle."

"Gentle?"

Again, another stretched silence.

"Gentle, Irini? Lykans aren't gentle."

"I mean in nature. She's soft. Calm ... I dunno."

"I noticed. She's so still. So not ..."

"Like us," Irini finished. "I know. I noticed it more and more as she grew. There was no fire, no tempestuous outbursts ... you can, you know ... tell-"

"Ssh," Ella abruptly cut her off, and Caia realized she must have been heard. Quickly, and as quietly as she could, she returned to her new room and shut the door softly behind her. She heaved a sigh leaning against it, trying to catch her breath. She laughed but it wasn't a happy sound.

"How did I get here?" she asked softly.

Caia shook her head. She couldn't let their conversation upset her, and she couldn't let herself dwell over what Irini was about to say or it would drive her crazy. She'd had enough crazy for one day. When the sounds of the pack leaving, one by one, filtered up to her room, and the final kicks of the gravel driveway as their cars drove off could be heard, Caia cracked open her window and carefully scaled the house, descending to the ground with the ease and agility of her species. Dropping to the grass with a soft thud, Caia breathed a sigh of relief. She let the smell of the damp earth and wet wood overwhelm her. It was wonderful. Glancing up at the moon, shining like a brilliant orb of comfort in the dark sky, Caia thanked Artemis that it had made an appearance from behind the clouds tonight; she could peel the anxiety of rejoining the pack from her human skin, and run.

Quickly, she removed all of her clothes, the night air cooling her anxious flesh.

And then... she let the change happen.

She felt the pain of her skin transforming. She could feel every piece of fur pushing through, and ironically, the pain was like that of someone pulling a strand of hair from your scalp - that unexpected wince, but thousands of winces all over your body. She relished the burning pain of her muscles stretching and straining as they reshaped. The almost satisfying cracking of her bones as they said goodbye to the girl and hello to the wolf. Rushing blood in her ears drowned out her surroundings as her heart grew larger in order to pump the extra that her other self needed. She watched her nose grow in front of her eyes into a long snout, felt the sharp watery pain of her eyes elongating, her vision defined and clear-perfect.

Caia came down onto all four legs, enjoying how soft the ground felt against her hard, leather paws. Then she laughed, a hoarse animal sound, at the tickling sensation that was left over when the change was complete.

It was exhilarating to be a wolf.

The trees were suddenly a blur as she took off through them, racing around the obstacles and leaping over bracken. She felt the warm glow of the moon on her soft pelt and knew that it didn't matter about the pack being home. She already had a home, and she was running with it, the night whispering comforting words in her ears as she soared.

Lucien stayed as far back from her as possible. She seemed lost in the feel of the run, which he was glad for, otherwise she would have felt his presence before now. Caia was extremely fast - faster than the other females of the pack - and this pleased him. She was a beautiful lykan but more than this he could feel her joy from a distance. Caia was part of the night, of the woods. He knew the others were worried about her, he himself was worried. But watching her, keeping her safe, he realized that perhaps she was more lykan than they could ever have hoped for.

That night Caia lay in bed, listening to the hushed noise of the woods outside her bedroom window. Leaves rustled in the gentle breeze, animals scurried among bracken and twigs, birds chirped sweet goodnights to one another. As her eyes bored into the moonlit ceiling above her head, she thought of the pack, of Magnus in particular. Of Magnus who brought with him a rush of memories of her father. Of losing him. Of her clinging to Magnus for safety, security, love.

A night long ago flickered across her eyes, Magnus holding her close as he rocked them on a rocking chair she'd loved, Albus seated across from them, a fire blazing and casting shadows over him as he regaled her with the history of the war. Irini sat at their feet, rapt. Magnus had told Albus she was too young to understand but Caia remembered hushing him, making his chest shudder with laughter beneath her. She wanted to hear, she wanted know, even though she was afraid. Magnus had sensed it, burying her closer to him, and Albus had leaned back in his armchair, his eyes faraway, somewhere else, as his deep rich voice resonated around the room…

The war has been raging for centuries; a war that breathed beneath human reality, lost in the labyrinth of their legends and folklore. It is a silent war of soundless screaming and invisible bloodshed.

And like many wars it is built upon a mindless prejudice.

The ancient Greeks had it right. They were not naive enough to believe they actually had any control over their fate. No. They knew the gods controlled all. They didn't believe a good crop that year had anything to do with luck in a poorly cultivated land - no, it was Demeter who'd blessed their farm. They didn't believe that one man was far superior in battle than another, thus tipping the scales of a battle in their favor - no, it was just that Athena took a liking to him, and so aided the warrior. Yeah, the gods were capricious, unmerciful, loving, and selfish; there was nothing that contented them more than making the human world their chessboard and humans their own personal chess pieces.

They gloried in their own supremacy.

But one day... the gods of ancient felt a pierce in each of their hearts. It was the day humans, who had once been under their thrall, who had loved them, and feared them, and prayed to them, turned their back upon the gods and their heart to a new one. As the centuries passed the gods were no longer worshipped by any human, no longer feared, or loved, or prayed to. The barrier of space that had allowed them to come down from their mountain, and interfere in the lives of humans strengthened as time forgot them. Indeed, their very existence would have been expunged from earth if not for their legacy: their children, the supernaturals of their own creation that still looked to the heavens and believed in them. They are the children of Gaia: Mother of all the gods. **We** *are the children of Gaia.*

We are the culprits of the silent war waging beneath the humans' very noses.

On one side of the war are the true instigators, those who call themselves the Midnight Coven: a community of magiks who believe above all in their own superiority. Gaia, perhaps in her infinite wisdom, had long ago blessed a number of humans by allowing them a taste of her blood, so that as the years turned a generation of magiks arose; witches and warlocks with elemental power, a race of children who would forever pray to her, and through them time would never forget her. They believed, however, that those lesser supernatural beings were abominations not fit to live side by side with humans, much less themselves. Their distaste for lykans – like us - and vampyres not only enraged those they sought to exterminate, but also their own kind: magiks who believe in the equality of the races. We call ourselves the Daylight Coven. You see, to our mind, Midnights hunted not abominations, but their own people, humans transformed and blessed by the gods, creatures descended from Gaia herself. This gaping split in beliefs between the dark and light Covens is shared by the magiks' contemporaries, the faeries of Hemera. As a primordial deity, the Goddess of Daylight and Sun, her children are almost equal to that of Gaia's. They are descendants of a young queen, who had sold her soul to her favorite goddess for the opportunity to take on the form of any living thing she wished, so that she would always know her enemies, and they would never know her. From her, to Hemera's delight, sprang a race of shapeshifters who held the power to take on the appearance of anything born of nature. They're mischievous and tiring, but useful spies on either side of the war.

Hades, God of the Underworld (and grandson to Gaia), created a race of children familiar to humans within their folklore: vampyres. His children were the souls who passed through the River Styx without toll, and whom Hades returned to earth to extort in blood, payment from those who dared to leave them to travel into the underworld without coin.

And the youngest of the children of the gods are the lykans: we are fierce, strong wolves consecrated with the power of regeneration. In the dying years of the ancient gods, Artemis, Goddess of the Moon, the Hunt and of Beasts, was called down to earth by the last human who prayed to her. His son was dying from his battle wounds, and Artemis in gratitude for his loyalty, replaced his son's wasted heart with that of a wolf's. To her supreme pleasure, for she had always been a competitive goddess, her own race of children was born, and she too is remembered by us.

In the early years of our existence, we children of the gods, cousins, wandered the world of humans at peace with one another. But the ages passed, and our forms changed - lykans producing lykans by humans, diluting the werewolf blood, and eventually becoming a non-violent breed of our original selves.

In other words, this rational (most of the time), articulate lykanthrope narrator before you is an evolved version of my ancestors.

Anyway, because of the vengeance taken upon Hades for his kidnapping of her daughter Persephone, the goddess Demeter changed the course of the vampyres, blessing them with fertility and diluting their undead souls with the light of humanity, until eventually adhering to the laws of the Daylight Coven, they withheld from killing humans.

The last century has seen calm before the storm. The Midnight Coven dissipated into a mist, a near invisible layer of destruction that touched those who did not seek it. We Daylights have waited with bated breath, aware that our enemy had retired a fearsome aggressive strategy. The Dark Coven has become wary of the war spilling over into the world of the humans, and instead has embraced a far more threatening silence.

But the attacks have started.

The subtle desolation of individual supernaturals: communities of vampyres, and packs of lykans; packs like ours, who want nothing to do with the war and have lived in relative peace.

Other than the faeries who share their beliefs, only the daemons, the beasts created from Midnights own magik, are allied with the Dark Coven. The Daylight Coven, with her allies of faeries, lykans and vampyres, can only hope to act fast enough to discover the target of the next Midnight attack in order to prepare the target for war.

Some supernaturals escape disaster.

Others slip through the cracks - targeted without warning, without preparation.

That's how the war stands.

But our pack, Pack Errante is untouched by the war, unpolluted by the world and as long as I have breath within me... it will remain so. You can sleep peacefully at night, young Caia, knowing Uncle Magnus and Uncle Albus are guarding your dreams...

Pulling back from the memory, Caia was surprised to feel the wet, hot slide of a tear down her cheek. She remembered how, despite Albus' history lesson of the war, she had gone to sleep that night feeling safe and protected and loved. It was only a few months later she was taken from the pack and hidden away. She hadn't felt safe since. Lying under the pack roof again, she wondered if that contentment would ever return to her.

4 – SCHOOL RULES

Irini had never been much of the mothering kind (having been so young Caia couldn't really blame her) so Caia was used to being up by the crack of dawn and taking care of herself. She had hoped to have the house to herself on her first morning in Lucien's home but as she crept downstairs she could hear the sounds of the living coming from the kitchen. Taking a deep breath she walked with what she hoped was a sedate confidence into the room. The sedateness and the confidence disappeared at the sight of Lucien at the kitchen table, hunkered over a paper and sipping coffee.

"Morning." He looked up in greeting. His metallic eyes were as hard as the day before, and he produced no smile for her. She answered exactly in kind. "You're up early," he observed.

She nodded, not really sure how to engage in small talk. Instead she shifted her weight onto her other leg, waiting for him to tell her where to find some breakfast. He said nothing, merely stared.

"Um," she glanced quickly around the kitchen and spotted some cereal on a far corner, "Can I help myself?"

He nodded. "Of course. This is your home now. There's coffee in the pot and orange juice in the refrigerator; bowls are in the second high cupboard to your left and utensils in the drawer below it."

Caia sighed inwardly. Obviously he was a 'throw 'em into the deep end' kind of guy. She was acutely aware of his gaze on her the entire time as she gathered her cereal, nervously finding her way around the kitchen. Being a usually very even-tempered lykan she was surprised by her overwhelming desire to snap at him and childishly ask him if he wanted to take a picture of her so he could cease staring. Yesterday he had definitely bothered her in some way. Evidently the feeling wasn't going away any time soon.

When she finally found a seat at the table across from him he was still staring. She tried to ignore the heat that blossomed beneath her cheeks at his scrutiny.

"Yesterday must have been a little overwhelming for you."

She looked up from her cereal. Goddess, he was huge. Struck dumb apparently, she merely nodded. Her reaction to him produced a quirk in the corner of his mouth which she suspected was a smile … or it could've been a smirk …

"You don't talk much do you?" His brow was furrowed and he was looking at her as if she was an unusually complex puzzle.

"Only when I feel like I have something useful to say. I prefer to listen. You learn a lot more a lot faster."

She was surprised when he actually chuckled, giving her a glimpse of his perfect wolf whites. "I suppose you're right. Magnus would approve." He smiled softly as he sipped at his coffee. "Big guy missed you."

"I missed him too."

"He all you really remember?"

Caia stopped eating and looked at him. His tone and the way he observed her told her that his question wasn't merely out of curiosity. Pack Leader was beginning his 'back to work' interview. "I remember Magnus the most." She looked over at the bulletin board he had pinned to the kitchen wall. Along with deadlines, memorandums and notes to one another, there were a number of photographs of the pack. "I do remember Ella though. I remember you, too." Her eyes turned back to him. His gaze was still fixed on her.

"I thought maybe you were too young. I must have taken off just before you left with Irini."

"Yeah, but I have this vague memory of you, too. Young, moody, avoided me like the plague." She smirked.

His face remained expressionless as he replied, "You were a kid. I didn't have time for you."

If he thought she was going to be upset or insulted by this he could forget it. Instead she continued, "I remember Dimitri and some of the other, older pack members that I met last night. I didn't think I would but... I don't know... they unearthed some latent memories I guess."

Lucien sighed. "Still, it's been a long time."

Caia finished her cereal and got up to rinse her bowl. "Are you asking if I'm ready to rejoin the pack?"

He made no sound but when she turned around he was standing right before her, so close she could feel the heat from his body stroking her skin. "You're seventeen and you've never ran with a pack," he murmured.

"No," she whispered. "And no, I don't think I'm ready."

He seemed surprised by her admission and pulled back a little. "You have a lot of learning to do. From what Irini has told me we have nothing to worry about your integration into the local high school. But you'll need to learn how the pack works."

"Learn how?" She gulped nervously.

Lucien stepped forward again. "From experience. We've moved our monthly run up to next Sunday. You run with us."

Her heart started racing a little faster at the thought. Unlike the pack she had begun to feel and enjoy the privacy of the change. She had to share her favorite thing? With these strangers? With him?

He seemed to understand, his large hand pressing onto her shoulder in what she guessed was supposed to be a reassuring gesture. Instead it felt a little threatening. "Loners don't fit well into packs, Caia. I won't have them in my pack. Especially not you."

What did that mean?

She started to ask but was stopped as his 'talk' triggered a far more pressing question. "I have to start learning huh?" she led.

Lucien nodded, all stern and in alpha-mode.

"Fine. Here's a question you can answer that Irini wouldn't." Caia watched curiously as his face hardened and he tensed as if ready to face something unpleasant. "Why … why did The Hunter pick me? My parents?"

The big lykan heaved a heavy sigh and leaned back against the counter crossing his arms over his chest. Caia almost gulped at the way his muscles rippled with the movement. "At first," he began softly, his eyes not quite meeting hers, "We thought it was an attack on the pack, that we were one of the unfortunates the Dark Coven had targeted. It was confusing because we're a small pack. Small packs don't tend to draw the eye of The Midnights. But we later realized it was a member of the Midnight Coven acting independently from it. Your mother and father had taken a trip and apparently while on it they came across a Midnight: The Hunter. Recognizing what they were The Hunter tried to take them out. Your father killed one of The Hunter's followers, and The Hunter tracked them back to us, and to you. He killed your parents and tried to get to you, but you were well protected. And as you know he didn't give up. He came back for you four years later and again, he failed."

Caia blinked, trying to take this new information in. "It doesn't make sense."

"Why?" Lucien frowned. "What?"

She shrugged. "Why, when he got to the pack did he just kill my parents? Surely he would have went back to the Coven and told them about the rest of the pack?"

Lucien shook his head, looking irritated by her questions. "No. He acted without orders from his coven when he killed your parents. He would have been reprimanded for his attack rather than rewarded. Besides, The Hunter is called exactly that because he was insane, obsessive. He wanted your parents dead and any trace of them – that would be you – gone, and that was that. There is no rhyme or reason to creatures like him."

Before she could reply a bright voice called from the doorway, "Oh how good it is to be home to a kitchen that's bigger than a cereal box."

Both she and Lucien turned to Irini who was practically crooning as she danced into the kitchen.

"Our kitchen wasn't that bad, Irini," Caia mumbled, not only reeling from Lucien's story, but also from having overheard Irini's conversation with Ella the night before. Irini didn't know she had heard and she didn't want her to. Instead she let a placid mask slide onto her face.

"Ha. Speak for yourself." Irini shook her head as she poured herself some coffee. "It was tiny for a girl who was used to … well … this." She gestured with both hands as she smiled at the room.

"Glad you're back." Lucien chuckled as he held out his own mug to be refilled.

Caia's mind wandered from the kitchen as brother and sister bantered easily with one another as if the last ten years of separation hadn't existed. She was lost in a mass of whys and hows - furious and relieved all at the same time. She was furious to realize that if her parents hadn't taken some stupid trip away from the pack they would still be alive; furious that Irini hadn't already told her and saved her years of worrying about the pack... which led her to relieved. She was relieved that her parents were the targets of some weird, persistent hunter, and not a soldier of war sent by the Dark Coven to wreak havoc and destruction upon their small pack. Boy, if she'd known that for the last ten years imagine the hours of sleep she wouldn't have missed. She looked at Irini and wanted to be angry at her, she really did. But it wasn't in her nature to growl and hiss and spit, and neither was it in her nature to hold a grudge. And how could she when Irini's face was flushed with a happiness she had never witnessed there before; her eyes light with what she could only imagine was a new lease of life. She looked so young. As if the ten years had melted away and she was eighteen again. No, Caia couldn't be angry with her. Irini was ecstatic to be home. If it hadn't been before, it definitely was obvious now, that she had genuinely been too upset to discuss anything of the past with her young charge.

Her thoughts and musings were interrupted by the sound of the doorbell, and both Caia and Irini's heads snapped towards the sound in alert. Lucien's eyes narrowed as if he understood; for years now both of them had been living quiet, isolated lives where the doorbell ringing signaled a potential threat.

"It's OK," he reassured them. "It's just Jaeden for Caia."

She frowned at this, her mouth forming an 'o' shape in question. But he was up and out of his seat before she could speak, returning to the room a few seconds later with a tall brunette who looked about Caia's age. The first thing Caia noticed about her was the warm friendliness in her eyes, but as her gaze travelled over her she realized that the girl, with her piercing blue eyes and luscious curves and curls, was as outrageously attractive as the rest of these creatures. She had a feeling her self-esteem was going to take a serious hit among this crowd.

"This is Jaeden." Lucien nodded to Irini and Caia. "Irini, you remember Jaeden, Dimitri's daughter?"

Irini smiled brightly at the mention of the Elder and got up to hug the girl who was at least three inches taller than her. "Of course,"

Jaeden laughed at that and Caia was warmed by the pleasant sound of her chuckle. The girl's blue eyes found her. "Do *you* remember me, Caia?"

Gazing at her in concentration she had the vague impression of a gangly young girl who used to have to coax her into playing with her. She nodded and smiled tentatively back at her. "Yeah. I do."

Lucien looked pleased. "Good. Jaeden's taking you to school."

"School?"

"School." He nodded, enunciating the word as if she were an idiot. "It's Monday. I've got it all sorted out. They're expecting you. I told them that your guardian died and as a minor you had to come here, so there shouldn't be too many questions about your transfer one semester from graduation."

"Oh. O-K." She was thrown by this news. She thought she might have at least been given time to settle in.

Obviously that was wishful thinking.

Goddess, she couldn't wait until she graduated at the end of the school year. "I'll grab my backpack."

It was awkward at first, climbing into Jaeden's …

"Can I ask… what is this?" Caia indicated the rust-colored rust-bucket she had just climbed into.

Jaeden laughed. "I think they call it a 1982 Buick Skyhawk."

"Wow, I've never even heard of a Skyhawk before."

"She runs like a dream," Jaeden reassured her, lovingly stroking the wheel of her car.

"Sorry, I didn't mean to be rude."

Again the girl laughed. "Don't worry. I'd fear for my life as well if I was taking my first look at this baby. But she's fine. I swear."

Caia didn't have a chance to answer because Jaeden launched straight into the questions. "So, what's it like living with Lucien?" She giggled, her eyes sparkling in excitement. She ran her tongue along the tips of her top row of teeth. "He's really rather delicious."

It was Caia's turn to laugh. "I suppose. To be honest, I really don't know what it's going to be like living with him. So far... pretty intimidating. The man is huge."

Another laugh. "Well, you get used to that. I forget you haven't been around males, they're all huge but yeah I suppose Lucien is one of the largest, he'd have to be to be Alpha, there are the Elders though and maybe Mal and you're just about to meet him." She had an endearing way of rushing one sentence into the other as if afraid she wouldn't have time to discuss everything she obviously wanted to.

"Mal?"

"Malek," she explained. "He's Morgan and Natalia's oldest son."

Caia looked at her blankly. She couldn't put names to faces quite yet.

"Mal," Jaeden insisted. "You'll recognize him when you see him; huge, dark and kind of twisted."

The vague image of a lykan she'd noticed standing heads above others in the living room last night flitted across her mind. "Actually

I think I know who you're talking about. He goes to school?" she asked incredulously.

"Uh-huh. All the human girls are in love with him."

"And you?"

Jaeden sneered. "No thank you. He's so arrogant. You think Lucien's bad? Ugh. Mal messes around with Dana. Watch out for her by the way."

"Dana?"

"Yeah, you're going to meet her. She's Daniel's twin sister, and you'll meet him, too."

"Anyone else I should know about?" Suddenly she was extremely nervous. She forgot that there were pack members her age, other than Jaeden, that she'd have to see every day. Would they all be as friendly as Jaeden? Somehow she didn't think so.

"There's Sebastian. He's the same age as the twins, so is Mal. Their little brother Finlay too, he's fifteen."

"So ... you're a senior, like me?"

"Yeah, so is Alexa. But, you know, we eat lunch with Mal, the twins, and Sebastian as well. So, you'll have nearly all of us to keep you company."

That's not what Caia was worried about.

Jaeden was full of questions about her life in isolation with Irini, and Caia tried to answer as many as possible, but the girl was like a machine gun. Before she knew it they were pulling into a parking lot behind a large, modern school building. There were lots of kids already buzzing around; the air filled with the scent of teenage pheromones. Caia blew out air between her lips. Although Lucien had come up with an excuse no doubt the school thought it incredibly inconvenient her transferring one semester away from graduation. It wasn't going to interfere with her school work, but she had a 3.8 G.P.A. and had scored a 1250 on her SAT's last year, which meant she would have to go another round of explaining to teacher's why she hadn't applied to any colleges. Irini had told her she couldn't because they didn't know when the pack would call them home, and since she didn't know where home was going to be, she couldn't even apply for a college nearby. However, Dimitri had told her there was a community college here. Joy.

Yup, she sighed, feeling the twinge of disappointment again that she wouldn't be able to go off and enjoy the thrill of college life elsewhere.

"Here we are." Jaeden smiled at her. Her eyes suddenly softened when she took in her expression. "You'll be fine. I promise. And if people think it's weird that you're transferring at such... well... a weird and pointless time in your high school education then we'll do what we usually do. Ignore their very existence."

Caia smiled tremulously, grateful to the girl. Her immediate acceptance of her into the pack was going to get her through what she guessed was going to be a rough first year. She took a deep breath, her nostrils filling up with those icky pheromones and a hint of damp earth scents mixed with individual fragrances she would soon come to identify with the other pack members her age.

They were close.

"I hope you're right." She blew out her breath and got out of the car.

"I'm always right," Jaeden teased. "Come on, the guys will be waiting,"

Jaeden led her across the parking lot towards a group of teenagers standing around a Ford SUV.

"Jaeden?" she asked, as her eyes wandered over the group. She recognized, due to his immense height and build for a sixteen year old, what could only be Malek. He was standing in the center with five other teenagers crowded around him.

"Yeah?"

"Do you know why Lucien pulled me out of school and back to the pack now? Doesn't it seem like a stupid time? Couldn't he have waited until after graduation?"

Jaeden smiled. "I heard my dad talking about this with Mom."

"You were eavesdropping?"

She shrugged, and grinned cheekily. "Well... anyway, I heard him say that Lucien wanted you to connect as much as possible with the pack. He thought a semester at school with lykans your own age would do that."

"I guess that makes sense." In actuality she wasn't entirely convinced by that excuse but it was just then that Mal looked up as they approached and any overhanging anxieties she had over Lucien's reasoning disappeared. She felt Mal's black eyes burn through her from head to foot. He murmured something to the others and they all turned towards her. Caia was struck by disbelief that humans could possibly think these 'kids' were just like them. They moved with an unbelievable grace that bordered on predatory.

"He's doing it again," Jaeden grumbled.

"Huh?"

"Looking at you like you're a snack."

Caia was confused. *Who? What?* "Huh?"

"Didn't you see the way Mal was looking at you last night? You're fresh meat, baby."

Caia winced at the thought. From what Irini had told her, when pack males turned sixteen they were fully matured (somehow she doubted that) and were more than welcome to start sniffing around the females to find a possible mate. Vice versa for the females. Caia had no intention of becoming involved in this part of the lykan life cycle.

No mating for her.

No. Uh-uh, Haaades no.

"Hey guys." Jaeden smiled as she drew up to them, standing as close to Caia as possible. She was surprised by how comforted she was by this small gesture of protection. "You all remember Cy, right?"

"Jae." A tall blonde stepped forward first smiling widely, his eyes twinkling as he turned to Caia. "Hey Caia, I'm Sebastian."

Caia was somewhat transfixed by him at first; he had this feral quality to all his movements, and of all the lykans she had met thus far he was quite simply the most beautiful - if it was possible to describe someone so masculine as such. The contrast between the smooth, aristocratic sculpturing of his face, and the sinewy wildness of his physique was intimidating; in fact he bordered on damn right scary, except for the gentle light that played in his eyes. Finally, Caia managed to nod back with a smile in acknowledgment, and was quickly introduced to them all. Finlay was the smallest - being only fifteen - as well as the shyest of the lykans surrounding her. The red-headed Daniel was as friendly as Sebastian, whereas his twin was practically spitting, her eyes flicking between Caia and Malek in outrage. Malek had stepped right up to Caia, closing her off from the others and deliberately surrounding her with his scent. He had reached out and taken her hand into both of his in a flirtatious shake. "Nice to finally meet you one on one," his voice rumbled.

OK, she could see why the human girls were falling over this one. He oozed charm and confidence and that illustrious hint of danger. *If only they knew.*

Fortunately for Caia - otherwise she might have found herself in a bitch fight with Dana - she didn't feel that explosive shiver of heat at his touch that a certain other someone had created. Instead she took a step back, releasing her hand from his and giving him a polite nod. His eyes narrowed but he covered his irritation with a smile, and stepped back to place an arm around Dana's waist. She curled into him like a happy kitten and flashed her blue eyes triumphantly at Caia.

"And this is Alexa." Jaeden indicated a girl who was so outrageously gorgeous it was almost sickening. She had long blue-black hair and large onyx eyes. She didn't say a word but her burning stare was enough to make the devil himself want to curl up and hide under the bed.

Caia had been right. Not everyone was going to be as friendly as Jaeden.

"Well guys," Mal was looking around at them all, "We better show Caia around."

Lucien *had* taken care of everything. All she'd had to do was go to the school office and pick up a timetable that had been produced based on the classes she was taking at her previous high school. Most of her teachers were OK. Only one of them, her calculus teacher, had decided to pull the 'stand up and tell us about yourself' card. The students were curious about her; they whispered to one another, the girls narrowing their eyes in instant dislike, the guys smiling and nudging at each other. Caia was used to this. Irini had explained that lykans were supposed to be natural predators. In their original state, when Artemis had first blessed them, their hunger had gotten the best of them and they had fed on humans, stealing their flesh and soul. The goddess' plan had been for them to mate with humans to produce a superior race she could call her own – it had taken a couple hundred of centuries for that to be the result – and one of her genetic gifts from way back then had been special pheromones that attracted humans. At first this had only made it easier for the wolves to hunt them but as the centuries turned so did they. Present day lykans were the product of the mixed heritage of lykan and human, and so their predatory instinct had died over the centuries; in other words they had learned to control their appetites. Nowadays it was rare for a human and a lykan to mate – supernaturals put this down to the fact that the humans no longer believed in the gods, and so Artemis was punishing them by refusing their entry into their wondrous world. Still, speaking of appetites, there was of course the odd lykan who got off on murdering humans - they were rogue, and always hunted down by their own kind. So thanks to the conflicting results of her special pheromones, Caia wasn't surprised when no one approached her to introduce themselves.

Back at her old high school she used to eat lunch in her car. Here, well, she had the pack.

Jaeden was in her French class just before lunch so they made their way to the cafeteria together.

"So," she smiled the wide smile Caia was coming to expect from this sweet girl, "How has the first morning gone at Human High?"

Caia laughed. "To be honest... not much different than before; classes are the same and the people are the same."

"Meaning... they don't talk to you?"

"Exactly."

"Oh you know why. We're all the same. Well ... except Malek. He's always flirting with the humans."

As they entered the cafeteria she zeroed in on the pack teenagers. They were sitting sprawled around a table together as other students looked at them, but didn't go near them. They were looking at her as well, huddling close to whisper when they realized she was with Jaeden. Caia couldn't understand how they were supposed to go undetected by these people when Jaeden and the others not only looked the way they did, but stuck together like ... well, like a pack. Nonplussed, she grabbed a roast beef sandwich and soda and followed Jaeden to the table. As it had been that morning, Sebastian, Finlay, and Daniel offered friendly smiles; Sebastian pulling out the chair next to him for her so she didn't have to sit beside Malek. Dana grimaced at her presence, while Alexa didn't even acknowledge it.

Malek smirked. "So?"

She shrugged. "It was fine. The usual."

He chuckled, his eyes sparkling. "You don't say much, do you? She," he pointed to Dana, "Never shuts up."

"That's what Lucien said." Caia shrugged again, frowning. Was she weird because she liked the quiet?

"What?!" Dana's mouth opened and shut like a fish, and everyone (even Alexa) laughed. Caia realized her blunder and blanched under the girl's glare.

"No. I mean ... Lucien said the same thing about me not saying much," her explanation produced nothing more than a look so evil she was sure the girl was muttering some kind of curse against her in her head. Caia felt Jaeden kick her under the table in amusement and decided looking at her new friend would only make her laugh, and *that* would definitely make these lykan girls hate her more than they already did.

"So," Malek continued again, ripping off a piece of his sandwich like the animal he was and then talking with his mouth full, "Were you dating anyone at your old high school?"

Her brows knitted together, as did Jaeden's she noticed. "No. It's frowned upon ... that's what Irini said anyway."

Malek laughed. "It's frowned upon. You're very cute, you know that."

"Mal," Jaeden warned.

"What?" He smirked, and then turned back to Caia. "It's frowned upon to try and make a 'forever' deal with one of them, but dating and sex with them isn't out."

"It's not in either." Sebastian glowered.

Daniel laughed. "Ah come on. It's harmless fun."

This set off a debate about the ethics of dating humans. She noticed they were very careful not to actually use the word human - it was always 'them'. Jaeden and Sebastian were obviously dead set against the whole idea so she had the feeling that it was definitely 'frowned upon' by the pack. As they argued among themselves, Caia noticed Alexa wasn't saying anything. Instead she was watching Caia with her dark eyes narrowed in dislike. Caia found herself flushing under scrutiny. If she didn't know any better she would guess that this lykan was threatened by her. Funny, how she worried only about returning to pack life - it had never occurred to her that she was returning at a time when many of the females were in competition with one another to snag the male of their choice. She sighed and looked at little Finlay who sat across from her watching the goings on. She caught his eye and shrugged as if to say she was sorry for causing the argument. He merely blushed and looked away.

"Ignore Mal," Jaeden finally spat, turning to Caia. "We're allowed to be friends with one of them, but nothing more."

Caia just nodded, while Malek chuckled at having so thoroughly annoyed the group.

His next question caused even more of an undercurrent, "So, Caia, you got your eye on anyone in the pack, yet?" He leaned back in his chair, puffing his muscular chest up and grinning at her, his eyes turning blacker than black with heat. She squirmed, completely uncomfortable with such blatant attention, but before she could say anything the table jumped and he let out a growl. Someone had kicked him hard and she had a feeling it was Sebastian.

Jaeden grinned. "Be warned."

Caia hid her smile. Oh boy was she in for a ride with this lot.

At least, she thought somewhat happily, she had a two lykans who were on her side.

As she climbed into Jaeden's Buick, Caia felt like she could breathe again. Her first day of school had gone as expected, except for the overwhelming sense of 'pack' that was being thrust upon her. It was strange but even when one of them hadn't been in a class with her she had felt their energy throughout the school.

She threw a tired smile at Jaeden. "That was interesting."

For once Jaeden didn't laugh. "Cy, I'm sorry about Mal."

"Don't be. I mean, he's harmless, right?"

"Oh yeah," she agreed quickly. "But, well, it can't be easy for you coming back to all this. You don't need a jerk like Malek sniffing after to you. It'll only cause you more grief."

Caia smiled at her. "Thanks."

"For what?"

Caia shrugged embarrassed. She had never had a friend so she wasn't quite sure how you were supposed to talk to one. "I don't know. For being cool I guess. You *and* Sebastian."

"Cool? About what?"

"Um... I don't know. You've just been really nice to me."

"Oh." She smiled, seeming to understand. "You mean because every other bitch at that table thinks you're a threat?"

Caia snorted at her bluntness. "Yeah, maybe."

"As long as you leave Ryder alone, we'll be cool my friend."

"Ryder?"

Jaeden turned to look at her quickly with a quizzical tilt to her brow. "You know, the big guy who was with Lucien last night. He's Lucien's best friend, and a Rogue Hunter."

She honestly hadn't noticed any big guy next to Lucien last night. She'd kind of been occupied with that big guy all by himself. "Nope. Sorry."

Jaeden laughed. "Well, you'll meet him soon enough. But things look good for us if you didn't even notice him last night. He's pretty hard to miss."

Jaeden grumbled away about French class and projects and, for what had to be the hundredth time that day, made Caia feel like she had been her friend forever. So lost in Jaeden's warm chatter, she was surprised to realize the car had come to a stop, not at the house, but in town.

"Why?" she asked, indicating their unfamiliar surroundings with a sweep of her hand. Jaeden nodded to the store they were pulled up outside of. It was called *Luar Furniture*. Moonlight Furniture. Caia snorted. "That's subtle."

Giggling, Jaeden reached into the back seat for Caia's backpack. "Yup, well Lucien's not exactly a subtle kind of Alpha."

"This is Lucien's place?"

"Yup. He asked me to drop you off after school."

"Why?"

Jaeden shrugged. "I have no idea, sorry."

"OK." Caia tried not to bite her lip anxiously. "Well, thanks for the ride."

"I'll pick you up tomorrow."

"Thanks." She reached for the door handle to get out, and then slowly turned back to Jaeden. "And thanks again for ... well ... you made today a lot easier for me."

The young lykan's smile lit up the whole car. "I'm really glad you're back, Cy."

Smiling despite herself, she climbed out of the Buick, and waving Jaeden goodbye made her way into the store. All was quiet with no one manning the front. Taking in a set of doors at the back of the room she guessed Lucien was in there somewhere. It was quite a large space; the showroom was filled with all kinds of pieces of furniture. She looked over some of it, awed at how beautifully crafted they were. His work came in all styles and woods. Stunning, she shook her head amazed, and then thoughtlessly turned over a tag on one of his rocking chairs. Her eyes widened. That's how Lucien was able to contribute so thoroughly to the already substantial pack inheritance. Entranced by the rustic whimsy of the chair, Caia didn't hear Lucien come up behind her.

"So how was school?" The dark voice rumbled in her ear.

"Wha..." She jumped, turning to face him, her hand floating to her heart in reflex. *Dammit*, she breathed closing her eyes. She did not want him to know how much he unnerved her. She opened her eyes at his gentle, mocking laughter.

"Didn't mean to scare you."

"Yeah, well, if your intention is not to scare people don't sneak up on them."

"I thought you would have at least smelled me. I picked up your scent, that's how I knew you were out here."

She shook her head gently, turning to look back at the rocking chair. She didn't want to analyze the rush of hot shivers that ran down her spine when he mentioned he'd followed her scent. She was acting like an idiot.

"I was too busy looking at this chair. It's really beautiful."

"Thank you," he acknowledged and took a step back from her. Her body appreciated it and was almost functioning normally again. "So how was school?" he repeated.

"Fine. I met Dana and Daniel, Sebastian, Alexa and Finlay, and their brother, Malek."

"How was that?" Lucien smirked, as if he knew how uncomfortable it must have been for her.

"Again, fine." No way was she going to let him think this was hard for her. From what she knew of Pack Leaders he'd treat her like a baby otherwise.

"Just fine?"

"They're nice."

Lucien laughed outright. "Nice. No. Uh, I've met Dana, Alexa, and Malek and they're not nice."

Caia rolled her eyes. "OK, well … the others were nice."

"And …?"

"And nothing."

He quirked an eyebrow in a very disarming way, something inside her stomach actually tugged in reaction to it.

"I'm trying to fit in with everyone here. If I have the Pack Leader running to them every time I've got a problem, they're going to hate me."

"So there is a problem?"

Caia felt a growl purring at the back of her throat. She never growled. "No," she said between clenched teeth.

He seemed to take the hint. Kind of. "Your classes OK?"

"Yes. Thank you. They're fine."

A moment of silence descended upon them. His silver eyes never left hers and she began to squirm, stepping from one foot to the other. She hated that he affected her so much. When she couldn't take it any longer she blurted out the first thing that came to mind, "Why did you ask Jaeden to drop me off here?"

She thought he wasn't going to answer. He stood staring intently at her for what seemed like hours, before he suddenly stood up from the desk he was leaning on. "I wanted to see how your first day at school had gone."

"Couldn't you have just asked me when you got home?" she asked a little mulishly, and then seemed to remember who she was talking to and blanched.

His eyebrows rose in amusement. "You're not used to people and the whole art of conversation thing yet, huh?"

"You talk about me like I've been locked in a dungeon for the last ten years." Caia sighed. "I have spoken to people you know. I've been known to converse with teachers, delivery men, the mail guy … all manner of folks."

He chuckled. "Were you rude to those people, too?"

She blushed. "I didn't mean to be rude. I was just surprised at being dropped off here, that's all."

He stared at her again, and Caia felt her blush deepen. Goddess, was the guy trying to make her appear like a bumbling backwoods person?

"I'm finished for the day. I'll drive you home."

What? Caia sighed in confusion as he strolled across the store and disappeared into his back room. "Couldn't Jaeden ha..." her voice trailed off as she glanced around, perplexed. "Never mind."

5 – Watering Hole

That night Caia experienced her first family dinner in Lucien's home.

The drive to his house had been interesting to say the least. Like her, he didn't seem to be much of a talker but it was obvious he was trying to make an effort. He had started by asking her questions about her old school, what were her teachers like, what subjects she enjoyed...

There was a lull of silence and he cleared his throat as if he was thinking of something else to say. Finally, a noise of what she assumed was satisfaction rumbled from under his breath as he apparently thought of a question to ask. "You like music?"

Caia nodded, trying not to smirk in amusement. The guy was pretty adorable, she decided, when he was attempting to be normal.

At that thought he glanced at her frowning, un-amused by her less than helpful response. "I'm trying here," he growled.

"I know." She nodded with laughter in her voice. "You don't have to."

The look he threw her was almost admonishing and she found herself frowning at the complexity of it. He was so serious, so worried. "Yes I do," he replied gruffly.

She was caught in his gaze, perhaps would have stayed trapped there if her brain hadn't suddenly realized that his eyes were on her and not on the road. "The road," she said pointedly, although her voice was a less controlled, husky version of itself.

Lucien smirked, flashing her a wicked look. Caia sighed inwardly, unsure whether he was mocking her for distrusting his driving or for her girlish response to him. *Men*, she groaned. How was she to cope with them after a decade without them?

"You OK?" Lucien chuckled.

"Fine."

"Fine," she heard him mutter, shaking his head. "Always fine."

At last, **she** breathed inwardly as they pulled up to the house. Just as she was about to release that sigh of relief, her eyes fell on the sight of two other cars in the driveway. She looked up at Lucien as they got out of his car.

He shrugged. "It's just Magnus and Ryder."

"They're here for dinner?" *Or are they checking up on me?*

She bit her lip anxiously as they walked towards the house. Ryder, Jaeden had explained, was the pack's own true blue hero. He was a Rogue Hunter, which meant he brought justice to any lykan who broke the law (killed humans for pleasure). Was the hunter inspecting her or something? Her thoughts must have betrayed her because Lucien explained to her, apparently amused, "You'll be seeing a lot of Ryder. He's a bachelor and can't cook so he either comes here for dinner, or goes to the diner owned by his mother, Yvana."

Oh, she let go of the breath she hadn't known she'd been holding. Her nerves really couldn't have taken the Spanish inquisition tonight.

As soon as Caia stepped through the front door she was brought to an abrupt halt by Irini who bounded at her, excitement sparkling in her eyes. "So how was school? Was everything OK? Were the others nice to you?"

Caia smiled. It was nice that Irini was still interested in her. She'd half expected that with her new found freedom she would want to forget the person responsible for her 'imprisonment'.

"Everything was fine. Really. I'm OK."

"You let me know if anyone bothers you."

Caia chuckled, remembering her giving a similar demand when she'd begun the ninth grade. "I will."

"Guess what?" Irini whispered, smiling widely as she changed the subject.

Caia's bag was heavy and her stomach was growling but she smiled as she asked the expected question. Irini didn't answer at first, just smirked mischievously at Lucien as he walked around them and into the kitchen. Caia could hear more than one male voice greet him, as well as the soft cadence of Ella's voice.

"We have guests."

Caia glanced meaningfully behind her at the driveway. "I gathered that."

"Aidan's here." Irini hungrily ran her tongue across the bottom of her top row of teeth.

"Aidan?"

"Ssh." Her eyes darted back to the kitchen. "Ryder's brother," Irini whispered. "The one that got away."

Her eyes were round, sad, but hopeful. Caia gazed beyond her to the kitchen door where she could hear those voices, before returning to Irini's face, capturing the anxiety there. It had never occurred to her that when Irini had ran into hiding with her that she was leaving more than her family behind.

"Irini, I'm sorry," she whispered, not even meaning for the apology to slip out.

"Wh-"

"Caia," Ella suddenly interrupted, appearing in the hallway. "How was your first day at school?"

She sighed. How many times was she going to have to lie today? "It was fine."

"Good. Come on in, Honey. Dinner's ready."

The sight that greeted her in the kitchen was more intimidating than having met all of the pack at the same time. The intimate setting, a table set for seven, four of which were for large lykan males, made Caia's smile of 'hello' tremulous. Magnus strode over to her immediately, drawing her to his side and giving her shoulder an affectionate squeeze.

"You OK, Kid?"

She nodded, craning her neck back to look up at him. His eyes twinkled happily.

"Cy, this is Ryder." He nodded to the lykan standing next to Lucien. He was about an inch smaller than the Alpha but shared a similar build to him. His face, however, was not nearly as severe as Lucien's. He had constant humor in his eyes and a warm quirk to his top lip. The lovably, shaggy, brown mess of his hair only added to his approachable appeal.

"And this is Aidan."

Aidan, an almost mirror image of his brother, except for the straight blonde of his hair, stood directly across from Ryder.

"Hi." They waved comically at her.

"You met them last night but I thought a second introduction might be needed."

Caia threw the Elder a grateful smile.

Ella had laid out a beautiful dinner; fillet of beef and all the trimmings, and Caia smiled secretly, thinking how Irini hadn't inherited her mother's ability to cook. For the longest time the two of them had enjoyed many a microwaveable meal until Caia was old enough to start experimenting with cooking. From then on she had cooked all of their meals.

She tried to offer Ella help but was shooed back into her seat between Magnus and Irini. She watched incredulously at the amount of food these males piled onto their plates. She hadn't touched her own plate yet, her eyes jumping from Lucien to Ryder, to Aidan, to Magnus, as they scoffed large amounts of beef down. Irini giggled beside her before elbowing her to get her to stop staring and start eating.

Ella laughed, obviously having noticed and understood the reason behind Caia's wide eyes. "Don't mind them, honey. They're just animals. You'll get used to them."

Ryder choked in amusement as he took a swig of water, and Aidan and Magnus joined his laughter.

Lucien merely shrugged. "What?"

This set them off again.

"Dude, we've frightened Caia with our non-existent manners," Aidan explained smiling at her.

"No, no-" she tried to protest.

Lucien frowned. "We're just eating."

"Caia's not used to eating at the watering hole." Irini giggled and smiled flirtatiously at Aidan, who winked in response.

"You *will* get used to us, Cy," Ryder assured her pleasantly. "Eventually."

Caia squirmed, hoping she hadn't made anyone uncomfortable. But as their amusement lingered she was put at ease enough to turn to her own plate.

"This is delicious Ella, thanks," she said politely between bites.

"Why thanks, honey," Ella preened, and then flicked her fork at the others. "This lot never say thanks."

A rumble of muted 'thank you's' swam towards her as the men spoke with meat in their mouths.

"Ugh, guys," Irini groaned, "Save the thanks and just chew."

"I don't remember you being so cheeky." Aidan smiled at her. Caia watched his eyes light with appreciation as they washed over Irini.

"I grew up." She shrugged.

"I noticed."

Magnus cleared his throat meaningfully, his eyes darting to Lucien, who had now stopped eating and was watching his sister and Aidan with a darkening suspicion. Caia snorted in her head. It had taken him long enough to realize they were flirting with one another.

"Sooo," Ryder drawled, breaking Lucien's scrutiny and saving his brother, "Caia, you like movies?"

Everyone except her and Irini groaned.

"What?" He laughed.

Lucien turned to Caia with an exaggerated look of weariness. "When Ryder isn't mutilating rogues with his bare hands, he's strapped to an armchair in front of his Blu-ray player."

"I love movies." Ryder shrugged, smiling at her.

Caia smiled tentatively back. She liked this lykan. "I like movies," she offered, grasping an opportunity to maybe bond with another member of the pack, particularly one who was so highly regarded by everyone else.

Ryder's eyes lit up. "Yeah?"

She nodded, stupidly pleased with the warmth in his gaze.

"Who's your favorite director?"

She mused for a bit as she chewed on a piece of exquisite beef. "Truth?" She smiled shyly.

He nodded expectantly.

"I can't quite make my mind up between Tarantino and Tony Scott."

The lykan let out a delighted laugh. "Well, I think I might be in love." He sighed dramatically, his eyes twinkling over mutual film love. Caia felt her cheeks go red with embarrassment at his attentiveness. She had never been a blusher before she returned to the pack. She bit the inside of her cheek willing the redness to go away and realized that, while she was blushing, Lucien had growled at Ryder.

Ryder ignored him. He smirked. "Have you seen *Underworld*?"

She chuckled, realizing where he was going with this, her eyes dancing with pleasure. "Yes, I have. I swear it was written by one of us."

"I think we could take those CGI lykans."

She laughed again, and he leaned conspiratorially across the table towards her. "Who do you think would win in a fight? Luci*en*," he indicated their Pack Leader with a tilt of his head, "Or Luci*an*?" he referred to the 'lycan' leader of the film franchise.

"What?" Lucien asked dryly. She suspected he didn't like being out of the loop on anything.

"Hmm." Caia pretended to think. "Luci*an* is pretty tough... he can squeeze bullets out of his head. I don't think even Luci*en* can do that?"

"Yeah, but silver hurts Luci*an*. Luci*en* would just laugh at a silver bullet."

"That's true."

"What the hell are they talking about?" Luci*en* grumbled to the rest of the table.

Magnus smiled. "I don't know, but it looks like Ry has found a fellow movie buff."

"Ry and Cy." Irini snorted like a teenager.

Aidan laughed with her and then quieted at the dirty look Lucien threw them.

Ryder smiled at Caia and returned to his food. She, however, was confused. She'd been getting along with the pack. Wasn't that what Lucien wanted? *Weird, moody, beast of a lykan.* She sighed and turned back to her own meal.

He would have to watch his reactions. Lucien gazed surreptitiously at everyone around the table. He was being overbearing and he knew it. His only excuse was that Caia's presence had left him feeling unbalanced. He was glad she was getting along with the pack, that she'd taken a shine to Ryder. Really. He was.

After everyone had finished dinner Caia offered to help Ella clean up. Magnus yawned and took his leave. Irini and Aidan on the other hand glanced at one another with an obvious hunger. Huh. He hadn't seen that coming.

"Uh, Irini, you want to go for a run... with me?" Aidan glanced nervously between Lucien and his sister. Irini didn't even bother to look back at her brother, just smiled beatifically at Aidan and nodded, jumping up from her seat in the same motion.

Ryder laughed softly as the two disappeared out of the back door and into the yard.

"I'm invisible," Lucien grumbled to his closest friend.

Ryder sighed, getting up. "Leave 'em be. I haven't seen my brother so happy in ages. He's been talking about Irini constantly since it was decided she'd be coming home."

Lucien was confused. "I can't even remember them having a thing together before she left."

"You were gone at the time."

"Hmm."

As they stood from the table Lucien's gaze was drawn to Caia as she cleared it. She tucked a lock of pale hair behind her ear before she picked up some plates, her long eyelashes fanning her cheeks as she looked down. He sighed softly. She seemed so fragile. She awoke every protective instinct he had.

Ryder clamped a hand on his shoulder, startling him out of his musings. He was guided from the room by that hand and out onto the porch. His friend chuckled, but it was more disbelieving than amused. He leaned against the porch frame and stared out at the woods. "Were you jealous in there?"

Lucien felt an unexpected blow of annoyance at that question. "What?" He frowned, more than irritated that he'd been that obvious. "No."

"You were certainly something."

Lucien shrugged, not meeting his friend's eye. "Well you were a little..."

"A little, what?"

"For a start, you said to the girl you were in love."

Ryder guffawed, "It was a figure of speech."

"It was flirting."

"I wasn't flirting with Caia. I was trying to make the girl feel at ease. She's had this pained look on her face since she arrived."

Ryder was right and he was wrong? Wow... that didn't happen that often to him. As Pack Leader he was pretty self-assured, and usually 99.9% right in most situations. Lucien sighed deeply and wearily. She was throwing him off his game. How was he supposed to handle all this? He groaned, running his hand through his hair in frustration. "I'm sorry... I'm just... It's just... I don't know, what-"

"Lucien, you can do this. You just have to keep your head on."

"By that you mean...?"

His friend glanced back inside, a sarcastic tilt to his mouth. "You can start by not getting all dreamy-eyed around her."

"Pfft! Dreamy-eyed. She's just a kid, I'm a grown man," he hissed, looking back inside, hoping their voices weren't carrying into the kitchen.

"She's not a kid. She's almost eighteen. And despite your status as Alpha I don't know if twenty four qualifies as a grown man."

Lucien glared at him. "This coming from a twenty four year old."

"Yeah but I never once stated I was a grown man." Ryder grinned cheekily making Lucien snort with laughter. Ryder shrugged, still smiling. "My point is… Caia's… different. And different can be fascinating."

"The only thing I'm fascinated by is her interaction with my pack. We're keeping an eye on her, but not that kind of eye. OK."

Ryder laughed, obviously unconvinced. "Man, whatever you say."

Lucien leaned casually against the doorframe of Caia's bedroom. He could hear her moving about in her bathroom, the water running. The laptop he'd bought her was open on the desk, but he couldn't see the screen from where he was standing. Her bed was neatly made, her room surprisingly tidy. She had placed her things throughout the space, which pleased him. When he'd checked earlier that day her suitcases were, worryingly, still standing at the bottom of the bed, unopened.

"Oh," her startled voice ripped him from his thoughts.

Lucien looked up and smirked at her. "Just checking you have everything you need."

She looked around the room and back at him smiling dryly. "More than."

"Good." He jammed his hands into his jeans, trying to think of something else to say. But then she moved from behind the bed to put a can of deodorant back by her toiletries and any thought of using actual words left him. His eyes unwillingly travelled down her body. She was wearing girl boxers and a vest. For a lykan who was shorter than most her legs certainly seemed to go on forever.

Suddenly, Caia cleared her throat, bringing his gaze back to her face. She'd scrubbed it clean, patches of her skin red from it. It made her look so young and so innocent. His heart beat harder at the thought of what was to come for her.

"Caia …" Lucien began.

"Yes?" she asked warily

Is she scared of me? He groaned inwardly. That was the last thing he wanted. "I want you to come to me if you need me. That's my job here."

She nodded at him, her green eyes round on his. "Thank you."

"You'll be OK," he promised, more for himself than for her.

Again, she nodded mutely, looking bewildered by his seriousness.

"Well." He heaved up from the wall. "Goodnight."

"Goodnight. Lucien."

6 – UNWANTED

Caia woke up the next morning feeling a little more optimistic about her return to the pack, and dare she say filled with that dangerous thing they called hope. Caia was calling last night's dinner a success. There had been a few awkward moments, but in general the mood had been jovial, and the brothers had actually seemed to like her. To her surprise, and perhaps disappointment (she was unused to the feeling, so she wasn't sure if that was what that little pang had been), Lucien wasn't at breakfast. With him having already left for the store, and with Irini sleeping late, Caia found herself breakfasting alone with Ella. Caia didn't mind in the least. In fact, she found the Elder's presence soothing, despite how anxious the lykan seemed about making sure Caia was OK and that her transition into the pack was going smoothly.

"You know, you have your father's eyes," Ella said, her smile bittersweet as she gazed down into her coffee.

"Were you good friends with my dad?" Caia asked curiously. This was really the first time anyone had offered a comment about her parents.

Ella chuckled at her obvious enthusiasm. "Actually, I was friends with Rafe before Albus was."

"Really?" She hadn't known that.

"We dated."

She hadn't known that either. She said so to her.

"It was a *looong* time ago. Your father was hunting a rogue and he stayed with my pack-"

Wait. "Your pack?" Caia interrupted in confusion.

Ella leaned back in her chair amused. "I was born into a different pack, Caia."

"Huh." She shook her head in amazement. "I didn't know that either. Or that my dad was a Rogue Hunter for that matter."

It was unfair that there was all this history, their history, her history, and she knew very little of it.

Damn The Hunter.

Ella frowned at her tone. "Irini didn't tell you much, did she?"

"It upset her too much to talk about the pack."

"Hmm." Ella was frowning again into her coffee, seeming lost in her thoughts, but Caia was eager to get more information about her father out of her.

"So you were in a different pack?"

"Hmm?" Ella blinked. "Oh. Yes. A younger pack. I met Rafe and we dated when he was with them. After he left I had a falling out with my family."

"What happened?"

"Well." She sighed heavily. "My father wanted me explore the possibility of mating with one of the males in my pack because he had the dominance of an Alpha, and they thought he might become Pack Leader. I hated the guy, so I ran away... to Rafe's pack."

Caia smiled, thinking of the result of that. "And you met Albus."

Ella chuckled, resting her chin on her hand, her eyes twinkling at the memory. "It was instant. We just wanted to be with each other. I laughed at first when I told my parents I'd mated with another Pack Leader... but... we never spoke again."

Having never been given the opportunity to know her own parents it seemed like a crime against nature that Ella's parents had, in their own way, made her as much of an orphan as Caia was. She mumbled an empathetic 'sorry'.

"Don't be. They were never the family this pack has been for me."

Caia nodded, letting that sit for a moment. And then... "So what happened with my dad?"

Ella smiled patiently, seeming to understand her curiosity. "Albus and Rafe had never been close. Albus really only trusted Magnus, and Rafe's father hadn't had the best reputation."

Caia took a breath, her mind spinning. "My grandfather?"

Ella nodded. "Yeah, he was quite the trip. He tried to take Albus' father's leadership from him."

"Wow."

"Yeah, but your father was nothing like him. I soon got Albus to see that, and they eventually became great friends."

"How..." Caia trailed off, wondering how her father could have been friends with them after having dated Ella himself.

Again, Ella seemed to understand. "Your father and I were just friends when I came to him after running from my parents," she explained.

"Oh." Caia smiled softly, looking down at her bowl.

"What?"

"It's just nice to hear something about him."

There was a moment of silence between them before Caia was jolted from her musings by the sound of Ella's chair scraping back loudly from the table. The Elder smiled down at her. "Wait. I have something for you."

She watched as Ella dashed out of the room and could hear her running quickly upstairs. The sounds of drawers being pulled open and shut and Ella's amusing mumblings filtered down through the ceiling. Caia wondered what on Gaia's green earth she was up to. It was a few minutes before she came sauntering gracefully back into the kitchen, something clasped tightly in her hand.

"Really," she explained, "You should have had these before we placed you into hiding. But everything was done in such a rush... anyway, you should have them now."

Caia took photographs from her hand. She gasped, gazing at the first one. It was of a toddler standing in between a man's knees as he bent down to huddle her close. Their green eyes matched, twinkling mischievously.

"Is this... my father and me?"

"Yes."

Goddess, her father had been just as gorgeous as the rest of them. She snorted as she looked at herself. Even as a toddler she had looked scrawny and weird, her head just a mass of blonde curls and her eyes too large for her face. There were two other photographs; one of her father by himself, gazing into the camera with this weary sadness in his eyes. The last of her and her father again, except a younger Magnus was in this one with them. Magnus had her on his shoulders and her father was trailing at the back of them, seeming to protest at her being up so high. His eyes were happier with her, his love palpable even in these old pictures. For the first time in years she felt that searing stab in her chest at the pain of his loss. She blinked, a tear falling onto the picture.

"Oh!" Ella jumped, and Caia looked up to see that the kitchen tap had come on full blast, splashing water onto the floor. She ignored it as Ella rushed to switch it off, muttering under her breath.

"Thank you." She smiled at Ella, brushing the tears from her cheeks. "This means a lot. Ella?"

Ella looked back her distractedly. "Yeah?"

"Do you have photos of me with my mom?"

Ella seemed to blanch. "Uh-"

"Hey, party people!" They both turned to see Jaeden bouncing in the doorway.

"Hi honey." Ella smiled brightly at her. She looked almost relieved by her appearance. "Well, I've got errands to run." She strode towards the kitchen door, brushing an affectionate hand down Jaeden's cheek. "Look after her."

She was gone before Caia had spoken another word.

Jaeden talked non-stop in the car on the way to school. Having learned that Ryder had made an appearance at dinner the night before, she was full of questions.

"And you... what... spoke to him?" she asked in awe.

"No, we had conversation through the power of thought," Caia answered sarcastically.

Jaeden rolled her eyes. "You know what I mean?"

"The guy is really not that intimidating. Not compared to Lucien."

"Pfft. Ryder makes Lucien look like a border collie."

Caia didn't believe that for a second. "He really is cool, Jaeden. You should try talking to him. Mention movies."

The girl shook her head in disbelief. "Here for two days and you managed to speak more words to that guy than I have in a lifetime."

Caia glanced sharply at her, worried that she may have annoyed her new friend already. She knew girls could get weird about guys, and Jaeden had kind of warned her. But no, she breathed a sigh of relief, Jaeden was smiling at her, her eyes laughing. "Movies huh?"

"Movies."

"I'll give it a shot."

"Class, this is our new student, Caia Ribeiro," the overly enthusiastic English teacher sing-songed. "Why don't you find a seat, Caia."

She wanted the floor to open up and swallow her. There were a few seats available in the classroom, but the problem was that one of the vacancies was beside Alexa. Everyone had seen her sit in the cafeteria with her yesterday, so if she didn't sit with her now it would look like she was snubbing her. Enter the real problem: Alexa's dislike of her. *Crap*, she thought, as she teased her lip between her teeth, nervously walking towards the seat. This was why she was a loner at her old school. She gave Alexa a small smile. The dark beauty almost snarled back at her. Groaning, Caia slid into the chair, fully aware of the students looking at her. It seemed like forever before the teacher finally started doing her job, and the class was once again preoccupied.

"You don't mind too much, do you?" Caia mumbled under her breath, aware that Alexa could hear her with her sensitive lykan ears. "About the seat?"

"You can sit wherever you want. It's a free country."

Caia let that go, listening to the English teacher as she handed out copies of Thomas Paine's *Common Sense* as part of the American Literature curriculum. She sighed. English Lit was her favorite subject, and she had sort of been hoping the class would be interesting enough to take her mind off the she-devil sitting on her left side, but she'd read that one already at her last school.

Around fifteen minutes into the class, an adult Caia didn't recognize walked into the room and murmured something in the teacher's ear.

The teacher sighed and turned to them. "Open your books and read the introduction while I deal with this," she grumbled, leaving the room. The hum of noise rose to an extraordinary level. Not that any of the noise pertained to the book that was being discussed.

"You understand I don't trust you," Alexa hissed from beside her.

Startled, Caia turned to the girl, curious as to what she had done to emit such a reaction. "Why?" She shook her head in confusion.

"You're not like the rest of us, Caia, and that's plain to everyone, even you." She sneered. "I bet you think you're better than us."

Caia's eyebrows puckered in confusion. There was that 'you're not like us' stuff again. She felt the heat under her cheeks and hoped to goddess Alexa couldn't see it. Unused to confrontations of any kind, Caia squirmed uncomfortably. "I don't think I'm better than anybody. You don't even know me."

"Whatever. Just know that I'm watching you. I'm not going to be taken in by your 'I'm so fragile and innocent' crap, and I'll make damn sure Lucien isn't either. And if you do anything to jeopardize the pack, I'll be the first one there to gouge a piece out of your hind."

She was being threatened? Unjustifiably? She felt a flush of what could only be described as white hot heat. It flickered over her skin, up her neck, and into her face. Of a sudden Alexa's chair was pushed with force away from Caia's body and into a startled girl, who started batting at Alexa to get off of her. The class was snickering, gazing at Caia like she had done it. Alexa's eyes flashed on her angrily, half collapsed on the girl, and half draped over the chair that was tilted up at a precarious angle from the crash. She was blazing with fury.

I didn't do it, Caia thought defensively, *why is she mad at me?*

"Girls, what on earth is going on over there?" The English teacher queried in annoyance as she re-entered the room.

Alexa got to her feet, glaring at Caia and pushing her chair back beside her. "Nothing," she replied smoothly, sweetly, not taking her eyes from Caia.

"Just stop the shenanigans."

"Sorry." She slid gracefully back into her seat and turned to Caia, whose eyes were still round as saucers with shock.

"You just made a huge mistake." Alexa smiled evilly. "Kicking my chair with the force of your strength in front of 'them'," she whispered, indicating the room of giggling human students, all of whom were still looking at the two of them. "Lucien would not be happy if he knew."

Caia shook her head rapidly. "I didn't kick you."

"Oh cut the innocent bull. Your ass is mine. You better keep me happy, or I *will* tell Lucien."

Caia tried to shake what had happened with Alexa, but found it difficult to concentrate on much of her classes before she broke for lunch. The success of last night's dinner was suddenly overcast with Alexa's clouds. Lost in her thoughts as she picked up some food for lunch, she only became aware of the whispering as she walked towards the pack. Looking around, she saw human eyes following her, and heard snatches of their conversation. They were discussing how another newbie had been sucked into the 'weirdo's' group.

Maybe they hypnotize pretty people.

Caia almost laughed at that, but was too concerned to make much of an effort. It did look odd, she thought, approaching these gorgeous creatures. Mal didn't even look like a teenager.

"Hey," she greeted them as she slid in beside Jaeden. She avoided Alexa's eyes.

"So, how was the second day thus far?" Jaeden chirped, biting into her sandwich with gusto.

Caia glanced at Alexa whose face was surprisingly smooth. She returned her gaze, but her dark eyes didn't narrow, and her full lips didn't pinch. What was she playing at now? "It was fine."

They began talking among themselves, with Caia barely paying attention. For some reason she was filtering them out and her hyper sensitive ears were filtering the human kids in. They seemed truly disconcerted by the pack.

"Don't you hear them?" she asked abruptly, and then wished she hadn't when the pack all narrowed their eyes in confusion at her.

"What?" Mal's eyebrows furrowed.

"Them." She subtly nodded her head, gesturing at the rest of the cafeteria.

"What about them?" Jaeden seemed concerned more than confused.

"They're whispering about us."

Dana shrugged. "So?"

"So, don't you think separating ourselves from the rest of them make us look more … conspicuous."

Jaeden smiled. "Caia, weren't you a bit of a loner at your old school?"

She nodded. *So what?*

"Loner's are just as conspicuous, but no one really said anything, right?"

Caia shook her head. "That's different. I mean, I just... listen to them. We unsettle them."

Alexa growled in irritation. "Look, they just see us as a bunch of really cool, hot kids who only like to play with other really cool, hot kids. They call us weird and whisper about us because that's what jealous biatches do. There's no need to worry." She heaved a dramatic sigh as if she was talking to a moron who should know this stuff already. "Lucien moved us into town gradually over five years. We didn't all just appear here together. One family moved in, and then another, and we gradually pretended to befriend each other over the years, just like ordinary folks. So … not suspicion." She gestured to 'them'. "Jealousy. Normal, teen, green envy. You should feel honored to be one of us … *Cy*."

Caia wasn't sure she was convinced. "Bu-"

"Why don't you *can* the questions?" Alexa glared at her meaningfully. "You don't want to annoy me."

What she really wanted was for her to go to Hades, but Caia was a little worried that Lucien might believe Alexa over her. It was definitely too soon to be getting in trouble with the Pack Leader. When it was obvious Caia wasn't going to retaliate, Dana snickered at Alexa's victory. It was a short-lived snicker, followed by an 'Ow'. Jaeden had kicked her under the table and was now turned towards Alexa. "Why don't you sheath your claws, *Alex*?"

"I hate that name," Alexa spat.

Jaeden smirked. "I know."

"Ladies," Mal growled, "Please. You're spoiling my appetite."

Caia looked down at her food, feeling Jaeden's gaze on her.

"So, that's why you didn't tell that spawn of the undead where to go?" Jaeden mused, as she drove Caia home.

"Pretty much."

"And you didn't kick her?"

"I swear to Gaia I don't know what happened in that classroom."

Jaeden shrugged. "Just ignore her then. You know Alexa's unbalanced enough to have pushed her own damn chair away from you."

"It was just... weird."

Caia was exhausted. She hoped everyday with the pack wasn't going to be as trying as today had been.

And she had been so stupidly optimistic this morning.

Jaeden pulled the car up to the driveway and Caia was surprised to see Lucien was already home; an unfamiliar car parked beside his.

"Is it always like this, do you know?" she quizzed Jaeden, gesturing to the vehicle.

Jaeden smiled in understanding. "He's Pack Leader, so you'll find the house pretty busy. You know, if you ever need space to breathe you're always welcome at my house."

It must have been the exhaustion but Caia felt her eyes watering at this young girl's kindness, her friendship like air to a trapped claustrophobic. Rapidly blinking to blot out the tears, she smiled wearily and thanked her.

"Cy?" Jaeden stopped her as she was getting out of the Buick.

"Yeah?"

She looked away from Caia, a deep frown creasing in between her eyebrows. She sighed, seeming unsure whether to say what she was going to say. She bit her lip.

"Jaeden," Caia prompted.

"OK." She sighed. "I... just... I want you to tell me if Alexa bothers you, OK."

"You know, contrary to popular belief I *can* take care of myself."

"I know. But I've known her my whole life and she's... manipulative." Her blue eyes saddened. "Her brother was Dermot... He died in the Lunarmorte against Lucien."

Caia's eyes widened at this new piece of information. "He tried to take Lucien's title?"

Jaeden nodded solemnly.

Caia was quiet for a minute, absorbing this. It didn't seem right to condemn someone for their family's mistakes. Then again, Alexa was pretty scary. Ruthless her middle name. But... nah... she shook her head. "That doesn't mean Alexa's the same. Look at my grandfather. He tried to take Lucien's dad's title and my father was nothing like him."

"Cy," Jaeden's voice was firm, "Alexa wants to be Lucien's mate. She'll stop at nothing to do it."

"I'm not standing in her way."

Her friend shrugged, starting the engine up again. "Apparently, you are."

Caia laughed humorlessly. "Are you all crazy?"

"Just promise if you need me you will come to me?"

"I feel like I've landed in a bad mafia movie."

Jaeden giggled as she started backing up the car. She leaned out of her window as she passed Caia. "You've lived the life of a human too long. Pack politics are normal for us."

Caia rolled her eyes. "Yeah, well, Irini could have at least warned me about them."

Jaeden pulled to a stop now that she'd turned the car around. Her face was suddenly serious. "Yes, she should have."

Caia raised a questioning eyebrow. These lykans confused the hell out of her. They were so blasé one minute and the next as serious as if someone had just killed their mom.

"See you tomorrow, Cy."

She waved silently as Jaeden pulled away, and then turned to look at the house. When she had stood in the airport unable to breathe for panic at the sheer thought of returning to the pack, she hadn't been afraid because she knew what was awaiting her, she'd been afraid because she *hadn't* known. If she had... well... she might have jumped on the next plane to anywhere else.

As she entered the house she could hear Lucien talking to someone in the kitchen and being answered by an unfamiliar female voice. What she really wanted to do right now was run upstairs to her bedroom, shut the door, and have an uncharacteristic crying session.

But that would be rude.

Heaving a sigh, she walked cautiously into the kitchen. Lucien had obviously caught her scent because he was looking towards the doorway when she stepped through it.

"Caia." He smiled, and she was surprised that he looked genuinely happy to see her. She tried not to blush and strolled slowly towards him, her gaze flicking between him and the attractive older blonde across from him.

"Hi."

"Caia, this Yvana, Ryder and Aidan's mother."

She smiled at the older woman, catching the resemblance now. She held out her hand formally. Yvana had been staring at her, expressionless, but as she'd stepped closer, freezing icicles had crept into her eyes, and she cringed back from Caia's outstretched hand. "I hadn't realized how much you look like your mother," she spat.

Caia flinched, completely taken aback. The venom in this woman's voice was uncontrolled and so heartfelt. First Alexa, now her?

"Yvana," Lucien's voice rumbled darkly in warning. Caia had never heard him use that tone before, but she was still too shocked by Yvana's reaction to look at him. She was caught in this woman's bleak gaze. What had she done to her?

"Griffin died because of your parents... because of you." Yvana was standing up now, trembling with anger and grief.

Caia looked to Lucien for answers. Who was Griffin? But Lucien's face was mottled with anger as well, the muscles in his forearms taut as he rounded the table. "You can leave now."

"Lucien," Yvana protested, her eyes breaking from Caia's as she realized how angry she had made him.

"What's going on?" Irini's voice drifted towards them from the doorway.

"You can't expect me not to be upset. That you would even expect me to be in the same room as *that*," she spat again, flicking her hand distastefully at Caia.

Caia recoiled as if she'd been hit. She staggered back, her mind roiling with confusion. This woman really hated her. Not the petty teenage hatred of Alexa, but real intense dislike. As if she had wronged her somehow. She felt the tears prick the corners of her eyes. She didn't want to be here. Where everything was unfamiliar and cold; where she was welcome, but unwelcome; where secrets hung in every doorway and no one trusted her enough to confide them. Instead of asking for an explanation, exhaustion defeating her, she turned and hurried from the room, brushing past a worried Irini who tried to stop her. But she didn't stop. Not until she was in her room with the door closed. The tears had cascaded down her cheeks now, her vision blurred as she stumbled past the bed, and into the bathroom where she could lock the door behind her. Relieved, she slid down and crumpled onto the bathroom floor. Big fat tears rolled down her cheeks for the first time in a long time. And she let them keep on rolling.

It wasn't long before she heard a soft knocking. Irini must have followed her.

"Caia?"

She tensed at the voice. It wasn't Irini. It was Lucien.

"Caia, open the door."

"I'm OK." But she knew he would hear the tears in her voice.

"I'll just break it down," he teased.

Sighing, she slid away from the door to the wall opposite it, rubbing the salt out of her eyes. She must look a mess. Sniffling, she stretched up and flicked the latch up on the door, and then settled back against the wall with her knees pulled up to her chest, her arms protectively around them.

"It's open."

Slowly it eased open and Lucien appeared. His hair brushed the top of the door frame as he stepped inside, his gaze soft as he looked down at her. In fact, Caia could have sworn there was anguish in his eyes.

"Yvana's gone," he told her quietly.

"I'm not crying because of that."

"Uh-huh."

For a moment Lucien just stared at her, and then sighing, he stepped towards her. She was surprised at how he managed to fold his huge body down into a sitting position next to her, his entire left side pressed against her right.

"So... why *are* you crying?" he persisted gently.

"Tired, I guess."

"It's been a long couple of days for you. But I thought... I don't know... I got the impression last night you enjoyed yourself at dinner."

Caia peered up at him from under her lashes. He was looking down at her, his eyes wary, sad even. She nodded. "I did."

"But today you don't want to be here," he guessed.

She didn't have to say anything. Why else would she be sobbing her guts out on the bathroom floor?

Lucien sighed again. "Yvana has her reasons, Caia. Not great ones. What she said she never should have, but the rest of the pack wants you here. You belong with us."

"Her reasons?" she whispered.

"Griffin was her husband," he explained wearily, grief in his own voice. "He died alongside your father... I mean, your parents... protecting you."

She blamed Caia then; blamed her, and her parents, for bringing The Hunter upon the pack. She guessed she could understand her rage. Most lykans when they mated, mated for life. It was said that when their mate died, a part of themselves died with them.

She let silence fall between them, relieved that it was actually a comfortable silence with him. For someone who could be slightly overbearing he had the ability to be patient when he wanted to be.

"Why?" she croaked, verbalizing the confusion in her head. "Why does Yvana hate me, and Ryder and Aidan don't?"

"She was his mate, Caia," Lucien whispered, turning to gaze at her intensely. "She can't see reason in this."

"I'm sorry." Frustratingly, the tears came even more intensely this time. Just as Lucien tut-tutted and leaned over to wipe the tears from her face, the tap in the sink and the shower blasted on.

Lucien cursed and jumped to his feet to quickly turn them off. He muttered under his breath and then turned to look back down at her. She felt his gaze, but her own was on the tap in the sink. A sense of déjà vu washed over her. It was insane, but that was three times in the last few days that the water had come on unexpectedly around her. Really, it was crazy for her to even think that she had something to do with it. Right?

"Is there something wrong with the pipes in this town?" she asked quietly.

"What?"

Caia looked at him intently; he had no idea what she was talking about. She groaned and whispered an unintelligible 'Forget it," under her breath.

"Caia." He was crouching down before her again, his hand brushing her hair back from her face affectionately and bringing her strange thoughts back to him. "You going to be OK?"

She nodded mutely, her heart suddenly thumping loudly at his nearness, his touch. Goddess, she hoped he couldn't hear it.

He smiled. "Why don't you come for a walk with me then? Get up off the cold bathroom floor?"

His change in tone made her frown and she quickly got to her feet. "I'm not five years old," she said dryly, brushing past him. She stopped abruptly and turned back to face him; he nearly crashed right into her having been tailing right behind her. She drew in a deep breath as her heart thudded again at his proximity. She had to crane her neck back to gaze up at his face. "And..." she managed. "Just so you know, I don't cry like that normally."

Lucien lips quirked up at the corner. "I actually believe that."

Hmm, she wasn't sure what he meant by that, or how she should respond.

It was quiet out here, just as he liked it. Being Pack Leader he didn't really have much time for himself, and so was always the more appreciative of quiet moments such as these. Caia walked a few steps ahead of him, stepping over bracken and rocks as they picked their way through the woods. Lucien let her have some space for a while, knowing she probably needed some time to collect herself. She seemed embarrassed for having been caught crying. Lykans were an emotional lot, he was used to women crying and shouting over nothing. But the sight of Caia curled up on the bathroom floor with true pain behind her eyes had done something to his insides. He never wanted to see her like that again. Damn these unexpected feelings towards her - they had hit him from the left field.

"It's heaven out here." She stopped in front of him, her head tilted back as she breathed in heady earth.

Lucien smiled, strolling towards her slowly. "It's why I chose the house."

"I can see that." She opened her eyes and smiled gently back at him. Her eyes were still red and puffy from her crying, but at the same time the green in them seemed to be electrified from all the tears. He felt himself caught in her gaze, feeling like a shy teenager all of a sudden. At the long silence she quirked her eyebrow in amusement. Lucien cleared his throat feeling himself flush. What on Gaia was going on with him?

"Uh-" He looked away from her, staring ahead into the deepening forest. "Uh... Oh did ah... Irini tell you the story about the pack history?"

"No. Apparently Irini didn't tell me much," she replied dryly.

Lucien thought he caught a note of annoyance in her voice and narrowed his eyes on her. "Are you angry about that?"

"No." She sighed, her sweet face crumpling wearily. "I even understand it. It's just... hard."

Her response touched him. Lykans were such volatile beings, usually quick to anger and frustration. But she wasn't like that. The kindness with which she seemed to approach everything and everyone appeared too honest to be anything other than the truth of her. It made it hard to keep his guard up around her. She seemed to pose no threat whatsoever.

He shoved his hands in his jeans pocket and started walking ahead.

"Where are you going?"

"Into the story. Are you coming?" He threw back over his shoulder.

He heard her laugh at his whimsy and then pick up speed until she was striding by his side. "Remember to slow it down a little. My legs are like an entire foot shorter than yours."

"Are they really?" He let his gaze wander over them flirtatiously and then laughed when he saw her blush. She was too easy to tease.

"The story," she reminded him wryly.

Lucien chuckled. "Right." He glanced at her as she stepped gracefully over a small fallen tree limb. "You know the pack originates from Portugal, right?"

She nodded, not taking her eyes from her path. "Some of our surnames give it away," she reminded him.

"Right... And you know about Lunarmorte?"

"Lunarmorte. Moon Death," she breathed. "I can't believe you fought one."

He felt a sharp pain in his chest at the reminder. "I don't like to talk about it." He was curt. He didn't mean to be, but discussing how he had killed a man he had grown up with, brought with it a hailstorm of pain that was just a little too overwhelming to bear.

"Of course. Sorry."

The patience in her eyes made him sigh in relief. If he'd spoken that way to his mother or Irini - or any of the women in his pack for that matter – they'd have more than likely snarled and stomped away from him, in hurt.

"Do you know why we have Lunarmorte and other packs don't?" He continued in her easy company.

Caia shook her head, her brow creasing. "I didn't know it was something only we did. I mean, I know we're the only ones that call it that, but I assumed the concept was universal."

"Not really. It has to do with where our pack began."

They walked further into the woods until he touched her shoulder and indicated for her to start walking in a different direction. She seemed more relaxed around him now, for that he was grateful.

He smiled slightly when she glanced back up at him, her eyes expectant for the story.

"The pack's story really began with our ancestor Aurelio Lorenço," he began. The words came easily to him as he had told this story a million times to the kids of the pack, who for some reason requested it as a bedtime story more often than not. He snorted, lykans really were weird. "You see many, many years before Aurelio's time the blood of the lykan had found its way into the family gene pool. We're not sure who, or when, as these things have a tendency to become confused and marred by rumor and gossip over the centuries. What we do know is that the Lorenço's were a prosperous family of aristocratic lineage. Aurelio was in fact the brother of a Baron, Godofredo Lorenço. They were lykans but … two very different kinds. Godofredo, like the rest of his family and his ancestors, did not harm humans, in fact he married one. Aurelio, on the other hand, believed humans were beneath the touch of his family and hunted them like game. He was furious when his brother married a human girl, and soon began causing trouble. Before, his murders had been committed outside of their county. Godofredo knew of his brothers crimes, and other than some fervent pleading with him, did nothing to stop him. He loved him, wanted to protect him. When Godofredo married, however, Aurelio began taking humans from their local village. The people only began to suspect the Lorenço family after Godofredo's wife became one of the victims, and Aurelio showed no signs of grief. In fact, he seemed to revel in her death quite publicly. Godofredo was devastated and banished Aurelio from the county. But it was too late. The people had grown suspicious of the true nature of the Lorenços, and they drove them from the county, and eventually the country. Our pack became nomads, visiting everywhere and settling nowhere. That's one of the many reasons this pack forbids marriage to humans."

He sighed and caught her gaze as she looked up at him. "We were settled before the Hunter, of course. And now, we're settled again. But the history of the Lorenço family gives you an idea of why we have the rituals we have. With some nobility, and as was with the Lorenço line, the line is held through primogeniture. However, as seen with human nobility, sometimes a first born son never comes along. That's why the Lorenço's created what we call Lunarmorte."

Caia shook her head, gazing in front of her, her cat eyes wide.

"What? What are you thinking?" he asked, and was surprised to realize that he really wanted to know. Ryder was right. Different *was* fascinating.

She laughed, a light feathery laugh that hit him low in his belly. "I'm just in awe, I guess." She shook her head. "I can't believe how old the pack is. I always thought we were a pretty young pack."

"Well we are." Lucien smirked. "We're early modern. There are packs out there that can trace their ancestry as far back to Charlemagne."

"Wow."

"I'll say. But that's nothing compared to how old some of the families of the other supernaturals are."

"I always liked history in school."

"You said." He smiled, and Caia caught his look, chuckling as she too remembered his awkward attempt at conversation with her yesterday in his car. It seemed a million years away now.

"Will we turn back?"

Caia nodded. "I'm pretty beat."

His eyes narrowed in on the dark circles under her eyes; the weariness in them matched the limpness of her body. He sighed. "Tomorrow will be a better day."

She nodded, but her eyes looked almost longingly behind him into the woods, and then she turned to gaze in the direction that would lead them to the house. Lucien felt his breath catch, watching the play of emotions across her face. She really didn't want to be here with the pack, with him.

Well, too bad.

Without thinking he gently took hold of her elbow and started guiding her back to the house. He let go when she complied and ignored the questions in her eyes.

7 — ~~Friend or Foe?~~

The rest of the week passed in a blur for Caia. There were so many members of the pack that came over to discuss their problems with Lucien, some even to introduce themselves to her again. It eased her worries a little. With the exception of Alexa, who hadn't spoken to her since their last exchange in the lunchroom, and Yvana, whom she hadn't seen again, the pack had so far been friendly and welcoming. Ryder hung around a lot and always made her feel like a long lost sister - joking with her, bringing her some movies to watch. It felt nice.

By the end of the week, she was sure her exhaustion was unparalleled. But she had one more performance to put in because Jaeden and her family were staying for dinner that night. She was up in her room, beating her head against the wall over a problem in her calculus homework, when she heard the two cars coming up the gravel driveway. She glanced at her watch. It was seven o'clock. The aromas coming from the kitchen had been mouth-watering since she had gotten home from school. Again, Ella had refused her help.

"I'd like to cook sometime. Do anything to, you know, do my bit," Caia had told her as Ella physically shooed her out of the kitchen.

"Oh of course, honey." Ella had smiled brightly. "And you will. Just not today."

"I could set the table."

"Irini is going to do that."

"I could tidy the sitting room." She'd gestured towards said room from the hallway.

Ella had frowned at that. "I did that already," she'd replied, sounding piqued.

Caia had laughed, abashed. "Of course you did. It looks great."

"Go do your homework."

She had obeyed the quelling look in Ella's eye and left her to it.

Caia sighed and looked back at her calculus problem.

"Caia! They're here!" Ella called from the bottom of the stairs.

"I'll be back," she growled at her homework. "Maybe, somehow by magik, I'll have the answer when I do."

Stopping to check her reflection before she left the room Caia was reminded once again, as her eyes washed over her jeans and plain white shirt, that no matter what she wore she really was the plain Jane of the lykan world. She glared back at her homework and then back into the mirror. Whoever came up with the phrase 'you can't win 'em all' obviously had at least *one* thing going for them; how about 'you can't win anything; nada; zilch', hmm?

"Ugh." She shook her head at herself. "Self-pity is not a good color on you."

They were congregated in the living room. Dimitri with his family and there seemed to be a lot of them. And then Magnus. She grinned at him, feeling her nerves dissipate a little.

"Hey kid." He grinned back.

This should be OK. Right? She glanced at Jaeden who smiled at her as she wrestled with a squirming toddler. Caia's nerves began to melt away as Dimitri hugged her, followed by Magnus, and then pretty much everyone else. It was nothing like her experience with Yvana. Warmth emanated from them all, Magnus sticking protectively by her side. Dimitri's wife, Julia, was introduced to her first. A gorgeous woman Caia presumed was ages with Ella - goddess knew how old that may be - Julia hugged Caia to her, and said it was good to have her back. Then there was Dimitri's eldest, Christian, and his wife, Lucia, who both were friendly and sincere. And then Jaeden came forward and introduced the bubbly three-year old in her arms as her niece, Jaela.

Caia was surprised as Jaeden suddenly pushed the child into her arms. "Say hello, Jaela."

"Uh, Jae …" Caia nervously wrapped her arms around the child. She tried not to blush as everyone watched her hold the little girl awkwardly, but then Jaela grabbed onto a strand of her hair and Caia's eyes locked onto the little one's big baby blues. She smiled sweetly at Caia and made some gurgling noises, trying to snuggle deeper into Caia's arms.

"She likes you." Lucien suddenly appeared beside her. He turned to Lucia. "I thought I was the only one she liked?" His disgruntlement amused everyone.

He was placated by the squealing Jaela when she realized he was there - she threw her arms out at him, hitting Caia in the face and crying out, 'Luchy!"

Wincing Caia turned to him. "I think she wants Luchy," she teased.

"Oh only Jaela is allowed to call me that." Lucien grinned, taking the girl into his arms. "Ain't that right, gorgeous."

Caia sat with them, enjoying the peace and comfort that this small group of the pack enjoyed with one another. They were obviously a family within a family, and so warm to her she felt herself being pulled in, despite her concerns.

"Dinner's ready folks." Ella smiled, looking sweaty from her slavery in the kitchen.

Dinner with them all was probably the best time Caia had had. She hated to admit it, but as Magnus and Dimitri took turns light-heartedly teasing her and each other, as Julia jumped flightily from asking her questions about school to asking Ella about cooking, as Jaeden threw her affectionate smirks, as Christian and Lucia whispered lovingly to one another, and as Lucien ate his meal while playing with Jaela and making her giggle throughout the entire dinner, she realized that this was what she had been missing her entire life. Not the pack. Just a family. An ordinary family having a meal together. It was so humdrum and yet at that moment it was the most wonderful thing in the world to her.

When dinner was over the family decided to settle back in the living room with some coffee and cake.

"I'll clear up, do the dishes," Caia said to Ella as they got up from the table.

"No-"

"I'll help." Jaeden grinned, and managed to do what Caia couldn't and shoo Ella out with the others. Lucien was the last to leave. He stood at the doorway, his eyes narrowed on Jaeden.

"All the times you've been over for dinner you haven't once offered to clean up. What are you up to?" His glance shifted between her and Caia.

Jaeden laughed at him. "You're so suspicious, Lucien."

"Always. For good reason."

She chortled at that and leaned past him, grabbing onto the door. "Bye, Lucien." She began closing it on him.

"If she's bothering you, let me know," he said to Caia, and laughed when Jaeden smacked him on the arm and pushed him out of the door. She turned back to Caia once they were alone, smiling at the bemused look on her face.

"He's not suspicious at all. He's just plain nosy."

They were standing together, Caia washing up, while Jaeden dried and put the dishes away.

"So how was that for you?" Jaeden glanced back at the table. "I know you were pretty nervous about it earlier."

Caia smiled shyly, not meeting her eyes. "Honestly... and you promise you won't tell?"

"Of course."

She sighed and shook her head. "Ugh, this is stupid. I don't feel like myself here at all-"

"Bu-"

"No, don't get me wrong, I don't mean that... I just... I feel really goofy because..."

Jaeden grinned. "Because?"

Caia shrugged embarrassed. "Because I've never had a better time," she spoke so quietly even Jaeden with her lykan hearing had to lean in.

"Aw, Cy." She laughed and shoved at her playfully. "Did you have *A Little House on the Prairie* moment tonight?"

At that, Caia splashed water from the sink up onto Jaeden's face. She merely sniggered and pulled back as Caia narrowed her eyes on her teasingly. "Oh I am never telling you anything again."

"You did." Jaeden wouldn't let up. "Aw, I think my heart hurts a little."

"Oh, you've done it now," Caia growled.

What ensued was a water/bubble/washing-up liquid fight that ended with the two of them slipping on the latter and landing hard on their butts, screaming hysterically.

"What the Hades..."

Giggling, and trying to catch their breaths after having chased each other around the kitchen - which now looked like the great flood had hit it– they glanced up at the kitchen doorway to see Lucien and Ella gazing around in wonder. Magnus stood chuckling behind them.

"What have you done to my kitchen?" Ella squeaked.

"It's totally her fault." Jaeden laughed, flicking bubbles at Caia.

"What..." Caia's mouth fell open.

They turned at the sound of Lucien's laughter. "If you were going to have a water fight couldn't you have told us? Some guys pay to watch that stuff, you know."

"*Lucien*," Ella admonished.

"What?" He laughed innocently, and then turned back to look at Caia. "Need a hand up?"

She shook her head, wincing at the pain from her butt when she'd landed on the hard floor. She laughed breathlessly. "I think I can manage."

"I might need a hand." Jaeden smiled flirtatiously.

"A hand? You need something but it's not a hand." Caia groaned, getting to her feet. She pulled Jaeden up with her before turning to Ella. "We'll clean it up, I promise."

"Hmm," she grunted, un-amused, and spun on her heel to leave.

Lucien and Magnus followed, and she could hear Lucien say, "Leave 'em be. She's just having some fun."

Jaeden raised an eyebrow as she turned back to Caia. "Sounds like Lucien's championing someone."

Caia frowned distractedly, looking around them at the mess. "How did we do this?" She snorted.

Jaeden laughed wearily. "I don't know, but we better clean it before Ella decides to *end* us."

Sitting down at her desk, Caia smiled sheepishly at Jaeden who was sprawled across her bed, now in dry clothing borrowed from Irini's closet. Caia's clothes were all a little too short.

"You think Ella will forgive us?"

The kitchen was now sparkling clean after a thorough tidy up. Tired and a little afraid of Ella, Jaeden had followed Caia up to her bedroom rather than sit with the rest of the family.

"She already has, I hope." Jaeden sighed, glancing down at the calculus work Caia had left on the bed. "Dude, what is this?" She tilted her answer book up at her.

"Drywall," she replied sarcastically.

"Haha, funny."

Caia smiled. "What are you talking about?"

"Uh, the genius solutions you're apparently capable of."

"What?" Caia knitted her brow in confusion and took the answer book Jaeden held out to her. Her eyebrows must have hit the roof. "What the Hades..."

Now in the once blank space next to the problem she had been unable to solve was a solution and answer. She had no idea if it was right. There was no way on Gaia's green earth she would have been able to come up with that. It was gobbledy-gook.

"I have no idea how this got here." She looked up at Jaeden, her eyes round with confusion. "Did you do this? Are you messing with me?"

Jaeden snorted. "Jeez, no. I wouldn't even know where to start with calculus. Or anything to do with math. Math hates me."

"Irini, maybe? One of the others?"

Jaeden sat up and stared at Caia like she had gone a little crazy. "You're saying you didn't answer this?"

"No!" Caia stood up abruptly. "This is just another in a long line of weird things that have happened to me this week." She grimaced, staring hard out of the window as if the forest would give her the answers. Images passed across her eyes - of water coming on of its own accord; of Alexa's chair flying away from her without anyone having touched it. What was going on here?

"What other weird things?" It was Jaeden's turn to frown.

Could she tell her? She felt like she could trust her, but she had only known her for a week, and telling her this stuff would probably only make her think she was a prime candidate for the insane asylum.

"I um..." Caia took a breath. *No*. This, she would have to keep to herself, until she could work out what was going on. "Nothing. You know... I forgot the teacher did this one as an example for me. I must really be exhausted, huh?" She laughed hoping it didn't sound entirely fake to her.

At first she thought Jaeden was going to argue, her gaze narrowing as if she were trying to see past something. It seemed she gave up, however, smiling gently. "You're cuckoo, you know that?"

"It's been drawn to my attention on occasion."

"Beside the cuckoo, I'm really glad you came back. You're sort of soothing."

She smiled gratefully. "You were right before. I'm not used to being around so many people. I hope I can keep the names straight."

"Yeah, you are kind of awkward."

Caia grunted. "Well, thanks."

Laughing, Jaeden threw a pillow at her. "I'm kidding."

There was a moment of comfortable silence, and then Jaeden giggled as if she had just remembered something. "So, you ready to get publicly naked on your first run with the pack?"

Caia's heart stopped. "Get what?"

"Are things going to plan?" he asked his agent.

"Very well. I nearly have all the information I need to execute Phase One," she purred back at him.

"You've raised no suspicions?"

"Not a single one."

"Good. Make sure it stays that way. I want the information I need soon. Very soon."

"You'll have it, sir."

"Hm, we'll see. I'll be in contact." He turned to Lars as he placed the phone down on the receiver. His assistant was hopping from one foot to the other, like a puppy dog waiting on a treat.

"Well?" Lars asked excitedly.

"Do you have to be right at my back? Go stand on the other side of the room."

"I take it things aren't going well." Lars's face fell as he inched away from his superior.

"According to our spy everything's going perfectly well. She'll be sending the information we need over the next few weeks."

"And Caia?"

"Integrating into the pack. By the time we get the little bitch, the pack may actually mourn her."

Lars sneered. "Yes, but by then we'll have all the information we need to destroy the rest of the mangy mutts ... they won't have time to mourn the abomination."

A slow, lazy smile spread across his face. He liked it when his lackeys were particularly enthusiastic. "Sometimes, I do like your way with words."

8 – SECRET WORLDS

"You nervous about the run tomorrow?" Sebastian asked, as he eased back on her bed. Caia had been hoping to maybe sleep late, what with it being a Saturday and all, but she'd been woken up by Ella, who told her she had visitors coming over. She'd reluctantly got up and showered, had a sleepy breakfast with Ella, while Irini sat sipping cup of coffee after coffee. She was venturing out to an early picnic with Aidan. Caia hoped Aidan liked grumpy for brunch because Irini really wasn't a morning person.

An hour after she had gotten up Sebastian and Jaeden came strolling in, bright eyed and bushy-tailed. Goddess, they *were* superhuman.

"I don't know. A little." She nodded from her position at her desk. "Especially after the little reminder that we'll all be naked... together."

Jaeden was on the floor doing sit ups. She smiled in-between them reassuringly. "There is nothing to worry about, I promise. It's a lot of fun, all of the pack running together, the sound of all those paws pounding into the ground."

"All those parts bouncing around," Sebastian teased.

Caia groaned. "There's a mental image I just didn't need."

"Oh come on, Caia, just keep your eyes at face level and you'll be fine."

They laughed together for a moment, enjoying Caia's embarrassment.

"What about the little ones?" Caia frowned. "Who looks after them?"

One thing Caia did know about the pack run, anyone under the age of thirteen was not allowed to take part.

"You mean like Jaela and Sunday and the others?"

Caia had no idea who the kids were, except Jaela, so she just nodded. "I guess I do."

Jaeden shrugged. "The moms take turns looking after them. For instance, Lucia will look after all of them one run, but for the next one Cera will, and then Imogen."

She found herself frowning again. "Whose Cera and Imogen?"

"Cera is Lucia's sister - and Ivan, Joaquin, and Kerianna's mom. Her husband died a year back ... *shot*," Jaeden whispered the word.

Caia's eyes widened. "Shot?"

Jaeden's eyes teared up. "Some stupid human wanted his wallet and he wouldn't give it to him. We guess it's because he thought he could take him, you know if it came to a fight, but he just pulled out the gun and shot Michel in the head. If it hadn't been such close range he would have been able to change so he could regenerate."

"My goddess... how awful."

They were silent a moment, all feeling awkward, especially Caia for having brought it up. Finally, Sebastian cleared his throat as he sat up on the bed, "Imogen is my mom, by the way," he offered. "Sunday's my little sister, she's five. I have another little sister, Seana. And Isaac's my dad."

Caia shook her head. "I'm never going to remember everyone, am I?"

Jaeden stopped exercising. "It'll take time. There's a few of us."

She nodded, and was quiet as Jaeden scolded Sebastian for putting his feet up on the bed.

"Hey, I have a question," Caia mused interrupting their squabble.

"Yeah?" They both quizzed.

"Where do we run?"

"At the back of your place." Sebastian shrugged, indicating her window with his a nod of his head.

"Lucien and my father bought acres of the woodland just outside Woodrush," Jaeden added. "It's so we have privacy."

"About that?" Caia leaned towards them, looking from one to the other. "How come you don't get caught?"

"We haven't had any trespassers." Jaeden looked at Sebastian for confirmation.

He nodded and continued for her, "Yeah, even in the past when there *have* been the occasional sightings, nothing ever came of it. We guessed they just couldn't believe what they were seeing. There have been teenagers who saw us and told but ... ach, everyone just thinks it's the retelling of the werewolf myth over and over again."

Jaeden snorted. "We're safe due to the modern age of cynicism. Thank the gods superstition's out right?"

Caia didn't laugh; she had a far more pressing question on her mind. "What about the war?"

Both Jaeden and Sebastian stilled, their entire bodies stiffening in alert, like prey catching the sounds of a hunter.

Sebastian cleared his throat. "Uh, what about it?" he asked nervously.

Caia just shook her head, pleading with her eyes for a response from the two of them. "You never talk about the war-"

"The war doesn't touch us. There is no need to talk about it." The three of them turned towards Lucien standing in the doorway. *What was with him and doing that?* Caia narrowed her eyes. Sebastian jumped up from the bed, reacting to Lucien's tone. The Alpha's eyes were glinting dangerously as they flickered over Jaeden and Sebastian. Was he angry at them?

"It's not their fault. I asked."

"Well stop asking," his voice was like ice.

She flinched as if he had struck her. Why was he was being such a jerk when he had been so kind and friendly all week? Now he had all of them acting like they'd been caught with their hand in the cookie jar. They hadn't done anything wrong, and neither had she for asking. "I have a right to know," she heard the steel in her own voice, watched her friends react in surprise to the strength she showed him, and it encouraged her to continue, "I withheld from asking Irini because it seemed to upset her, but I have a right to ask now."

"No, you don't," Lucien countered, stepping towards her. "I will not have the war brought up. We are peaceful, and the pack does not need those kinds of memories being dredged up at the moment."

Caia didn't back up. Instead she took a step towards him, telling him physically that he didn't frighten her. "The Hunter was part of the war. He took my parents from me before I had the chance to get to know them. I deserve to know the whys and the hows."

"I told you all there was to know a week ago, so drop it."

She glared at him for a moment, her green eyes clashing into his silver ones with heat and anger. She was flushed with the warmth of her annoyance and could feel Lucien's anger melding into the air around them with hers until it was hard to breathe in the stifling atmosphere. Slowly realizing that Jae and Sebastian were shifting uncomfortably, she backed down, forcing on a tranquil expression. She felt like she had the day she'd encountered Yvana in the kitchen. Just when she was beginning to feel a part of these people...

Lucien must have read something in her eyes because he sighed deeply, running his hand through his hair as if frustrated. "Jae, Seb... give Caia and me a moment please."

They couldn't have scrambled out of the room fast enough.

"Caia, I'm sorry," Lucien said softly, closing the door behind them.

She nodded, a little unsure of him now. "You don't have to treat me like a child, you know."

He nodded, lowering himself onto the bed across from her. His eyes were kind, the ice melted. "I know. I am sorry."

"So, what?" she grimaced. "I'm not allowed to talk about the past? I have questions."

"I get that. I do. But..." He shook his head. "I don't know how to say this without hurting your feelings."

"Why don't you just rip it off like a band aid."

His mouth quirked up at the corner, his eyes holding hers fast. "OK. I don't want you mentioning the past, or the war, or The Hunter, because I want my pack to accept you. Reminding them of all of that will just make things harder on *you*. No one else."

"I thought no one blamed me," her voice was a little unsteady. Had everyone been faking it? Even Jaeden and Sebastian?

"They don't. But they've also gotten past what happened. Refreshing their memories isn't going to do anyone any good."

She guessed she understood - but she wasn't giving up. She'd give them all time to get used to her, and when enough time had passed, she would get the answers she wanted. "OK," she exhaled.

Lucien smiled widely, breathing a huge sigh of relief. "OK." He slapped his knees and stood up. "Still friends?" he asked, smiling softly at her, his eyes locking hers to his like a magnet.

Caia felt her heart thump a little irregularly. "Still friends," it was a miracle her voice came out as strong as it did.

"Good. I'll send them back in."

"Wow," Jaeden whispered when she re-entered the room with Sebastian. They were both smiling like small children. "I've never seen anyone stand up to him like that, except for the Elders."

Sebastian chuckled. "It was pretty awesome."

Caia laughed at them. "It was nothing. Really, we're fine."

Jaeden laughed. "He got his way though, right?"

"For now."

By eight o' clock the next evening the pack had gathered outside at the back of Lucien's home. Caia walked towards them all, Sebastian on her right and Jaeden on her left. Having them beside her was comforting, but it didn't diminish the flurry of butterflies in her stomach. She took in Lucien, standing tall, straight, and powerful in the middle of his pack, angling his head to listen to whatever Ryder was telling him. Jaeden stopped beside Magnus - deliberately it seemed – and the Elder smiled softly at Caia before coaxing her into his side.

"You'll be OK," he whispered, stroking her cheek. "Your eyes give away your panic. Don't let them see."

Caia nodded gratefully, taking a deep breath. She squeezed Magnus' hand, reassuring him she was alright.

"You OK?" Sebastian asked as she returned to them.

"I'm fine. I promise."

She turned back to the rest of the pack who were gathered in little groups. Irini was cuddling up to Aidan. Ella and Magnus were talking quietly with one another. Dimitri and Julia stood with Christian, but Lucia was nowhere to be seen. She'd obviously gotten babysitting duty this time round. Her eyes swept the circle catching sight of Alexa, Malek, and Finlay standing with their family; Dana and Daniel with theirs.

"That's my mom and dad," Sebastian whispered in her ear, pointing to a young looking family. "And my kid sister, Seana. She's a pain in my ass."

Caia smiled, detecting the affection in his voice. He waved at his parents, who smiled back and nodded politely to Caia. She returned the gesture, and smiled at Sebastian after he nudged her teasingly with his shoulder. She glanced around them all again, and then realized there was someone missing.

"Where's Yvana?" she whispered to Jaeden.

Jaeden screwed up her face. "Everyone heard about how she reacted to you. Lucien banned her from this run. As punishment."

Caia's eyes widened. She hadn't expected that. She glanced shyly over at Lucien only to catch him watching her intently. His silver eyes flashed concern at her, and she nodded her head gently to let him know she was OK. Goddess they were a protective lot; it was wearying, but nice. He nodded back and turned to Ryder to murmur something.

They stood for a few more minutes, talking among themselves, until a hush fell over the pack as they all turned to gaze up at the quarter moon.

"Tonight is a special run," Lucien's voice rumbled through the pack, drawing all eyes to him. "Tonight we run in honor of the safe return of my sister, Irini, and our brother, Rafael's, daughter, Caia."

Caia felt her face warm as a hum washed around them. She waited for him to say more, her eyes drinking in his own silver pools as they scanned the pack. He was born to be a leader; his magnetism alluring, his strength and assuredness comforting. She could feel it drifting over the other pack members, wrapping around them. They were happy with their young leader that was for sure.

"Artemis, go with us," Lucien rumbled.

"Artemis, go with us," the pack repeated, and then, just as she had felt herself easing in to the moment, they began to undress. She turned away as Jaeden and Sebastian stripped without any hesitancy; gaped as Irini and Aidan undressed each other, grinning wildly as they touched one another. It wasn't just them, Caia realized. Couples watched each other intensely as they disrobed, regardless of the other lykans. Everyone was just so at home in their own skin. She felt a pinch on her arm and turned (keeping her eyes at face level) to find Jaeden pointedly raising her eyebrows at her. Sighing, her fingers trembling, Caia began to undress. *No one's looking, no one cares, pretend this is just an ordinary run, and it's just you. You do this all the time.*

The mantra may have worked but as her last piece of clothing dropped to the slightly damp earth and goosebumps erupted across her soft skin under the cool night breeze, she made the mistake of looking up and found Lucien gazing at her. Not just gazing either. His eyes were running the entire length of her body, and when he finally realized she was looking back, he didn't smile as if he was teasing her. His jaw was clenched, his eyes darkened to a coal grey. Her breath caught, and she felt glued to the spot. Finally, Caia mentally slapped herself, as she realized she was staring at him also … really staring … at everything, and enjoying the view. She tried not to blush, looking around to make sure no one had noticed. And of course Alexa had. She was glaring at Caia like she wanted to rip her throat out. Her eyes narrowed, and Caia could almost hear her threatening to tell Lucien about their little incident earlier on in the week. She couldn't have that. She was still trying to figure things out herself.

As the moaning and growling of the pack drifted into her awareness she shoved aside the animosity pouring out of Alexa. The pack were all changing around her. A tingle of anticipation rushed through Caia at the sound of their cracking bones as they contorted and reshaped. She closed her eyes and tried to clear her mind, feeling the breeze, hearing the whispering of the trees, bathing in the glow of Artemis.

And then it was there, the pelt pushing through, the change burning like growing pains. Before she knew it she was thudding to the ground on all four paws, her sharp wolf eyes taking in the sight of the pack, now seeming pretty huge in its wolf form. It was an impressive sight, so much so, she took an involuntary pad backwards, watching them all shift and nudge each other. And then a huge, black, and superbly powerful lykan padded into the center of the wolves, his large silver eyes sweeping them all.

Lucien.

She followed the others' example as they bent their hindquarters and lowered their head to the ground, bowing to their Alpha before the run began. She had very little time to enjoy the awe of the moment. To bow with them all to Lucien tugged at her more than anything had thus far. She felt part of the pack, part of their history.

She felt extraordinary.

And just like that the pack took off, running so fast earth and dirt kicked up in the aftermath. With one last look, Caia burst out after them, extremely conscious of how aware they were of her movements. Knowing this, she couldn't quite enjoy the run as she would have done, too busy watching them as they played with one another, never realizing the comradeship and intimacy that was possible even in lykan form. She realized relationships could actually be built out here. Like this. Unused to the idea, slightly uncomfortable with it even, Caia raced past them all, ignoring them and enjoying the rush of the wind on her pelt. She was fast, possibly faster than the rest. She laughed a little, enjoying the thought. But her laughter was cut short by the thunder of someone chasing her, and before she had time to react a weight crashed into her side, sending her paws out from her under her. The impact didn't hurt, it barely winded her, but she turned to growl at her attacker in instinct, only to find her nose inches from silver eyes. Caia stumbled, taken aback that Lucien had come after her. She would have thought he would have been too busy overseeing the pack. She watched in amazement as he began to almost dance around her, butting her playfully with the top of his head. He wanted to play with her as she had seen the others play! Caia sensed his amusement at her uncertainty and couldn't help but smile inwardly when he butted her again and then rolled away from her. He made a choking sound like laughter, and slowly Caia began to relax. Eventually, without thinking, she was moving forward with great speed and grace, dancing around him, disconcerting him, and in doing so finding the opportunity to butt him back forcefully. Again, he made the choking sound as he got back to his feet, bowing his head appreciatively at her efforts. Caia had no idea how it happened but she found herself rolling and tussling in the dirt with this huge lykan, knocking him back just as hard as he did her, and enjoying this moment of freedom with one of her own.

But when Lucien nipped her a little hard and she made a noise in reflex, he was quickly beside her, bussing his head against hers. If that hadn't been enough of a surprise, he then licked the spot he had hurt. At this Caia jumped back, wary of the intimacy in his action. Was it intimacy? She had no idea, she was just getting used to this whole thing. Lucien seemed to sense this, and turned, gesturing with his head for them to return to the rest of the pack. She was grateful. She ran with him, managing to keep pace with him even though he was extremely fast. They were upon the pack within minutes, racing by many of the members. Of a sudden she was flanked on either side by a brown lykan female more long and languid than she, her laughing blue eyes drifting questioningly between her and Lucien. The other lykan was larger and sinewy, his sandy pelt and soft eyes so like the human version of Sebastian, Caia almost found it comical. She enjoyed the playfulness of Jaeden and Sebastian, who seemed to want to ease her into the play much more slowly than Lucien had. So caught up in her new friendships and this bizarrely, wonderful experience with them in lykan form, Caia didn't notice the black wolf who sidled up near them, her paw striking out deliberately. She heard the choking noise of laughter, however, when she found herself tumbling hard into the dirt. Surprised by Alexa's deliberate trip, Caia shook her head, slowly pushing herself back up on all fours, aware of Jaeden and Sebastian's annoyance and the wary presence of Lucien, who had reappeared. His hovering and questioning eyes demanded reassurance that she was alright. She dipped her muzzle and watched as he thankfully eased back. Alexa, however, just as dangerously beautiful as a wolf as she was in human form, twitched her nose from Caia to Lucien, her wolf eyes narrowing in irritation, her hostility palpable. Her back went up, tensed, her hindquarters bent, and Caia realized she looked ready to pounce on her. In barely a second of blurry movement Lucien was in front of her, growling in irritation, making Caia's heart pound. He wasn't going to fight this small female over her, was he? Never had she been so grateful for the silliness of Jaeden and Sebastian together as they dispelled the moment by throwing themselves playfully at Alexa. She at first continued in aggravation, snapping her jaws near their throats.

But soon realization must have dawned on Alexa: they had diffused a situation in which she would have found herself out of favor with the Pack Leader.

The last thing she wanted.

Caia gazed up at her ceiling, her muscles weary from the most energetic night she had ever spent as her wolf self. It was a pleasant, physical exhaustion that had taken over her previous mental exhaustion, and for this she was thankful.

Tonight had been an unexpected one. She had feared losing something special by running with the pack, but instead she had touched what it really meant to be a lykan. There was this incredible freedom in being in wolf form. A freedom in expression; to show affection that she might not normally show as a human; a childish, animal playfulness that was frowned upon in human society, and yet was probably the most fun she had ever had. More than anything it made Caia feel a part of something, a part of a family, like she had done on Friday night with Lucien, and with Jaeden's family. It was intimidating, and scary, and exhilarating all at the same time. She turned on her side, her eyes drifting out of the window and into the dark of the trees where she had played merely hours earlier.

Still, what was she to make of the pack?

Jaeden and Sebastian she got; Irini and Aidan; Magnus too, and even Ella. *But Lucien?* She felt something for him. *Attraction?* She didn't know. She had never felt it before. Whatever it was, it was making her dream of him. And after tonight and his long, languorous perusal of her, she imagined she would be dreaming of him again. Caia sighed, and flipped onto her back. She couldn't have feelings for Lucien. She just couldn't.

Alexa would kill her for starters.

9 – By Artemis' Will

The next few weeks with the pack seemed to drift by quickly in a massive blur of new emotions and experiences. Her friendships with Sebastian and Jaeden had deepened surprisingly fast, particularly with Jaeden who was her constant companion. If anyone had asked her just a few months before how she would feel about that, she would have readily replied that she disliked the idea of having her privacy intruded upon so much. To constantly be surrounded by people? No thanks. But these weeks with the pack had changed her. If she came home to a quiet house, which was a rare occurrence indeed, she felt her mood darken, an inexplicable anxiety pressing on her chest. Part of her resented this chip that had been knocked out of her fierce independence, and another deeper, hidden part of her that she was reluctant to accept, was glad of the company and happier than she had ever felt. She was also gradually getting to know the rest of the pack as they sought advice from Lucien. Moreover, she had enjoyed another run with them, wherein it was easier for her in wolf form to have fun with others, out-with her circle of friends.

It was beginning to feel like home.

And soon there was celebration within the pack as Aidan and Irini announced their plans to mate. Irini was fighting Ella not to go overboard with the ceremony and party she planned to have at the house. Caia was happy for Irini, and intrigued to see what the ceremony entailed. After all she had never been to one.

"Is it like a wedding?" she asked Ella one Saturday afternoon as they shopped for dresses. Caia had tried to tell Ella that she wasn't an evening dress kind of person, and Irini had tried to back her up. Ella had put her foot down. No, no, no. Caia was to wear a dress in the same shade as herself and Irini.

"So, it *is* like a wedding?" Caia asked for the fifteenth time. Ella was so preoccupied at the moment it was like pulling teeth to get an answer from her about anything.

"No, and yes." She smiled, holding up a bronze silky thing in front of Caia. Caia wrinkled her nose at the color.

"No, and yes how? That's not really a good color on me."

"I agree," she tut-tutted, and shoved the thing back in the rack and started shuffling through more. "Irini, how's it going in there?"

Caia's gaze wandered to the changing stalls as Irini called from behind the curtain, "I never knew dresses could get this complicated. I don't think this color will suit Caia."

"I think it's going to be difficult to get a color that will suit us both," Caia replied doubtfully.

"This is a nice shade," Ella mused, pulling a dusty pink satin dress off the rack.

Caia took it from her and held it up in front of her, gazing at her reflection. "It's actually quite pretty," she relented.

"Ooh." Irini appeared from behind the curtain, wearing a long citrus colored gown.

"Oh no." Ella shook her head at her appearance.

Irini sighed. "I know, Mom, told you so. I look like a giant tangerine. Anyway I was oohing at Caia's dress." She gestured to her. "I like that color. I think it would work with our coloring, too."

Ella nodded contemplating the situation like the world depended on her decision. "Yes. We'll find dresses to match."

"Shouldn't I try it on first?"

"Well, duh." Irini laughed. "I can't believe it. I'm going to-" she stopped abruptly as a sales lady walked by - "Be getting *married*," she finished instead. "And you're trying on an evening dress. My world is all askew."

As Caia trundled reluctantly into a changing stall, she called through the curtain, "So you never answered my question..."

The sales lady had gone. She could hear Ella sighing. "No. It's not like a wedding, in that there are no vows. One of the Elders, in this case Magnus, recites the binding ritual in Greek in front of the rest of the pack, who stand as witnesses. Then the ceremony is over and we go and have a party... yes, like a wedding reception."

"Soo... the color co-ordinated dresses?"

"Political propaganda, if you like. I suppose they are a bit like bridesmaid dresses, except we wear the same color as the bride. I want everyone there to see you as my family."

Caia didn't know what to say. She would thank her but Ella would only shush her. Apparently she was supposed to be used to Ella's kindnesses by now – the rest of the pack just expected and assumed such loyalty. She heaved a sigh and pulled the curtain back. "So... is it OK?"

Irini and Ella turned to her and gasped.

Caia's face fell. "That bad?"

"No." Irini laughed, and pulled her out to have a look in the mirror. "You look stunning."

Caia grimaced. That was taking exaggeration to a new level. Then her reflection appeared and she stared wide-eyed. The color of the dress was just the right shade for her peaches and cream complexion, making her hair seem lighter and her eyes greener. For once she actually felt pretty.

"It's nice," she admitted, nodding shyly.

Ella and Irini laughed. "I think it's a winner."

Caia had thought finding one dress would make the task of finding Irini and Ella one easier... but no. By the end of the afternoon her feet were killing her and they had been in every dress store in town. They had eventually found a dress for Ella, and Irini was in the changing rooms trying on their last three options for her.

Ella for once was relaxed. "We'll get shoes later. I'm too exhausted to go on."

Thank goddess, Caia breathed.

"I just can't believe this is finally happening." Her eyes sparkled like a typically ecstatic mother-of-the-bride. "You know, Irini and Aidan had a thing when they were younger."

She nodded. "I'd heard something like that."

"Yeah, Irini was the popular girl of the pack back then." She smiled fondly remembering. "And very sought after. Dermot and Aidan were her avid followers."

"Dermot? Alexa's big brother that..."

Ella nodded, her expression somber. "The very one. Thankfully, Irini had seen past Dermot's charm and straight into his ambitions. Every time he came around to 'see' Irini he was always seeking Lucien. But Aidan ... aww goddess, that boy had it bad. It was like something out of a nineteenth century novel, flowers and chocolates, kisses on her hand. Irini loved it," Ella tittered, and then her expression became bittersweet. "Aidan was so despondent when she left."

"I'm sorry." Caia winced.

Ella blanched, realizing her blunder. "Oh no, Cy, no. It's not your fault. And anyway, now we know the two of them were truly meant to be mates. I'm so happy for her."

"Me too."

They were silent for a moment as Ella smiled softly to herself, and Caia pondered another question. Finally she felt brave enough to ask, "Ella?"

"Hmm?"

"Is it true that... that when a lykan mates... they mate for life?"

Her adoptive mother nodded, her eyes soft. "I keep forgetting there is so much about this life, the life that was always meant for you, that you don't know," she tsked and sighed. "Most lykans find their mate, but not all of us. I was lucky to meet mine, and Irini's lucky to meet hers. What it means is that we literally can't have children with anyone other than our mates."

Caia's eyes widened as she tried to take this in. "I remember Irini mentioning something, but I guess I didn't really understand. You mean, we can have relationships with other people, but if we don't find our mate ... we can't have children?"

"Well, it's more that if Artemis doesn't bless the union between the two of you, then you're not mates, despite what your heart may be telling you ... and you can't have children."

Caia blinked. "So, it's entirely up to Artemis. But what if you don't find your mate? Or, what if you really think someone is *the* one but Artemis disagrees?"

Ella's eyes were saddened at the thought. "Then Artemis is right and that person isn't your mate. No children. That's why it's imperative that our Pack Leaders find mates... otherwise Lunarmortes would be occurring all the time. The pack's been lucky, however."

"So Lucien..."

"Will have to find his mate if this family is to continue leading the pack."

This left Caia reeling. Artemis had really done one over on her children with this one. "So you can never love anyone again?" She winced when she realized how blunt and insensitive that had sounded, but Ella shook her head, seeming not to mind.

"No honey. I can love, just not like I loved Albus."

"It sounds like we got screwed in the relationship department."

Ella laughed, but looked aghast. "Caia, that's blasphemous."

"Sorry. I just-"

"Cy, I'm not lonely," she interrupted, her eyes softening as she said quietly, "I have Magnus."

She thought her eyes were going to bulge out of her head. Magnus and Ella? Since when? "You..."

The Elder was obviously delighted to have shocked her. "We take comfort in one another. He lost his mate when she was very young, and after Albus... we love each other, Cy. Just ... not the way we loved *them*."

She smiled softly at Ella. She was glad actually. Ella and Magnus were two of her favorite lykans. That they had one another was a comforting thought.

"One day you'll find your mate, Caia," she said softly, her eyes warm and wise.

Caia snorted. "I don't see that happening. I'm not really cut out for the whole marriage thing."

Ella chuckled knowingly. "It's not really up to you, one way or the other."

Lucien needed to run tonight. His mother was driving him, and everyone else, crazy with this whole mating business. He was happy for his sister and Aidan, he really was, but did it have to be the topic of conversation at breakfast and dinner? His mother was even calling him at work to ask about icing colors and paper napkins. The ritual couldn't come fast enough.

He sighed and ambled outside of the surprisingly quiet house, rolling his eyes as he passed the kitchen, which was covered in recipes, and cakes, and fabric swatches. The breeze was relaxing as it caressed his face.

"Heaven," he breathed and began stripping down. He let the change happen, enjoying the burning pain and pressure of it, as always. Without thought, he took off into the dark woods, relishing the freedom and the feel of the wind on his pelt as he rushed through the trees. Despite the autonomy of the run his thoughts soon turned to that of his pack members and their problems. Yvana, whom he'd only begun to forgive for her rash treatment of Caia, had just asked permission to hire staff for the diner outside of the pack. He was wary of the decision, since many of the pack ate there, and often conversation wasn't human friendly, but he also realized her need to keep her business going. She was running out of staffing choices within the pack itself. Then there was Morgan, who was worried that his son, Malek, was having too many casual, sexual relationships with human girls; he needed the authority of Lucien to put a stop to it. And then there was Cera, who was struggling financially with her three young children, since Michel had been killed. He knew her family, Dimitri and gang, were doing their best to help out, but it wasn't enough. Lucien was going to have to find a way of giving her money that wouldn't offend her pride...

So lost in these thoughts, he didn't hear the sound of the other wolf before she was nearly upon him. He stopped and lifted his nose to the air. *Caia.* She suddenly came into view, sliding to a stop before him, her green eyes surprised and wide. His heart did a little unexpected thump. By the look in her eye she hadn't been running after him; obviously she had just been running and had been surprised to hear another lykan. *She must have followed my scent to find me*, Lucien watched in amusement as she lowered her head and bowed to him. He admired the way the moonlight shone through the canopy of the forest and filtered across her blonde pelt. Even in wolf form, he thought ruefully, she looked more vulnerable than the others. That fierce feeling of protectiveness washed over him again, and he involuntarily took a pad towards her. When she raised her eyes back up to him they seemed to detect his still lingering amusement over her submission to his authority, because they narrowed warily. She huffed on her four legs pacing in front of him, clearly unsure of whether he wanted her there or not. He was glad she was as unsettled by whatever was between them as he was. Bowing back at her, a chuckle erupted hoarsely from the back of his throat, and he looked up in time to see her fur bristle at the sound of his laughter. Caia turned as if to leave and his heart stopped. She couldn't leave. He threw himself into her side to stop her, and pulled her unwillingly (at first) into a tussle with him. Like their first run together she smacked him back and nipped playfully at him. And so began a teasing play of rough and tumble. He enjoyed this freedom with her, away from the eyes of the pack, but as their play continued a new feeling began to rush through him and he pulled back instantly. He couldn't hurry things with her, it would only frighten her. Green eyes seemed to dance mockingly at him, as if she had won their little tug of war. He bowed to her in defeat and watched as she suddenly took off with a snort, running fast towards the house. She was incredibly swift, but he was just as, and they entered into the back yard at the same time. He watched her silently for a moment as she turned to gaze back at him, her tongue hanging out in a comically wolfy grin. He laughed, she had run harder than she had wanted him to realize in an effort to beat him. His hoarse laughter stilled as Caia padded over to him, and softly, almost caressingly, nudged her head against his own. He felt all his muscles strain in reaction to her touch. Finally, it registered that she was indicating for him to turn around so she could change. Lucien laughed again. He had already seen her naked at the pack run and he hadn't been particularly gentlemanly about looking away then… but he acquiesced to her request because he didn't want to upset her. By the time he turned around again Caia was already in human form and clothes, scaling the wall of the house, and climbing into her bedroom window. Lucien quickly changed and grabbed his clothes that were lying in the dirt near the door. Just as he pulled his t-shirt back on, he looked back up at her window to see her standing looking down at him. She wore a small smile, her eyes really soft on his for the first time. She gave a slight wave, and moved away from the window into the darkness of her room.

Something inside Lucien split open.

With a shock of awareness that set him back on his heels, Lucien realized that all he wanted in this life … was to melt into the darkness with her.

10 – Behind Enemy Lines

Lars looked over worriedly at his superior, who, in a matter of minutes, had obliterated the furniture in the room with a flick of his wrist and the point of his finger. His superior did not care a whit for the nervous fear oozing out of his assistant, who still hadn't mastered the basic communication spell he had given him. Now, he realized that all warlock and witches had different levels of talent and ability, and Lars's did not lie in the communication and transportation division, but surely to Gaia he could master a basic communication spell! He heaved a huge sigh, pulling his temper back in. He unfortunately couldn't blame his rage on Lars. He was waiting on his damn, stupid agent to phone him so he could blast his rage down the telephone at her.

The phone thankfully rang then, making Lars jump high and yelp. With a withering look he flicked his wrist and encased his assistant in a glass cage so he couldn't hear him and couldn't be heard by him during this very important telephone call.

"Boy, are you in trouble," he growled down the phone.

He heard the sharp intake of breath before she hurriedly went on, "My lord, please. I'm doing the best I can. Things are progressing well, I think."

"No," he snapped. "The information you have sent me tells me nothing. We have no 'in' yet, and we need an 'in'!"

"I'll get you an 'in'," she whispered.

"Oh, you will," he demanded menacingly. "In fact, if you don't get me the information I need to wage war with this despicable race of … of *dogs* within the next few months, I am going to have to go in all spells blazing. And if that happens, my dear little spy, you *will* be the first casualty."

11 – TRADE OFF

The intimate run with Lucien had given him a permanent starring role in her dreams. Sometimes the dreams were so real she felt absolutely consumed by them, lost in them, finding it difficult to fight her way through the sleepy fog into reality. The fact that the dreams inevitably ended with Lucien kissing her, however, was the wakeup call that she needed. Kiss. Bam! She was awake, and Lucien-less. Caia was trying to control her fantasies, she really was. She lived with the guy. He was Pack Leader for goddess-sake. But it wasn't like she could avoid him. When he wasn't at work, he was usually hanging around the house with Ryder, so that people always knew where to find him. And Ryder and he were always so friendly, welcoming her into their company. They were her friends. It was during these little gatherings that her eyes would drift over Lucien's face, with its fierce silver eyes and sultry mouth. And then lower, to his strong sinewy forearms and large capable hands. The tug in her lower belly would just get more insistent. She had no clue what was happening to her. She was even day-dreaming in class, and she was not the day-dreaming kind. Caia doubted he was day-dreaming back. She was just a kid to him, right? Ugh, she didn't even want to think like that. Of course she was just his friend. Didn't she get that feeling when they playing during their run together - he suddenly pulled back like he didn't want to cross some line with her. She had been disappointed, but amused at his tentativeness at the time. But in truth it was kind of hard to get over her crush when he acted like such a gentleman.

A week after the infamous run with Lucien, a run that she hadn't even told Jaeden about, he called to her from the hallway as she was finishing her breakfast. Caia frowned and glanced at the clock. Jaeden was late to pick her up. After Lucien called her again, she took her last bite of toast and curiously strolled out of the kitchen to find him standing at the front door with a big grin on his face. "I want to show you something?"

Caia shook her head, stepping back. "Uh no. I'm not falling for that again. Last time you and Ryder said that to me I had heart failure."

He had the decency to look sheepish. "How were we to know you were afraid of spiders?"

"Spiders?" Caia spluttered. "It wasn't just a *spider*. It was the *mother* of all spiders."

Lucien laughed. "This isn't a spider. Will you please just come?"

Huffing somewhat as she remembered the huge, brown, spindly creature they had thrust in her face about two weeks ago - thinking she'd find the alien monster from Hades as amazing as they did - she walked cautiously after Lucien. She followed him outside and stopped short on the porch as he approached a brand new car.

"I know it's no sports car." He slapped the roof of it, like it was an old friend. "But it's brand new."

"What is it?"

"The new Ford. You like the color?" He watched her carefully for a reaction.

Caia smiled in confusion. It was gold pistachio; metallic; very pretty. "Yeah? Why?"

He grinned. "Because it's yours."

Her jaw must have hit the floor. Was he kidding? Nope, not by the cheesy grin on his face. "Lucien, I can't accept this." But she was already gravitating towards the vehicle. She ducked her head inside the passenger window, checking out the color co-ordinated interior, and inhaling that wonderful new car smell. "I really can't accept this."

She heard him grunt from the other side of the car. "No can't about it. It's yours."

"Does she like it?"

Caia straightened to see Ella rushing excitedly out of the house. "Huh, what d'ya think, Cy?"

"I think it's too much," she said regrettably. It was such a nice car.

Ella's face fell. "But... Lucien went to a lot of trouble-"

"Mom." He stopped her, shaking his head in what Caia had come to recognize as irritation. His gaze swept back to her. "You're taking the car." It was a demand.

"Bu-"

"No buts. Jaeden's not picking you up this morning so unless you're going to change into the wolf suit and run there you're going to be late."

They were waiting for her, standing around Mal's SUV, as she pulled into the parking lot in the Ford. It was a dream to drive. She'd actually forgotten how much she'd missed having a car, although back in her life with Irini it had been a beat up Mustang she'd driven. Caia felt a little self-conscious as she got out of the vehicle and headed towards the pack. Jaeden was smiling devilishly at her.

"You knew about this," Caia stated grimly, coming to a stop in front of them.

Jaeden nodded impishly.

"Nice ride." Mal laughed. "Looks like you're all set to be a Soccer Mom."

"Shut up." Jaeden slapped him across the head, incurring a low growl from the back of his throat.

Caia looked thoughtfully back at the shiny machine. "I was actually thinking that if he was going to get me a car he could have gotten me a nice, cheap, old thing."

"Yeah." Jaeden laughed, and eyed her meaningfully. "He could have."

She rolled her eyes. Jaeden had begun making little innuendos about her and Lucien for the past few weeks now. Just because he was being nice to her and trying to make sure she integrated back into the pack without any problems, Jaeden thought his preferential treatment meant something. The only feelings between Caia and him were the private ones emanating from her fantasies, and she was telling no one about those, not even Jaeden. Not that it mattered as she had a feeling Jaeden was aware of her crush. Her perceptiveness could be a little disconcerting sometimes. Besides, Caia thoughts depressed as her eyes fell on Alexa, why would Lucien be interested in the little orphan Annie when he could have the gorgeous Alexa?

"Lucien is being generous," Dana's annoying voice cut into her thoughts. "You should be a little more grateful."

Alexa smirked. "Yeah, Caia. If he could hear you now... tut-tut."

Caia felt like hissing. The terrible twosome still didn't like her. "I didn't say I wasn't grateful."

"Back off." Sebastian sighed, clearly as fed up with their sniping as Caia was. He drew her towards him protectively, a gesture Caia accepted, and she and Jaeden followed him towards the entrance of the school. "You know, I wish they'd get over it already," he voiced her thoughts. "You haven't even looked at Mal twice since you got here, so what's Dana's problem?"

"She's a sheep," Jaeden chimed in. "She does whatever she thinks will make Alexa happy."

"You know." Alexa made them tense as she appeared suddenly, striding up to them. "That was kind of rude, Sebastian." She moved past them gracefully, an ugly twist to her mouth. "But I forgive you. I'll have to get used to being magnanimous. It's what a Pack Leader does."

Jaeden guffawed, "What?!"

"Are you completely psycho?" Sebastian asked incredulously. "You are aware that you're not Pack Leader?"

Alexa smiled evilly, her eyebrow quirking up as she drew them to a halt. She turned that wicked smile on Caia. "But I will be mate to Pack Leader. The party at Lucien's will be a perfect opportunity for me to show Lucien what a mistake it'll be if he chooses differently." Her eyes narrowed in calculation. "He wouldn't want to choose someone, say, who would jeopardize the pack by foolish displays of strength in front of 'them'."

Caia heaved a sigh. She had hoped Alexa had forgotten that by now. No other weird occurrences had happened since the calculus solution, so Caia was left without explanation for it. She was afraid there would be questions, and trouble, if Alexa did mention it to Lucien.

"You know I didn't do that, Alexa."

She snorted. "Oh goddess, are we still on that track?"

The bell rang. Caia shook her head in disbelief. "I actually thought you were off my back. No one here cares about your designs on Lucien." OK, that was a lie. "Do what you want. Stay out of my way, and I'll out of yours. OK."

"You don't fool me, Caia."

Sebastian groaned. "Oh come on." He tugged Caia and Jaeden past the she-devil. "You're delusional, you know that."

They had gone only a few steps when Jaeden threw over her shoulder, "In more ways than one. Lucien will never choose you. Don't you think he would have already?"

"She's exhausting," Caia growled, as they walked towards class. "Every time I get into it with her I feel like I've stepped into an episode of *Gossip Girl*."

"What *girl*?" The two of them asked in unison.

Caia shook her head. She forgot that because of her long period of isolation from the pack she'd watched a lot more television than they had.

"TV show."

"Oh, yeah." Jaeden nodded. "I never watched that one. Is that the one with the annoying girls with so much money they have to resort to cruelty and manipulation out of sheer boredom?"

"Yeah." Caia snorted, eyeing her suspiciously. "Sure you haven't watched at least a couple of episodes?"

"We-"

"Don't let her get to you," Sebastian said softly, interrupting them, and returning the conversation back to Alexa. His eyes were concerned as he rubbed her shoulder comfortingly. "Ignore her."

Caia nodded. She'd try.

But that day in English, with the she-devil sitting right beside her, she couldn't help but have a different kind of day-dream. One in which Alexa was Lucien's mate, and she kept Caia in a cage as an amusing pet. Lucien would come over to the cage to poke and prod at her with a stick, to the delight of his new bride.

"Miss Ribeiro?"

"Hmm," she mumbled, wincing as if she really felt the prod of that stick.

"Caia?"

"Huh?" She blinked, and realized her English teacher was asking her a question. She straightened knocking her book to the floor. The class snickered and she tried to hide her blush.

"Thank you for joining us, Miss Ribeiro," the teacher said sarcastically.

"Sorry," she mumbled and glanced at Alexa. The girl was gloating at her like she knew what she'd been day-dreaming about. OK, the girl was gorgeous, but could Lucien really be attracted to her? Caia sighed. She needed to stop thinking about her Pack Leader. She didn't even recognize this whiny person she'd become. She should avoid Lucien at all costs.

Lucien was happily surprised when he heard the chime on the front door of the store sound, and then the familiar, sweet scent of Caia drifted into his workroom. He smiled and wandered out into the store front to see her running her hand along one of the rocking chairs he'd designed.

"Like it?"

She spun around in surprise. "I don't know how you manage to do that?"

"This." He tapped his nose. "You need to focus on using it more. You don't get taken by surprise as much. Although this is a surprise." He gestured indicating her presence.

He thought he sensed shyness in her smile as she walked around the room, keeping her gaze on his furniture. He watched her furtively, enjoying the way her long hair slid across her shoulders like silk. When his thoughts wandered to wondering what that hair would look like spread across his pillow he gave himself a mental slap.

"You here for a reason?" Lucien prodded, hoping his thoughts weren't clearly written on his face. Instead he concentrated on trying to keep amusement at her presence out of his voice. It seemed to annoy her when she thought he was laughing at her.

Finally Caia looked up, stopping and sitting in one of the dining room chairs. She halted abruptly and flushed. "Do you mind?" she asked.

"No." He smiled. "It's what it's there for."

She relaxed and eased back into the chair. "I'm actually here about the car."

Lucien groaned. She was keeping the damn car. He was about to tell her so when she lifted her hand up to stop him from saying anything.

"I'm keeping the car."

It was his turn to relax. "OK. Good."

"But on one condition."

His eyes narrowed. He was used to giving the orders around here and setting the conditions. Usually, that would be his reply to such a statement, but it caught in the back of his throat. He cleared it. "What condition?"

"That you let me get a job."

That wasn't what he expected.

No. He had the luxury of being able to take care of his kinswomen. His mother didn't have to work, and he hadn't demanded Irini get a job when she'd come home because she'd been working her ass off all the time she'd been gone. Now, he wasn't some old-fashioned chauvinist, but the women of his family only worked if they wanted to, but if they didn't need to, then he didn't want to make them. Besides, Caia was too young for a job. She should be concentrating on school.

"I don't think so."

She smiled that crazy sweet smile that seemed to work its charm on all the men in the pack. Magnus and Ryder crumbled under it.

"I thought you would say that. So, I was thinking that I could work for you here, at the weekends or something."

"For me?" he asked incredulously.

He watched as her expression turned unsure. "Well... I just thought you know... you don't have anyone manning the store front, and you can get busy at the weekends..."

Lucien grinned. He was sold. "I think it's a great idea."

Caia grinned back at him. "You do?"

"Sure. This Saturday OK?"

She nodded happily, and he realized she was just glad to be contributing something to the family. He understood that. But for him, it was a perfect opportunity to keep an eye on her.

12 – Witches, Vampyres and Faeries, Oh My

Jaeden couldn't help herself. She told everyone at lunch the next day that Caia was working for Lucien. Alexa's reply had been to cause a scene by storming away from the table. The humans had watched them for the rest of the lunch period, wondering what an earth had happened at the 'pretty people' table. Caia knew Jaeden was just as pissed as she was that Alexa and Dana wouldn't get off her back, but really, telling Alexa that she was going to be spending even more quality time with Lucien was just asking for the girl to tear her apart. For the rest of the week she was met with icy resentment, which as far as Caia was concerned was better than the girl actually speaking to her.

It was with a huge sigh of relief that Saturday rolled around quickly. She hadn't seen much of Lucien lately, and although it had been her intention (before she went and asked him for a job working beside him) to avoid him, she was missing him a little. Moreover, she was more than a little relieved to be getting out of the house. She assumed she hadn't seen much of Lucien because, what with Irini and Aidan's mating only a week away, Ella had turned the house into party planning central.

As Lucien always left for a work a few hours before the store actually opened so he could get a start on his furniture before the interruptions began, Caia didn't arrive for her first day until eight forty-five. She was surprised to see Ryder was already there. He smiled teasingly at her as Lucien gave her a run through of her duties. There was nothing major to undertake - the cash register seemed easy enough to understand, and besides, he had told her if she was asked any questions she couldn't answer to just give him a shout.

"I can't believe you're working here." Ryder smirked, settling into a rocking chair as Lucien departed into his work room.

"Should you be doing that?" Caia asked, sliding onto the stool behind the front counter.

Ryder chuckled and shrugged. "Dunno, you tell me. You work here now."

Caia laughed. "Why is that so amazing to you?"

His eyes twinkled but he shook his head, refusing to say anything. She felt her stomach flip. Ryder didn't suspect her feelings, did he? Holy Artemis, that would be awful. Worse than awful. Utter mortification was in sight. "You haven't had a job lately," she stated, trying to turn the conversation away from her.

He nodded. "True. Things have been quiet for a while."

She leaned against the counter, her eyes wide as she asked, "So you must have come across other supernaturals on all your trips, right?"

"Sure."

"I haven't met any." She sighed, thinking of all the creatures out there that shared their world, and she had no idea what any of them were like.

Ryder frowned. "What about Marion?"

"The magik who put the protection spell up around me?"

He nodded.

It was her turn to shrug. "I never met her."

Ryder grinned. "I can't believe that. Marion is great. You'll really like her. Powerful witch too. You know her sister is the Head of the Daylight Coven?"

Caia shook her head. She had had no idea. That meant that for ten years she had had actual royalty looking after her, watching and protecting. Wow, the pack really did have connections in high places. "How do you know a witch that high up in the circle?"

He winked. "How else?"

She shook her head. "What's that supposed to mean?"

"I keep forgetting you're only seventeen. Mind you when I was seventeen I knew-"

Caia frowned. "Ryder, the point?"

The hunter laughed at her impatience. "OK, OK. The pack is good friends with Marion because once, a long time ago, Magnus was *really* good friends with Marion."

It took a moment for that to sink in, and then she gasped, "Magnus was with a magik?"

"Hey, there is nothing wrong with a little variety in life."

The leer on his face made her ask quietly, so that her voice wouldn't carry through to Lucien, "Have you ever...?"

Ryder seemed to be enjoying her awkwardness. "What? Enjoyed some vanilla instead of chocolate?"

She rolled her eyes at his metaphor. "Yes."

He nodded, taking his turn to glance through to the work shop to make sure Lucien wasn't paying attention. "Many times. You know there are some lykans who have mated with other supernaturals."

Her mind whirled with the revelation. She had had no idea that was possible. She brightened; suddenly her options were a little less confining. "Really?"

"Sure. I have a friend from another pack. David. He mated with a faerie."

"A shapeshifter?"

"One and only."

"Wow."

"You really didn't know that was possible?" Ryder queried leaning his elbows on his knees. "Your education is kind of spotty."

She twisted her lips peevishly. "Tell me about it." Then she frowned. "But they can't *actually* mate, right? Ella said that you can't have children unless you mate, and you can't mate unless the gods bless the union so..."

Ryder nodded. "And what goddess should bless a union between a lykan and a faerie, Artemis or Hemera?"

"Exactly."

"Hemera." He smiled. "She has precedent, since she's all primordial and shi-"

"So they can have children?" Caia interrupted, amazed.

"They'll have faeries for children in that case."

Caia's mind hurt with how many scenarios this new situation created. "But, if a vampyre and a lykan mate, then who-"

"Well there's the thing. Vampyres can only have kids with their own kind. And to be honest they don't view mating the same way we do. Hades doesn't bless the union or anything you know. He didn't exactly expect his nasty little undead to refine their ways and start living like humans. Apparently, the story goes that Demeter, the Goddess of Fertility, granted the vampyres the ability to give birth to their own kind in vengeance against Hades for kidnapping her daughter Persephone and making her Queen of the Underworld. With this gift, vampyres became even more human."

Caia shook her head, astounded by all the new information. Ryder grinned at her.

"You want to hear some of my personal stories?"

Caia nodded her head enthusiastically and leaned back to enjoy Ryder's colorful storytelling. They were interrupted a few times as customers came in, but for most of the morning he held her enthralled. He told her about a group of vampyre hunters he'd stayed with for a few weeks; how, although many vampyres were able to sustain themselves on the blood they bought from butchers and slaughterhouses, these hunters preyed on animals to hone their skills for hunting the rogue vampyres that killed humans for pleasure.

"So," Caia searched for clarification, "It's against the law to hunt a supernatural that isn't of your own race?"

"Completely," Ryder told her, his eyes serious. "If I were caught hunting a rogue vampyre I could be pulled up before the Council. It's a huge breech of Coven laws."

"So vampyres," Caia went on, "What are they like? I mean, we don't die by silver bullets so what's the true story behind them? Do they sleep in coffins?"

Ryder smiled at her innocence. "No. They walk in daylight, they're not afraid of crosses or holy water-"

"I didn't think they were, considering they're pre-Christian."

"Smart ass." He shook his head teasingly at her. "Basically, they look like humans, just like us, except they move faster, they're stronger, and they live on blood. To kill them, you've got to cut off their heads."

"What about the heart?"

"Well, unlike the myths, vampyres hearts actually do beat, but it's encased in thick bone so... you really have to cut off the head to end the bloodsuckers."

"Wow. Their hearts beat. I feel like I've been lied to my whole life."

Ryder chuckled at her faux look of disappointment. "Yeah, well I love the movies, but they certainly have a hell of a lot to answer for, huh."

She smiled, but then promptly frowned. "What's up with the bone encasement around the heart?"

"Don't ask me, ask Hades." Ryder shrugged. "Oh, and they have this thing for coins."

Caia screwed up her face in confusion, reeling from these new found facts on vampyres. "Coins?"

"Yeah." He grinned. "Think about it. The reason they're here at all is because Hades sent them back after they crossed without coin into the underworld."

"So big coin collectors, huh?"

"Huge. Don't try to touch any of them either. They do *not* like that."

Caia laughed, shaking her head at all the new information. "We belong to a world that is just..."

"Just what?"

"Amazing. And I know nothing about it."

His smile was soft and sympathetic. "You're getting there. You want to hear about this faerie I met in Italy? She was the first faerie I met, and boy did I learn my lesson..."

She laughed as he told her about this gorgeous woman who had stolen from him not once, not twice, but three times when he was on a job in the southern climes of Italy. She had disguised herself as three different people; all women he couldn't resist apparently.

"Yeah, I don't like faeries," he finished.

Caia was confused. She thought some faeries worked for the good guys. She mused aloud about it.

"Of course." Ryder nodded, and leaned back lazily as he looked at his watch. She could hear his stomach growling. "The Daylight Coven employs them, just as the Midnight Coven does. Marion has her very own personal faerie... now *she* is annoying."

Caia liked the sound of Marion. "Will I get to meet her? Marion I mean."

Ryder straightened. "Sure. Probably pretty soon actually-"

"Ryder." Lucien appeared in the doorway to the workshop. Caia watched his eyes harden on his friend. "I need your help back here with something."

Ryder sighed and stood up slowly like he'd been caught doing something he shouldn't have. Her eyebrow quirked up in curiosity as he strolled slowly after his friend. Lucien shut the door behind him and Caia tip-toed over to press her ear up against it. She had a feeling Ryder was in trouble.

She was right.

"Watch what you're talking about," Lucien hissed.

"I didn't say anything," Ryder protested.

"It was close."

She heard Ryder sigh at Lucien's tone. Even he wasn't allowed to cross the Pack Leader. "Sorry. I'll be careful."

Caia pulled back as she heard movements towards the door. She tried to look as innocent as possible as Ryder returned to join her in the store front. She was bemused when their conversation turned to movies. Lucien was hiding something from her. This meant he didn't trust her. At this thought, hopes she hadn't even known she'd had deflated, and she had a feeling she was going to be abysmally depressed for the rest of the day. Whatever these feelings for him were... well they really sucked.

Fifteen minutes later just as Ryder was complaining of the need for lunch, the front door chimed, and in stepped the unexpected. Alexa strolled in, graceful as a ballerina, holding two brown paper bags in her hand. She was wearing a figure-hugging short skirt and tight shirt, topped off by a cropped leather jacket. She looked a million bucks. Caia glanced down at her plain t-shirt and ragged jeans. Oh yeah, no comparison. What was she doing here? Caia groaned inwardly.

Alexa smiled sweetly at her, obviously for Ryder's benefit. "Ryder." She turned that smile on him and swayed over to him seductively. "Your mother said you would be here so I brought two." She handed him one of the paper bags that smelled of meat and then turned to Caia with a flash in her eyes. "I didn't know you would be here," she lied and smiled flirtatiously at Ryder again. "I'll just take this to Lucien."

Caia watched in confusion, and admittedly annoyance, as Alexa swayed those hips out of the front room and into Lucien's workshop.

Ryder must have read her confusion and smirked knowingly. "Alexa comes by every Saturday with lunch from my mother's diner for Lucien," he explained in a lowered voice.

Well, she hadn't known that. "Oh," was all she managed, curling her hands into tight fists. She had no reason to be mad, she knew that. She was the newcomer. But still, the girl was so obvious. She flinched at the sound of Lucien's laughter. She made him laugh? Caia groaned, and was thankfully saved from Ryder's questioning eyes as a customer walked in. He was a tall guy, possibly in his late twenties, attractive in a human sort of way. His eyes seemed to light up as Caia approached him in greeting.

"Can I help?" She smiled, and then flushed at his appraising look; even Caia, the oblivious, recognized male appreciation in that answering grin. She could feel Ryder straighten up from the counter where he was standing, tensing protectively.

"Yes." The guy's smile widened. "*You* definitely can."

"Is there something in particular that you're looking for?"

Another laugh sounded from Lucien in the workshop. Her smile tightened.

"Well." The guy sighed dramatically. "My sister tells me I'm never going to keep a girlfriend with the crappy, old furniture I own at the moment. She recommended here for a dining room set."

"OK." Caia nodded, trying to focus. "Well," she began, walking towards one of only three sets Lucien had on display. It was the least stylized, solid, straight-edged mahogany. It looked the most masculine of them all. "There is this one."

The guy nodded, running his hand along the back of one of the chairs. "It's nice. Mahogany?"

Caia nodded again. "Yeah. If you have any particular questions I can get the owner, Mr. Líder. He crafts everything."

The guy's eyebrows rose. "So, it is all handcrafted?"

"Sure. If there is a design that you would like to discuss with Mr. Líder, I can give you a copy of his portfolio, or as I say, you can speak to him personally."

The customer grinned, eyeing her again. "That's very cool. Mr. Líder is a lucky man to have such a competent assistant."

Yeah, she was sure it was her competency he was ogling. She laughed softly at his obvious come on. He was as bad as Alexa. "Be sure to let him know that."

"Oh I will." He grinned, obviously assuming she was flirting back. He leaned over the dining table, lowering his voice. "You know, I'm not definite on the furniture, but I'll certainly take *your* number,"

"Can I help?" Like a sword unleashed from its scabbard, the steel in Lucien's tone rang throughout the store. Caia turned sharply. He only used that tone when he was seriously pissed. His silver eyes shifted quickly from her to narrow on the guy.

The guy seemed to sense Lucien's annoyance and, arrogantly leaning against one of his tables, he drawled, "And you might be?"

Lucien strolled with a fake casualness up the steps from the doorway of his workshop onto the shop floor, and Caia watched as the guy's expression changed when he saw how huge Lucien was. His eyes flickered to Ryder and back. "I'm the owner. Lucien Líder."

The guy grinned now and offered Lucien his hand. He indicated the room with a sweep of his free hand. "Your furniture is well crafted."

"Thank you," Lucien replied stiffly, refusing the proffered hand. He glanced up at her, and Caia blanched. What in Hades was he doing? Her own gaze drifted past him to Alexa, who was directly behind him, looking less than amused that his attention had been diverted from her.

"Oh." The guy followed Lucien's gaze, seeming unconcerned by Lucien's rudeness. "Your assistant has been very helpful."

"Is that right?" Lucien murmured, still looking at her. Caia narrowed her eyes on him in annoyance.

"What?" The guy grinned, noticing Alexa behind Lucien. His eyes washed lasciviously over her. "Another assistant?" He smirked at Lucien as if they were friends. "You certainly know how to do business."

Caia sighed. If this guy knew that he was in a room of lykans, two of which who looked as if they could happily rip him apart, the cockiness would soon dissolve and the peeing of the pants would commence.

Lucien growled, shifting his gaze between Caia and Alexa. He turned back to the guy. "We're closed."

"I... I'm sorry?" the guy asked, completely bewildered by the turn of events.

Ryder took over, obviously reading something in Lucien's demeanor that she didn't. He clasped his big hand on the guy's shoulder and started leading him towards the door. "We forgot to put the sign up, sorry. You'll need to come back during business hours."

"Bu-"

"Goodbye now," he said cheerfully, and shoved the guy outside.

Caia scowled. "You just lost a customer."

"So?" Lucien snarled. "Remember," he pointed to his ears, "lykan hearing. He wasn't interested in the furniture."

Caia rolled her eyes. "That was just talk. I could have gotten him to buy that furniture," she retorted incredulously. "The guy wanted an entire dining set. Have you had something bad to eat, or something?" Her eyes narrowed on Alexa, who was looking suspiciously triumphant.

He drew her a look of annoyed bafflement. "What?"

"Well, something is pissing you off. Your attitude with that guy..." she looked to Ryder for an explanation. "I mean, I know lykans have an issue with temperament but please..."

Alexa sighed and strode over to Lucien, laying a possessive hand on his shoulder. Caia flinched again at the gorgeous picture they made together. Both tall, and dark, and tanned. "Lucien was just being protective," Alexa purred. "That guy looked at me like I was a whore."

Caia snorted at that and caught Ryder smothering a grin with his hand. It was nice to know they shared a similar sense of humor.

Lucien shrugged as if it was no big deal. "The guy was a jerk. I don't sell my furniture to jerks. I have a specific clientele."

"So what." Caia shrugged. "I've not to serve people you think might be jerks? If so, you're really going to lose a lot of business."

Lucien looked uncomfortable. His jaw was clenched and a flush had appeared on his cheekbones.

"Uh." Ryder coughed. "Why don't I take you for some lunch, Cy? You haven't eaten."

Caia blinked. "Huh? Wha-"

"Come on." He grabbed her jacket and her elbow, and started guiding her towards the door.

"Um... okaaay." She glanced back at Lucien, who was still standing tense, his gaze strange on her. Then her eyes drifted to Alexa, who was leaning into him, smiling smugly. She couldn't believe Lucien had actually lost a customer over that she-devil. Her heart went limp at the thought as she followed Ryder.

Yeah, today was definitely going to be a depressing one.

When Caia related the story to Jaeden later that night at her friend's home she was assured by her that it was nothing weird for Lucien and Ryder to have acted the way they had if the guy had been even the slightest bit lecherous.

"You know how temperamental we are. Well, males tend to get a little possessive over their womenfolk, even if said womenfolk aren't their mates."

"So, that was just testosterone?"

"Yeah."

Caia grimaced. "How disgusting," she replied wryly.

Jaeden shrugged, her smile sheepish. "I don't know. Don't you think it's a little hot?"

She guffawed. "No. We live in the twenty-first century. And we're lykans. We don't need any man to take care of us."

Jaeden didn't look convinced. "Sorry. I just think it's kind of nice that they care enough to want to smash some human jerk's face in when he gets a little too friendly."

"Well it was embarrassing." Caia sighed. She felt her cheeks turning red at the thought of that poor guy. What must he have thought when Ryder shoved him out of the door? Plus, she mused, biting her lip, he thought she was attractive. It was kind of nice. Her self-esteem wasn't really up to much lately thanks to the rest of the women in the pack all looking like glamour girls. Her eyes flickered over Jaeden who was beautiful without even having to try.

"I know you don't want to hear this." Jaeden was smiling cheekily at her. "But maybe Lucien kicked the guy out because he heard him asking you for your number."

The thought made her heart kick. It was a nice thought. It was based entirely outside the realm of reality, but it was still nice. She shook her head, her eyes wistful. "I don't think so."

"You sound disappointed by that." Jaeden was grinning, her blue eyes sparkling with mischief. "Am I to assume one has feelings for our glorious leader?"

Oh crap, Caia groaned. In her depression she had let too much show on her face. Trying desperately to cover her slip she shook her head, laughing as if that was the most insane idea on the planet. "Oh please. Of course not."

Her friend looked unconvinced. "Uh, yeah... sure."

"I don't," she retorted, through gritted teeth.

Jaeden's expression changed. She slumped and looked serious. "I really think he has feelings for you, Caia."

"Don't say that to me." She got up and grabbed her bag, shoving her feet back into her shoes. Jaeden jumped up, anxiously following her as she made her way out of her bedroom and down her staircase.

"Why? I really think it's the truth?"

Caia ignored her, her heart beating faster as she rushed down the stairs and out of Jaeden's front door. Her eyes fastened on her car with relief as she strode towards it.

"Caia." Jaeden stopped her, spinning her around to face her. "What's wrong?"

She felt the threat of tears and gulped a lump back down in her throat, holding them at bay. Before returning to the pack she hadn't cried since she was a little girl. These days it was all she seemed to do. She was so tired today. Shaking her head, she pulled her car door open and threw her bag inside.

"Caia, please."

She drew to a stop at the worried look on Jaeden's face. She realized Jae was afraid that she'd offended her somehow. She heaved a sigh. She should trust her; she owed her that much.

"I just..." she stopped, trying to gather her thoughts. "I'm happy here, Jae."

"So, what's the problem?"

"The problem is... I'm happy here, and I never have been before. But this... this is all new, and the pack is just getting to know me. If anyone thought, for one second, that I had designs on Lucien..."

Thankfully she watched the light dawn in Jaeden's eyes. "I see."

"I don't have any," she rushed to explain, "It's just... he's been kind. And not everyone is accepting of me as you are."

Her friend drew her into an unexpected hug. "I won't tell anyone you like him. I understand. I won't tell."

Caia breathed a sigh of relief and hugged her back tightly.

"Why are you calling?" he asked coldly. "I told you not to call me unless it was necessary."

He heard her sigh sweetly on the other end of the phone. "Well," she replied breathily, "Last time we talked you seemed anxious that things weren't progressing as quickly as you would have liked. Today, I have reason to believe that Phase Two won't be as far off as we thought."

He smiled into the mirror above his phone table. He liked the sound of that. "Oh?"

"The girl and the leader are becoming attached."

"You know this for certain?"

He clenched his fist, knowing she was insolently rolling her eyes. She thought he couldn't see. "Yes," she said evenly. "My eyes and ears are everywhere."

Despite her insolence he felt his shoulders relax a little. This was good news indeed. "What about the others?"

"With the exception of one or two, they actually seem to be rather taken with the little abomination."

"Good. We are depending on that."

She chuckled. "Yes, we are. How's my little pet faring by the way?" she purred.

It was his turn to roll his eyes. "*My* pet, don't you mean?"

"Well, of course, my lord,"

"I'm enjoying it. I find it is an excellent outlet for all my pent up aggression."

"I'm sure."

Actually at this moment he rather felt like visiting it. Bored with her now, he shut down and said, "Call when there is no doubt about their alliance. We'll move in for Phase Two."

"Of course, my-"

He hung up before she was finished and gazed into the mirror again. His eyes narrowed at how unkempt his hair was. Smoothing it with his hands and straightening his collar, his eyes brightened with anticipation, thinking of the pet his spy had given him. It was just a bonus in this tense and frustrating business. He strolled through the house until he came to the large kitchen. At the end of the kitchen was a pantry, and in it was another door. The door led down old wooden stairs to a deep, dark pit. At the bottom he stopped and took in a lungful of the air. He winced at the damp earth that attacked his nose.

Damp earth and fear.

With a snap of his fingers a flame appeared in thin air, dancing in front of him, lighting the entire room and waiting for his command. It followed him as he strode to the end of the dark dungeon-like basement, and came to a stop in front of a large cage. He bent down, his eyes lighting up with delight at the creature inside. "Hello again."

The fear roiling inside of it him hit with full force. He shivered in delight at the tingling warmth of excitement spreading through his body.

"Did you think I'd forgotten you?"

13 — First... Everything

There was a dark cloud over her head for the next week. She would fall out of bed in the mornings, and go through the routine of washing and dressing, having breakfast, and then heading off to school...

And then she'd see Alexa's triumphant face, and whoosh! The dark cloud burst overhead, drenching her in a self-pity she had only ever read about.

"I don't like this," she muttered to Jaeden during their study period.

"What?"

"This." She indicated herself dramatically with a wave of her hands. "This person I've become... dear goddess, I'm like one of *them*." She flicked her pencil at the humans in the room.

Jaeden laughed under her breath. "Caia, it's called a crush. Believe me, Ryder makes me feel the same horrible mixture of happiness and despair. Add a pinch of lykan volatility and you've got yourself the teenage hormonal party from Hades."

She snorted, but Jaeden's comforting words of assurance didn't make her feel any better about the fact that all she had been doing for the last few days was moping about Lucien. Last night at the dinner table she had even been reduced to monosyllabic sentences in his presence.

"I heard Alexa's been visiting his store after school." Jaeden twisted her face in disgust.

"Who told you that?"

"Sebastian's seen her when he's been coming home from Yvana's."

Caia moaned, cupping her chin forlornly in her hand. "I can't even imagine what my life will be like if he actually mates with her."

"If who actually mates with whom?" Sebastian whispered, sliding into the seat beside her.

"If Lucien mates with Alexa," Jaeden answered.

"Why would that bother *you*, Caia?" Sebastian looked suspicious, pulling his chair closer to hers.

Her heart picked up tempo, as her eyes flew wildly to Jaeden. Sebastian couldn't know. No one else could.

"Uh." Jaeden swung her pencil about as she tried to think of something. "Um... oh, because Alexa hates Caia. If she was Lucien's mate, I mean ... she could cause trouble for her."

Sebastian smirked and put his arm around Caia's shoulder, his tawny eyes twinkling as he looked into hers. "You don't have anything to worry about. I'll protect you."

Caia grunted and pulled from his embrace as the bell rang. She gathered her things and stood up before them. "Thanks Sebastian, but no. If the worst comes to the worst... I've always wanted to go to China."

Saturday morning arrived quickly. The nervous energy in the house was at breaking point as Ella flew between Irini's and Caia's rooms to make sure their preparations for the mating ritual were going well. Eventually, Caia had decided to leave Irini in the capable hands of her mother and Lucia, who was fixing her hair for her, and stay out of the way in her bedroom. She had changed already, her slender figure wrapped in the dusky pink satin dress they'd chosen. It was floor-length and figure-hugging, creating the illusion that she was taller than she was. She was a little self-conscious of the thin straps and low cowl neckline, but Ella assured her she looked perfect. Lucia had twisted her long, pale hair into a French twist, and placed tiny pink rose buds into the style. She sighed, turning to the side to make sure the dress wasn't wrinkled from sitting in it. She didn't care what Ella said, this certainly felt like a bridesmaid dress. Caia turned at the sound of someone clearing their throat, and immediately flushed at the sight of Lucien standing tall and elegant in a dark suit. Oh my, he was handsome, her heart fluttered uncontrollably.

He smiled at her, his eyes drinking her in. She flushed again.

"You look..." he stepped into the room and stopped a few feet from her, his hands jammed casually into his suit trouser pockets. "Wow." He met her gaze and grinned. "You look beautiful."

Oh boy, she was sure he must hear her heart thumping rapidly in her chest; she felt like it was going to explode. Did he actually say she looked beautiful? Was he just being polite?

"Thank you," she managed, and then had to clear her throat when it came out all breathy. *Dammit*. "So do you." She flushed again and stammered. "I... I m-m-mean you look nice."

Lucien laughed and her eyes got caught in his. They weren't as electrifyingly silver today, more of an intense dark smoke. "Don't be nervous, Caia."

"Nervous. Why should I be nervous?"

He shrugged. "Because you've never been to one of these before."

"Oh, right." She rolled her eyes at her own obtuseness.

"Why aren't you with all the other females, primping and fawning over Irini?"

Caia laughed dryly. "Ah, no thank you. I'm safer here."

Lucien smiled softly. "You're really not like the others, are you?"

She stilled under his gaze and gulped. Well she'd heard that before. "Is that a bad thing?"

He took another step towards her, his voice low as he said, "No. Not at all."

"Caia, there you are." Ella came bustling into the room, unaware of the electrical tension that was miraculously sparking. She brushed by Lucien, smiling distractedly at him, and grabbed Caia's wrist. "You're needed for pre-ritual photographs."

Caia docilely followed her, her gaze glued to Lucien until Ella pulled her out of the room, jerking her eyes unstuck. Her mind was whirring. Had they just had a moment together? It had certainly felt like a moment. She had goosebumps. You didn't get goosebumps from ordinary interactions... right?

Her mind was distractedly on the dreaded Alpha for the rest of the morning and into the afternoon as they bustled about with setting the house up for the post-ritual party, and settling Irini's nerves. The backyard had been set up with white lawn chairs for the ceremony, all facing towards the woods where Irini and Aidan would stand before Magnus. The ritual would take place as darkness fell, when the moon was out, and they could call upon Artemis to bind their two souls. By six-thirty the driveway was chock full of cars and the pack were settling themselves in their finery out back in the chairs. The thrum of their voices floated through the quiet house. Caia took a deep breath. She would sit in the front row beside Ella, Lucien, Ryder, and Yvana. As Ella had already mentioned, her seat with the family and the fact that she was wearing the same color as Irini and Ella was deliberate, so that the pack viewed her as family as much as they themselves did. She would sit in between Ella and Lucien, since Yvana, although she had apologized for her outburst, was clearly still affronted by Caia's mere presence.

"It's time." Ella took hold of her hand and led her through the kitchen behind Lucien and Aidan's family.

"Ella, are you crying already?" she whispered, aghast at the tears in the Elder's eyes.

"I'm just so happy and yet so sad. I just got her back, you know."

Caia squeezed her hand and pulled her closer. "You still have her. She's not going anywhere."

Ella smiled, and they quieted as they strolled towards their seats. Seeing the family of the mating couple, the pack's voices dissipated into silence.

Irini and Aidan approached Magnus from either side. He stood with his back to the woods. He smiled at the couple and welcomed the pack. When he stilled so did everyone else, and Caia's skin prickled at the hush that washed over them all. Magnus tilted his head back and gazed up at the moon. Caia followed his movement, but then looked back at him when she realized that was what everyone else was doing.

"Artemis," he called in his brandy warm voice. "Potnia Theron," he appealed, using the lykans 'mother' title for the goddess. The rest of his recital was in Greek - the mystery of those words floated across her skin, as gentle and as awakening as the night's breeze. "Artemis," he finished, taking Aidan's hand and placing it on top of Irini's and holding the two in a bind. "Potnia Theron," he continued in English, "Bind these two souls together in eternal devotion to each other and to you, their mother."

Caia gasped as Irini's and Aidan's eyes widened, watching as they did as a moon-colored light emanated from their clasped hands and rushed exquisitely through their bodies. Magnus' expression remained unchanged, but Caia was in awe, her gaze turning to Ella and Lucien to see if they were just as astounded. But no, they remained as still as Magnus, watching as the light burned brighter and then dissolved just as suddenly. Magnus grinned and stepped back releasing their hands. "Artemis has blessed this union."

Aidan grinned and pulled Irini into a heated kiss that made Caia blush. Irini laughed and pulled back, and turned to smile happily at her mother. The pack was suddenly on their feet, whooping and rushing towards the couple in congratulations. Caia took a step back to let the others by.

"Amazing, huh?" Jaeden suddenly appeared, resting her chin on Caia's shoulder, draping an elegant arm over the other.

"It was beautiful," Caia whispered.

"I remember when I saw my first. It was for Christian and Lucia. Pretty awesome... to know that Artemis is really out there, watching over us."

Caia turned to her with sadness in her eyes. "If she hadn't bound Irini and Aidan together that would have meant they weren't soul mates."

Jaeden shrugged. "Yeah. But supernaturals rarely confuse these things."

"But it happens?" Caia bit her lip, sympathizing with lovers who had gone before Artemis, believing they were in love, only to have Artemis refuse to mate them. "Artemis says no and a couple can't... have children together."

Jaeden nodded distractedly, her eyes on the happy couple. "Yeah, exactly. Come on." She grabbed her hand and pulled her towards the kitchen. "Get your head out of the dark clouds and into the house. We need to choose the music before someone else destroys the night with ABBA, or something."

"What's wrong with ABBA?" Caia mumbled, glancing back at the crowds around Irini and Aidan. She was glad for them. They seemed safe and happy in their little world. She hoped it would always be so for them.

His house was filled with laughter and warmth; people in the sitting room, kitchen, and hallways, all drinking, and dancing, and celebrating. It was a fantastic atmosphere, and he really should be more into it than he was. But he was distracted.

Lucien sighed and leaned against the stairwell in the hallway, beer in hand, watching the festivities around him. Aidan was dancing to Jeff Buckley's *Hallelujah* with his elder sister in the sitting room. Her face was flushed with happiness and excitement, and Lucien was more than glad for her. One of his biggest regrets was that Irini had had to leave her pack behind. Ten years was a long time to be away, but she was home and in love, and she was safe. That was all that mattered now. He sighed again and turned to surreptitiously watch Caia laughing with Jaeden and Daniel in the kitchen. He'd been doing that since their 'moment' in her bedroom this morning. The sight of her standing in the dress as the sunlight filtered across her face just... ah, it was like he'd been punched in the gut, the force of the feeling was that strong. He had been going to kiss her. He knew he would have if his mother hadn't walked in. That woman had good timing; kissing Caia then would have been a mistake; it would have frightened her and... well... it just wasn't the right time.

"Why are you standing out here by yourself?" A familiar voice brushed his ear.

Lucien felt like rolling his eyes. *Alexa*. Instead, he turned and threw her a patient smile. She was standing too close to him, trying to impress him with her low cut dress that fit her like a second skin. Now, he wasn't immune, and the girl was gorgeous, but her machinations were so obvious. She wanted him because he was the Pack Leader and nothing more. She was just her like brother. And that hadn't ended well.

"This is a happy occasion, Lucien. You should act like it." She ran her hand seductively up his arm. "I could make it happier," the provocative comment was followed with a wink.

Lucien shrugged her off, wondering how long his patience was actually going to last. He hadn't been bothered by her showing up with his lunch every Saturday because... well, he was usually hungry by the time she did and... she *was* fun to look at. But the past week her visits had become daily, and her flirtations more dangerously obvious. Ah, he sighed inwardly, wincing at the hope in her dark exotic eyes. She would find out soon enough that even if he might have been interested, there was no way he could make her his mate.

"I'm going to get another beer." He walked away from her, pretending he hadn't seen the petulant twist in her expression. Wandering towards the kitchen, he frowned, realizing Caia and the others had left. Where was she? He strode in, dumping his empty beer bottle in the trash in time to hear her familiar laughter. Following that sound he stopped in the kitchen doorway and watched as Sebastian pulled her along to the end of the right side of the back porch.

"Sebastian, what is going on?" Caia laughed again as the young male pulled her up short and pressed her into the back of the house. Lucien frowned, keeping hidden, but close. He'd had his suspicious about Sebastian's feelings for Caia, the way his eyes followed her when she was in the room, his constant protectiveness of her. But Caia seemed oblivious. Even now, when Sebastian had her positioned against the back wall and leaning into her, she was smiling up at him without a clue that the boy was about to make a move. Lucien groaned. Sebastian was a good kid... he did not want to have deal with him.

"I thought we should talk." Sebastian's grin was loopy, his eyes dazed.

Lucien rolled his eyes. The kid was drunk, too? Goddess it took a lot to get a lykan drunk... how much had he consumed?

"About?"

"You and me." He leaned in even closer.

Lucien watched as Caia straightened, her eyes narrowing, "Sebastian, how much have you had to drink?"

The boy shrugged. "Enough. That's not the point, though. I need to tell you something."

"Well, tell me so we can get back to the party."

"Caia," he groaned, and leaned his head against his arms. His bright eyes opened, looking down at her. "Caia."

"Sebastian?" She was laughing, amused. "Goddess, spit it out. I've never seen you like this before."

Lucien smirked, *I'll bet she hasn't.*

"OK." Sebastian straightened, rolling his neck on his shoulders as if preparing for a fight. "Caia. I want you to know... I want you to know I don't care that you're different."

Lucien frowned. *Uh oh, where is this going?*

Caia stiffened, glowering at Sebastian. "Different?"

Oh yeah she's pissed.

He nodded, continuing on foolishly, "I want to be here for you, Caia, when things get rough... and they're going to. I think we should mate, Caia, before your po-"

"Hey!" Lucien boomed, cutting the boy off before he said something they'd all regret. "What are you guys doing out here? You should be inside enjoying the party." He smiled for Caia's sake, but inside he was burning mad. He was going to kill this kid. His step faltered in front of Sebastian and he glared down at him. The boy at least had the good sense to look nervous. "Sebastian, I think you've had enough to drink. Why don't you go inside and start chugging back some water. That's not a suggestion."

He nodded blearily, glancing quickly at Caia, before rushing off the porch and inside. Lucien watched him go and then turned back to her.

Her light eyes were wide with confusion. "Did you hear any of that?" she asked.

He nodded and took a breath. He just needed to be calm and smooth, and he would have her thinking nothing of it. "Drink. That's why there's an age limit."

She narrowed her eyes on Lucien, her mind still whirring with Sebastian's proposal for them to mate. She hoped Lucien was right and it was just the drink talking, but she hadn't even realized

Sebastian had been thinking that way about her. And what the hell had he meant about protecting her when things got rough?

"What was he talking about?"

Lucien shrugged at her and grinned. "Oh, it was just the ramblings of an inexperienced, underage drinker. You guys were supposed to be sticking to soda."

Caia was unconvinced. His reprimand sounded like a tactic to throw her off the scent. "This whole 'different' thing keeps coming up in conversation," she persisted.

He threw her a look as if to say she was crazy. "I don't know what you're talking about?"

She sighed, so sick of games. "I'm talking about secrets. There are secrets here."

"What kind of secrets?"

"I..." she heaved a sigh, throwing her hands up. "I don't know."

"Caia-"

"No." She shook her head at him, annoyed. "Don't use that patient tone with me like I'm a child, Lucien."

The man had the audacity to smirk at her. "Stop acting like one."

She fixed him with one of her finest glowers. "I am not."

"Are too." He grinned.

She felt her stomach twist at his smile. Dammit, did he have to be so hot and so... *so*. Caia sighed, trying not to smile back at him. The only way to not fall for his charm was to keep at him about the secrets. "For instance," she placed her hands on her hips, straightening to her full height, not that it did any good standing next to a live action *He-Man*, "Why don't you want me asking about the war? I mean really, not the phony answer you gave me when I first asked? Why does no one speak about the war?"

Lucien groaned, running his hand through his hair. "Caia, this is a party, why can't you just enjoy it?"

"Because I'm asking you a question, *oh chosen one*."

"Caia," he said softly and started towards her. Taken aback, she stepped away from him and tripped on her heel, falling against the wall of the house. "Caia, there *is* no big secret," he said as he reached out to steady her. His gaze moved from her face to sweep the backyard and the woods. "The war is such a part of our daily existence that we just don't talk about it. It's like breathing. You do it. It's there. But you don't talk about it."

"Unless you're an asthmatic," she countered.

He turned back to her with a comically baffled look on his face. "What?"

"If you're an asthmatic you talk about breathing because it doesn't come so easy. Well I'm an asthmatic."

"No you're not."

She rolled her eyes. "It's a metaphor, Lucien. I'm asthmatic because I've been a part of the war. I was a target and may still be.

Which means the pack could still get targeted. I'm just saying, maybe it's something we should talk about."

He nodded at her, understanding. "I get it. I really do. But the Daylight Coven do all they can to find out the targets of the Midnights. We have an extra close relationship with them through Marion so … I think we're good."

"If you say so."

Irritation flickered across his face. He took another step towards her, close enough that she had to crane her neck again to look up at him.

"Caia," his tone was a warning.

She shrugged, pretending to be un-intimidated. "I guess it's just easier to worry about the war when you were once the target of it."

He looked incredibly uncomfortable as he swallowed and shook his head, his eyes darting away from her. "You weren't a target of the war."

"No. But I was the target of *a* war. Makes you nervous."

"Caia," Lucien growled softly, "I will protect you. You have nothing to fear. I won't let anything happen to you."

Caia stilled, trying not to make more out of his promise. He was the Pack Leader; it was his duty, nothing more. They were silent together a moment, and then she raised her eyes to look into his. They were filled with sincerity and determination. He really meant what he was telling her. The silence seemed to stretch thin between them, and suddenly the air around them changed. It became electric, crackling and sparking. After a long moment, embarrassed and awkward, she moved to go. She hadn't taken more than two steps when she was abruptly crushed against him, his warm lips pressing against her own. Shocked at first, her mind taking its time to catch up on the fact that he, *Lucien,* was kissing her, she stood immobilized. Having never been kissed before, she didn't know what to do with her lips, and she strained a little as if to pull away. Lucien held tight and kissed her harder, and all thoughts of pulling away just dribbled out of her brain. Her legs began to tremble as if her nerves had snapped, leaving every part of her body shaking. Lucien made a soothing noise in the back of his throat, and left her lips to brush soft kisses across her cheek. He then moved his lips to her ear, his warm breath sending shivers running throughout her as he whispered for her to open her mouth. Her final thought was obliterated and she obediently complied. At the feel of his tongue against hers, another wave of rippling shivers cascaded over her. She stood dazed until instinct took over, and she was kissing him back, in love with the feel of his mouth fused against hers. Lucien's strong arms tightened in response as she slid her hands up over his arms and entwined her own around his neck. Forever, they seemed to be locked in that kiss, each moment building something new in Caia. It was like a spring tightening, all these feelings she didn't know what to do with. Her skin grew hotter and hotter, her body losing her usual tight control one burning step at a time.

"Lucien!"

They pulled apart at the sound of Ella calling his name, Caia gasping, trying to catch her breath. She felt caught in his surprised gaze. And then he smiled softly, brushing his thumb across her lips. Her heart thudded. Had that really happened? Did all first kisses turn out that good?

"Lucien!"

He pulled back cursing under his breath, but his eyes never broke contact with hers.

"There you are," Ella called, striding towards them. "Lucien, the pipes have all burst!"

That got their attention.

"What?" He turned to her.

She heaved a huge sigh throwing her hands up in bewilderment. "A few seconds ago I heard Alexa squeal in the kitchen, and the pipes have burst. Water, everywhere! Then Julia comes running from the downstairs bathroom, Morgan from one of the upstairs, and they're the same. Magnus is checking Caia's bathroom while Isaac and Draven take care of the plumbing. But there's water, *everywhere*," she ended on a whine.

Lucien cursed again, and started heading towards the kitchen.

"Can we fix it?" Caia asked nervously, still reeling from Lucien's kiss.

Ella nodded. "Thankfully, Isaac and Draven are plumbers, but it's put a little damper on the party."

Caia nodded numbly and followed after them. She stopped in the doorway, watching as the others mopped up the small flood in the kitchen. This couldn't be happening. Her gaze flitted back towards the end of the porch where she and Lucien had shared their explosive kiss. Could it have been explosive enough to have done this? She bit her lip, her heart thumping louder and louder. First, the pipes in the airport, then her bathroom... oh, and that morning with Ella when she'd cried over her father's photograph. Was this her doing? She shook her head and pulled back from the doorway. Kicking off her shoes she turned and ran down the porch stairs, past the lawn chairs and into the woods, not stopping until she was at least five minutes from the house. Leaning against a tree to catch her breath, and trying to slow her panicking heart, Caia shook her head in disbelief. "It can't be me," she whispered. "How could it be?"

What was going on? Is this what the pack meant when they called her different? But pipes bursting? No, that was crazy. No one else would even connect the two.

"No," her moan turned into a gasp. And suddenly she knew. She could feel something inside of her pulsing. It had always been there, throbbing like a barrier below the energy she tapped into when she changed. It was alien and strong.

"What's happening to me?" she pleaded with Gaia, as she felt tears prick her eyes, the fear readying her heart for explosion. Growling a profanity she would never have dreamed of using before, Caia pulled off the satin dress in haste and ripped her hair out of the French twist. And then she began to run; faster and faster, her feet tearing on bracken, her toes sinking in moss and dirt, her muscles aching; and with one final spurt of fear she dove arms first as if she were diving into a pool, high into the air, pushing the change like she had never done before. As she landed, it was on her graceful pads, her wolf legs pushing her further into the forest, and away from her fears.

14 – THE CHANGE

The school was quiet. The bell for first period sounded at least ten minutes ago so everyone else was inside. Everyone except Caia. She felt limp, as if she were no longer a part of her body. That night she had ran as hard and as fast as she could from the house, pounding out her anxiety with the dirt beneath her paws until a resolution had fallen upon her. She hadn't wanted to be alone in whatever was happening to her and, although she loved Jaeden, there really was only one person she had felt safe enough to turn to.

Lucien.

By then she had been away from the party for well over an hour, so she returned as quietly as she could, finding her torn dress, and then scaling the house to enter her bedroom. She had taken pause as she remembered Magnus was supposed to be checking the water pipes in her bathroom. But the room was dark and quiet, and there was no light filtering from under her bathroom. Sighing and aching, she had tried to squelch the butterflies in her stomach enough to focus on what exactly she was going to tell Lucien.

He was going to think she was crazy.

Caia had moaned and fallen back onto her bed. Lucien was so good, so caring and fair. He took time with his people, took their problems upon his shoulders as if they were his own. He would need someone just like him, not some troubled girl who was falling to pieces. And what if what was inside her was bad? He'd only try to help because that was who he was. And what if she hurt him? Hurt any of them?

No. She would just have to deal with this on her own like she had everything else.

Eventually Jaeden had been sent to find her, but Caia hadn't opened the door to her or anyone, claiming she was tired and just needed to sleep.

She had kept herself shut in her room the next day. Jaeden had called, Ella had hovered, and Lucien had threatened to break down the door. At that, she had whispered through the wood that she was OK, she promised. She was just exhausted, but they shouldn't worry. But they had. She could feel it radiating throughout the house. She hadn't known how she could feel their emotions as strongly as she felt her own and her anxiety had only worsened.

Jaeden hadn't accepted her feeble reassurances. She had dragged Caia over and into her car as soon as she had arrived at school on Monday.

Neither of them had said a word yet.

Jaeden sighed. Caia looked out of the passenger window at a cat that was dashing from belly to belly of the cars parked around them. Its simple happiness made Caia envy it.

"Caia." Jaeden finally gave in, pulling her around to face her. "You have to tell me what's wrong."

She realized her friend wasn't going to give up, and she wasn't going to tell her the truth, so she decided to waylay her with the other something that was pressing on her. "Lucien kissed me on Saturday."

Jaeden's eyes widened, her jaw dropped, and she let out a startled whoop. "Oh. My. Goddess."

Caia managed a wan smile. "Yeah."

Jaeden grabbed her arm, shaking her. "Caia, are you crazy? Aren't you happy? I thought this is what you wanted?"

"It's just a crush, Jae."

Her friend shook her head, refusing to accept that. "You can't say that."

"Yes I can, and it is."

"Cy... a crush is what I have for Ryder. He's gorgeous, and he has a cool, dangerous job." she snorted. "But I don't know him, not the way you know Lucien."

Caia frowned, her head throbbing. "What are you getting at?"

"Well," she shrugged, "Have you considered the possibility that what you feel is more than crush? That, you might be falling for him... and he for you?"

Caia twisted her lips in thought and looked down at her hands. They clutched the straps of her backpack so tightly they were white. She liked Lucien. A lot. And she was of course attracted to him. But in love with him? Did she really know him well enough for it to be that? Did she even want it to be that?

"No."

"No?"

The sound of laughter from inside drifted towards her ears. She could hear a teacher telling a student not to write on the desk; a class giggling at one of the few funny teachers they had in there; a girl stuttering over a class presentation. It was all so normal, so human. But she wasn't human. She wasn't even sure she was a normal lykan. The only examples of reality she had in her life were the bonds of friendship she had with ones such as the girl by her side. And goddess forgive her, but, all she wanted right now was for Jaeden to go away. To leave her alone so she could go back to ignoring the fact that something was happening to her - good or bad, she didn't know. And to top it off, her crush on a lykan she could never have had gone from hot to sizzling in a matter of twenty four hours. She sighed, and glanced back out the window at that cat. If what was inside her was dangerous she would take herself far away from these people she had begun to love. She smiled humorlessly as she thought of the day she had told Sebastian that China was always an option if the worst came to the worst. She *had* always wanted to see The Great Wall.

"Caia?" Jaeden begged.

She looked back at her friend and placed a reassuring hand over hers. "I'm not meant for him, Jaeden."

"Maybe that's not your decision."

Caia sighed. She really couldn't take a speech about the gods and fate just now. "I better get going."

"Caia ..."

She shook her head and got out of the car. "We'll talk later."

Alexa was smiling like the cat that ate the canary. Caia's back immediately went up as she slid into her seat beside her in English. She didn't even want to know what was going on with her.

When fifteen minutes had gone by, and Alexa hadn't said anything, Caia relaxed minimally, trying to concentrate on the passages the teacher had asked them to read. As per usual the class was rowdy and obnoxious, and the poor teacher was having trouble controlling them.

"So, you missed all the excitement on Saturday night," Alexa purred and Caia groaned.

"Really," she murmured back, uninterested.

"Mm," Alexa continued smugness in her voice that alerted Caia. Her skin began to prickle unexpectedly, the hair on the nape of her neck standing up. What the Hades? She turned to look at the girl. "Yeah. While you were gone, the gods knows where, I helped

Lucien mop up. He was very grateful." She sighed breathily. "And then we got to talking. Really talking, you know."

Caia shifted uncomfortably, and her stomach began to roil with anticipation.

Alexa giggled softly and ducked her head closer to Caia's as if they had been best friends all their lives. Her eyes were sparkling. "And I dunno, maybe we had too much to drink... before I knew it we were in his bedroom."

It was like someone had literally slapped her across the face. Her eyes narrowed on the girl. Alexa didn't mean what Caia thought she meant, did she? Lucien wouldn't kiss one girl, and then...

A white heat prickled across her skin, boiling her blood as it passed inch by inch from her feet up through her legs. It was a familiar heat she had felt only once before.

"And there I am, waking up next to his gorgeous body. I think the pack will be celebrating another mating soon, and when we do," she smiled and touched her flat belly, "This will be a whole lot rounder."

At those last words, without warning and with no way to control it even though she knew what would happen, the white heat blasted out from her body like a force and sent a horrified Alexa flying across the other side of the room. The sound of her peers gasping and chairs scraping back was lost on her. She stared at Alexa in horror, her hands trembling, the blood pounding in her ears.

And then the worst happened.

A familiar wincing pain radiated from her left hand. She glanced down and saw her fair pelt pushing through the soft flesh there. She slapped her other hand over it so they couldn't see. No! Oh goddess. She couldn't breathe.

"What on earth?" she heard the teacher cry as Alexa stumbled to her feet.

She heard the 'oh my God's' of everyone, even some snickering, but they were all staring at her like she'd gone mad.

"Caia Ribeiro, what has gotten into you?!" The teacher was shrieking.

"I have to go," she mumbled, ignoring Alexa's snarl of her name as she fled past her classmates and out of the door. Her eyes never left her hand as more and more of her pelt started pushing through. She swallowed a groan at the feel of her muscles burning, readying themselves for the change.

"Watch yourself, young lady." She looked up as someone steadied her, and realized that there was a small crowd in the hallway. "The water." The janitor pointed to the floor a few feet from her. "The pipes in this place have all gone crazy... water getting everywhere..."

Caia didn't stop to hear him finish. The water was her fault again, but with the change coming fast that was the last thing on her mind. Her pelt was pushing through her legs now, her feet shifting in her shoes. Holy Artemis, she wasn't going to make it out of here.

"Caia!"

Sebastian? She heard running footsteps and turned to see him running towards her. He stopped and tried to halt her too, locking onto her elbow. "Caia, I need to talk to you about Saturday night."

"Sebastian," she growled, her voice changing, too.

His eyes widened, and he gripped her tighter. "Caia?" He looked terrified.

Tears spilled over her lids, rolling hotly down her cheeks as she leaned into him, pleading with her eyes. "I'm changing, Sebastian. I can't stop it. I didn't... you have to get me out of here."

She was never so thankful for his quick thinking. He didn't say another word, just grabbed her, and started running with her towards the parking lot. She tripped as her left foot completely changed inside her shoe and he swung her up into his arms, running towards his car. She was aware of him almost ripping the car door off, and then he was none too gently throwing her into the backseat. The door shut behind her and she clawed onto the leather seats as her back rippled. She heard Sebastian getting into the front seat, and then a blanket was thrown over her, launching her into darkness as she changed completely, her clothes tearing and ripping painfully. Her heart slowed, somewhat, as she realized they had made it, and she sat panting as the car spun around and sped off at high speed.

"Lucien," she heard Sebastian say and realized he must be on his cell, "We have a problem. It's Caia. It's happening, man. Meet me at your house."

What is happening? she screamed inwardly, and let out a low growl of anguish. Did they know already?

Daddy, she thought for the first time since she was a little girl and she used to speak to him in her thoughts, *Daddy I'm scared.* But, unlike when she was little when an imaginary strong voice would always reply, Caia heard nothing… nothing but the steady thud of her heart and the squeal of Sebastian's tires.

15 – TIME

Lucien flew up his driveway, the gravel rioting against his paintwork as he skidded to a stop two seconds behind Sebastian's car. His heart was hammering in his chest and pounding blood in his ears as he jumped out of his car and strode towards an anxious and flustered-looking Sebastian. He knew it, he cursed inwardly, he had known yesterday something was wrong with her, it was just he had been self-absorbed enough to think it had something to do with the kiss they'd shared. "What's going on?" he asked in a low anxious voice as he reached the young male, looking beyond him and into his car. He could see a lump under a blanket in the back seat. "What the..?"

Sebastian raked his hands through his hair and Lucien noted how they trembled. "I caught her in the hallway. She was so scared, Lucien... and she was changing."

Lucien flinched at the thought. She must have been terrified. Growling, he brushed past Seb and pulled the car door open with enough force to unhinge it. He ignored Sebastian's squeak of protest and pulled the blanket out of the car. Caia was revealed, lying towards him in her lykan form, her snout nestled between her forepaws, her large green eyes staring up at him, blazing with fear.

"Caia," he whispered, reaching for her. At the sound of his voice, she stood up and leapt out of the car, running past him and up into the house.

Sebastian shrugged nervously at his questioning look, and then followed Caia inside. Lucien took a huge gulp of air, feeling his own hands tremble a little. Guilt pounded along with each of his steps as he followed the two inside, trying to focus enough to form an explanation for her. Inside he found Sebastian in the sitting room, his neck craned back as he stared at the ceiling. Lucien frowned, and then understood as he heard the noise of Caia's movements from above. She was obviously trying to change.

He waited tensely in the sitting room, his heart thudding louder and faster, his jaw clenched in self-directed anger, his brain refusing to formulate the explanation he knew Caia deserved.

"Do you think this is it?" Sebastian asked in hushed tones.

Lucien threw him a look that clearly said 'you think?'

He growled again and threw himself into his armchair. "We need to ask her what triggered it."

"Should we call anyone else?"

Lucien nodded. "Call Magnus. My mother will be with him. And Dimitri."

Sebastian nodded back distractedly before wandering into the kitchen to use the phone. Lucien shook. If it was happening he had left Caia scared and unprepared. Magnus was right. They should have told her as soon as she had arrived. How would she ever trust him now?

His gaze shot back to the ceiling at the sound of a thud and he was out of his chair within seconds, storming up the stairs to her bedroom. At the sight of her crumpled on the floor he drew in his breath and rushed to her. He pressed his fingers against her neck and sighed in relief at the healthy pulse he felt there. She had changed back, and had obviously been in the middle of getting dressed when she had passed out, no doubt from the shock. She had thrown on a long t-shirt and had been pulling on her jeans, so Lucien, trying to be as much of a gentleman as possible, pulled the jeans back off of her, and quickly picked her up with the intention of sliding her under her covers and into bed. But as he did so, she unconsciously snuggled her head into his chest, making mewling sounds that sent his heart hammering. He held her like that for a while, knowing that this was probably the last time she would accept his touch for a time. His eyes drifted over her peaceful face as he pulled her tighter into his chest. When had she become so vital to him? He sighed deeply, and was finally able to let her go, laying her in the bed and pulling the duvet over her. He pressed a soft kiss to her forehead. She had no idea what was to come. The guilt he felt for having not told her sooner was burning in the back of his throat. He'd done what he thought was best for the pack at the time. Dimitri had been his voice of reason, telling him that no one knows what the deep darkness can do to a person. But now he felt sure of Caia. Sure that she was good, that she wasn't a danger.

"Is she OK?"

Lucien turned to find Sebastian standing gazing at her, worry tormenting his young face. An image of a drunken Sebastian leaning in towards Caia on Saturday flitted across his mind and he realized he wasn't the only one who was worried that they wouldn't be forgiven for their deceit when she woke up and learned the truth. He didn't want to think about that. On the one hand he could empathize, but on the other he didn't want this stupid kid anywhere near her in that respect. He was beginning to understand the possessiveness of the mated guys in his pack. "I need you to call Ryder," he ordered gruffly, turning to look back at Caia, his hand involuntarily brushing her hair back from her face. "He's on a job for Marion."

He looked back at Seb, whose eyes were round as he watched Lucien's behavior with her. His face crumpled as if he understood. "Are you-?"

"Call Ryder," Lucien demanded, making it clear his private business was exactly that. "And tell him to bring Marion back with him. Tell him... tell him it's time."

Magnus, Dimitri, and his mother had all returned home. Ryder was already on his way back with Marion. Apparently they had news of their own. Lucien wasn't sure he could take any other news at the moment. He had sighed and told Sebastian not to tell his parents anything yet but to go home and get some sleep. He would call him when it was time. His mother was trying to ease his guilt, assuring him they had all done what they thought was best.

But none of them knew what had been happening to Caia lately. None of them knew the extent of her fear.

Lucien could feel Magnus' disapproval rolling off him in waves. He deserved the Elder's anger; he relished it in fact.

As for Caia, she made no move towards waking. They checked on her regularly, until Dimitri assured them it was just exhaustion that was keeping her in bed.

Finally Lucien had sent them all to bed, while he himself hadn't been able to sleep, at all. And that was why he found himself alone in his kitchen at 5am, dressed and drinking coffee, his stomach rolling at the deed that was to be done as soon as Caia woke up.

At 6am he heard the sound of a car approaching, heavy feet on the porch steps, and the front door swinging open. Lucien trudged out to investigate.

There before him was Ryder, his face tight with anxiety, and next to him Marion. She was a small woman with flaming red hair that reached her buttocks. She had the largest pair of violet eyes Lucien had ever seen, and pixie features that gave away her heritage as a magik.

"That was fast," he said in appreciation.

"It sounded urgent." Ryder grimaced.

"It's time."

"Apparently so," Marion's voice was like a wind chime, a tinkling, musical sound so in contrast to a husky lykan's. Lucien watched in bemusement as she looked around the home, wandering from room to room, and eventually falling into an armchair in the main sitting room. "I can feel her."

Lucien was unsurprised by her comment, having expected that kind of power from her and from the little he knew of magiks. He turned back to Ryder. "Why were you already on your way back? Seb said you had some news."

"That would be because of Saffron," Marion replied instead.

"Saffron?" His face was scrunched in confusion. When no answer was forthcoming he turned to Ryder with a growl curling his lip. He wasn't in the mood for a mystery. Sleep deprivation and his worry for Caia didn't exactly bring out his sunny side.

Ryder sighed. "Saffron. She's Marion's faerie."

"And?"

"She was the one who came for me to tell me about the rogue. Well, she waited until we got back to Marion to tell us she had felt energy in our town." Ryder's eyes snapped to Marion in irritation. Lucien could feel an argument brewing between them and managed to refrain from yelling at them to explain to him what was going on. Instead he said it slowly and quietly, with a growl coiled around the last few words, "Would someone please explain to me, in full detail, what the hell is going on?"

Marion's eyes flashed. "There's no need to be rude, Lucien."

He growled again.

"Oh, alright." She sighed. "Saffron, my faerie," she now spoke slowly as if to a moron, "She came to get Ryder for me because we'd encountered another pesky rogue lykan, and when she came back with him – after some ill-treatment from your lykan there by the way -" she gestured to his friend with a look of reproof, "she told me that she had sensed the energy of another faerie in town."

"Another faerie?" The blood drained from Lucien's face. "As in an enemy faerie?"

Her face was grave now. "Well, the Daylight Coven would know if we had a faerie in town with you."

"You're sure this Saffron is right about this?"

"Of course I'm right!" A voice squeaked from behind him. He whirled around but could see no one. He looked at Ryder in confusion, but his friend merely rolled his eyes and shrugged.

"Where are you?" Lucien snarled.

"I'm right here," the voice answered just as testily. His lykan ears strained, swearing the voice was coming from the window, but he couldn't see anything.

"Marion," he growled, warningly.

She sighed again. "Saffron, stop playing games. I'm afraid our young friend is in no mood for it."

"The window!" The voice cried.

Lucien took tentative steps towards the large window in the sitting room, his eyes straining to see anything.

"Here!"

That time he caught a flicker on the pane and his eyes narrowed on the small face smirking at him. He should have known. The faeries' face was in fact a spot of sun dapple filtering onto the window through the branches of the surrounding woods. "Goddess," he muttered, amazed by their abilities and how treacherous they could really be as spies. Turning back to Marion he glared. "Make her appear."

"They do like to show off, don't they?" Marion chuckled and then turned to the window. "You heard him, Saffron."

He heard a weary sigh, and in the matter of a few blinks a tall, willowy blonde stood before him, her hands on her hips, her ice-blue eyes glaring between him and Ryder. "Your kind needs to learn patience."

Lucien let a warning rumble sound from the back of his throat. "Patience? I think I've shown quite a lot of patience considering I've just been told there is an enemy in my town and no one will get to the point and tell me exactly what is going on."

Saffron shrugged gracefully and walked over to stand beside Marion's chair. "Faeries have an energy like all of us beings-"

"Trace." Lucien nodded. Everybody knew about trace, it was a part of their energy, their existence.

"Yes. Trace. Only a very, very old faerie can mask their trace. I'm talking half a millennia old, and there are only a few of those old spies kicking around, not to mention that every single one of them works for Daylight."

Lucien nodded, crossing his arms over his chest. "So this Midnight faerie... it can't mask its trace, so you sense it here?"

"Exactly."

"Yeah," Ryder growled, slapping at Lucien's shoulder to get his attention. "The dumb tree sensed it, and didn't say anything until we were at the Coven with Marion!"

"Am I the tree in that sentence?" Saffron hissed, her eyes narrowing on Ryder dangerously.

"Children, please." Marion sighed, rubbing her temples at their exchange.

"Yes. Children," Lucien agreed, smirking at Ryder and turning back to Saffron. "So, can you follow this trace?"

She quirked her lip, shaking her head softly. "Unfortunately, only the Head of either Coven is blessed with that ability."

His gaze snapped to Marion who was already shaking her head. "Nope, no, Lucien. My sister and brother-in-law are in the middle of their own little mess at the moment. Marita does not have time to come down here, I'm sorry. At times like these you're lucky to have gotten me and Saffron."

"Lucky isn't the word I'd use," he heard Ryder mumble under his breath.

"Lykans aren't the only ones with good hearing," the faerie snapped at him. He smiled innocently, which seemed to annoy her more.

Usually their childish banter would have amused Lucien, but now he was too nervous. Spinning around to face Ryder he let his emotions play on his face, as he only could with his closest friend. "This is about Caia."

"I tend to agree with you there," he could hear Marion whisper, and so turned back to her carefully.

"I need your help with Caia, she's showing the signs."

"Have you told her the truth yet?"

"No."

"Well, I can't help until you do so."

He was irritated by the demand in her voice, not used to having his decisions made for him, especially when he'd already decided on that course of action. "I'm going to," he growled lightly. "But only about The Hunter and her heritage. The other... well... she needn't know about that just yet."

"You're sure?"

He felt his shoulders tense, his teeth clenched. "Yes," he managed.

"OK then."

Her eyelids felt as if a pile of lead had been piled on top of them, refusing to let them open. Come to think of it, her face felt pretty heavy, too. Slowly, Caia managed to open her eyes, the sleep easing from them until she had focused on the ceiling. Ugh, what a weird, deep sleep she'd had. She felt her right arm lying across her stomach, but her left one, she couldn't. Groaning, Caia turned and used her right arm to pull it out from under her pillow. Numb. She used her right hand to shake her left into waking, until gradually she was moving each finger. Flexing it, she sighed as the sharp burning tingles brought it back to life. Flopping back onto her pillow, Caia's gaze found its way back to the ceiling, her mind assailed with images. Her fingers unconsciously brushed her lips as she remembered Lucien's kiss. It had been a great kiss. Her first kiss. At the mere memory, an eruption of butterflies exploded in her stomach, their little wings flapping rapidly against her heart, and kicking it into an erratic speed. And then memories of the day before intruded, obliterating each and every one of those butterflies with the force of a shotgun.

Alexa taunting her about having slept with Lucien.

Caia cursed them both, groaning at having stupidly fallen for Lucien's easy charm. And that hadn't been the worst of it. Her heart sped up again, remembering how she'd had no control over her change at school, at Sebastian having saved her ass and the pack's, from exposure. She felt a wave of sickness. Climbing out of bed, she dozily made it into her bathroom and breathed with relief when the nausea passed. She braced herself against the sink and stared deeply into the mirror above it, hoping to find answers to the questions she saw in her eyes. But none were forthcoming. Instead she ran the cold water and, cupping a handful of it, threw it up and into her face, enjoying the icy rivulets running down her skin. And then an invisible hammer hit her head as she glanced back at the mirror, the conversation she heard between Sebastian and Lucien yesterday when she'd been changing in his car, rang in her ears.

Her eyes flashed and she growled, wanting to rip the sink off the wall.

They knew!

She tore out of the bathroom, hurriedly pulling on a pair of jeans, and then tore down the stairs as if the hounds of Hades were nipping at her ankles. Her bluster, however, slowly died at the sound of voices coming from the living room, bringing her to an abrupt halt. She sniffed the air and found the familiar scents of her housemates, plus Magnus, Dimitri and Ryder. Among the scents were two unfamiliar ones – of the non-lykan variety. She grumbled, realizing she couldn't exactly rip Lucien's head off in company. Oh, but he had it coming.

Sighing heavily, she finished her journey to the doorway of the living room, only to be taken aback by the sight of all them. They were all turned towards her, as if waiting for her. Her eyes immediately went to Lucien and she was angered by the tenderness she saw in his face. She flushed as she remembered the hot kisses they had shared, and how Alexa's taunt had sent Caia into a blazing rage, enough of one to have been able to what... throw Alexa telekinetically across the room? Frowning at him, and at her own anxious thoughts, she took in the rest of the group. Ryder stood beside Lucien, and on his other side were two unfamiliar women. The first was a small woman with long red hair and wide violet eyes. She was attractive and very delicate, like a doll, and Caia guessed, by the way she held herself, older than she looked. The scent Caia picked up from her, surprisingly, was a strong vanilla, so strong she could almost taste it. And next to this woman was the most stunning creature Caia had ever seen. The woman was tall, only a few inches shorter than Ryder, with a slender figure and graceful limbs. Her perfect face was framed by short, sharp blonde hair that followed her jaw line in strands of thick silk. Her ice blue eyes were watching Caia curiously.

"Hello." The red-head stepped forward, her words tinged with an accent. "I'm Marion."

A wave of feeling rushed up and over Caia, a safe feeling, like she could trust this woman with anything. Engrossed in the feeling, she almost forgot her manners. "Sorry." She took the woman's hand in her own. "It's nice to finally meet you. I have a lot to thank you for."

She shrugged, laughing warmly. "Not at all. Oh." She seemed to remember herself, and turned back to her companion. "This is Saffron. My faerie."

A faerie? Caia blinked, remembering the amazing stories Ryder had imparted. "Nice to meet you," she said, trying to hide her awe.

She watched as Saffron wrinkled her nose and turned to Ryder. "She smells different from the rest of you."

"Shut up," he hissed back, glaring at her.

"Wh-"

Before Caia could ask her question Magnus stepped forward, interrupting her. "We need to talk," he said softly. His worried eyes made the hair on Caia's skin rise. If she had been in wolf form her ears would have twitched, her hair would have spiked, and she would have lowered to her haunches, awaiting the attack.

They knew!

They all knew what was wrong with her... and no one had told her.

Even the witch and the faerie knew.

She could feel everyone's anxiety over having to tell her. Angry tears pricked the corner of her eyes. All this time they had been keeping something from her. She had trusted them.

Her gaze blazed with accusation as it moved from one to the other. She took perverse delight in watching them squirm. "Is someone finally going to tell me why every time I have an emotional outburst water pipes instantaneously rupture? Why I can throw someone across a room without even touching them? Why I started to change in front of a class of humans yesterday, and could do nothing to stop it?! Why I can actually feel your emotions right now?!"

Their mouths had fallen open, ears disbelieving at what she was telling them had happened to her.

"Caia." Lucien made a move towards her, his eyes full of guilt and anguish.

"Don't." She stepped back from him, her eyes accusing and filled with dislike. He was the last person in the world she wanted touching her right now. She took satisfaction in the way he flinched, hurt by her rejection.

He sighed and looked at Magnus, and then back to her. "You should know Magnus wanted to tell you from the start, but he was outvoted."

Caia looked at her uncle, and nodded, as if she had known all along he would not hurt her. "Then you explain, Magnus. Please, just tell me what's happening to me?" She crumpled into a chair, hating the way her eyes filled with tears as they pleaded with his. "I'm scared."

She looked at Lucien sharply as he made a sound of distress. His emotions hit her like a wave and she gulped under the force of them. Despite whatever had happened between him and Alexa, he had some caring feelings towards Caia - enough to feel hurt when she was hurting. She didn't want that. She just wanted to be mad at him. She looked away, as Magnus approached her, ignoring her feelings for her Pack Leader, and taking comfort in the strong arm her uncle placed around her shoulders.

"You don't have to be scared, Cy. We'll get you through this."

"Get me through what?"

"For you to understand, we have to go back to the beginning." He sighed, rubbing her shoulder in comfort.

And then he began to tell her a tale that threw her back into a past she had never known existed. To a history that had been rewritten.

16 – THE AWFUL TRUTH

19 years ago

"How could you, Mikhail?" Albus burst out in rage, his hands trembling with so much emotion, so much confusion.

His older brother shrugged, defeated and weary. "I don't know."

"You're the Pack Leader. To have an affair... with the enemy?" Rafe added in disbelief. Albus was glad for his presence. It calmed his fiery temperament.

Mikhail's eyes flashed at the young man. "Why are you even here? This is between me and my "Mikhail," Albus warned, angry at the obvious blow Rafe took. He tried not to show it but Rafe's eyes darkened with sadness. It had taken Ella's persuasion for them to see that Rafe was an excellent man, a young man who had suffered for the sins of his father. Albus knew he thought of himself and Mikhail as his own brothers. For Mikhail to hint otherwise was a verbal punch to the stomach that Albus wouldn't stand for. "Don't take your own foolishness out on Rafe."

Mikhail groaned, "Nothing will come of this. I promise. The affair is over with Atia."

"You had an affair with the wife of the Head of the Midnight Coven! If Devlyn finds out, this will never be over!"

"**Well, Atia.** You have been a naughty wife, haven't you?" Devlyn murmured as he circled her like an animal. His eyes raked over his beautiful wife as she dangled by her arms, arms that were clapped in chains attached to the ceiling. A long time ago he had thought Gaia had created this enchanting creature just for him. Now his stomach turned just thinking about where her body had been. "How was it? Sex with a dirty animal? Not even an influential Pack Leader... some small time piece of filth who has the audacity to call himself a leader."

He watched as her eyes began to tear in rage and frustration. She pulled at her chains, her body swinging from the motion. "I told you I killed Mikhail! It is over, and there is one less lykan in the world!" she cried, her tears turning to blood as they ran over the wounds he had inflicted on her. "Please, Devlyn..."

He laughed humorlessly. "What? You think I'm happy with the death of just one of those mutts? More of them must know that my wife had an affair with one of them. If the Coven ever found out..."

She pulled again at the chains, and looked at him wildly. "They're strong, Husband. Small-time they may be, but they can't be killed easily." Her eyes widened as she thought of something, licking her lips in excitement. "Yes, you won't be able to kill them unless you infiltrate them. I can help. I can find out their weaknesses, and together we can take them out."

Devlyn stared, amazed that she would think he would fall for that. "My dear, why would I ask your help to take out this pack, when you're the reason I have to do a black ops against them in the first place?"

"Devlyn...," she begged.

It was the last thing she said.

His name.

A plea for his mercy.

He felt nothing after he killed her. Just stared at her in disgust, and turned away from her body. His eyes found his son, who stood in the doorway, his hand on his elder sister's shoulder protectively, even though he was three years younger than she.

"The Coven is never to hear of this," Devlyn commanded. He watched as they nodded their heads, their faces belying their own disgust at what their mother had done. He felt their anger hit him like a heat wave, and smiled at their loyalty. They were furious that their mother would have even dared to betray him, let alone with a lykan.

"Adriana," he coaxed, and his young daughter stepped forward from the shadow of her brother, Ethan. She was just as beautiful as her mother, and the perfect weapon. "Your eighteenth birthday is in what... three months?"

"Yes, Father."

"I want you training intensively until then."

"Of course, Father."

"Don't you want to know why?"

"Of course, Father."

He smiled. He had raised his children well at least. They hadn't been poisoned by their mother's weaknesses. Adriana would make a fine Head for the Coven once he was gone. "I'm sending you into the pack."

Her eyes widened at that. "You want me to infiltrate the pack, Father?"

"Yes. I don't want anyone other than my children knowing of this." He strode towards her, putting his arm around her small shoulders, leading her to Ethan. His other arm went around his son, and he guided them both from the room in which they'd watched him punish and execute their mother. "If the Coven was to find out, children, this family would be stripped of its title. We go from being royalty to traitors."

"We understand, Father." Adriana nodded determinedly. "So, I will infiltrate this pack of mangy dogs and find out all there is to know about them." She stopped and stared at him with determination in her eyes. "Who their strongest warriors are; their relationships with one another, and thus where their weaknesses lie."

"Good." Devlyn was pleased. She had been taught well. He turned to his son. "Why is Adriana's plan the best we have, Ethan?"

His fifteen year old son pulled himself up straight, his eyes blazing with a hatred that would see him through the worst of the war. "Because there are only three of us, Father, and many more of them. If we can understand their weaknesses, we can exploit them. An emotional lykan is one that we can take by surprise, before they make the change into their... disgusting animal forms. In animal form they are protected from our magik. But as humans..." Ethan smirked. "They're putty in our hands."

Devlyn chuckled and squeezed his children closer to him. "Exactly."

"Albus," Rafe said *quietly, placing his hand on his friend's shoulder, "I've returned."*

Albus turned, his eyes sad as he looked over his friend. "You look well. I take it that last rogue didn't give you too much bother?"

"No. Not really." Rafe shrugged, and then took a seat beside him. "Ella says you are adjusting to your duties."

It was Albus' turn to shrug this time.

"Al." Rafe sighed. "It has been months now. I wish you would stop blaming yourself for Mikhail's death."

"I should have known that bitch would come back for him."

"You did all you could for him. I know you don't want to hear it, but Mikhail had to have known what he was doing when he got

mixed up with a dark witch... for goddess sake, Albus... he signed his own death warrant."

Albus flinched and Rafe immediately felt terrible. "I'm sorry. I just don't want you blaming yourself any longer. You have a pack who cares for you, a pack that are now your responsibility. Not to mention a great wife, and two kids that she's having a hard time controlling while you are out here in your garage... blaming yourself."

His friend's silver eyes flashed at him in pain. "Why did he do it, Rafe? I can't understand."

Rafe shook his head. "She enchanted him. It could even have been a spell."

Albus nodded. "Yes, I had thought of that."

They sat in silence for a few moments longer until Rafe couldn't help himself. "I've brought someone home with me, Albus."

His friend, and leader, quirked an eyebrow at him. "Someone?"

Rafe smiled, thinking of the blonde-haired beauty that was sitting in Ella's kitchen with her. "A young woman I met on my travels."

His friend smiled his first genuine smile in months. "Oh?"

"I was hoping she could stay with us."

"You're taken with her," Albus stated in amazement as he stood up. "Which pack is she from?"

He sighed. This was going to be the difficult part. "She's not from a pack. She's a magik."

"What?!" Albus shouted in instant anger.

"A Daylight witch!" Rafe cried holding his hands up in defense. "She's good, Albus. I swear."

His friend shuddered in pain. "Rafe..."

"Albus, it's OK. I promise she's not a bad guy."

Adriana sighed, watching the handsome lykan sleeping peacefully beside her. She wondered if she had inherited her mother's perverse nature, because sex with this beast had not been nearly as intolerable as she had thought it would be. She smiled wryly, remembering her inward reaction when her father told her she was to attach herself to this lykan; to give herself to him, in every way, if needs must. Her anger over that had been obvious. She was the highest ranking lady of the Dark Coven, and she was to give her virginity to a... mutt? And then she thought of her mother's betrayal, and the thought of that betrayal becoming public, and no sacrifice was large enough. Luckily for her, Rafe had been enchanted with her from day one. Within a week she had managed to weasel all his secrets out of him, including that his former Pack Leader had had an affair with the leader of the Midnight Coven's wife.

Who else knew this? she had asked, all innocent and sympathetic to his pain.

Everyone, he had groaned, everyone except the children.

Children, she sighed, and rubbed her rounded belly. *She flinched at the thought of her father's fury when she had returned to him with the news.*

"Pregnant!" *he had screamed.* "It's not possible!"

She had cried, kneeling at his feet. "It's not my fault, father. Please..."

He had sent for their prophet. And then the horror of her situation was realized. Years ago the Prophet, an old immortal man who never spoke to or saw anyone except the leading family of the Coven, had told of the coming of the child of mixed race, who would contain such power that they would bring about the end of the war.

"Gaia has grown weary of her children's war my lord," *the old man had wheezed.* "She has blessed your daughter's union with the lykan male, out-with a mating ritual, in order to bring forth a child from the prophecy."

Devlyn had destroyed everything in sight while she had sat terrified of the thing growing inside of her.

"The only way to kill it, is to wait for the birth... or kill your daughter."

Her eyes had flown wide to her father's face, his dark eyes fierce on hers. The silence had stretched between them like a twanging wire.

"And the child will definitely not just be a magik? It will have the genes of both my daughter and that... thing?"

The prophet had nodded wearily.

His eyes had burned on her as she'd begun to cry harder.

"Father, no." Ethan had stumbled up from his seat in the corner of the room. Adriana's heart had pounded for him. How brave of him to face their father for her sake.

Devlyn had shaken his head. "No, old man, I won't kill my daughter when she has done only what I asked of her."

She'd drawn in a huge breath of relief and smiled tremulously at her brother.

"What is to be done then, Father?" Ethan had asked for her.

"Adriana will return to the pack," he'd told them, taking them by surprise. "We don't want them suspicious. The child must be killed but so shall the pack be. We have everything we need to destroy them and the abomination growing in your belly. After the birth."

"I'm sorry, Albus," Rafe groaned, tears spilling down his cheek as he cradled his baby daughter to his chest. "I'm so sorry I've brought this upon you."

"You didn't," Albus bit out, anguished at the sight of his friend in such a state of grief. "My brother brought this upon us. If anyone should apologize it is my family."

"I can't believe... Adriana...," he moaned, and held the baby girl closer.

"She... her family is not finished with us, Rafe. We must leave."

Rafe nodded, but made no move.

"We have to leave now, friend," Albus demanded, and pulled him to his feet gently. The rest of the pack was already headed where he had told them to go, and Marion, who had revealed Adriana to them when she visited with Magnus, was protecting them on their journey from any attack.

Rafe nodded again and followed him outside to the car. Ella waited anxiously with Lucien and Irini who, although young, were unusually quiet, fully aware something was wrong.

"Albus." Rafe stopped him before they reached the car.

"What?"

"You'll protect her, if something happens to me," he pleaded, his eyes falling lovingly on his daughter. "You'll protect my Caia."

Albus nodded vehemently. "I already have a suggestion... but it can wait for now."

17 – ALONE

"Three years after your mother's escape, she returned," Magnus continued her tragic story quietly, "The pack's guard was down and she tried to get to you. Your father got to you in time but Adriana... she killed him," he whispered, grief cracking his voice. "Again, she escaped the pack, and again she waited. It was another four years... she returned for you, but Albus was ready and he sent you and Irini into hiding under Marion and Daylight protection. Albus, as you know, went after your mother and she killed him. That's when Lucien went after her." Magnus looked up at Lucien and Caia followed his gaze. Lucien stared back at her, his jaw clenched, his fists tight, pain screaming across his eyes.

"It took me five years, Caia," he croaked, "but I finally got the opportunity, and I killed her... to protect you, to protect the pack."

She felt her head shaking back and forth as if trying to shake their words, the truth, out of her ears. All the secrecy, the vague comments, the weird crap that she had been going through, all had been this, lies covering up the awful truth.

"So, I'm what... a magik?" her voice sounded dead to her. "Am I a witch?"

Ella leaned forward. She could smell her, could see her hand reaching to clasp her own, but she couldn't feel her touch. "Yes.

You've been showing signs towards the approach of your majority. Your eighteenth birthday. That's why Marion is here."

"By the sounds of it," Marion added, "You're a water witch."

She pulled out of Ella's grasp to hug herself, to keep from falling apart. *A water witch?* She felt like laughing hysterically, *what does that even mean?*

The table in the center of the room began to shake as she watched it, and she felt everyone's eyes fall on her worriedly.

"My mother killed my father. Tried to kill me?"

"Yes," Lucien answered her softly. His strong hand reached for her, and she could hear him telling her to stay calm, but the words didn't sink in.

"And you killed my mother?" The table started shaking uncontrollably now.

"She has a lot of raw power," Marion murmured in surprise. Caia could hear her telling her she needed to stay calm. Was that her? Was she making the table do that? Of course, why not? She'd made Alexa fly, burst water pipes!

A wave of nausea swept through her entire body, and with her lykan reflexes she ran from the room, out onto the porch, where she leaned over the railings to vomit the horrific truth into the bushes below. She couldn't seem to stop, until eventually all she had left were dry heaves. It wasn't until she came up for air she realized someone was holding her hair back. Lucien. She sighed, feeling his warmth at her back. Too exhausted to be angry at him right now, she couldn't help but lean back into his comforting heat. "I'm OK," she whispered, feeling the tension in his body.

She felt his lips in her hair, and then his strong arm came around her waist and she was pulled tightly against him. He hushed her, and she suddenly realized she was crying. "It's going to be OK," he whispered soothingly.

Caia shook her head. "How?" she heard the weakness in her voice and hated it.

"I'm sorry," she could hear the sorrow in his words, "I'm sorry that I killed her, but I had to."

Angry now, Caia pulled from his arms and spun to face him, batting furiously at her tears. "I'm not," she growled loudly, the sound of the wolf distorting her voice like she had never heard before. "I'm not sorry you killed her! She was a monster, Lucien!"

Of a sudden Marion appeared on the porch, her hand reaching to Caia beseechingly. "Caia, you have to calm down. Your power is based in your emotions, you must calm down."

She shook her head. "My parents... in my head... they were the one thing..." she couldn't finish, the pain... it hurt all over. Splinters of wood started ripping up off the porch, one slicing her cheek. She didn't even flinch. Her angry eyes bore into her Alpha. "And you didn't tell me!"

"Caia." Lucien tried to reach for her but the world suddenly grew very loud. All she could hear was this monstrous, soul-wrenching sound filling her ears, as if the world was falling apart. A wooden floorboard began jerking up from the porch.

"Caia, you have to pull it together." she saw Marion mouth. No she was shouting she just couldn't hear her voice. The woman stepped towards her, and she seemed to say something else but Caia couldn't lip read those words.

And then she didn't care about not knowing. She didn't care about anything as the world turned black.

18 – UNRAVELING

Lucien was lost in his own thoughts, his eyes gazing at the ceiling, worrying about Caia knocked out on her bed. Her reaction to the truth was the worst he could have feared; it had bled all her usual strength from her, and obliterated the cool, tranquility of her character that he had come to find so soothing. He was oblivious to the others and their conversation until Magnus looked worriedly at Marion and asked, "Will she be alright?"

"Yes. It was a pretty powerful spell. She will be out for a while, but she'll be fine."

Lucien sighed heavily, his eyes sweeping his family. "I knew she would take it badly, but I wasn't prepared for that reaction."

To his annoyance Saffron snorted, shifting her weight on the arm of the chair she was perched upon. "Yeah." She shook her head, her eyebrow raised sardonically. "Man, was that an overreaction. I mean, come on, it's not as if she woke up one day in a dysfunctional pack of lykans, who, as far as she was aware, were keeping her from the inner circle of the pack like she wasn't really one of them, and then they tell her that she's only part wolfie because the rest of her is part evil witch, and, oh, that's cos' her mommy and daddy didn't die due to some weird hunter guy, but actually her mommy killed her daddy and then tried to kill her too. Oh, and that while all of you were going about your daily lives, she was frightened to cry in case the house flooded, scared, not knowing what the hell was happening to her, when right next door her Pack Leader had all the answers for her. Not to mention the icing on the cake... being prophecy girl an' all..."

He was proud of his own restraint; rather than lunging at her he merely curled his lip back and growled. He wasn't the only one.

The faerie wasn't intimidated in the least. She just shrugged her elegant shoulder. "What?"

Ryder beat him to the punch. "Can you shut up for just one second, never mind a minute?"

"Why would I do that when you so obviously love the sound of my voice?"

"One day you're going to turn into something real small, and I'm going to be there... to put a cup over you, and trap you... *forever*."

"Look, don't push your weird, sexual, *'I dream of Jeannie'*, fantasies onto me OK. I'm not interested."

"Sexual f-," he spluttered, his face growing dark red with anger.

Lucien raised an eyebrow. It really took a lot to get under Ryder's skin but obviously this faerie had the knack.

"I despise you," Ryder growled.

Saffron clutched her chest mockingly. "I'm wounded. Really. Ow. My heart is breaking."

"Would you two quit it." Lucien sighed. "We have things to sort out. Like another faerie in town."

"Caia should know." Magnus pierced him with a fierce stare.

"I don't know about that." Lucien shook his head. "I don't think she can deal with it right now."

"Try me," her soft voice cut straight through him. He turned to see Caia leaning against the door frame, exhausted but looking calmer. She refused to meet his gaze and he frowned, remembering to be confused by the fact that she had been cold towards him before she knew he had deceived her.

"How did you..." Marion squeaked. "How can you be awake?"

"Caia, maybe you should lie down." His mother stood up and went to her, drawing her against her side protectively. He watched her eyes. She looked so wary of them. If only she knew how much they had all come to care for her.

"But how is she awake?" Marion cried, her hands flailing in frustration. "That is one of my very powerful sleeping spells."

"Marion. Please," he shushed her, and turned his attention back to Caia. "Are you OK?"

"I'm calm, if that's what you're asking."

"No. It isn't."

"Look, just explain to me what's going on. I think I've been lied to enough for one lifetime."

"Caia-" Ella began, her eyes full of apology, but Caia shook her off, pulling from her embrace and walking slowly, further into the room.

She looked directly at him, her green eyes so damn unreadable. "We should put this behind us and just get on with it. From the sounds of things there's more to this story."

"OK," Dimitri spoke before Lucien could, "Then you should know that there is another faerie in town."

She frowned in confusion, rubbing her forehead in tiredness. He wanted to reach for her and hold her close, but he knew she would only reject him. "What does this mean?"

"I felt another faerie's trace here. It's energy. It's from the Midnight Coven," Saffron explained.

"And?"

Lucien cleared his throat, "It can only mean that you've been found. We all have."

He watched her grapple with his statement. "I... I'm confused. I thought that what happened... that woman," she seemed to choke on the word, refusing to call her mother. "I thought..." She stopped, and her eyes widened. "Is Devlyn still after me?"

Lucien made a face. "Not exactly. The only reason a Midnight faerie would be here is because of your uncle."

He let that statement sink in, studying her face as it immediately tightened at the news. "My uncle? My moth- Adriana's brother?"

"Yes. Ethan. Devlyn died, so Ethan's the Head of the Coven now and a very powerful warlock."

"So he's after me," Caia whispered. "He wants to end this, even though the pack has clearly protected the secret. He still wants me gone."

"I won't let anyone hurt you," he found himself promising fiercely, desperately wanting to reach out and ease her worry.

She ignored him again, and again he felt it like a pierce to his heart, rubbing his chest as if she really had hit him.

"So this prophecy... what does it mean exactly?"

Magnus looked to the others and then back to her. "We didn't know anything about the prophecy because the Prophet is from the Midnight Coven. We discovered it when we sent a faerie in as a spy around the time of your first birthday and she told Marion's family about the prophecy. Gaia wants the war ended."

"And I'm... supposed to be able to do that how?" Caia whispered, fear in her voice.

Marion shrugged. "Your mixed race must do something to your powers. I've already witnessed first-hand how strong you are and you haven't even begun to harness them."

"That still doesn't explain how I'm supposed to bring an end to the war."

They were silent. For having a number of years on her identity, they were as clueless as she was.

She chuckled humorlessly. "Devlyn had no idea that it would be his own actions that would bring me into creation."

"No." Dimitri shook his head. "But he and his family wanted you gone, not just because they think of you as an abomination, and not because they were even thinking about what your powers were. They want you gone because the prophecy didn't say which side you would bring an end to the war on."

Her mouth fell open in disbelief, her eyes wide with pain as she began to understand the significance of his statement. The table began to shake again and Lucien felt like cursing. They were putting too much on her too soon. He was about to say so when she fixed her eyes on the table and it stopped. She took a deep breath.

Lucien smiled softly, pride shining in his eyes. She was learning to control it already.

"That's why you didn't tell me the truth from the very first day I got here," she whispered, the accusation in her words slapping the smile right off his face. "You're afraid of me, afraid that... whatever is inside me might be evil. That I'll help *them* win the war."

Everything inside Lucien cried out against that. He didn't believe that of her. "Caia, no."

"Not now, though," she snapped at him, her eyes full of a betrayal that ripped at him. "Not now, that you've kept a careful watch on me, and spent time with me... like you were my friend."

He sucked in his breath. She thought that was it. She was accusing him of pretending to feel something for her in order to spy on her? "Caia..." he growled, his anger boiling over.

"Stop. I don't want to hear it," her voice broke with exhaustion as she looked anywhere but at him.

Ryder cleared his throat, trying to ease the tension between the two of them. "Do you really think this guy wants the pack gone as well?" He directed his question at Lucien and Marion. Lucien shrugged.

The witch sighed. "It's what we assume."

Saffron reiterated her sigh and stood up in agitation, "You all know the truth as well. If I was him I'd want you gone."

"Thanks," Ella snarled, "That's very comforting."

"I try."

"Seriously," Ryder muttered at Ella, "Cup."

"What was that?" Saffron asked sweetly, knowing full well what he'd said.

"I said why don't you do something useful for a change and try to find this other faerie?"

She turned red in the face. "I already told you I can't. I can feel the energy but I wouldn't know who it was until they were in the same room as me."

"Marion." Lucien blew air out between his lips in an attempt to ease the tension gripping his entire body. "Isn't there something we can do? We have to know what his next step is going to be."

Marion sighed. "Well, usually I would send Saffron in to spy on the Coven but since they don't know anything about it that would be pointless."

"But Ethan obviously has someone working for him."

"Yes. I imagine just a few that he trusts." She stood up with a shake of her head, her mouth set in determination. "No. I think our best course of action right now is to get Caia trained."

"Speaking of which." Ella smiled nervously. "The school called about an incident between Caia and Alexa in a classroom, and Caia leaving the school grounds."

Caia groaned. "What did you say?"

"Well, Alexa was smart enough to lie and say she had tripped and well... the teacher didn't seem to be buying it, but what else can she say?" Her smile was sheepish. "I lied and told them there had been a death in the family and that Caia was just very upset, and that she would be out of school for a few days."

Lucien nodded, glad he didn't have to deal with inquisitive humans. Before he could say anything on the matter Ella asked,

"Caia, why did you... magikally *puff* Alexa across the room? She wouldn't say."

Did Caia blanch? He frowned watching as she flicked a nervous look at him. "Uh-"

Well this is interesting.

"-I Uh..." she shook her head as she struggled to explain, and finally snapped her head back defiantly. "You know what? I'd rather not say, and given your own little penchant for secrets, I'm sure you don't mind if I keep my own."

Damn, that was annoying.

Caia received a phone call from Jaeden shortly after, begging Caia to forgive her for her own part in the deception. But it wasn't Jaeden she was mad at, neither was it Sebastian or Magnus. Her anger was directed solely at Lucien and the other Elders. As everyone else in the pack had to do what they and Lucien advised, she realized how difficult it must have been for her friends. As she remembered past conversations with them she realized they had even hinted at the truth. Sebastian had almost said it to her on Saturday evening when he had been drunk, but Lucien had intervened at the moment of truth, and then kissed her. Which brought her to the question of why he would do that, but then sleep with Alexa? She concluded that he was trying to a) distract her from Sebastian's faux pas and b) butter her up and keep her on their side so that she wouldn't fight against them with the Midnight Coven in the war.

"Do really believe Alexa?" Jaeden asked her softly.

Caia glanced once more at her door. She was paranoid that the pack would be keeping an ever careful eye on her now, to even go so far as to spy on her. An annoying thought suddenly occurred to her. "Saffron?" she asked, her gaze scouring the room. She heard nothing, and felt no one else's energy.

"What?" Jaeden asked in confusion.

"Oh sorry, not you. And to answer your question, no, I'm not positive that Alexa was telling the truth. But if so, she's a helluva liar and well... you know how cozy the two of them were in his store and she's been there every day of the week since."

"Yeah but, Cy, Alexa is the mistress of lies and manipulation. She could cover the lie easily... I just don't see Lucien sleeping with *her*."

Caia heaved a massive sigh. "I don't want to believe it either but I'm not exactly going to ask him about it. I'm not really in a talkative mood with the *master* of lies and manipulation. See, they're perfect for each other."

"I don't believe her."

Caia groaned and slumped back on her bed. "Well, it doesn't matter at the moment. Right now I have uncontrolled powers and a prophecy to deal with. The part where my mother murdered my father is getting tucked to the back of my brain for now."

"You're compartmentalizing the situation."

"Is that what you call it?"

"Sure," Jaeden said with a smile in her voice. "It's what Sydney does in *Alias* all the time. Talk about dysfunctional families. Woof."

"I thought you didn't watch that much TV?"

"I don't, but *Alias* isn't just any old TV program. It's *Alias*."

"OK. Well, never mind that it's fictional, Jae, my reality is that my mother killed my dad."

"Sydney inadvertently killed her mother."

"I'm a lykan and have to hide within a human world."

"She's a spy and has to hide her identity from everyone she loves."

"I'm prophecy girl."

"So was she."

Caia sighed. "OK, again … I actually exist, Jae... I think I win."

"I guess you do. I was..." Jaeden exhaled noisily, and Caia could feel that she felt helpless for her. "I was just trying to make you feel better in a situation where that can't possibly happen."

"The fact that you tried means a lot."

"I'm here for you, always."

The sound of the floorboards squeaking outside her room brought her bolt upright. She narrowed her eyes as she felt waves of curiosity, mixed with guilt, filtering through the walls. "I'm going to have to go, Jaeden."

"Wait!"

"What?" She really didn't want whoever was outside listening to hear something they shouldn't. She sniffed and Lucien's scent hit her. He really wanted to piss her off didn't he?

"I was just wondering what happens now?"

"Training with Marion. You'll cover for me at school?"

"Of course."

"OK. I gotta go, Jae. Talk later."

"Bye."

Caia hung up the phone and tip-toed over to the door. He was still standing outside, she could feel him. With perverse satisfaction she pulled the door open with lightning quick motion. Lucien stood looking at her aghast, his ear turned towards the door. If she hadn't been so angry at him, the sheepish look on his face would have been comical. "I can feel you, remember," she snapped.

"Oh. Right." He straightened to his full six-six and shrugged the sheepishness from his face and demeanor. "I was just making sure you were OK."

"That's not really your problem anymore."

He growled, his face flushing with irritation. "I'm still your Pack Leader, Caia."

"Do you lie to every member of your pack or am I just special?"

He sighed, running his hand through his thick dark hair. "Caia, I am very sorry. I made an error in judgment but... can't you understand? After everything this pack has been through, I was just trying to protect them."

She did understand. It didn't change the fact that he had hurt her like no one else had before. "I do understand that, Lucien."

His body seemed to relax, the tension easing from his muscles. "So we're going to be OK?"

"You and I?"

He moved towards her, taking her by surprise as he cupped her cheek gently with his large callused hand. "Yes. You and I. We can get through this together."

A silence stretched thinly between them as their gazes locked, and for that moment Caia forgot her anger and could only remember the feel of his lips on hers at the party. As the moment continued to build, Lucien growled from the back of his throat and lowered his head towards her, his silver gaze caught intently on her mouth. She began to tremble with the desire to give into him, her heart beating erratically at his overwhelming closeness. But as his lips were about to touch hers, his warm breath fanning her face, sending shivers over her already confused body, an alarm bell rang inside her head, jerking her back from him.

Lucien frowned, trying to urge her closer, only for her to push his hand off and step back into the safety of her bedroom. "There is no you and I, Lucien." She gripped the door and began to close it on his face. "Just Pack Leader and Prophecy Girl."

Caia turned around and braced her back against her closed door, listening as his footsteps slowly moved away. The feelings emanating from him were so raw, her rejection genuinely hurting him deeply. Maybe Jaeden was right. Maybe Alexa had lied to her, and just maybe Lucien wasn't trying to butter her up. His emotions told her that his caring feelings were real. It didn't matter. She and Lucien couldn't be anything, now that she was some freak of nature who could bring total destruction to the pack and to him. No. She was going to train with Marion and then take on her uncle so that the pack would be safe from him. Once she was certain of their safety, she would leave the pack and Lucien. Her heart thundered in her chest at the thought, and she felt sick, a feeling likened to grief wrapping itself around her body.

Caia cursed, hearing the water in her bathroom rush on. "Let's just work on controlling the freakish powers first, huh, Cy," she muttered, and made to turn the water off.

"**We have a** slight problem."

When did they not? Ethan thought in agitation as he zapped the mutt in its cage, its shriek of pain easing his headache. "Spit it out."

"They're training her," his spy murmured, obviously not wanting him to hear correctly. He could feel his muscles tensing, a warm heat of angry power flushing across his skin from his feet up. A bolt of white heat flew out of him, and an even louder, agonized howl deafened him.

"Damn." He sighed, and crouched down to peer into the cage. He hoped he hadn't killed the thing; it was important leverage.

"My lord?"

"Shut up," Ethan snapped, turning his ear to the cage. He sighed in relief when a whimper escaped the creature. "Oh thank, Gaia."

"My lord?"

"Stop 'my lording' me. We'll need to take her sooner than we thought, that's all."

His assistant hissed, "There's more."

Ethan wanted to reach down the end of the receiver and choke the living daylights out of her. Unfortunately, he needed her for the time being as she was one of only three people within the Coven who knew about Caia: himself, her and Lars. Of course, he'd have to kill them both when this was over.

"What else?" he asked between clenched teeth, half afraid of the answer.

"Well, it appears Lucien and Caia's relationship has now been put asunder due to a female member of the pack's jealousy."

That was the last thing he wanted to hear. Another wave of heat flew from his body but he made sure it wasn't directed at the mutt in the cage.

"My Lord?" she asked again, worriedly.

He waited a few seconds so that he didn't accidently kill her down the phone line. When he was sure he was under control, he said in restrained breaths, "You will need to go in as quickly as you can and reunite our lovely couple."

"Yes, my lord."

"I don't have to remind you that Caia's relationship with her animal friends is pivotal to weakening the pack. Particularly her relationship with Lucien."

"I'll go in immediately. As soon as I'm allowed. They have her under lock and key at the moment."

"Then break the damn lock." *Jeez, you just can't get reliable help these days.* "You can't wait any longer than a few days or else her powers and control will develop. Get in there and get those two lovebirds together or... I will personally eviscerate you."

Her breath caught in the back of her throat and he reveled in the power he held over her. She knew he was perfectly serious. "Of course, my lord."

"And Xylena?"

"Yes, my lord."

"Once your mission is complete I want your first kill to be the bitch lykan female that put a kink in Caia's relationship with the Pack Leader and a kink in our plans."

"Gladly."

19 – LESSONS

"That's it, Caia. Hold it... hold it... hooold iiiit."

Caia sighed, her head aching with the exhaustion of trying to contain the water. Marion had set up a heavy duty hose out in the backyard and was attempting to train Caia in controlling it. Right now, instead of the water pouring out directly and falling with gravity, she had Caia separating the water flow into two halves, each spraying in the opposite direction. It was the strangest feeling, having to reach deep inside and tap into the energy that she now felt hovering above the energy she used to tap into her wolf side. The trace buzzing above the lykanthrope energy was sharp and airy - like steel vapor - her lykanthrope more a tingling heat. The first day of training had been excruciatingly frustrating as she kept tapping into her lykan trace, fur exploding across her body at the slightest attempt to harness her magik. But the amount of focus it took was keeping her heartache at bay and allowing her to function normally.

Well.

As normal as she could be.

Although she felt heartache at the truth of her family's past, she also felt a weird sense of relief and freedom from finally knowing the truth. She doubted the new lease of life she felt was an entirely 'human' or normal reaction to the situation, but her embarrassing emotional breakdown when she first heard the news was human enough for her, thank you very much.

So there she was, on the third day of training, and she had finally managed to conquer her dueling energies when Marion began throwing her off her focus with her obnoxious cheerleading coach persona. She'd obviously had way too much caffeine.

"Marion," she warned between clenched teeth, the pain in her forehead increasing.

Marion laughed, clapping her hands together. She was being wonderful, she really was, but she also had a perverse sense of humor. At Caia's warning, Marion magiked a whistle out of thin air and started blowing on the damn thing, jumping from one foot to the other. "Go, Caia, Go, Caia. Go Go Go, Caia. Whhhiieettt!" She blew the whistle shrilly and was silenced abruptly by a spray of water in her face.

Caia laughed, letting the water return to its natural flow.

Instead of frowning, Marion smiled brightly. "Very good, Caia. You managed to direct a third stream of the water in another direction. We'll just forget the fact that it was on my face..." she did frown now, glancing down at the whistle around her neck. "I think you literally wet my whistle, though."

Caia chuckled and then collapsed onto the grass. "My head aches."

"It will at first." Marion gracefully settled down beside her.

"What next then?"

"Well, I think we should soon begin on creating water from air."

She rolled her eyes. "And I do that how?"

"You think about it, and it will happen."

Caia grunted. She made it sound like a piece of cake. It wasn't.

She had asked from the very beginning of her training why she had the power to harness water. If she was going to be this weird hybrid of lykan and witch shouldn't she have really cool powers? Not some weak ability to quench her thirst whenever she wanted. Marion hadn't been amused by her blasé opinion on being a water witch. Apparently it was one of the most powerful kinds.

"You see, Caia," she had relayed patiently, as if to a child, "There are four kinds of magik. Water, Fire, Air and Earth."

"Wasn't that a band?"

Marion had rolled her eyes. "I'm sure you're thinking of Earth, Wind & Fire. Please, Caia, can you take this seriously? It is pivotal to everyone that you take this seriously."

She had sobered at the reminder of her great destiny, whatever that meant. "So the elements, huh?"

"Yes," Marion had said primly. "I'm a fire witch. I can harness fire." She'd stroked the air with her fingers and a flame appeared in front of her.

Caia had jumped back in surprise with a childish 'whoa'.

"I can control it." The flame had started to dance across the room, while Marion sat, just looking at it, not moving. "I can manipulate it." The flame had suddenly roared, nearly scoring the ceiling.

"Holy Artemis!" Caia had cried. "You could warn a person before you do that."

The witch had merely smiled and turned back to her, the flame disappearing as if it had never existed. "A fire magik is one of the most powerful," she'd explained without arrogance. "However, a water magik is more powerful because of the obvious."

"In a fight we can douse you." Caia had nodded in understanding.

"Exactly. We can use fire to destroy, but so can you with water. I actually fought a water magik from the Midnight Coven a few years ago. He almost killed me," her had voice lowered at the memory. "He was able to fill my lungs with water so that I was asphyxiated. If it hadn't been for the opportune arrival of my brother-in-law, Vanne, who is a powerful water warlock himself, I most certainly would have died."

"What did Vanne do?" Caia had asked in awe. This woman had seen and done things she couldn't even begin to imagine.

"He wrapped the enemy warlock in a cocoon of water and he drowned. In doing so his power over me was broken, and the water disappeared out of my lungs."

The thought had terrified Caia. That she had the ability to do something so horrendous to a person. That she would most definitely have to do something like that to Ethan in order to protect the pack.

A more terrifying question had pierced her mind.

"Do you know what kind of warlock Ethan is?" She'd asked quietly.

"Fire." Marion had smiled triumphantly.

Caia could see Marion thought she was more than capable of taking Ethan on because she was a water witch. Caia wasn't so sure. She had only just discovered she was a water witch. And now here she was, three days later, exhausted and in pain from the smallest of tasks.

"Do you need to take a break, Caia?" Marion asked gently and then she stroked the air with her fingers, a glass of lemonade appearing in her hand. She handed it to Caia, who took it, blinking incredulously.

"If you're just a fire witch how can you conjure things from nothing, and if I'm just a water witch how could I blast Alexa off her feet and make furniture move?"

Marion smiled smugly. "The element is just the basis of our power. Gaia would never be so selfish as to bestow only measly gifts on her children. We can have, and do, whatever we want, but we have rules to protect ourselves and the human society."

"I guess you should tell me about them."

Marion groaned at the monotony of it. "I'll get around to it."

"But what if I break a rule in the meantime?"

She sighed, rolling her eyes again. "Are you going to utilize your magik to kill a human?"

"No."

"Are you going to utilize your magik to force a human or Daylight supernatural from their own free will?"

"No."

Marion grinned. "Then I think we're OK for now."

Caia smiled back at her. "It's kind of like you're Robin Williams and I'm Aladdin."

"Excuse me?"

"You know... 'Genie I want you to make me a prince!'"

The witch shook her head in confusion, and apparently worry. "Are you OK? Maybe you're getting too much sun."

Caia sighed in frustration. "*Aladdin*? *Disney*? Can't kill anybody, can't make people fall in love, can't bring anybody back from the dead...'It's not a pretty picture, I don't like doing it!'"

"I have no idea what you're talking about."

"You're killing me here," Caia sighed. That had been her best Genie impression.

"Maybe we should just proceed to manipulating water."

Caia nodded, feeling more of an alien freak than ever in the company of her pop culture free companion. "I was kind of hoping you could help me control the whole telekinetic thing first. I'm getting tired of being my own personal poltergeist."

Marion shook her head again, pulling Caia to her feet. "You are the strangest girl."

"Ryder gets me."

Lucien tried not to wince as he watched Marion train Caia on how to control her telekinetic abilities. The first few hours had been grueling as the witch taunted Caia with her past, and insulted her abilities in every possible way in an effort to incite her temper. At first it didn't seem to be working, and Lucien had laughed quietly from his place at the kitchen door, amused at Marion's disgruntlement and Caia's ethereal coolness. But when she mentioned Adriana's name, the hose pipe they had been using earlier suddenly whiplashed into the air and missed knocking Marion's head off by an inch. The witch had smiled triumphantly and continued to push Caia until the young lykan-magik was able to control the telekinesis, even when her emotions were toyed with. Now they were working on Caia's ability to utilize the telekinesis whenever she wanted. Marion had nearly been killed by many a flying object.

"Shi-" he hissed, and ducked his head as a large branch flew at him. It crashed past him and into the kitchen, skidding across the table and smashing his mother's fruit bowl and some glasses that had been left there. He turned wide-eyed to see Caia smirking at him. "It's OK!" he called. "I'm OK."

Marion walked towards him sheepishly. "Sorry, Lucien, that was an accident. Didn't know you were there."

"I did." Caia shrugged and smiled too sweetly.

Lucien groaned. "Still like that is it?"

"I don't know what you mean."

Marion frowned at her protégée. "I think we should take another break."

Caia nodded and turned away from them, heading into the woods. Lucien sighed, his eyes following her closely. When was she going to come around and stop being pissed off at him? He had said he was sorry.

Marion strode up the porch steps and glanced back at Caia before she reached him. She smiled sympathetically when she turned back to him and gave him a reassuring pat on the shoulder. "She doesn't hate you, Lucien. She just needs someone to be angry at right now."

He grunted. "That makes me feel so much better."

The witch chuckled, her eyes twinkling. "Well, the fact that she's chosen you as the one to be angry at *should* make you feel better."

"And how's that?"

"Well, generally to be angry at someone they have to have done something to upset or hurt you, and to be able to upset or hurt someone means you having to have meant something to them in the first place." She smiled as he took this in, and then slid past him gracefully into the house.

Lucien sighed, gazing at the spot Caia had entered the woods. He hoped to Gaia Marion was right about her, because if they were going to get through the next few weeks together, Caia was going to have to like him enough to trust him.

20 – REPLACED

The wave of energy sparked her senses as she drove closer towards the house off the highway. *Crap,* she groaned. It definitely wasn't energy from someone from the Midnight Coven. She cursed profusely as she pulled over to the side of the road and quickly dialed Ethan's number on her phone.

"What?"

Ah, he was as pleasant as ever.

"My lord, I think we may have a problem."

"You know, I'm seriously considering having a t-shirt made for you with those exact words on it," he sneered and then snarled, "Why am I not surprised? What the Hades is going on now? Incompetent wench."

She flinched and bit her tongue. If she said anything disrespectful to him she would be dead in seconds. "I can feel unfamiliar energy radiating from the house. I think it's Daylight. I'm just parked off side their driveway."

"That's why you're calling me?"

Duh.

"Yes, my lord."

"Xylena, do you remember why you're going to the house?"

What?

"Yes, my lord."

"And do you remember to whom you are going to visit?"

She rolled her eyes. He really was a jackass. "Yes, my lord."

"And do you remember that Caia has just been introduced to her new powers? That the energy coming from the house is most probably hers?"

Oops.

"No, my lord. I didn't think of that."

"Yes. Obviously."

"I apologize for disturbing you, my lord." She was lucky he hadn't fried her already.

"Just get your ass in there, already."

"Of co-"

He put the phone down on her. *Charming. Prince of the Coven ... My ass*, she snarled and threw her phone down. *Frickingcenter toad.*

Caia took a deep breath and smoothed her hair back before she opened the door. She had been training constantly for the last week with Marion and hadn't seen anyone other than Marion, Saffron and the Elders since the revelation. Everything seemed to be going well so far. Marion was impressed by how quickly she was learning to control her powers, and awed by the range of said powers. But Caia was exhausted and missing her friends. And to be honest, despite all the sadness and madness, she was a little excited by her new powers and wanted to share it with Jaeden and Sebastian. So instead of her working at Lucien's this Saturday, Jae and Seb were on their way over to visit with her.

"Sebastian." She smiled and drew him into a hug. He squeezed her back tightly and placed an affectionate kiss on the top of her head. "How are you?"

He chuckled and brushed a loose strand of hair behind her ear. "How am I? You're asking me how I am?"

"Yes."

"Well, I'm OK, now I know you're not angry at me."

Caia shoved him playfully and then made for him to follow her upstairs. "Angry at you? Seb, you saved my life at school, getting me into your car so fast. Thank you."

He looked adorably embarrassed by her gratitude, shrugging and mumbling incoherently under his breath. She laughed and then stopped him as he blushed. She wanted him to know that she was serious. He had been a true friend to her throughout the whole ordeal. "Honestly, Sebastian. Thank you." She exhaled slowly. "I mean you even tried to tell me the truth that Saturday..."

"About that." He blushed again. "Caia, I'm really sorry if I made you uncomfortable. I was wasted."

She chuckled. "Yeah, you were. But you were also sweet. Wanting to mate with me so the pack would accept me." She smirked, brushing his hair from his face.

Sebastian laughed and pushed her away. "Will you stop? I'm dying of humiliation here."

"Don't be humiliated, Seb-"

The doorbell rang cutting her off.

"Just go up into my room. That'll be Jae, we'll be a sec."

He nodded and headed towards her bedroom while she ran back down the stairs, throwing the door open, and then throwing herself into her best friend's arms. Jaeden laughed, but hugged her close.

"Whoa, Cy. You OK?"

Pulling back, she was shocked by the strange feeling of unfamiliarity that hit her. She smelled like Jaeden, her energy felt like Jaeden, but there seemed to be something else there. It was the strangest trace she had ever encountered, thick, smog-like, icy. It was difficult to describe the feelings that ran through her. She blinked, trying to clear her mind, and then noticed how uncomfortable Jaeden was. Her eyes were darting all over the house, into the hall, the kitchen, up the staircase.

"I'm fine. Just glad you're here," she answered. "Are you OK?"

She nodded and smiled a little falsely. "Of course. Is Sebastian coming?"

"He's already here. Let's go up." Jaeden nodded and Caia followed her, frowning. "You sure you're OK?"

"I'm fine. Really. Anyway, you're the one that's been through all the crap. How are you really? How's the training?"

"Good, I think."

Once they were seated in her bedroom with Sebastian, Caia frowned at how stiff her friend seemed to be, still trying to identify the unfamiliar trace that Jae reeked of. Jaeden narrowed her eyes at her scrutiny and then shrugged as if remembering herself. "So, Cy, everyone at school has been talking about your meltdown with Alexa last week."

"Oh great," she groaned. Just what she needed, gossiping kids when she returned to school on Monday.

"I wish I had been there to see Alexa fly across the room."

Sebastian laughed. "Right. Man it would have made my year."

"Aaaahhheeeeaaaahhh!"

"What the-" Caia jumped to her feet at what sounded like a cat being tortured. Saffron's energy hit her before she physically appeared and Caia's eyes rounded as Jaeden shrieked in outrage, her chair flying away from her. Her body wavered, flickering in and out of existence, as she began muttering something in Greek under her breath, her eyes now a blazing onyx instead of their natural blue.

Before Caia could do or say anything, or even comprehend what was going on, Saffron materialized behind Jaeden and placed a hand firmly on her shoulder. Jaeden slumped immediately and collapsed on the floor with a thud. Saffron's own eyes were onyx as she cursed at the girl she had just knocked out. She kicked her and Caia cried out to her to make her stop. She did, catching her breath, her eyes changing back to ice-blue.

"Would someone like to explain what just happened here?" Sebastian whispered, staring in horror at his friend's unconscious form.

Marion suddenly flew into the room, her wild red hair plastered to her head with dark gunk in it. She glared at Saffron. "I'm getting tired of your dramatics, Saffron. My head is burning."

It was then Caia noticed Saffron was wearing plastic gloves covered in hair dye.

Marion mistook her questioning gaze for the gunk on her head because she shrugged looking sheepish. "It never comes out the right red. I've tried all kinds of magik on it but *L'Oreal* does it every time; it's just th-"

"If you are done," Saffron snapped, and pulled Jaeden's body up off the floor and dumped her into a seat. "Marion, put Hephaestian ropes around this one."

"Why?" Caia snapped, making a move towards Jaeden. She was blown back by Marion.

"Good grief," the witch cried before Caia could complain, her gaze switching between Saffron and Jaeden. "Dimitri will be devastated."

"Why?!" This time both Caia and Sebastian yelled in fear.

"Caia." Marion's face crumpled in sympathy, causing Caia's heartbeat to pick up speed, those old butterflies flapping their wings around the pit of her stomach. She looked at Jaeden, now tied to the chair unconscious, and she remembered that unfamiliar trace.

"What's going on?"

"That's not Jaeden. That's a faerie from the Midnight Coven."

Jaeden tried to contain her sigh of relief as Ethan walked away from her cage. He always came back if he felt her relief, and he would push the pain to her limit. She had also learned quickly to try and suppress the urge to vomit. He enjoyed her fear and pain too much. It spurred him on.

Once the light from his flame had disappeared and she could no longer sense him in the dank basement with her, she began to shudder and whine with her fresh burns. The bastard had put a spell around the cage that stopped her from being able to change into a lykan; otherwise he would never have been able to hurt her. But trapped in her human form, naked as the day she was born, Jaeden was covered with healing wounds that would have mended much faster had she been allowed to change. The new burns sliced across her back. He must be in a good mood. When he was angry he had always targeted her stomach, one of her more vulnerable areas as a lykan.

She unconsciously pulled her knees further into her chest so that she would be curled up as tight as she could be in a fetal position, but the movement tightened her back and thus her burns, sending another involuntary whimper into the darkness.

When they had first taken her - drugged her - she had woken up in the cage and had tried to keep an ear out and listen to what was happening. She knew this had to do with Caia. And soon she knew that Ethan was Caia's uncle. She waited, hoping and praying that her rescue would be soon. Her father would have the entire pack after her once they discovered her gone.

She clung to that hope through his torture and his taunting, but as the days passed - or was it weeks? She couldn't tell anymore - her hope began to crumble. Where was the pack?

And then Ethan, in one of his more sadistic moods, had told her about the faerie that had infiltrated the pack disguised as her. He'd had to blast her unconscious after his revelation sent her into an uncontrolled rage.

Now there was only darkness and pain, and the never ending breath of time. When once she had waited here hanging onto her hope, she now waited for the moment when Ethan would go too far ... and end the agony of her twisted body and mind.

21 – REALITIES

Caia watched numbly as Lucien and Dimitri manhandled the faerie that looked like Jaeden. They were trying to secure her so she couldn't pull any funny stuff while they took her down to the basement.

"What are they going to do?" she asked softly, bleakly.

Magnus stood by her protectively, his eyes blazing with anger and sadness. Before he could reply Caia jumped at the hideous crack of Dimitri's hand across the faerie's face. "CHANGE!" he roared at her.

Caia flinched, an unexpected tear rolling down her cheek. Dimitri was bristling with rage she had never witnessed before, and he no longer wanted the evidence of his daughter's disappearance in his face.

The faerie spat out blood and glanced anxiously at Dimitri. "I can't with these ropes on me."

Lucien sighed, his eyes fully of sympathy and anger, too. "I'm sorry, Dimitri. We can't take them off her."

"I can do it." Saffron sneered at the faerie in the chair.

"How?"

"Faeries can unmask one another." She stepped forward and put her hand on top of the faerie 'Jaeden's' head. Saffron's beautiful face crumpled into a mask of distaste at having to touch her, but a wave of energy hit them all as the faerie's form began to waver in the chair, and finally Jaeden disappeared from them. For some reason that made Caia want to cry even harder. She glanced at Sebastian, who was trembling with fury. His best friend had been gone and in the hands of the enemy for how long? Her eyes flashed back to the faerie, who was now a serene looking blonde with velvet brown eyes.

"Your name?" Saffron hissed.

The faerie said nothing. Saffron did the honors and slapped her with a surprising amount of force.

Caia was troubled with more than the faerie's name. She stepped towards the faerie involuntarily and her brown eyes locked onto her.

"How long has Jaeden been gone?" she choked.

The faerie shifted nervously.

"How long?" Caia repeated.

Nothing.

"HOW LONG!" Dimitri bellowed. He was immediately restrained by Magnus and Lucien. They couldn't chance him ripping the supernatural apart before they had the information they needed.

"Let's get her down to the basement." Lucien sighed heavily. He did not look pleased by this.

"The basement?" Caia asked in confusion. *Why the basement?*

Magnus cleared his throat. "They need to get Jaeden's whereabouts from her, one way or another."

She understood, and a shudder ran through her body. They were going to torture this creature.

No.

Without thinking, Caia hurried to the faerie to question her once more, and placed her hand on her shoulder. Before she could say a word a riot of images blasted her mind and threw her physically back. She landed hard on the floor and, although she could hear the chaos it caused in the room, her mind was too busy being assaulted by the dark images of rusty bars and the smell of fear to care. Unfamiliar faces hit her, and blood. Lots of blood. The most prominent images, however, were of those bars. Caia tried to hold onto them. And then she saw her. Jaeden lying naked and bleeding - her skin ripped and torn and burned - behind the bars of a cage. White heat shot through Caia's body and she came back to the room she was in, Lucien bending over her anxiously and Magnus holding Dimitri back, while Saffron interrogated the faerie.

Caia looked at the remorseless creature in front of her, and tears of fury trembled down her cheeks at the images of Jaeden. They were real. She knew they were real.

"They have Jaeden in a cage," her voice came out in a growl. Her wolf had taken over her in her own frightened fury.

Dimitri let rip another roar.

"Caia, how do you know?" Lucien asked tentatively, helping her to her feet.

She shook her head. "When I touched her I saw things. About her," she bit out and glared at the murderess. The faerie looked frightened now. *Good.* Caia glanced up at Lucien who still held onto her. "Take her to the basement, Lucien. Find out everything you can... however you can."

He nodded, but his jaw tightened. He wasn't happy about torturing any creature, for any reason, and he seemed even less happy that Caia was ready to do so.

"You didn't see her," Caia choked an explanation.

"Is she alive?"

She nodded, her head dropped. "Barely."

It was as if someone had died, the dark tension of grief that gripped the house was so intense. Sebastian was sent home despite his protesting, while Dimitri, Lucien, Saffron, and Marion interrogated the prisoner in the basement. The basement must have been soundproofed because no noise filtered up to Caia's ears as she sat anxiously with Ella and Magnus in the kitchen, cupping a now cold mug of coffee between two frozen hands. Magnus sat close to Ella, his big hands wrapped around hers on the table, offering her comfort. Her steel grey eyes were puffy from crying. She had just gotten back from Julia's, having left her in the care of Christian and Lucia. By the strained look on her face, Caia knew that Julia had collapsed at the news. She hissed. The tension was making her angry. Everyone, including Jae's own mother, was acting as if Jaeden was dead. She wasn't. Caia didn't know why she was so certain, but she was sure that Jae was alive somewhere. The handle on her mug broke off in her hand and she glanced up sheepishly at Magnus and Ella's enquiring eyes.

"Sorry," she mumbled.

"A few days ago and this place would have been flooded. Furniture would have been broken." Caia gazed blankly at Magnus, who smiled. "I'm saying I'm proud of how quickly you've mastered your powers, Caia."

Oh. She flushed a little at his praise and shrugged. "Marion has been very patient."

The Elder sighed at her modesty. "She says she's never seen anything like you. Marion's not one for exaggeration." His lip curled as if he was remembering something. "Or praising for that matter."

She shrugged again. "It's no big deal."

"Cai-" Magnus began only to stop quite abruptly at the sound of feet stomping from the basement door into the hall. They waited expectantly and, while she knew Ella and Magnus could smell that it was Lucien and Dimitri approaching, only Caia knew that Dimitri's rage was now mingled with grief, and Lucien oozed anguish. Her heart faltered. She must have been wrong.

Oh Goddess, Jaeden.

They appeared, their expressions mirroring the emotions rolling off of them. Not only that, but Dimitri's knuckles were smeared with blood. Caia sniffed subtly. Not his. She winced, but then stubbornly stamped out any sympathy for the faerie that had caused more bloodshed than Caia cared to know.

"Well?" Ella trembled.

Dimitri turned away, his head bowed, his breathing erratic as if he were drowning. Lucien sighed heavily, running his hand through his hair in that familiar gesture of frustration. "She's alive."

They all let out a collective breath of relief.

"But?" Caia asked, bracing herself. Jaeden may be alive but there was reason Dimitri looked like a grieving father.

"They've had Jaeden for weeks."

An unexpected growl erupted from Magnus, and Ella squeezed his hand tightly, trying to rein in his angry shock.

Caia was angry too, but at the moment confusion won out. "How weeks? I... I sensed something different in Jaeden's trace today so I assumed that..." her voice cracked, "I assumed that she had been taken recently."

Dimitri snapped around to look at her, his dark eyes blazing angrily as he snarled, "What do you mean you sensed something different?"

She stumbled back under the force of his fury. "I just thought something was off... but-"

"You knew!" he yelled and moved towards her. Lucien jumped in between them, his hand halting Dimitri, his teeth bared and a low menacing growl purred in his throat. Caia's heart raced frantically.

"It was the transition," Marion's mellow voice broke some of the tension. They all turned to her as she walked calmly into the room, her gaze on Caia. "With her powers under control, her senses have opened up. Caia would not have sensed the unfamiliar trace on Jaeden until afterwards. And as far as I'm aware this was their first meeting since Caia became aware of her heritage and started training with me."

Dimitri seemed to relax and Lucien followed suit. He moved to stand beside Caia, though, proclaiming his position as her protector. For once she was glad of his nearness.

"How long has Jaeden been gone exactly?" Ella asked softly.

Lucien hissed, "According to that thing downstairs she was kidnapped and replaced two weeks after Caia's return."

Oh my –

Caia's head swam with the news, and she grabbed her stomach feeling nauseated. She had only known Jaeden – the real Jaeden – for two weeks. Her best friend had been some scheming faerie bitch from Hades! *Oh Jaeden.* She whimpered inwardly, as images of her friend in a cage burned behind her eyelids.

Magnus stood up from the kitchen table. "We need to start a search. Did she tell you anything?"

Lucien nodded, pain flitting across his face. "She gave Jaeden to Ethan. She wouldn't give us a location, but she hinted he wasn't too far away. Obviously Dimitri and Christian will be in on the search and I'm going to send Ryder and Aidan with them."

"Shouldn't you send more?" Caia practically whispered, concern crinkling her forehead.

He shook his head. "No. I don't know what Ethan's plans are. She refused to say anything more-"

"Refused?" she interrupted, noting his use of past tense.

He shrugged, obviously no longer bothered by what he had had to do now he understood the reality of the faerie's crimes. "Marion's spoken to the Daylight Coven. She's not a useful POW if she's not talking, so they told Saffron to take care of her."

Her eyes widened and she gulped, glancing towards the hallway. After everything she had been through it took the fact that downstairs in the basement there was a dead faerie - an executed faerie – for her to fully comprehend what their war meant. She had a feeling that this was just the beginning.

"Anyway," Lucien sounded weary now, "She wouldn't tell us what he plans. So I'm staying here, and so is Magnus, to protect the pack. I'm afraid it will just have to be enough that I'm sending my strongest males out to find her."

"It is," Dimitri assured hoarsely.

"Right, we better get ready then-"

"I'm sorry to stop you all," Marion interrupted again in that soothing voice. "But you all seemed to have missed a very pertinent fact. Understandable under the circumstances."

Annoyed at the interruption, no one said anything. Caia tensed up, however, when Marion's gaze rested on her once again.

"If you have learned anything in the last few days, you should remember that only a faerie can sense another faerie's trace with the exception of the Head of the Coven it belongs to."

"What are you getting at?" Dimitri snapped, his patience nonexistent.

"Caia sensed the faerie's trace."

A silence descended across the room as the weight of her meaning fell upon their shoulders.

"It's not possible," Caia whispered.

Marion nodded, a smile playing on her lips. "Not only sensed the faerie, but with a single touch, garnered much about that faerie including the conditions of Jaeden's kidnapping." She shrugged. "Adriana was the heir to the Midnight Coven and you *are* her daughter."

"What does this mean?" Ella asked flabbergasted.

"It means we know how desperate Ethan is." Marion strode further into the room. "He's not the Head of the Midnight Coven, and the Coven has no clue. It also means that he has none of the powers which accompany it."

"Such as?"

Caia wasn't even sure who asked that. Her brain was overloading on information and a cold sweat was breaking out across the top of her skin.

"In time Caia should be able to trace every member of the Midnight Coven, no matter where they are."

It was like a bomb that kept on exploding.

"Don't you see?" Marion was getting excited now. "This is Gaia's plan. The Midnights won't be able to attack anyone without Caia knowing exactly when and where. The war will eventually come to an end once they know there is no hope of victory."

Caia trembled at Marion's announcement. "Wait. Wait." She shook her head, terrified by the hope that seemed to be blooming in all of their eyes. "I don't feel anything. I only sensed some trace. I can't even tell you where Ethan is. If what you say is true I should be able to do that!"

Marion shook her head refusing to be wrong. "It's something that will come with time, I don't know how long. But you are the rightful Head of the Coven."

"I think I'm going to be sick."

She felt Lucien's hand clasp her shoulder and in her weakness she took comfort from him.

Dimitri cleared his throat, "This is good news. But I need to move and get my daughter back."

Caia was busy reeling, her gaze on the floor, as she heard him stride towards the hallway. "Caia?" She looked up at him as his eyes blazed back at her from the doorway. "If what Marion says is true... if these powers come to you... you'll inform me right away of Ethan's whereabouts?"

"Dimitri-" she wanted to protest. She didn't want anyone's hopes high because she didn't believe for one second she was capable of the kind of power that Marion was hinting at. However, one look at those eyes, eyes that not too long ago had held strength and warmth and were now shattered by guilt and fear, Caia could only nod. "Of course."

Knowing members of the pack were out searching for Jaeden and she could not made Caia feel useless. She had changed and run through the woods for hours in the hope that it would do something for her angry restlessness, but by the time she crawled through her bedroom window she was even angrier, felt even more useless. But most heavily weighing on her shoulders was the guilt. If she hadn't returned to the pack none of this would have happened. Sighing, she peeled back her covers and slid in between her cool sheets. If only there was a way to get in contact with Ethan. To trade herself for Jaeden. Surely he would go for that. If what Marion said was true then Ethan needed her out of the picture in order to be the true Head of the Coven. She moaned and turned onto her side, gazing out into the woods. Could she sacrifice herself for the pack? An image of Jaeden in the cage sent pain shooting through her chest. The image was replaced with something that knocked the breath right out of her body.

Lucien. Dead. Trying to protect her.

Hell yeah, she could sacrifice herself for the pack.

"Jaeden, where are you?" She tried to see through the darkness. Wherever she was smelled of sewage, but underneath the stench was the smell of damp earth and... fear. "Jaeden!" she yelled now.

A flame suddenly lit up in front of her, illuminating a small part of the room - enough to show the corner of what looked to be a cage to her far right.

"Jae." She stumbled towards it, but the flame went out, bringing her to a standstill in complete darkness again. "Jae?"

A whimper.

"Oh goddess," Caia breathed, her panic easing somewhat at the sound of her friend's nearness. Carefully, she lowered herself to the damp floor and started crawling on her hands and knees towards where she thought the cage was.

"Ow," she whined, as her nose came up against cold bars, bringing stinging tears to her eyes. "Jaeden?" She couldn't see anything but she could smell Jaeden, and the area in front of her was rife with fear.

Another whimper. Closer now. Much closer.

"It's me. Caia."

Suddenly another flame burst inside the cage illuminating Jaeden, who was curled up in a fetal position at the back of the cage, her back beginning to heal from long diagonal burns that scored her from shoulder to hip.

"Oh... Jaeden!" Caia cried, pulling at the bars in desperation. She scrambled around the cage looking for a way in, but there was no doors, no lock. She braced her feet against the bottom of the cage and pulled at the bars with every last drop of strength she had.

"Aaahhhhrrrrggggh!" She growled in frustration as the bars refused to give.

"Jaeden?" She heaved out of breath. "Jaeden, it's Caia. Can you hear me?"

Her friend made no move, just continued to shudder and whimper, unaware of her presence.

"Jaeden!"

"Caia," a voice called from behind her. She turned to look but there was only darkness. "Caia."

"Caia, wake up."

Slowly the dankness of the basement faded to nothing and she pushed her eyelids open with effort. Lucien stood looking down at her, his forehead creased with concern, his silver eyes sad.

"What?" She shook her head in confusion and pushed herself up against her headboard. Lucien was on her bed, his hands stroking her hair back.

"You were shouting in your sleep."

I was? "I was?"

He nodded and sympathy melted into the sadness. "You were shouting for Jaeden."

Her dream came back to her immediately and she scrambled excitedly for Lucien's arm without thinking. "I dreamt of her."

"What?"

"Jaeden."

"What was the dream about?"

"I think I was where she was."

"What was it like?"

Caia couldn't help but smile softly in gratitude. He wasn't even questioning the madness. He believed her. With that she sighed and went on to tell him of her visions.

22 – REVELATIONS

"So, are you still pissed at Lucien? Cos' it didn't look that way this morning," Sebastian asked quietly, almost tentatively, as they walked towards the main entrance of the school.

Caia sighed. Before her powers had suddenly shifted into gear she would have unobservantly answered Seb's question. Unfortunately, now she could feel the jealousy rolling off of him and she winced. Their relationship had been so much easier when she hadn't known he had feelings for her. She blanched at all the times she had playfully shrugged off his embraces. Could she be any more of a bitch?

"We're OK," she answered carefully, ignoring the smirks she was receiving from her human school mates. They were whispering about her alleged attack on Alexa. Well not so much 'alleged' as *actual*. She huffed. "I'm trying to forgive him for deceiving me. I know he only did it to protect you all."

Sebastian nodded but wouldn't meet her gaze.

Dammit. It was going to be difficult if he kept this up, and frankly he was the only friend she had right now. Mal and the others were suspiciously off to class when Sebastian, who had decided to drive Caia to school today despite her protesting that she had shiny new Ford, had pulled into the parking lot. They weren't standing in their usual spot around Mal's SUV waiting on them.

Caia had laughed. "What, are they scared of me or something?" She had indicated the abandoned SUV.

"Actually, yeah." Sebastian had chuckled and taken her book bag from her like a true gentleman. She had let him. It was easier that way...and kind of nice.

As they approached Caia's locker, Sebastian sighed. "So, no word yet from Dimitri and the others?"

More comfortable to be on safer ground she nodded. "Actually, yeah, but no good news. They've searched the eastern and southern boundaries but nothing. They're going to cross state lines next. But Lucien seems happy with the speed of their progress in the search."

"Yeah, they've accomplished quite a lot in a few days. They would have accomplished even more if they had let me in on the search."

Caia touched his arm, drawing him to a stop. "Lucien wants you here, protecting the pack."

That garnered a snort. "Yeah right. He thinks I'm a useless young male." His golden eyes flashed. "I'm not useless. And..." he growled, not meeting her eyes. "She was my best friend, Cy."

"*Is*. Not was," she warned him.

He nodded, although his jaw clenched in anger. "Sure."

The bell for first period rang and Caia impulsively pulled him into a hug. "I'll see you at lunch," she mumbled in his ear, and then immediately regretted the hug when his arms tightened around her.

She felt his anger dissipate into comfort mixed with lust. Teenage boys, she huffed inwardly, even immediate danger and war doesn't cool their libido. Pulling away from him gently she sent him her most platonic smile and wandered off to class.

"Oh sorry," a voice full of laughter said as a large body bumped into her. Caia turned to see a boy from her biology class stumble back and then smirk when he realized whom he'd walked into. He nudged a guy Caia didn't recognize because she didn't have a class with him. "Dude, it's psycho Ribeiro."

'Dude' chuckled, his dull eyes drinking her in from head to foot. "Man, how is it even possible that she launched some other chick across a room? She doesn't look like she could lift a pencil." He laughed raucously at his own lame joke.

The boy from biology curled his lips. "Dunno man, but she did it." He stepped closer to her and Caia flinched back. A human had never attempted to intimidate her before. Was there something off with her pheromones? "You like it rough, Caia? How about you play it rough with me after school, huh?"

She felt a growl begin at the base of her throat and had to remind herself to exert some self-control. "Why don't you go play rough with your 'Dude', jackass."

His eyes narrowed as he closed the space between them. She refused to back up even though he had a good six inches on her. Seriously… why wasn't he afraid of her?

"Maybe someone needs to teach you some manners, little girl."

"Maybe you need to back the hell off."

"Or what?"

"Or-"

"Or you'll be eating out of a straw for the rest of your life," a rough voice rumbled from behind them.

The boy pulled back enough for Caia to see Malek standing beside 'Dude', towering over them all, his muscles rippling as he crossed his arms over his chest.

She was surprised to say the least. Mal had flirted with her and had also been downright rude (she had shrugged that off because he was rude to everyone) but he had never, however, shown her much interest other than wondering what she looked like naked. And from his absence this morning, she had a feeling he was now wary of her, afraid of the Midnight blood that ran in her veins. But there he stood, un-amused and defensive because someone had been threatening her.

A warm rush ran through her. She was still his pack.

The boy's face turned a yucky sick color. He mumbled something about making a mistake before he brushed past her into the biology lab. 'Dude' made a quick getaway.

Caia smiled and flicked a look up at Malek. He nodded sharply at her. "See you at lunch."

"Sure." She grinned despite his abruptness. "And thanks."

He shrugged as if it was no big deal, and then grinned back at her. Well, leered back at her. "Can't have 'them' sniffing around our females now, can I?"

She rolled her eyes and started after biology boy. The truth was ... it was nice knowing Mal still felt that she deserved his dominant male protection – annoying but reassuring.

And later, halfway through biology, with a little concentration on the boy who had been trying to intimidate her, Caia managed to tip his opened bottle of water into his lap (he was wearing crème khakis) from all the way across the classroom. Immature 'he peed himself' jokes floated around for a good ten minutes, his angry blushes only making the class laugh harder.

Yup... being a magik had its perks.

Her mood abruptly changed at lunch with the dark pall that hung over the table. The news of Jaeden's kidnapping had reached all of the packs' ears by the weekend and had affected everyone deeply. Dana and Alexa didn't bitch at her, and Daniel made no attempt to make her laugh with his stupid jokes. Only Malek seemed to be himself, cracking out lewd comments and then teasing Caia quietly about being a witch. His first mention of it caused everyone to tense except for Caia. She was glad he had brought it up.

"I didn't see your car outside, Cy," he snickered. "What, you fly in on your broom instead?"

"Your wit astounds me," Sebastian grumbled.

Caia actually laughed though. She was the only one, other than Mal, who wasn't acting like she should be grieving because she knew Jae was still alive and was comforted (despite Jae's conditions) by her nightly visitations to see her. The night before she had actually seen how the scars on Jaeden's back had completely healed. And on the plus there were no fresh ones. Jae had even stopped whimpering and was sitting upright, although she was still unaware of Caia's presence.

"I really hope you're joking, Mal, and that you know a little bit more about witches than you're letting on."

Alexa snorted. "I think all we really want to know is if you're going to kill us in our sleep?"

Sebastian growled and Caia had to kick him under the table. It had been fairly loud and she had seen some humans glance around in confusion at the animalistic sound.

"No," she warned him, pressing a reassuring hand on his arm, "It's fine. I even understand the hostility now." She smiled sweetly at Alexa, being deliberately irritating. "You're worried that because of my heritage I'm a bad guy. I'm not."

"No one is saying that." Mal glared at his sister and Caia drew a puzzled look at his out of character behavior. "Are they?"

Alexa hissed, glaring back at him. "Just because Dad said... ugh you are so whipped."

"And you are so dead if you don't get your attitude in check."

"What, you're going to tell Dad on me?"

"You bet your ass I am."

"Well, I'll tell him all about your little sexcapades with 'them'."

Mal shrugged, ripping into his sandwich carelessly and answering with his mouth full, "He already knows."

"Uh-huh, yeah sure."

"Yeah-huh. Lucien had a *word*." He winced and then snarled, biting harder into the sandwich. "And believe me, it sucked. So if you want to keep that little ass intact I'd shut. The hell. Up."

Alexa snapped her teeth and stood up from the table to repeat her dramatic performance of leaving the pack in a huff. It was a ritual she had perfected to once a week ever since Caia's arrival. Today it presented an opportunity for Caia. She stood up too and to everyone's surprise rushed after Alexa.

As Sebastian had noted that morning, Caia and Lucien were talking, but things were still strained between them and the cause of it was swinging her ass out of the cafeteria. With her new found 'emotion radar' Caia was going to put to rest some serious doubts.

"Alexa," she said, grabbing the lykan by the arm and hauling her into the ladies' toilets. She kicked at the stall doors to make sure there was no one in the room with them and turned back to Alexa only to be confronted by a scared female. Caia rolled her eyes. "Relax. I'm not going to hurt you."

Alexa's upper lip curled and she bent her knees, lowering her body into a defensive stance. "What do you want then?"

"An answer."

She snarled but Caia wasn't fooled. She could sense the fear rolling off of her and, sadistically, felt a little good about it.

"Did you sleep with Lucien or not?"

This visibly surprised Alexa and she straightened from her stance to cross her arms over her ample chest. She huffed in amusement. "So that bothered you, huh? I thought that was why I was blasted across the classroom but I couldn't be sure. Well," she shrugged her shoulders elegantly, "You should really put that to rest, honey, because there is no way on Gaia's green earth that a tainted being such as yourself could ever be Lucien's mate."

Caia tried not to flinch at the insult. She was actually proud of herself - she really, truly had her powers under a lot more control. "Just answer the question."

"Yes." Alexa smirked. "Yes, I slept with Lucien."

The lie swelled out of her skin and settled into a smile on Caia's face.

"What are you grinning at?" Alexa snapped.

"You're lying. I can feel it."

"What?"

Caia inhaled deeply and gave the lykan one last sweet smile before turning out of the door with a, "Pathetic," as she sailed out of the ladies, feeling a little lighter than she had in days.

23 – DUPLICITY

Ethan was furious. More than that, he was anxious. Xylena hadn't called in when she was supposed to and, without what should have been his right by birth, he couldn't feel out her trace to see where she was, or if she still even *was*. He tried not to panic. He had royally pissed her off last time they had spoken and perhaps this was her shallow attempt at getting back at him. No. He would give her until tomorrow. If there was still no word then, he would have to change the plans a little.

He yanked at his hair in frustration and then blew the television set up without thinking. Damn. There had to be a more constructive way to deal with his fury.

Oh yes, he smiled evilly, getting to his feet. There was.

The smell of fear and sweat hit him before he even reached the bottom of the stairs in the basement. His own personal punching bag. Sometimes he just liked to come down in the dark, when she couldn't see or feel him, and watch her suffer. It soothed his pain. Yes, her spirit was waning every day. He chuckled, thinking about the uncontrolled rage that would greet him when the lykans found their filthy female in such a twisted mess. They would get stupid and he would get revenge.

"Morning, Jaeden!" he called out as he slithered towards the cage.

Caia had been feeling better after her confrontation with Alexa. Not only had the knowledge that she was half-witch, half-lykan boosted her confidence rather than drained it, but the heavy raincloud that had been hanging over her heart had cleared up a little: that is the corner that belonged to her Pack Leader.

She might as well admit that she had forgiven him for keeping her heritage a secret. The pack had no way of knowing who she was going to be since the last time they had seen her, or how in fact she was going to react to her magik. Lucien had just been doing what he did best: protecting his pack. But since then he had made it perfectly clear that she was just as much a part of the pack, and that he didn't hold who her mother was against her. It meant a lot, considering none of the pack, except for those closest to Lucien and his family, had visited the house since, and the usual pack run had been cancelled due to Jaeden's kidnapping. She knew for a fact that Yvana still hated her and now she could understand why.

You look like your mother.

Yeah, definitely not the greatest thing ever… being the spitting image of the snake that had killed a few of the most beloved members of a small pack. If Yvana hated her then she was pretty sure there were others who were only civil to her for Lucien' sake.

For that she was grateful to him.

And now she knew with absolute certainty that he hadn't kissed her and then went off and had sex with another female. So what did that mean? That he meant to kiss her? Unlike Sebastian who was so open his emotions were pretty much a neon sign blinking in his aura, Lucien was good at masking how he felt. Yeah, now that the pack were slowly finding out that one of her abilities was being able to sense surface emotions, they had all gotten good at strapping them down and shutting her out. Caia had, however, felt that Lucien at least cared about her, but then she had felt that same stirring feeling from him when it was directed at other lykans. What use was being a magik if you couldn't even tell if the guy you like liked you back?

These wicked, girlish musings had been progressing into mush after lunch and she barely paid attention to her classes. She was kind of disgusted with herself actually.

Mooning over a guy when she had a war on her hands.

It didn't stop her mooning, though.

It wasn't until the last hour of the school day when said mooning was brought to an abrupt halt by an intense pain ricocheting behind her eyes. She hissed loudly and slammed back in her chair. Feeling the stares of some of her classmates, she quickly righted herself and pretended nothing had happened. But what the hell had happened?! The lingering nausea from the pain was hard to control. She took a few deep breaths, praying she wasn't going to be sick. Just as she was beginning to relax another bout of lancing pain shot through her head.

"Aah," she whimpered quietly, slapping her hand to her eyes.

"Caia, are you alright?"

She managed to push her eyes open and through the blur of tears saw she had captured the teacher's attention, as well as everyone else's.

"I'm not feeling well," she managed.

"No, you don't look it." The click-clack of the teacher's heels grew closer. A gentle hand helped ease her out of her chair. "Let's get you to the nurse."

She shook her head adamantly. The last thing she needed was the nurse. "No. I just need a minute. Can I get a bathroom pass?"

The teacher clucked her tongue. "Oh, I don't know, Caia. You're very pale."

"I always am," she whispered weakly, and then realized she had better stop clinging to the teacher's arm or she would definitely get sent to the nurse's office. She straightened. "I just a need a moment. I promise."

"OK."

After the teacher had let her go she began heading towards the nearest toilets to pull herself together. Then the pain, ten times intensified, blasted her head, and with it her body, against the lockers in the hallway. She wasn't even aware of smacking the back of her skull against them or sliding to the floor. What she was aware of was the icy cloying she had felt on the faerie who had pretended to be Jaeden, and with it disrupted images of blood and a horror-filled eye. The eye was a familiar dark blue.

Caia snapped her eyes open breathing rapidly, glad to be alone in the halls. And then the panic set in, and tears of frustration and anger began pouring down her cheeks. Angry at her own weakness and damnable habit of crying she swiped at the salty streams with enough force to leave red splotches. Once they were gone, however, another set waterfalled over her lids.

"Jaeden," she whispered in agony.

Jae was being tortured again. Right now. As Caia lay there in a useless lump of girlish hysterics, Jae was in extreme physical pain. But what terrified Caia the most was the bleak numbness she had felt swelling out of her.

If they didn't get to her soon it wouldn't matter if they found her breathing or not.

They would be bringing back a dead lykan.

Cutting class was nothing to Caia's mind. The world had shifted enough on its axis for such things as war, torture, and imminent death to put perfect attendance on the back burner. After giving herself a good talking to, Caia had scrambled to her feet and had gone after Sebastian. He was in Shop and had managed to sneak out easily enough.

"What's happening?" he finally asked as they slid into his car.

"It's Jae," she whispered, choking on the name. "She's... it's getting worse."

His hands tightened on the steering wheel, knuckles going white with rage. "What's happening to her?"

"Believe me, Sebastian, you don't want to know."

"Yes I do," he snapped.

Caia drew a breath, grabbing either side of her seat as he whirled them out of the parking lot. "You might want to cool it or we'll never make it to my house."

After he eased on the accelerator, Caia explained to him what she could of the images she had seen.

"And you're sure that it definitely means Jae's being-" he cut off, flinching. The thought of a sweet girl like Jaeden being subjected to anything as horrifying as torture was just too unbearable to voice out loud.

"Yes. It's not dreams. I don't know how or why I know with such certainty, but I do."

"I believe you. I wish to Artemis I didn't, but I do."

They remained in tense silence until they pulled into Lucien's driveway. Sebastian exhaled, "Dimitri and the others are back."

Caia didn't even wait for him to shut the engine off. She was out of the car and rushing towards the house with him on her heels.

He caught up to her just as she was about to open the door. His hand gripped her wrist almost painfully.

"What?" She whirled on him, trying to pull out of his grasp.

Sebastian looked pained, his eyes flicking from hers to the house. "Are you going to tell them what you saw?"

Dimitri. He would go ballistic at this kind of news.

"Oh." She heaved a sigh. "I didn't think."

They stood for a moment in silence.

"Well," Sebastian was whispering now in case of nosy lykan ears nearby, "I don't think it would be wise. It would be different if you knew where she was. I mean, they obviously didn't find her or you wouldn't have had those visions."

She nodded, her shoulders slumping. "I don't want to lie."

He seemed to understand and he drew her into a hug, his chin resting on top of her head. "No one blames you, Caia, for who you are. How many times do you have to be told?"

She didn't say anything. It wouldn't matter how many times they told her she was blameless, she would never believe that. If they had just left her in isolation none of this would have happened.

Seb's arms tightened around her and she knew before the familiar dark voice said, "Am I interrupting?" that Lucien was standing in the doorway.

She drew out of Sebastian's reluctant hold and winced. Crap. She didn't even have to be half-magik to understand Sebastian's body language. He looked Lucien straight in the eye and kept a possessive arm around Caia's shoulders. Jeez. She really had to remember to lay off touching Sebastian. It was sending him the wrong message. A little worried, for some unknown reason, she glanced up at Lucien from under her eyelashes. And immediately wanted to flinch back. He looked furious.

Sebastian's arm was abruptly shrugged off.

"I have news," she said softly. "But I don't want Dimitri to know."

Lucien's expression changed, his eyes widening in horror. "Jaeden's not-"

"No," she reassured quickly, still whispering, "But I think our time is running out."

He nodded and stepped out onto the porch with them, shutting the door behind him. He brushed past them, perhaps knocking Sebastian back deliberately, and they followed him as he wandered down into the driveway so that they were further from the house.

"Speak."

Caia drew in a breath. "I had another vision. At school."

"That's why you're both cutting class."

Trust him to notice that in the midst of a crisis. Caia waved the comment off as if she were batting at a fly. "Lucien, she's in a bad way."

"What I don't get is how you can see Jaeden," he replied, off topic as far as she was concerned.

"What?"

"Marion said you would be connected to the Midnight Coven, but Jaeden's Daylight."

Understanding dawned. Caia had already thought of that and shuddered at her theory. "I don't think the visions I had before of Jaeden in the cage came from Jaeden. I think they were from Ethan."

Silence.

"And today I think I was seeing through his eyes as he... well..."

More silence.

Caia bit her lip looking between the two males. They both had paled, forming mirror images, shoulders hunched with their arms crossed over their chests, legs apart. They still didn't say anything. Oh goddess, they were just as creeped out as she was. Maybe this had finally toppled them over the edge. Until now, there had been no *real* evidence of her connection to the Midnights. She was just a magik and really a Daylight one at that. But forming some scary mind connection to Ethan... well... it was disconcerting to say the least. "Oh!" She threw her hands up. "For goddess sakes, say something."

"Does this mean you can trace Ethan to Jaeden?"

Caia glared at Lucien. "You know if I had balls that would've really hurt."

Sebastian snorted at her uncharacteristic comment and Lucien smirked. "I'll take that as a no then."

She nodded sharply. "I don't know what Marion meant about me being able to trace Midnights but I feel nothing. I couldn't tell you where he or any other Midnight was unless they were right here with us."

Lucien nodded and then looked back at the house, his eyes narrowing against the sun. Caia's heart stumbled as she let her gaze wander over his face.

"I'm not telling Dimitri," he agreed. "They've only come back for some more supplies and are heading out into the west. Nothing so far. Telling him this would just disrupt the control he's managing to maintain during the search. An uncontrolled werewolf is not exactly my idea of a party right now."

"Especially not one like Dimitri," Sebastian added, his eyes betraying his anxiety at the thought.

"Exactly. OK." Lucien turned back, glancing at his watch. "School's out now anyway so I doubt they'll question your presence, Caia. Go inside."

She wanted to protest at his command and then rolled her eyes. He was still the Pack Leader and that would pretty much be his argument if she snapped at him. Instead she nodded, jaw clenched, and muttered goodbye to Sebastian as she slumped off towards the house. As she opened the door she turned to look back at the two wolves. They were standing facing each other, and whatever Lucien was saying was having a decided effect on the younger male. Sebastian's face paled and his shoulders drooped, his hands now hanging by his sides. About to go back and see if he was OK, Caia was stopped as a force pulled her inside the house.

"Ella?" She winced at the female's tight grip. The door slammed shut behind her.

"Not thinking of disrupting pack business were you?" Ella mused, a smile tilting her lips, although her eyes were deadly serious as she indicated the driveway with a flick of them.

"Pack business?"

"Lucien needed to speak to Sebastian about something. When your Pack Leader asks you to do something, like say coming into the house and giving him some privacy, you do it."

"You know even for a lykan your hearing is unnatural."

"Supernatural, don't you know."

Caia smirked but couldn't shake off her worry for Sebastian. Whatever was going on out there was seriously upsetting him.

"Do you understand then?" Lucien sighed, hating the look in the young male's eyes. He had always liked Sebastian and had not wanted to tell him what he'd had to today. And the news may make him hate Lucien, but that was something he was just going to have to live with.

"Why tell me?" Sebastian snapped.

"Because I don't want you to get hurt."

The boy laughed but it wasn't a happy sound. "Too late."

"I can trust you with this?"

Sebastian's gold eyes blazed at him, but he nodded, his jaw clenched so tight it looked like it would shatter. "I won't tell anyone."

"Good. You better go home."

Lucien turned to leave, but Sebastian stopped him. "She forgives you for deceiving her."

His heart slammed, and he turned back to the tawny lykan who seemed ready to kill him at any moment.

"She told me so today," he continued. And then his eyes narrowed. "She won't forgive you this, though."

Lucien cracked his neck. Artemis give him strength because, no matter how kind he was trying to be to Sebastian, the kid was really pushing his buttons. "Why?" his drawl was deceptively lazy. "Because she has feelings for *you*?"

Sebastian winced at his Alpha's mockery and he shook his head. "No. Because she has feelings for *you*."

Well that shut him up.

"And when she finds out, you'll kill those feelings. And I'll be waiting."

Lucien growled, "I think you better leave. *Now*." Sebastian nodded, gloating over the fact he had gotten the better of his Pack Leader. As he turned to get into his car, Lucien said softly, "And remember who your Alpha is, Sebastian Trey."

No matter what issues arose within the pack, respect for their leader was ingrained in their souls. It was evident in the way the light of anger dimmed reluctantly in Sebastian's eyes, and the slight deferential nod he gave as he climbed into his car.

Lucien heaved a heavy sigh, running his hand through his hair. He hoped Sebastian wouldn't take too long to get over it. The pack had enough to deal with as it was.

He wandered back into the house, dreading the return. Dimitri was almost unbearable to be around, his anger and pain so thick it was contagious, and Lucien needed to keep a level head. He found Caia in the kitchen with the others, as Aidan and Ryder packed what seemed to be the last of the supplies needed. Dimitri gulped down the dregs of his coffee and clambered off his stool. Lucien noted how Caia watched the Elder's every move, as if waiting to catch him when he finally broke.

"That's us," Dimitri said gruffly, grabbing his rucksack. "We're heading out."

Lucien merely nodded and placed a hand on Dimitri's shoulder as he passed. The Elder stopped, touched his own callused fingers to Lucien's in acknowledgement and then gruffly left. His son followed him, Aidan striding at the back of Christian. Only Ryder stayed back a moment.

He, like Lucien, was watching Caia's face. His eyes met Lucien's over the top of her head and he read what he was thinking. She was never going to stop blaming herself for Jaeden's disappearance.

"I'll watch out for Dimitri," Ryder said. He squeezed Caia's shoulder gently and she smiled at him gratefully as he passed.

Lucien nodded at him as he walked by him. "Be careful."

"Always am."

When they were gone Lucien slid into the seat across from her. "Where's my mother?"

Caia blushed. "Upstairs with Magnus."

Lucien laughed at her red cheeks. "You'll need to get used to how open we are around here?"

"It doesn't bother you?"

"It's my mother, it bothers me a little."

"Where's Marion and Saffron?"

Lucien poured some coffee for himself. "They had to report back to the Coven, but they'll be back."

"For my training?"

"Partly. Marion says you're doing fine, though."

Caia just shrugged and kept looking anywhere but at him. "Is Sebastian OK?"

"Do you want to practice with me?"

The questions were asked in unison. Lucien glowered at her question. "Sebastian's fine. Pack business."

"I was just asking."

"I was just answering."

She rolled her eyes at him and sighed. "Practice what with you?"

He smiled, trying to shake off his jealousy. "Your magik."

"What could I do?"

"Marion said you still needed to practice telekinesis."

She looked him in the eye as she sat back in her chair. Her green eyes washed over his face with a perceptiveness that made him want to squirm. But he was Alpha. So he remained cool and expressionless.

"Well, it sounds like you're getting daily reports."

He nodded. "Of course."

Dropping her gaze she fiddled with a fraying edge on Ella's tablecloth. She was quiet for so long Lucien began to worry. Had he said something wrong? Without thinking he leaned across the table and pulled her hand gently away from the thread she was pulling at and laid it palm down on the table. "What's up?" he asked drawing back. He wondered if she realized how gentle he was with her in comparison to how he acted with the rest of the pack. It had certainly come as a shock to him.

She shrugged her delicate shoulders, her hair falling across her face. "Nothing."

"*You* are a terrible liar."

"Good to know in times of war you can't bluff for shit."

He chuckled and sat back. "With great powers comes great attitude apparently."

Her lips twisted in petulance but at least she was looking at him again. "I don't think that's how the saying goes."

"I don't think a Spiderman quote counts as an actual saying."

"Pop culture reference. Ryder would be proud."

Lucien smiled but leaned towards her. "Stop avoiding my question."

She rolled her eyes again and sighed.

"You know you keep doing that and your eyeballs are going to be permanently stuck facing the wrong way."

She laughed and he relaxed at the sound. "I'm being a teenager again, aren't I?"

"You *are* a teenager."

She shuddered and sat back. "No, I'm a hybrid. There should be a difference. No rolling my eyes for a start."

"Well, I'll try not to say anything that makes you want to roll your eyes."

They smiled at each other, their gazes caught, and suddenly they were back where they had been before he had started kissing her that Saturday night. The moment seemed to stretch, twisting tighter with tension and he was a second away from launching across the table at her like some uncontrolled pubescent male when suddenly the back door flew open, leaves scuttling in with the wind.

He shot out of his chair, sending it flying behind him.

"Sorry." Caia smiled sheepishly, standing too now. "You said I could test out my telekinesis on you."

Lucien groaned and narrowed his eyes on her. "A little warning first perhaps."

That night Caia fell into bed, her emotions ripped to shreds. She had spent most of the day with Lucien, showing him what she could do so far. For hours they had stood together in the back yard as she moved things with her magik and created water from nothing. In all that time her heart had ached in panic for Jaeden, and just ached for the male standing next to her. She had never wanted to feel anything for anyone and now her heart was breaking for two lykans.

Not once did Lucien touch her, it was almost as if he was afraid to. Instead he encouraged her and smiled proudly at her accomplishments like any Pack Leader might do. When she pounded a tree branch like a spear into the thick trunk of a tree she pretended it was Ethan she was obliterating, soothed by the splintering sounds of wood and Lucien's snort. He was impressed with the speed and power she could put behind her telekinesis.

It took her what seemed like years before she fell into the blackness of sleep and as soon as she got there her mind fought to be free.

"Please," Jaeden whined, pressing her body against the back of the cage.

"How many times do I have to tell you, you mangy mutt, that begging won't get you anywhere?"

Caia had her face pressed against the cage, could hear those awful words tumbling from her mouth. But no, it couldn't be. It hadn't been her voice; it was cold and clinical and decidedly male.

"I can't breathe," Jae whimpered.

Anguished, she tried to push her arm through the bars to reach for her but her arm wouldn't move. Instead her left arm gripped a bar tightly. She looked at the hand and gasped, but no sound came out her mouth. The hand was large and elegant, but masculine.

"Well we wouldn't want that, would we?" The cruel voice taunted. "I still need you alive, after all."

His hand let go of the bar and he flicked his wrist, sending a flare up into the ceiling of the cage. It burst into beautiful light and then filtered down like golden petals. As it touched Jaeden her eyes closed, and her breathing returned to normal as she fell asleep.

"Sleep well. Tomorrow it's going to start all over again."

"NO!" Caia tried to scream and rip his body away from Jaeden, but he wouldn't move. Desperate and terrified she kept screaming for him to get away from her but not once did he even acknowledge her presence.

"Jaeden!" she screamed hoarsely.

"Caia."

"Caia."

She was being shaken all of sudden... and finally she was able to move her body. Her eyes flashed open and she was back in her room. Lucien had a hold of her, his arms gripping hers painfully. Ella stood in the doorway, fully dressed, but her hair was wild, as if she had been sleeping.

"Are you alright?" Ella came forward.

Caia blanched, embarrassed, as Lucien eased her back against her pillows. "Was I dreaming again?"

Ella glanced anxiously at her son, who met her gaze with his own concerned one. "I wouldn't call that dreaming, honey." Ella shook her head. "More like a nightmare."

"I was calling out?"

Lucien snapped his gaze back at her and for the first time she realized that he was half-dressed, his muscular torso bare and gleaming in the faint light from her bedside table. He at least wore jeans, merciful Olympus. "Calling out?" he asked hoarsely, incredulously. "Caia, you were screaming so loud and hard I nearly had a heart attack."

She bit her lip. "I'm sorry."

"What happened?" Ella pressed a comforting hand on hers.

But Caia didn't get a chance to answer as Lucien turned to his mother, towering over her. "I'll talk to, Caia. Make sure she's OK."

Ella must have read something in his gaze because she just nodded, pressing a motherly hand to his arm. "OK. I was just going over to Irini's."

"At this time?" Lucien frowned.

"She called." Ella sighed. "She's lonely and upset without Aidan. Newlyweds separated and all."

Was that admonishment in her voice? Caia frowned as Lucien tensed. "He's needed elsewhere."

"Magnus could have gone in his stead. I've been comforting him because he feels useless."

"I need him here." Lucien stood firm, obviously annoyed at having his decisions questioned by his mother.

Ella didn't reply, she just smiled at Caia and left the room quietly, closing the door after her.

Lucien blew air out between his lips and turned back to Caia. He slid down onto the side of her bed and she scrambled for some equilibrium, bringing herself into a sitting position against the headboard.

"Your nightmare?" he asked softly, his silver eyes gazing at her fiercely.

It was Caia's turn to exhale. "It was horrible. Like I was inside Ethan, hearing what he was saying and doing?"

Lucien grasped her wrist all of a sudden, his eyes blazing. "Do you know where he is?"

At that she wrestled her wrist free. Every time he asked her that she felt more than a little useless. "No," she didn't mean to snap, "I didn't."

"What did you see?"

Oh Gaia, did she want to cry right then, but she swallowed the burning lump in her throat and managed to meet his eyes, tear free. "He was sending Jaeden to sleep because she was in so much pain. But he plans to do the same thing to her tomorrow... all that... torture. He burns her, Lucien. Tears her skin with flames and gets off on her screams." A ferociousness forged into her features. "He's not just some soldier on the wrong side of a war, he's darkness and perversion, and completely devoid of a soul. Just being inside his mind is a violation." Lucien tried to shush her rant but she shook him off, her green eyes huge and pleading. "No! He's sliced into every inch of her body with fire and she bears it. When *I* should. It should be me in that cage, not Jaeden. Me!"

Lucien made a choking sound, and before she knew it she was being pulled into a tight hug, his huge arms enveloping her so that her face was pressed against his throat. Without thinking she wrapped her own small arms around his back, pressing her hands into his shoulder blades. His skin was hot, and as she brushed her cheek across it she inhaled his comforting scent of storm and damp earth. The feel of him was like silk over steel, and for the first time since she had learned of his deceit, she felt truly safe with him again.

"We'll get her back," he whispered into her hair. "We will get her back. I won't let him hurt you. I won't let him have you."

Caia's mouth fell open as she drew back to look up into his face. He wouldn't release her, though.

"Lucien?" she whispered, drinking in the pain in his eyes, wishing she could soothe it somehow. "I-"

Before she could tell him she forgave him for keeping her heritage a secret, his mouth was on hers, and it was literally as if he were kissing the life out of her, as if he could steal her very essence into himself.

And she wanted him to.

Caia gasped against his mouth as his hand slid up her waist and grazed her breast. She was rewarded with a guttural moan from him that reverberated throughout her entire body. So involved was she in his heated kiss, so desperate to forget all the pain of the last few weeks and find that sense of the peace she had felt with the pack before learning the truth, Caia was surprised to find herself on her back and Lucien braced above her. The shock of it lasted all of two seconds, his lips burning everything from her mind as they trailed tingling kisses down her neck and chest. She shivered as his work-roughened hand slid up her thigh and onto the bare skin of her stomach. Then both his hands were there, pulling her camisole up and over her head.

She lay panting underneath him, her eyes wide on his as he gazed back at her with such tenderness and lust she thought she would shatter. And then his gaze travelled lower and she remembered she wasn't wearing a bra. She should feel embarrassed shouldn't she? Instead she just shivered under his hot look, a whimper escaping her lips, a whimper he seemed to understand more than she did.

Smiling softly, his lips caught hers again and she clasped him to her, pressing his chest against her. He growled from the back of his throat and Caia erupted into flames. She could barely breathe her skin felt so hot, so tight.

"Caia," he whispered into her ear before he bit her lobe, "Caia."

He repeated her name like a mantra and it seemed so full of... love? she questioned distantly. And then she forgot the thought and anything else as he cupped her breast. She gasped again and arched into his touch and they were both lost.

"Are you sure?" he was whispering hoarsely and she knew what he was asking. For a moment she froze at the importance of what was about to happen. Could she be with him? Could she lose her virginity to Lucien? And if they did this, what did it mean for them? For the pack?

"Caia?"

His hand slid down to her hips and pressed her against him.

Oh my.

What had she been thinking again?

Did she care?

He did it again, his breath heavy and faltering.

Insistent flames licked across her skin.

She nodded, incapable of forming actual words.

Lucien was shrugging out of his jeans and pulling her pj bottoms off in almost the same motion. And when he returned to her he held her gently as she wrapped her slim legs around his waist in instinct. He kissed her deeply, intoxicatingly. He kissed her everywhere. *Everywhere.* Her eyes rolled back in her head a couple of times as her fists tightened around her bedsheets. Finally, after a forever of kisses, Lucien braced himself above her, pushing inside of her. A moment of pain dissipated into a blaze of heat that built and built, their gasps filling the night as she held onto him for dear life, unaware of the scores she made across his skin with her nails… marking him.

Eventually the sweet tension he created inside of her shattered into a million brilliant pieces.

He shuddered above her and collapsed on top of her, a heavy weight pressing her into the bed, his hot breath against her neck. After a moment, when she felt she might have to ask him to get up because she couldn't breathe, he kissed her throat and rolled off of her, only to pull her across his chest, his hand grasping hers tightly.

"Caia," he mumbled, sounding incredibly satisfied. She smiled almost smugly and his eyes cracked open in time to catch the look. He chuckled and his grip on her hand tightened. "I'm sorry. I should have taken this a little more slowly but..." Lucien laughed softly as if disbelieving. "But I can honestly say I have no control over this."

Caia was about to smile in understanding because it was exactly how she felt, but the smile was halted by a strange tingling sensation crawling up the hand he held. They both tensed.

"What the-" she tried to scramble away but he stilled her, his eyes wide on hers before returning to their hands. A moon-colored glow was spreading with slow intensity through their hands and up their arms. It settled through their entire bodies like a peaceful warmth, before melting into nothingness.

Caia had seen it before.

She ripped her hand out of Lucien's and gathered her quilt to cover her naked body.

How was that even possible?

Had they just been mated?

About to form the words and ask Lucien what was happening to them, Caia stilled at the panic in his eyes.

"Caia," it sounded like a plea, "I'm so sorry, Caia. I was going to tell you."

She stiffened. "Tell me what?" she croaked.

Lucien tried to reach for her but she flinched back, making him growl in irritation. He glared at her and sat up, pushing at his hair - his hair which she had mussed up when they had... ahem... lost control. She fumbled trying to distance herself from the look in his eye. It was now a fierce mixture of pleading and possessiveness.

"Tell me what?" she repeated.

Not taking his eyes off her, and apparently unabashed by his nakedness, Lucien stood up quite casually and pulled on his jeans. "That we're mated."

It felt like a bomb had gone off in the room and with it the bulb in her bedside lamp shattered, throwing the room into near darkness, the only available source of light cast from the bright moon outside her window. She saw Lucien frown at the lamp and then back at her, his eyebrow raised in questioning.

Yes she had broken the lamp! It really was the least of their problems at the moment, however.

"Mated?" she asked, her voice an octave higher than normal.

He sat down on the bed and she couldn't help but pull back again. Jeez, she wished she wasn't naked for this.

"Our parents asked Artemis to betroth us when we were kids. You were just a baby, a few months old, I was only seven."

"How is that possible?" Caia managed to whisper, a lump forming in her throat as she tried to process this news.

He shrugged. "Back then we weren't sure why She agreed but now we think perhaps it was because of Gaia. If you are the child from the prophecy then it stands to reason She wanted you protected. My father offered me to your father as an assurance that the pack would always protect you."

She understood now. "Because only a Pack Leader had that authority."

"Exactly."

"It's why you ran away," she mumbled, everything making so much sense now, "When you were fourteen."

"Yes," he whispered, "But I've accepted my responsibilities since then." *Responsibilities?* She jerked as if he had hit her and he noticed. "No, Caia I didn't mean-"

"Stop." She was suddenly desperate to be away from him, scrambling from the bed, tugging at the sheets to hide her body from him. "Don't."

"Caia, please let me explain-"

"Did you know? Did you know that sleeping with me would close the deal?"

He groaned edging around the bed. "Caia, no I didn't think-"

"I swear to Artemis Lucien Líder if you come any closer to me I will kill you."

Perhaps it was the quiet stillness in her voice that stopped him in his steps. It was more cutting than any shrieking female.

"Caia," she heard the trembling anger in his voice and she looked up to meet his furious gaze. The silver in his eyes shone against the moonlight and she knew she was about to commence a miniature war with the Pack Leader. "It doesn't matter now. You're my mate. End of."

She scoffed and flashed daggers at him. "I don't think so. Once again you lied to me, and there isn't even an excuse for it. Does the rest of the pack know about this?"

He shook his head. "Only the Elders, Ryder, and now Sebastian."

"Sebastian?" And then she chuckled, a hysterical little laugh. "That's what you were telling him today."

Lucien nodded. "I had to. He thinks he's in love with you."

"And what, you think this apparent mating between you and I means that he's not allowed to be?"
Well that was the button. Lucien moved so fast she barely saw him until he had her caught up in his hands, his hand cupping her neck, holding her head back as if she were an offering. "Let's get this straight," he snarled. "I don't care how angry you are with me, you are mine, Caia, and I will kill anyone who takes what's mine."

She shivered but not from the cold. "I belong to no one," she said bravely. "And I definitely don't belong to you. How could I be with someone who doesn't trust me? Who *I* can't trust?"

He pushed her away as if he was disgusted and stepped back from her. "You've had a shock, you're not thinking clearly. We'll discuss this in the morning."

Caia didn't say anything. She didn't think she could, she was on the precipice of launching herself at him, claws unleashed. Her breath fell rapidly, waiting as he silently left the room, and then she collapsed onto her bed.

How could this be? She shook her head and winced at the spot of blood on her bedclothes. Her blood.

Blinking back sudden exhaustion, Caia looked away. Tonight, he was supposed to have been her comfort, her safe place, and that's why she had given herself to him without thought, without hesitation. And the way he had looked at her, as if she were the only thing worthwhile in this world.

Lucien may have come to terms with their parents taking away their choice when they were children. He may even want her for real now. But he wanted her on his terms, and the more and more he kept things from her, important things that concerned not only the pack but this entire war, the more and more he made her feel like a pawn. And she wasn't a pawn.

With that she tore away from the bed and clambered out of her bedroom window. The change burned out her exhaustion and soothed her jangling nerves as she rushed into the woods with renewed energy. She found the clearing where she and Lucien had first played together, and stood strong gazing up at the moon, the scents of the night fluttering up her snout and spreading through her body like rightness. She knew Lucien would hear her howl but she didn't care. She trusted at least that he would leave her in peace for the moment. After howling her heart out, Caia sighed inwardly and padded around in a circle, back and forth, around and around, her mind whirling. What she needed to do was be in on finding Jaeden. She couldn't just let others do what they could while she stayed back home twiddling her thumbs like the little Mrs. *Ha!* She snorted at that, and bared her canines instinctively. *Bastard*, she whined.

No, what she needed was to find out where Ethan was, and to do that she needed to connect to him again. She glanced back through the woods towards the house. Unfortunately that meant returning to the scene of the 'crime': her bed. She needed to sleep, and she needed to hope that in her dreams, Ethan would inadvertently lead her to her friend.

24 — RESOLVE

"She sounds impressive, Marion," Vanne mused begrudgingly, his eyes flicking to his wife as if to see if she agreed. Marion waited. If anyone thought Marion was hard to impress they hadn't met her sister. Marita was the most difficult person to please in the Coven. That proved intolerable at times... considering she was the Head of it.

Sometimes Marion thanked Gaia for sending a magik with Vanne's stubborn patience to deal with her. Her gaze lingered on him for a moment too long.

Sometimes.

She looked away as Marita held her husband's gaze, the connection between them evident. Marita nodded. "Somewhat, yes."

Sighing, Marion reached for her coffee, and then eased back into the huge sofa that faced its twin on which Vanne lounged casually. As per usual Marita acted the diva queen, perched primly on a Reproduction Louis XIV chair at the head of the coffee table. Her sister's suite was an amusing clash of tastes — Vanne's rustic coziness and Marita's stern elegance.

"I said I would return to the pack as soon as I could. With Jaeden's kidnapping I'm sure Ethan's closing in. Perhaps reinforcements?" she queried casually.

Marita sniffed. "If what you say is true then surely Caia will sense the Midnight's attack before it happens. Reinforcements will be sent then. For now, we are struggling to deal with infighting in Italy over territory between the largest packs in the North, a potential rogue Daylight magik in Caithness, and we've received Intel that there is a planned attack against the Króls."

Marion's mouth fell open. "The New York Króls?"

Vanne nodded, his lips pressed thin with tension. The Króls were one of the largest vampyre covens in the United States and a highly respected, powerful member of Daylight. That the Midnights would even contemplate such a direct attack reinforced their fears that the war was picking up speed again.

"I see." She sighed wearily. "I will return with Saffron then, and continue my training with Caia, hoping for the best that her heritage pulls through in time to save the pack. I think perhaps I will-"

Marita made this humming noise at the back of her throat, a warning that she was after something. Marion stopped talking and waited for her sister to speak.

Marita smiled appreciatively. "I was just thinking."

"Yes?" she and Vanne drawled at the same time.

"Well, I understand that Caia will wish to stay with the pack until this business with her friend is concluded. However, I think it would be best for the Coven if Caia is brought back here to continue her training."

Marion shook her head. "I don't know about that, Marita. Cai-"

"Here me out," her sister interrupted impatiently. "If Caia is going to be this important in the war it stands to reason that she should be brought to the Center, where she can benefit from our best magik's training."

"What are you saying? That I am incapable of training her?"

Her sister seemed to realize her insult and actually blanched. "Goddess, no sister. I wouldn't have allowed you to be Caia's protector all this time if I hadn't thought you were capable. I merely meant that she should be with those who share her magikal abilities, and with those who are heading this damn war against the Midnights. What's the use of having a weapon at our disposal if it's not *at* our disposal?"

Vanne cleared his throat and straightened in his seat. "I agree with Marita, Marion. The girl should be brought back here."

"The girl," Marion replied between clenched teeth, "Is as much a lykan as she is a magik."

"So." Her sister shrugged. "We have plenty of lykans at the Center. And vampyres and faeries. Caia should become acquainted with her allies if she is to help lead us to victory."

Although Marion could understand her logic, it grated that her sister was happy to forget that the girl in question was exactly that - a being with thoughts and feelings, not merely a weapon at their disposal. If Marion's suspicions of Caia's magik were realized, her sister and husband better hope in Hades that Caia came down on their side of the war. Not that she sensed any darkness in Caia.

The opposite in fact, which was comforting.

However, this was not her argument against her sister's proposition. "I think you've forgotten the part where Caia is mated to Pack Errante's Alpha. I doubt he would be happy to have his mate carted across seas, out of his reach."

She smirked at their silence.

"I see you had."

If she thought that was going to stop her sister she was wrong.

"It doesn't matter." Marita shrugged. "It will be up to the girl. Explain to Caia our wishes, and explain all the benefits of her coming to us, to the Center. We won't force her-"

"You wouldn't dare," Marion drew a breath. "That would be idiotic."

Her sister snapped back as if she had been slapped. "You forget yourself."

"I do not. You may be the Head of this coven but I am still your blood and I refuse to bend to you when you spew nonsense."

She barely listened to her sister rail at her about insubordination and yaddah yaddah yaddah. Vanne yawned. As sisters, with only a year between them, they had been arguing from the crib.

"Marita," Marion cut her off mid spewing. "Calm yourself, and remember how delicate this situation with Caia is. I will return to the pack and to Caia's training and I will offer her the Center as an option. But if she refuses and wishes to stay with the pack and with Lucien, then that will be her will. With her tracing magik she can fight a war against the Midnights from any location."

Her sister glared at her, looked to her husband for support, and then turned back with a regal nod. "Fine."

Marion smiled softly and was about to reach for another sip of coffee when her sister said quietly but authoritatively, "But weave your words with persuasion little sister. I want that girl here so I can see her capabilities for myself."

Caia groaned as soon as she entered the kitchen and was appraised by Ella and Irini. Their wide eyes travelled over her body and she flinched inwardly. She had forgotten that when two lykans mated, the other's scent clung newly to their skin so that other lykans would know they had been claimed.

She reeked of Lucien.

"Morning," she mumbled, her cheeks two bright red flags as she slid into a seat at the table.

Ella cleared her throat, "I take it you know, then?"

Caia nodded and grasped for the orange juice without looking at either of them.

"Lucien told us," Irini explained quietly.

"As if he would have had to."

They didn't reply, they just let her gulp at her juice.

"He said you're angry?" Ella prodded.

Caia nodded her head in answer but refused to say anything. She almost smiled at the tendrils of frustration that whispered out of mother and daughter.

"He's already called around the rest of the pack and explained the situation."

Orange juice flew everywhere.

"He what?"

Irini shrugged. "He had to. You wouldn't believe some of the grumblings. They don't like being left out of the loop."

"What?" Caia actually laughed at that as she jumped to her feet. "*They* don't like being left out of the loop?" She shook her head at the audacity of it and strode out of the kitchen without another word. Hearing Irini's chase she flicked her hand behind her shoulder, enjoying the sound of the kitchen door slamming closed and cutting off Irini's trail.

"Ugh!" she heard Irini's shriek. "Damn her magik!"

Caia did chuckle then, grabbing her book bag and dashing out of the house. As she drove to school she managed to tame an anger that fought to rise. There was no time for anger. This morning she had awoken with one purpose, and that was to concentrate her all into saving Jaeden. Lucien needed to be tucked to the back of her brain and this whole mating fiasco thrown out of the window. She may be able to trust Lucien when it came to pack politics and maybe even this business with war, but she didn't think she could hand over her heart into his safekeeping. The truth was, after she had fallen asleep last night, she had returned into her connection with Ethan. She could feel the house he was in, Jaeden in the basement below him; she could feel his frustration and anxiety over something, and the more he paced towards the doorway of the home, the closer the fingers of her trace reached for his location. She was close to finding him, she knew it. And with that certainty came the realization that Marion was most probably right about her part in the war. Maybe not now but soon Caia was going to be a frontline soldier, and love just didn't come into that equation.

No matter how good Lucien's scent felt on her skin.

"Caia." Sebastian was at her side as soon as she stepped out of the car. He inhaled and then paled, his eyes flashing their hurt. "It's true."

Damn, she had forgotten to expect this reaction. "No, it's not."

His eyes widened and he glanced behind him to Mal and the others crowded around the SUV. By the lecherous smirk on Mal's face, and the fury on Alexa's, her scent had already drifted up wind to them and they knew the truth of what their parents had told them this morning.

"But you smell like him," Sebastian replied in confusion, his expression wounded.

"It was a mistake. And please don't look at me like that."

"But you did..." he trailed off.

Not wanting to go into the details of that with him, Caia shrugged past him, heading towards school. "Yes. I was upset OK, it just happened. I did not expect to find myself spiritually and fertilely bound to Lucien."

She sensed Sebastian's smugness before he said, "I told him you'd be mad."

"Oh yeah, you already knew right. He warned you off."

"Sounds like you're mad about that, too."

She winced at the hope in his voice. How could he still want her even after she had been with Lucien? She sighed. "I'm just mad he told you before me." Caia stopped and glared. "No, let's rephrase that. I'm mad he didn't even tell me."

"What does that mea-"

"Forget it." She blushed, realizing that none of them knew that Lucien *had* to tell her because of the whole "sex=moon=glowing hands" thing. "I don't want to talk about it. I'm trying to concentrate on getting Jaeden back."

Sebastian grabbed at her arm bringing her to a standstill again. "You have news?" he asked eagerly.

She nodded, knowing her eyes emulated the eager hope in his. "I'm getting closer. I can feel it."

"What are you planning?"

Caia didn't hesitate. "When I find her I'm going after her. And you're coming with me."

Sebastian grinned. "How are we going to do that?"

She shrugged. "If I'm the one finding her I'm in a good position to make demands. Anyway Lucien owes me this."

Before he could say anything the pack's scents hit her. She turned to watch them heading towards her and braced herself. She was grateful for Sebastian who edged closer to her, offering her comfort and reinforcement. She just had to ignore the niggling possessiveness that still lingered in his emotions.

"Well." Mal grinned as the group reached them, his eyes full of mischief and laughter. "Go, Caia. I guess I've got to be extra respectful to you now."

She narrowed her eyes at him. "What?"

"Hey, I'm not saying anything. I'm impressed. You got yours."

"I got mine?"

Sebastian growled, sensing her tone. "Back off, Mal."

He just laughed and shook his head. "You need to watch yourself there, Sebby boy. There's a difference between *protecting* the Alpha's fêmea as we all should... and *coveting* her."

"The threat of Lucien's wrath doesn't seem to bother him." Dana whistled. "How hot, Sebastian."

Caia blanched at the flush on Sebastian's cheeks. "Leave him alone."

"Well," Alexa spoke for the first time, her eyes spitting fire, "I guess we better do as she says."

The rest of the pack tittered and moved to pass them. "Whore," the word whispered from Alexa's spiteful mouth to find Caia's ears. Sebastian bristled and she had to lay a hand on his chest to stop him going after the female.

They stood in silence for a moment and then the bell for first period rang. Caia turned back to Sebastian, her eyes sad now. "I don't think I'm ever going to get used to the pack's temperament. Only yesterday Mal defended me against 'them' and now…"

Sebastian snorted, "He may be obnoxious, but he's not spiteful. He's just having fun, enjoying us squirm a little. It's Alexa and Dana I'd worry about."

"I'm not worried," she said softly. "I have no intention of taking up my position beside Lucien."

"What?" Sebastian gasped. "Are you serious?"

"I told you it's not even a discussion. All I care about is getting Jaeden back."

His eyes brightened considerably, and he smiled, trying to look nonchalant. "And after that?"

She shrugged. "I need to speak to Marion about it. I guess more training. For the war."

"Caia-"

"Please, Sebastian. I don't want to talk about it. I need to concentrate on Jaeden."

Sebastian sighed but nodded, and led her into the school. "Let me know when I should put my game face on."

Caia grinned, feeling a rush of anticipation. For the first time ever she felt in control and certain that she was capable of bringing her friend home, even if it meant facing off with Ethan. For the first time since she was told about the prophecy, she believed she actually stood a chance.

Ah, the arrogance of youth.

Ethan smirked at Lars as he railed on and on about how he would never have been so stupid as Xylena had to have walked into the hands of the Daylight Coven. *Lars*, who was twenty-five years old and could barely master a basic communication spell. Xylena had been a two hundred year old faerie who had worked her way up the ranks from peasantry to Ethan's right hand. There was no comparison between the two.

"Caia didn't detect your presence?" Ethan interrupted.

Lars shook his head quickly, sending sparkles of sweat flying from his hair. Ethan curled his lip in distaste. "No, my lord. In fact I was extremely fast in getting the information you needed. Xylena is dead and the pack now know about their missing pup."

Just what he needed. He grumbled and restrained himself from throwing something at the vainglorious idiot. "Fine. Change of plans. We don't want the pack finding us here-"

"But, my lord, I thought this was what you wanted? The pack weak and emotional over the loss of one of their own?"

"Don't. Ever. Interrupt me again," he hissed.

Lars blanched and backed up. "Forgive me."

Ethan jumped to his feet and began pacing. "Jaeden was never meant to be that kind of pawn; she was just a bonus punching bag. Now the pack is looking for her and I don't have any inside information on what's happening with Caia and her Portuguese lover." He stopped and made a clicking noise with his tongue as he thought.

After a tense few minutes he huffed and turned back to Lars. "We need to kill Caia."

"Isn't that a little hasty? We don't know for certain how things have progressed with her and the pack."

"Lucien's her mate. It's enough to send him crazy and obliterate order in the pack. We need Caia gone before they become aware of her trace magik. They'll know for certain that Caia is the-" he choked off, hating to admit it. "Is the true Head of the Coven, and that the Midnights are incredibly vulnerable with her in Daylight hands. Once she's dead we'll attack. The pack will be too grief-stricken to keep up much of a defense."

"I don't mean to question you my Lord but won't that draw the attention you specifically wished to avoid?"

"No," Ethan sneered. "Why would it? It will just be you and me taking them down."

Lars paled. "Two of us against an entire pack?"

"For Gaia's sake man, they're a tiny pack and we have everything we need to know about them from Xylena's findings. We'll sneak in after Caia's death and take them out during their mourning. They'll never see it coming."

"But won't they be expecting our attack if we kill Caia."

Ethan smirked. "I didn't say *we* were going to kill Caia."

"You ready to talk to me rationally yet?"

Caia groaned and twisted around on her bed to see Lucian leaning casually against her doorframe. "Let me see. It's been less than twenty four hours since I found out that you lied and possibly tricked me into becoming your mate. What do you think?"

His face darkened and she took some satisfaction in his anger. "Tricked you?" he seethed quietly, prowling into the room and slamming the door shut behind him.

"Uh-uh." Caia scrambled off the bed and onto her feet. She flicked her hand and the door whooshed back open.

"Getting pretty good at that," he grumbled and threw himself into her computer chair.

"Lucien, get out."

"No."

"Fine. I will," she huffed and headed towards the door. He cut her off in seconds, looming over her like a giant cliff face.

"Look, finding myself bound to a teenager is bad enough, but to a magik. Thanks." He laughed humorlessly up at the ceiling as if talking to the gods, and then he looked back down at her, glaring. "So, why don't you cut me some slack and help me deal with this."

Caia snorted and crossed her arms over her chest defensively. "Deal with this? This is how I'm going to deal with this. I am *not* binding my life to a guy – any guy – especially not some jumped up Alpha who doesn't trust me, let alone love me. How's that?"

"Caia." He looked pained as he rubbed the back of his neck, clearly uncomfortable. "I do care about you. But you have to understand this has not been the usual situation and yeah... I've screwed up."

She wanted to believe him. Gazing up into those intense silver pools, feeling his heat so close to her, Caia was dealt with unfortunately timed flashbacks from last night. A flush erupted across her skin and she cursed inwardly. Lucien's own eyes darkened having felt her heat. He made as if to move towards her and she backed up, holding her hand up, warding him off. "Whoa, stop. I know enough about a mated couple to know that the attraction thing is just part of the deal OK, but this," she gestured between the two of them, "Will not be happening again."

"Caia, you can't deny a mating."

"Doesn't it bother you? Don't you feel cheated? What if you fall in love with someone, Lucien, and you can't have a family with her?"

He shrugged. "I'm not falling in love with anyone. Neither are you for that matter because you are my mate. Mine. So deal with it."

Silence descended over the room like a thick, uncomfortable blanket.

Caia cleared her throat. "I'm not going to be your mate, Lucien. You deal with *that*."

She flinched as a snarl ripped from the back of his throat - her hair even blew back from the deep breath of his growl.

And then he was gone, slamming the door so hard the entire upper floor shook.

"Well, that could have gone better," she muttered and turned determinedly back to her bed. Time to connect to her evil uncle and see if Jae was alright.

25 – PERSONAL DAEMONS

Two days passed. Caia was growing increasingly more irritable. Two nights now and she hadn't been able to connect to Ethan in her dreams, and she was beginning to worry what that meant for Jaeden. On top of that, Lucien was thundering around the house like a lion with a thorn in his paw, refusing to look at her or to acknowledge her existence.

Jeez, you would think he was the one who had been deceived.

In fact, everyone was being pretty lousy to her, except Sebastian, and it might have had something to do with Marion and Saffron's return. They had shown up the day after Lucien had stormed out of her room. That morning had been her first edgy, downing coffee, snapping at burnt toast in frustration, morning, because she hadn't dreamt of Jaeden. It did her nerves no good to have to be sociable to her mentor, who had wandered into the quiet kitchen with a warm smile.

"Morning, Caia."

"Mmmff," she'd mumbled, chewing angrily.

"Where is everyone?" Marion had queried gently, sitting across from her, while Saffron wandered around the kitchen looking bored.

"Bed," she'd snapped.

"Oh my, we are in a good mood," Saffron had drawled behind her, but Marion held her hand up to shush her, sensing Caia's mood.

"I guess we are a little early."

Caia hadn't said anything. She just kept chewing and frowning and wondering what on earth she had done wrong last night not to have been able to connect to Ethan.

"I can feel an awful lot of tension in the house, Caia. And you smell... different... Oh." Caia had glanced up to find Marion's eyes had widened. "You and Lucien... he told you."

"You knew!" Little bits of toast and coffee had projected out with the accusation.

Marion had ahem-ed and wiped delicately at her face. "Yes, I knew."

"Always the last to know, huh? Don't know why I'm surprised. I suppose the tree knew too." She'd thumbed behind her at Saffron.

"Oh, dear Gaia, no." Saffron had appeared in front of her, her slender hands sitting defiantly on her narrow hips. "Please do not even think of imitating that idiot."

"Ryder's my friend, watch your mouth."

"Oh my." Marion had exhaled. "You're really not taking this well. I don't remember you having this much attitude."

"It's called being lied to too many damn times to count."

Marion had shooed Saffron away again and had leaned across the table, gripping one of Caia's hands comfortingly. "I know you must be upset, but it doesn't take away your choices, Caia. You're too important for that."

She had her interest. "What do you mean?"

"Yes, what *do* you mean?"

They had looked up as Lucien sauntered into the kitchen, his body language had said casual while his expression had yelled 'warning, warning!' Ella and Magnus had trailed at his back. Caia hadn't even known Magnus had stayed over. He'd smiled weakly at her but she'd looked away. She was mad at everyone.

Marion's smile hadn't faltered. "Perhaps you should all take a seat."

Hmm, Caia had thought, *this was going to be interesting.*

When they had all been seated Lucien, just as mad at Caia, had thankfully sat as far away from her as possible.

"I spoke with my sister and her husband," Marion had begun.

"And?" Ella had asked, pouring her and Magnus some coffee.

"Well." Caia might have been seeing things but Marion's smile had looked a little nervous. "Marita and Vanne are impressed with what I had to tell them about Caia, and of course very anxious that she remain safe."

"Of course." Magnus had nodded.

"They are aware of the situation with Jaeden and understand that Caia would like to stay here until its conclusion."

Lucien had drawn in a sharp breath. "I don't like the sound of where this is going."

"Caia." Marion had ignored him and Caia had happily followed suit. "Marita would like to offer you a home within our Center, where you can train with the very best in magik. Where you can train to be a soldier for Daylight but most importantly where you can really put your tracing magik to good use and help us to prevent anymore Midnight attacks."

No one had breathed. Caia hadn't been able to look at anyone but Marion - Marion who had come back and with her brought a huge gust of air, allowing Caia to breathe again.

"Really?" she'd asked, trying not to sound so excited.

"Over my dead body."

She'd closed her eyes and slumped in her chair, refusing to look at the big oaf.

What had ensued was one of those seething, quiet controlled arguments fired back and forth between Marion and Lucien, but as it had stretched and heightened their voices had started to rise, and with that Ella and Magnus joined in trying to smooth the situation over. Caia had sat there listening to the argument but not really processing the words, all she had been able to think about was how she was being given the opportunity to be somewhere where they really accepted her, and where they really needed her. Wouldn't her father have wanted her to do everything in her power to stop the Midnights after all they had done to him and the people he loved?

"...don't care. You are not dragging my mate off to be used as a weapon-"

Caia had cut him off by standing so abruptly her chair clattered hard against the island behind her. "Marion," she'd said evenly, feeling everyone's eyes on her, "You would be right that I'm not going anywhere until I get Jaeden back, so my answer right now is that I will think about it. I will really, *really* think about it." She'd smiled a real smile for the first time in days. "And thank you."

She had thought Lucien would start yelling and railing at her, but when she was met with only silence Caia had dared to look at him. And he had looked back at her as if he had never seen her before. A hurt, a deep hurt, had burned his eyes and swelled out of him to gnaw angrily at her heart. She hadn't had to look at Ella and Magnus to see their reaction because she'd felt their hurt and astonishment, too.

They all thought she was betraying them.

And so that was why everyone was treating her with icy disdain.

Sebastian had been different. He swore he just wanted her to be happy, going on and on about how even if she did go it didn't mean he couldn't come visit her. He had heard the Center was full of lykans and vampyres. Hey, maybe he could even train to be a soldier, too. Yeah. He was surprisingly chipper about the whole thing and Caia suspected it had more to do with it meaning she wouldn't be with Lucien than anything else. So now it was just the two of them against the world, and two days gone and no such luck on her mission to rescue Jaeden.

"Ignore them," Sebastian said as they sat alone in the cafeteria. He was referring to the way she kept guiltily glancing over at the others who refused to acknowledge her. She found it especially weird being confronted with Mal's *actual* anger. He had never been serious about anything in his life, but there he was glaring at her. "You know they're just being loyal to Lucien."

"I can't believe it made the rounds with the whole pack so quickly."

"Gossip travels fast among wolves."

Caia snorted and played with her food, her expression grim. "What if I can't reach her again?"

Sebastian didn't even mention her change of topic. "You will. Keep faith."

"I swear to Gaia if this has anything to do with me stressing over other things, I will be supremely pissed."

"Caia."

She looked up at him to be met with his strange, focused, tawny gaze. "I believe in you."

Those words struck her so hard they knocked the breath out of her and she had to stop herself from reaching over to touch him like she wanted to. He really had become her rock. Her frown melted into a smile and the tension eased from her body. "Then I guess I better find her quick."

Magik was exhausting.

"I think you've killed me," Caia wheezed, flopping onto the ground.

She heard Marion's soft chuckle and resisted the urge to flip her off.

After she had gotten home from school (to an empty house for the third night running) Marion had pushed Caia right back into her training, and this time it was all squadrons go. The backyard was now a battle zone where plants were either drowning or dying in ashes. For the last two hours Marion had chased Caia around the yard, throwing fire at her while she had to douse them with water or duck. The strain on her focus, and not to mention the non-stop running out of lykan form, had reduced her ribs to a tapestry of stitches.

"Was that really necessary? Ella's going to kill you for destroying her yard."

"There's nothing wrong with the yard."

"Are you kidding me?" Caia sat up and shut up just as she was about to gesture at the war zone. There was no war zone. Everything appeared just as neat and alive as it had two hours ago. She turned wide-eyed to the witch. "You did this?"

Marion nodded and strolled gracefully over to her. "Of course."

"Wow."

"You'll learn soon enough how to do it. It's called glamour."

"I see."

"No, you don't, but you will. I'm starting off with the hard stuff. We'll get to the easy stuff later."

"Glamour is easy?" Caia asked incredulously.

"Believe me, in comparison to what we've been doing for the last few hours it is."

Caia didn't reply, just gazed around in wonder at the yard as Marion folded herself in sitting position beside her.

"You know, Caia, normally I would never do an exercise such as what we've been doing this afternoon with someone so early in to their training. The fact that you not only rose to the challenge but doused ninety percent of my fire is..." She chuckled sounding amazed. "Impressive."

Caia wanted to blush. Marion was this mega magik and she was telling her that she was impressive. She listened as the witch rambled on and on about the extent of her power, what she could be capable of doing. Her abilities with trace magik for the Midnights was what really fascinated Marion, and the more and more she talked about it, the more and more Caia wanted her to be right. She needed her to be right.

After a while, the sun had fallen beneath the trees and the moon danced in the sky, Caia decided it wouldn't be rude now to take her leave and head off to bed. She was buzzing with a new found desperation to find Jaeden.

"Caia," Marion called back to her as she wandered up the back porch.

"Yes?"

"I know what you're trying to do. In your dreams."

"What about it?"

"Marita told me a little about how it feels to be connected to Daylights. She's dealing with a potential rogue magik who is in Scotland at the moment. To find him she delves into his head in her dreams like you're doing with Ethan. She told me when she's inside, it's like she's sharing his body more than his thoughts and that to tap into that part she can't just sit docile and wait."

"I don't understand."

"She said she visualizes the space she occupies inside him as a room with a door that leads to his thoughts. Some are easy and all she has to do is open the door and everything she needs floods into her. Others she spends some time kicking the door down."

Huh, Caia breathed, "You think that'll work?"

Marion shrugged, smiling apologetically. "I wouldn't know, I don't have trace magik. But I believe Marita when she says that's what she does."

Caia stood a moment, just looking at her. If what she said worked Caia was going to kill somebody. *I mean something that simple and it's been within my grasp all this time.* She wanted to huff and scream like a petulant teenager. Instead she just smiled tightly, thanked her, and headed up towards her room.

*"**Well now,**" **Ethan** breathed and she felt his excitement as he gripped the cage bars. "You seem to have recovered nicely from your wounds."*

He was rewarded with a meek whimper.

"Sounds like I've definitely broken you now, girl."

NO! Caia screamed, desperate to claw at him somehow, maybe take those evil mitts of his and rake his own damn nails down his face.

He was smiling as he bent down to the floor. Caia could see Jaeden, sitting upright, her slender arms wrapped around her knees drawn tight to her chest. She had lost so much weight, her cheekbones sharp, her blue eyes stark in her narrow face. Her eyes didn't flinch away from his, but Caia saw no emotion there either. She just stared numbly at him, like a zombie. "You know, I was going to kill you since I really have no military use for you anymore but... I think I'll just keep you as my punching bag until you die of... well... unnatural causes." He laughed and stood up and began walking away.

All the while Caia screamed and screamed trying to make him walk back so she could keep an eye on Jaeden. Finally she exhausted herself, and by then he was back in the old-fashioned sitting room, gazing at the television. Across from him was a young male magik Caia had seen once before. Unfortunately, they had never said anything interesting to one another while she had been... visiting.

Suddenly Caia remembered why she was here.

Right, right, she wanted to smack her own head. She was to visualize a room. Right... and a door. She took a deep breath, closed her eyes and did just that. A long, narrow cold room with the stench of evil, and at the end... a black door. She walked towards it, trying to stay calm. She stopped outside of it and smirked at the sign on the door - 'Ethan's Evil Brain'. Who says you can't have a sense of humor even in the darkest of times. She tried for the door handle, and not to her surprise, she found it locked. Oh yeah, Ethan was going to be a tough door to break down.

Aaaaaaaaaaaaahhhhhhhh! She threw herself with everything she had against the door but it wouldn't budge. Next her legs were flying at it. Thump thump thump – oof! Marion never mentioned that this was would actually hurt! Frustrated as all Hades Caia took a running throw at it and despite the burning pain in her ear where *she had smacked up against it, she was happy to hear the splintering of wood. She got back to her feet and stared triumphantly at the cracked middle paneling on the door. A few more beatings and the place would be hers for the taking.*

Ten minutes later Caia stepped through the door and into a world of pitiless darkness.

"Holy Artemis!" She shot up in her bed, drawing in gulps of air. Sweat ran down her forehead, had gathered under her arms and her pj's stuck to her like second skin. Her whole body ached as if she really had been throwing herself against the door. Glancing at the clock, which read 22.15, Caia hurried out of bed and into her bathroom where she did a quick clean up. No one was in the house, she couldn't feel any of them, so she threw on some jeans and a sweater, grabbed her car keys and headed outside.

She knew where Jaeden was.

She couldn't stop grinning, her heart pounding, her adrenaline rushing. She almost wanted to change.

The Ford flew smoothly into town as she headed for Lucien's store, where she knew he had been hanging out til' all hours in the night trying to avoid her. But right now he couldn't avoid her. She needed him to help her get Jaeden back to the pack.

As would be expected, the mall she had to park her car in was completely empty, except for Lucien's truck. She smirked and got out of the car, shivering at the cold night air and the five minute walk she had to Lucien's place. Woodrush Point's parking facilities really sucked.

At the opposite end of the mall lot was a narrow pathway, almost like an alley, between two stores that she would have to walk through to get onto Main Street. She glanced around very aware of being on her own and tried to shrug off a sudden blast of ice that tingled across her skin in a perverse caress.

"Stupid... wimp," she muttered as she headed across the lot.

And then she stopped.

Her ears pricked, the hair on the back of her neck rose, and her animal instincts told her to run.

By then it was too late. The ice blasted through her veins at the same time something solid crashed against her back sending her flying through the air. Sickening pain exploded through her body when she landed on the asphalt, the flesh on her hands and legs scraping off in burning tears. Her head snapped back with the impact and her front teeth jarred, rattling her brain then piercing through her bottom lip. She tasted the blood and hissed, turning over with her fast reflexes in time to watch the approach of something she had never seen the like of before.

It could have been a human except for the swirling vortex of hell that was its mouth, its mouth that had no lips, its nose that was merely two small holes in the middle of its face where smoke belched out with its excitement as it neared her. Caia's heart demanded to explode in her chest but she refused it, breathing in out, in out, as she scrambled away from it like one of those chicks in a really bad horror movie. The thing's eyes blazed at her like two white glowing orbs. It had no hair and stood at least seven feet tall, towering over her in nothing but leathers and twisted muscle for a torso. Its skin was burnt red and deadly roped.

A daemon.

Caia knew instinctively that was what it was. Ryder had come across a few in his time and he had described them in perfect detail.

Oh, I am so screwed.

She hopped to her feet, crouched low in a defensive position. "What do you want?" her voice was impressively steady considering.

The hole that was its mouth widened into what could have been a smile (it was hard to tell) and a soft eerie voice escaped it, "It's not what I want little wolf, it's what your uncle wants."

"Ethan?"

It nodded and smiled again. "Aren't you going to ask what he wants?"

Caia shook her head. There was no need to. Ryder had told her that daemons were only utilized for two purposes. Security and assassinations.

Quickly, she scanned the area trying to gauge what her best move would be. She didn't know if she could outrun this thing. She could maybe if she was in lykan form, but did she really have time for that?

No.

And then her eyes alighted on her car and she gasped, looking back and forth between it and the daemon. Could she? She'd never moved anything as large as it before.

The daemon took a step towards her. Caia threw all her energy out towards the car and it strained, the metal crunching under her pull. It stopped the daemon in its tracks.

It looked confused as it took in the crunching car that had begun squealing slowly towards them, and turned its gaze back on Caia. Seeing her concentration it stood stunned in disbelief.

"I hadn't thought it true," it grumbled that echoing voice and picked up its pace, striding towards her.

"Aaaaaaaarrrrggggh!" Caia reached out with both arms and pulled on the car with all her magik, sweat breaking out in beads across her body. The car soared into the air and came hurtling back down, knocking the daemon over like a bowling ball hitting a pin. Caia didn't hang around. She took off in the direction of the store, flinching at the deafening sound of the car crashing to the ground and rolling and rolling…

It sounded like it was rolling towards her.

"Fu-" she whipped around and stared in shock as it bounced in tumbles across the lot, still coming at her. How much power did she put into the damn thing?! "Waa-" she shrieked and dove to the side, out of its path. Lying panting in disbelief Caia watched as the Ford finally lost momentum and drew to a screeching halt on its left side.

"My car."

It was completely wrecked that was for sure.

"Don't mourn your car, little wolf."

"Aw come on!" she yelled in frightened irritation at the gods, and then turned to see the daemon sneering down at her from a few meters away.

Getting back on her feet was the toughest thing she had ever had to do.

"I'm angry now," the daemon said serenely.

"Gee, I couldn't tell."

She really couldn't.

So what was she going to do now?

Her best bet would be to turn lykan and run.

The thought hadn't even left her head when the daemon pulled out of nowhere a long, thin metal chain-link with spikes. The daemon lassoed it above its head and then, to her horror, whipped it out at her. All she was aware of was the lashing, breath-stealing pain that lanced across her stomach as the spikes ripped her open. And then she was on her back gazing at the sky numbly for a moment.

When the pain hit she couldn't help but scream, clutching at her stomach only to feel warm thick fluid coat her hands. Blinking, terrified, Caia craned her neck and sobbed at the bloody mess that was her belly.

"Don't worry," the daemon's voice carried from a distance but she couldn't see it. "It will be over soon."

No, she shook, her head falling back to the ground. She couldn't die. She had to get to Jaeden. She couldn't die.

Biting back more screams, Caia managed to turn onto her side and then over onto her knees, saliva dripping from her mouth with the effort.

"You've got heart, little wolf."

I'm going to rip your throat out.

She had no idea how she managed the next feat. All she knew was that she needed to change in order to heal, and in order take this dick out. Maybe it was her magik but the change rippled through her in a second, no crunching, no tingling, wincing pain - just one minute human, the next a wolf. The intense, ferocious pain of her belly wound was enough to make her want to pass out for relief but she mentally shook herself, forcing herself onto all fours. She took a few steps, ignoring the blood that dripped onto the ground below her as the wound tried to heal itself with her transformation.

She looked up with her sharp lykan eyes, pulled back her muzzle and growled ferociously at the daemon as it stood amazed and surprised by what it had witnessed. It was all she needed.

Ignoring her wound, Caia ran and pounced into the air, pushing her wolf until she hit the daemon, her claws piercing its burnt flesh giving her a stranglehold. The daemon didn't even have time to throw her off before she widened her jaws and sank her teeth into its jugular, tearing its neck open and dousing her mouth and fur in blood. She gagged a little at the amount that flowed down her throat and then salivated as the daemon began to struggle with her. It had a grip of her body and it punched at her wound causing her to whine in pain. Its actions only made her angrier. Aggressively she ripped and tore at its neck… until eventually the damn thing rolled right off its body and fell with a thud. She collapsed with its decapitated body onto the ground and backed up off of it, her belly weeping in agony.

Lucien. She had to get to Lucien.

Lucien didn't know what he was thinking when he had asked Marion to come to his store to discuss what she'd offered to Caia. The witch was like a brick wall and she wasn't moving.

"I've told you I can't take back my offer because it isn't my offer to take back."

He tried not to growl and instead opted for intimidating pacing. "Marion, I thought you were a friend to this pack."

"I am."

"Well, how can you possibly think about taking an Alpha's mate from him?"

Marion heaved a huge sigh and collapsed onto one of the stools that he kept in the workshop. "I told Marita all of this but I have to do what she asked Lucien and... Caia has the right to make her own decisions."

He knew that. He did. Really. He just hadn't thought that she would even contemplate leaving him, leaving the pack, once she knew how tightly bound they were. Mates did not leave each other for Gaia's sake.

But she was leaving him.

Or seriously thinking about leaving him.

Lucien shook his head. He couldn't believe it. Rage flowed through his veins as thick as the blood it rode and he clung to it desperately. It was better than allowing him to analyze just how hurt he was by her. And you could only be hurt by someone you cared about.

Right now, the last thing on earth he wanted was to care about her.

"I know you care about her, Lucien," Marion said softly and he snarled, irritated that she could read him so easily. He forgot that magiks did that. Sensed emotions. What crap.

"She's my mate," he answered coldly.

"She's more to you than just a responsibility. I'm not blind."

He flushed, wanting to hit out at something, and instead turned his back on the witch, trying to control his breathing and his anger. The last thing he needed to do was insult the sister of the Head of the Daylight Coven. Although insulting the Head of the Coven sounded like a good idea right now. Interfering wench.

"You should tell her you have feelings for her. Maybe that's all she wants."

Lucien shuddered trying to control himself and he turned back to her, deliberately infusing ice and intimidation into his gaze. "I don't want to discuss this with you. I just want you to tell your sister where to stick her invitations."

"Now Luc-"

Scratch, scrape, scratch. Lucien's ears pricked up at the eerie noise. "Ssh."

"What?" She frowned.

Lucien shushed her again and listened. There it was again. A scraping noise coming from the front of the store. He strode out of the workshop and stopped.

"What is it?" Marion whispered.

Lucien sniffed and then turned back to the magik, puzzled. "Caia?"

The scratching sounded again followed by a whine, and Lucien was racing to pull open the store's front door. He watched in silent horror as a blonde wolf limped into the store and collapsed, leaving a trail of blood in her wake.

"Oh my goddess." Marion fell at her as he stood staring numbly at the sight of his mate bleeding to death on the floor.

"Caia?" he whispered.

"It's her belly." Marion's lips trembled as she turned to look back up at him, her hands covered in Caia's blood. "She's lost a lot of blood."

The copper smell pounded his nostrils like punches knocking him out of his daze and sending his heart into palpitations.

"Caia." He threw himself down on the floor next to her and looked into green eyes that gazed up at him in fear. She whined, and he ran a comforting hand down her bloodied blonde coat, noting a strange black dried blood around her muzzle.

"What happened to her?" he choked, anger increasing the tempo of his heart.

"Now, Lucien, stay calm," Marion muttered. "Her wound is bad but it's healing as we speak." She stopped and looked up. "Saffron!"

Suddenly the faerie was in the store looking nonplussed until she took in Caia. "Oh my."

"Saffron, I need you to follow Caia's trail of blood and see if you can find out what's happened here."

The faerie nodded militantly and left quickly.

Lucien looked down at his hands now coated in Caia's blood and he clenched them into fists. "This is her uncle, isn't it?" he growled and watched Marion flinch at the sound of the lykan in his voice.

"I told you to stay calm. She needs you to stay calm while I salt the wound closed."

He nodded and stroked Caia's head. She whined again and gazed back up at him and all his anger towards her just fell away.

"Caia," he leaned down to whisper in her ear, while he continued to stroke her soothingly, "It's OK, querida. You're going to be OK."

She growled and flinched as Marion literally poured some kind of salt onto her wound and Lucien had to hold her down so she didn't snap her jaws at the witch. He hummed low in his throat to calm her and watched in amazement as the salt glowed like fire on a stick of dynamite, before it burned out, leaving a closed wound.

He frowned, realizing Caia had stilled beneath him.

"Caia." He shook her head until Marion placed a hand on his forearm.

"She's passed out. She's fine."

His heart beat ferociously. "She better be," he threatened.

Marion chuckled. "Why, just five minutes ago I thought you couldn't care less about her?"

"I didn't say that," his snarl of outrage shut her up and he guessed she realized now was not a time to tease him.

"Do you have a blanket?"

Lucien shook his head, not taking his eyes off of Caia. A blanket suddenly appeared over her small furry self.

"It's for when she comes around. She'll need to change in order to get proper rest."

Lucien choked again, not wanting to think about what Caia had just gone through and he hadn't been there to protect her. "What do you think happened?"

"Well," Marion sighed gravely, getting to her feet, "Saffron will fill us in but... I can feel something unfamiliar in her energy... "

"Unfamiliar?"

"Daemon." Saffron strode through the door, a grimace on her face. "Daemon," she repeated and then looked down thoughtfully at Caia. "Is she OK?"

"She will be. What do you mean daemon?"

Saffron eyes flicked back and forth between the two of them. "The blood led to the parking lot at the mall, where I found Caia's car obliterated and turned up on its side. It was cast in magik, Caia's magik, so I'm guessing she used it as a weapon. Smart girl."

Lucien couldn't even process that. Caia had used her car as a weapon? He looked back down at her in awe. Who was this kid? "That doesn't explain how you know it was a daemon."

"Well." Saffron actually looked gleeful. "I found a decapitated daemon several yards from the car. He had a spiked chain link coated in Caia's blood so I'm guessing that's how she got wounded.

She must have changed into lykan to heal and then literally tore his head off. I'm impressed." She chuckled. "That girl has some serious attitude."

Marion was smiling as well. Lucien wanted to hit them both. Caia had just been attacked by a fricking daemon for Gaia's sake!

"Well," Marion said briskly, catching his murderous look. "I better head out and clean up the mess. You two get Caia back to the house."

The throbbing pain in her stomach woke her up with a start. It felt like her lower belly was on fire. "Ow." She trembled, opening her eyes and reaching for where it hurt, but just as quickly as she moved, her hands were clasped tightly away from her torso.

"Caia, don't."

"Lucien?" she asked, wincing at the pain. "It hurts."

"I know, querida, I know. Marion will be back any time now, I'm sure she can take care of the pain."

"What happened?"

"You don't remember?"

Slowly, painfully, Caia peeled her eyes open. She was lying in her bed. Lucien was sitting beside her, her wrists clasped gently in his hands. He had a blood smear on his cheek and his eyes were filled with something she had never seen before.

Lucien was scared.

She tried to reach for his cheek, concerned. "You're bleeding."

He just shook his head. "Not my blood."

"Sss," she hissed, another rip of pain lancing across her stomach. "Daemon."

"You do remember."

Yeah, she remembered alright. The bastard tore her stomach open. She tried to pull at her wrists to inspect her wound but Lucien held firm.

"My stomach, Lucien," she complained, hating the fear in her voice.

"It's OK. Marion closed the wound but you're still weak from blood loss, not to mention burning a fever."

Caia slumped back against her pillows, exhausted from that little attempt at movement and in a blinding agony that rippled through all her nerve endings. She curled her toes down into the mattress her fingers mirroring the action, as if anchoring into the bed would take away the pain. "Where is Marion? I think I need drugs."

He chuckled softly, letting go of her hands and tenderly brushing her hair back from her face. She opened her eyes to gaze up at him as he bent over her, and again she was taken aback by the emotion roiling in his silver gaze and off of his body. "She'll be here soon. She's cleaning up the mess you made in the mall lot."

Of course. And it was quite a mess. The Daylight Coven would have her killed if a human happened by the dead daemon and the upturned car.

"I uh, guess you heard about the car," she whispered sheepishly.

Lucien snorted. "Heard? I saw it. Really, Caia, did you have to destroy the car I gave you? I know you're mad at me... but it was brand new."

She cracked a smile and then remembered in the pain that, yeah, she *was* supposed to be mad at him.

"Ah no." He shook his head comically. "You smiled, you can't take that back."

"It's my smile, I can do anything I want to." But she couldn't stop herself from smiling weakly again. It was nice to have him near.

Quirking an eyebrow, he shifted even closer and leaned over her. "Does that mean that you forgive me?"

"Well..." Caia groaned, "A daemon almost killed me tonight. What you did seems paltry in comparison."

She had meant it as a joke, but Lucien's eyes darkened and he drew in a sharp breath. "I nearly lost you."

Caia didn't know how to reply to that. It was the first time she had seen him so lost looking... and all because she gotten hurt. As she gazed at him, wishing she could read his mind, Lucien slowly lowered his head and pressed a soft, sweet kiss to her lips. When he pulled back the look of anguish still strained his expression.

"Hey," she cracked, wincing again at the sharpness in her wound. "No taking advantage of the patient."

"My thoughts exactly."

Marion suddenly swooped into the room and nudged a reluctant Lucien out of the way. "OK." She smiled softly at Caia, taking her by the chin gently. "Well, you gave us quite a fright young lady."

"You should see the other guy."

"Oh I did." She laughed. "Quite an impressive decapitation."

"Well, you know – aahhhh… OK, drugs would be good now."

What followed was a spell that Caia wished she had been more in the frame of mind to pay attention to. Whatever Marion was doing the room smelled thickly of...

"What is that?" Lucien asked from the corner of the room, where he now stood with a worried Ella, Irini and Magnus.

"Partly it's Malaysian Kratom. I'm using a spell to run it into Caia's blood stream. It's a natural pain killer and I've amped it up a little with some magik so that the pain should completely disappear."

"The pain is completely disappearing," Caia vouched, feeling a little loopy.

"Uh, is it making her high?" Irini asked worriedly.

"Oh no, that's just the magik. That'll wear off in a few minutes."

Marion was right. A few minutes later and Caia couldn't feel a thing. She pushed herself up into a sitting position, batting away the many arms that tried to still her movements. And then she took a deep breath and lifted her pj top to inspect her stomach. A deep diagonal slash marred her pale skin but she could see with relief that it was already healing and should be non-existent in a few days.

"How are you feeling?"

She couldn't even tell which one of them said it. Maybe all of them. As her weary eyes took in the sight of her family gazing at her in concern, she thought of the people who weren't here. "You have to call Ryder and Dimitri."

Lucien frowned and strode towards her, ignoring Marion who was trying to keep the bed clear. "Why?"

"I was coming to you for a reason, Lucien." She blinked and looked behind him at Marion and the others. "I dreamt of Jaeden and Ethan again. I know where he is."

A collective hush fell over the room.

"You're sure?" Lucien almost vibrated with excitement.

"Completely."

"Where?"

Caia shook her head. "He's about a day and a half drive from here. I can show you on a map."

He nodded sharply and pulled his cell out of his jeans. "I'll bring them home."

"Caia! Caia!"

"Sebastian?"

They all turned to hear footsteps thomping up the stairs. Lucien groaned, "Who called him?"

Irini shrugged. "He's her friend. I thought she would want him here."

It was sweet of her, but Caia really didn't want any more people worrying about her. Sebastian almost fell into the room, his eyes widening when he took her in lying on the bed. He ignored everyone else, practically shoved Lucien out of the way, and collapsed on the bed next to her. "Caia Ribeiro, I'm going to kill you," he vowed hoarsely and then dragged her into his arms for a tight hug.

They both ignored the warning growl from Lucien.

"Seb, I'm fine." Caia pulled back from him smiling. "Really."

"Irini said it was a daemon." His eyes were huge with awe. "You killed a daemon?"

"Yeah, but he got a lucky swing in," she joked again, uncomfortable with all the attention.

Sebastian drew in a sharp breath. "Let me see," he demanded and when she made no move he huffed. "Caia let me see you're OK." When again she made no move his hands went to the hem of her top as if to lift it and in two seconds he was off the bed and pinned to the wall next to it.

"Touch her again and I will kill you," Lucien snarled into his face.

"Lucien." Caia threw off her bed covers, ready to pull him off. That sent everyone into pandemonium. Marion swooped down on her tut-tutting, while Irini and Ella shouted at Lucien to let go of Sebastian. Magnus was the only one to stay calm. He strode forward and peeled Lucien off the boy without breaking a sweat.

"Overreacting much." Magnus smirked, holding him back.

Caia had to admit she was impressed with Sebastian. He just shrugged his t-shirt back into place and frowned calmly at his Pack Leader. "I only wanted to check her wound."

Lucien shook Magnus off, who came over to Caia to make sure she was OK. She nodded numbly at her uncle but kept her eyes on the two males who looked ready to battle it out. And over her. Oh goddess it was like an episode of *The Vampire Diaries*, she groaned.

"She doesn't need you checking her wound. You're not her mate."

Sebastian smirked. "Well, neither are you, apparently."

Magnus had his arms clamped across Lucien like a vice before he could swipe his claws out at the young male. Even Magnus was frowning at Sebastian now. "Show some respect you damn pup. That's your Alpha you're deliberately bating."

The smirk slipped from Sebastian's face but he still looked less than deferential. "My apologies," he bit out and then turned to look back at Caia. "Sorry if I upset you." That at least sounded more sincere.

Caia nodded. "Look, let's forget about it. I'm OK. OK? And I know where Jaeden is." She grinned and flushed at the beaming grin of appreciation and love that Sebastian threw back at her.

"I knew you would find her," he breathed reverently.

"You've seen she's alright. You - leave now," Lucien demanded in a stony voice.

The young lykan turned back to his Pack Leader and then flicked his gaze back to Caia, questioningly. She groaned inwardly. She couldn't believe Sebastian would even attempt to deny his Alpha over her. The trembling tension in Lucien's muscles and the winds of possessiveness that blew from his body told Caia all she needed to know. "I think you better go, Sebastian. Thank you for coming though."

His face fell but he nodded and with one last act of defiance, pressed a tender kiss on her forehead. "You'll be OK?" he whispered intimately.

She nodded frantically, feeling Lucien's anger building. "I will. I'll call with any news," she promised and sent him a silent message with her eyes. He would be in on the search for Jaeden too; she would make sure of it.

When he had gone, some of the tension melted from the room, but Irini and Ella looked shell-shocked and Magnus almost as angry as Lucien. Looking mildly amused on the other hand was the sedate

Marion, who was watching them attentively as if enjoying an episode of *The Jerry Springer Show*.

Magnus huffed and looked around at his pack mates. "Someone needs to teach that boy a lesson."

"Magnus, no," Caia pleaded softly. "He doesn't mean it."

Lucien snorted and turned away from her, leaving Magnus to shake his head disapprovingly at her. "Even you should know, Caia, a male that young does not disrespect his Alpha the way that pup just did. Lucien would have had every right to tear him apart."

"No," Caia grumbled. "Sebastian was just worried about me."

"Humph," Magnus huffed and then turned to hit Lucien on the shoulder. "Come on, son, let's call Dimitri and then grab a drink. Got any of the scotch I like... "

When they had left Caia looked to the females for reassurance. But they were frowning at her, too.

"You really should discourage him, Caia," Ella advised sternly.

Irini bit her lip. "I would never have called him if I knew the boy was in love with her."

"He's not in love with me."

"Humph."

"You'll have to put a stop to it."

"Oh yes, or Lucien will end up killing him."

"That would devastate Isaac, and Lucien respects him."

"Caia, please-"

"Ladies," Marion didn't shout but her voice resonated around the room with authority, cutting off Irini and Ella's little tirade of advice. "You're disturbing my patient. Please leave."

26 – ROAD TO WAR

Ryder and Dimitri must not have been far from them because Caia awoke the next morning to the sounds of shouting from downstairs. One of the voices belonged to Dimitri. As she awoke, drowsy, but thankfully still in no pain, her brain began to function and process what the argument was about. Lucien had ordered that Dimitri stay home. The useless searching he had done had driven his grief in on him and he was like a snarling, caged animal who no one could help. As far as Caia could gather, Lucien and Magnus both thought it unwise that Dimitri go with them to rescue Jaeden. His emotions would just put them all in danger.

She bolted up in bed at the sound of a scuffle and a crash. Growling was interrupted by a quiet voice and Caia felt the glow of magik descend upon the house. The scuffling stopped.

"What did you do to him?" Lucien demanded.

"I put him to sleep," Marion replied serenely. "It was in everyone's interest."

"Yeah, and what about when he wakes up?" Caia was sure that the demanding voice belonged to Christian.

"While you're gone I'll take care of him, don't worry."

"Take care of him," Christian spluttered, "What does she mean by that?"

"Marion would never hurt your father," Ryder assured him.

Caia heaved slowly up off the bed, stretching her limbs carefully and checking out her mobility. As far as her body could tell this morning there was no wound, 'daemon who?' it said, and she smiled, only now truly understanding how wonderful lykan regenerative powers were. In fact, over all, she mused, as she pulled on some clean clothes and brushed her teeth and then her hair, she was feeling rather chipper. She'd survived her first daemon attack, which was technically her uncle's first assault on her, her powers were obviously growing *and* she had found Jaeden and was about to go and rescue her. Not a bad day's work.

Her smile didn't last long.

"What do you mean I can't go?" she growled through clenched teeth, glaring at Lucien. He stood dominantly in the center of the room, the map spread across the coffee table. Ryder, Aidan, Christian and Magnus were all gathered around it, while Ella and Irini popped back and forth with refreshments. Marion and Saffron were conspicuously absent.

Caia was seething. She had just spent the last hour with Aidan downloading detailed maps of the area. A big red circle now pinpointed her uncle Ethan and Jae's position on the print out. Uh the big red circle *she* had magic-marked!

"You're not coming." Lucien shrugged casually.

OK, Caia, breathe, she told herself, making little crescent shapes on her palms with her nails from curling her fists so tight. "Yes. But why?"

Lucien sighed as if he was talking to a moron. "Um, OK, let's see. You were just attacked and should be resting in bed for one," he ticked off his reasons one finger at a time. "Uh two, I'm not going to hand you over to your uncle like a Christmas present when it's obvious he now wants to kill you. And three, you're still in training, and I'm not taking the chance that you'll blow us all up with your magik."

Caia flushed, shifting from one foot to the other. "Well... I... " she stammered and looked around at the others for back up. Every single one of them lowered their eyes. She snapped and turned her blazing green gaze on her 'mate'. "Yeah, well... you need me to take you right to the door... *jackass.*"

Lucien stiffened at the insult while the others smothered their laughs behind their hands. "I'll let that slide because you're my mate," he drawled dangerously, walking slowly towards her. He stopped inches from her so she had to crane her neck back to meet his gaze. "But don't call me a jackass again."

She refused to be intimidated. "Jackass."

Lucien narrowed his eyes and cupped a large hand around the back of her neck, holding her imperceptibly tighter. She gulped.

"We don't need you now we know which area she's in. You've gotten us close enough to find her with this." He tapped his nose with his other hand and then drew her closer as if for a kiss. "Good thing you destroyed your car so I wouldn't have to confiscate the keys," he whispered across her lips and she tried not to shiver in reaction. And then she came back to herself and pushed him away, blushing furiously. He had just provided the pack with a deliberate display of dominance and she had fallen right into it. Bastard.

"I will never forgive you for this," she whispered angrily.

Lucien shrugged nonchalantly, though she saw his eyes had darkened with emotion. "Well, I would never forgive myself if something happened to you, so I guess I'll just have to live with that."

Caia wouldn't come out of her room as the males made their preparations for their journey. Irini and Ella were making snacks, while Ryder hunted down a motel for them to stop off on the way.

"There's the *Motel En El Camino!*" she could hear Ryder shout as he walked from the office to the living room.

"That'll do," Lucien responded. "We just need a place to rest our heads for a few hours, nothing more."

Caia picked up her lamp and threw it with considerable force against the large cabinet that housed her television. It shattered with enough noise to wake the dead and she smiled, momentarily appeased at the following silence from downstairs.

"She's really pissed." Aidan chuckled.

"She was such a quiet girl when she arrived," Ryder teased.

Lucien merely grunted.

Tantrum over, she waited and waited for them to leave, but Marion arrived with Saffron, postponing their departure further.

"I'm glad I caught you. I just got back from the Center." It sounded like she was out of breath. "I'm so sorry but Marita won't allow either me or Saffron to come with you."

Caia hurried over to the door, holding her breath. Why wouldn't the Head of The Daylights help them out? They were supposed to protect everyone from Midnights, no matter what.

"Marita believes Caia is more than enough artillery for you to deal with this."

"Caia's not going." Lucien slammed that door closed.

"I didn't think she would be. I am sorry," Marion sounded genuinely anxious. "Marita doesn't want to draw attention to this. She's just as fearful of anyone finding out that Ethan isn't the Head of the Midnights as he is."

"Why?" Ryder snapped.

"Because we have no way of knowing how the Midnights will react. It could be explosive. The Center is not fully prepared for that just yet."

"It's alright, Marion," Lucien reassured her. "We weren't asking you to come anyway. We can take care of this."

"But Ethan..."

"We're going in as lykans. He won't be able to touch us with his magik."

No one said anything after that and Caia slid down the door, her heart pounding. She wanted to go with them. She needed to go. And unfortunately it wasn't just about being the one to get Jaeden back.

She couldn't bear it if something happened to Lucien and she wasn't there to help him.

"Damn him," she hissed and jumped to her feet as the car wheels spun on the gravel driveway, the noise of the engines gradually fading into the distance.

"Caia?" Ella knocked on her door.

She braced her magik against it so that no matter how hard her adoptive mother pushed, the door wouldn't budge.

"Caia, please."

"I don't want to talk to anyone."

There was a moment of silence and then the Elder sighed. "OK. But there's food downstairs if you decide you're hungry."

"OK."

As soon as Ella's footsteps disappeared, Caia was clambering out of her window and down the side of the house as quickly and as quietly as she could. Once on the ground, keeping her back pressed against the wall, she sidled ninja-style along the porch and glanced quickly into the window. The kitchen was empty. Thanking Artemis, she ran full speed into the woods and began shedding her clothes at the same time. Like the night before, Caia was able to transform momentarily into a lykan, and she whooped inwardly as she tore through the woods, ignoring spiking bracken and branches that caught on her fur. At some point she was going to have to tell Lucien about her new cool ability. Just as soon as it entered her mind she dismissed the thought, wondering if it would only alienate her further from the pack. It didn't matter she supposed. If she was going to live at the Center she wouldn't have to tell Lucien anything. Not that Marita was sounding a whole barrel of fun at the moment.

It took her only fifteen minutes going at full pelt to get to Sebastian's house. She crashed out of the woods that cornered his neighborhood when she remembered she was a wolf. Sheepishly, she cowered back, and fell down into the grass so she could gaze around at the surroundings. It looked like she was going to have to go through the backyards and hope to Artemis no one saw her.

There were a few hairy moments. Such as when she thought the first backyard was clear and made to shoot through it and under the fence into the neighboring yard. She just managed to squeeze herself back behind a garbage can when a short, squat woman trundled out the back door with a pile of laundry in her arms. As soon as the woman's back was turned Caia streaked across it and out of sight.

Two houses from Sebastian's and her coat was soaked with sweat.

"Is that a dog?"

So startled at the booming male voice that came from behind her, Caia tore off, not even pretending to hide, and jumped the six foot fence that bordered Sebastian's house. There was some commotion behind her so she scuttled to the back door scraping and whining as loudly as she could.

Caia had never been so thankful to see anybody in her life.

"Caia?" Sebastian asked in amazement, his eyes darting around and then coming back to her. "What are you doing?"

She whined again and he ushered her inside.

"My mom and dad are visiting Cera. The kids all like each other," he explained.

She whined again as if to say 'and I give a rat's ass?'

"I'll get you clothes." He nodded and hurried out of the kitchen.

Back in a flash he held a pair of jeans and a large *Killers* t-shirt. "The jeans are my mom's. I couldn't find a shirt for you, though, so you'll just have to wear mine."

Caia waited for him to leave but he just stood there with his hands jammed in his jean pockets watching her. After a moment's padding, she growled politely, and he took the hint and left.

Her change back was just as quick and again she marveled at it. It felt almost like cheating, she thought as she pulled on the clothes. Sebastian's mom's jeans were a little on the long side so she rolled them up as best she could, and pulled on Seb's shirt. It smelled of him and she wondered momentarily if he had lied about not being able to find her a shirt from his mom's closet just so she would be encased in his scent. Shaking it off as paranoia, Caia wandered through the house until she found him sitting, waiting for her in his living room.

He smirked, drinking in the sight of her and she felt his rush of pleasure at seeing her in something he owned.

"I need shoes." She distracted him.

"What size?"

"Seven."

He grinned and got up. "My mom's an eight, that'll do, right? Mom has really small feet for a tall chick."

"You call your mom, chick?" she called after him.

"Not to her face."

Once she had on sneakers and socks Caia was able to explain the entire mess to Sebastian.

When she was finished, Sebastian shook his head in disgust. "I can't believe he did that."

"Yeah, well, I should have seen it coming. He's so..."

"Obnoxious," Sebastian supplied cheerfully.

"I was going for overprotective, but obnoxious works just as well."

He grinned and then stilled, looking serious and very grown up all of a sudden. "So what's the plan?"

Caia began to pace, hoping to Gaia that Sebastian would go for it. "The guys are staying at a Motel called *Motel En El Camino*. I thought we could take your car and head out after them and meet up with them there. Once we're halfway there, they're not going to send us back, and if they try to, this time I'm pulling out the big guns."

Sebastian looked worried. "Magik?"

"Yes. If it's the only way."

"Caia, you sure you want to do this?"

Yes. Didn't he understand? Jaeden had been kidnapped because of *her* and now four of the pack's strongest young males were headed out after her. *Lucien* was headed out after her. And they didn't have the backup they needed. She wouldn't let them do this alone.

"I have to."

Sebastian nodded. "Then let's go."

"Sebastian, you don't have to. You could just give me your car."

He chuckled and shook his head. "No way are you leaving me out of the action."

27 – THE FIGHT BEFORE BATTLE

Sebastian left a note for his parents telling them he was at Caia's. He guessed once they found out the truth they would already be with Lucien, who would most probably call Ella to let her know Caia and Sebastian were with him.

The drive was quiet except for when Caia gave him directions. The closer they got, the stronger the icy pull she felt from Ethan was. What disturbed her more was the shades of familiarity that hit her every now and then as they passed a town; incoherent thoughts would reach out at her, some dark, some dismal, some mundane. But she could have pinpointed the exact location of those thoughts, told Sebastian to turn the car around and drive right up to the spot of those thoughts.

This is what Marion is talking about, she sighed, leaning her forehead against the car window. Her body was humming with connections that grew more numerous as the hours ticked by, until Caia felt like she could burst out of her skin. It scared her more than she liked and she put a plug on her emotions so that Sebastian wouldn't scent her fear and mistake its reason. She was frightened by the thought of being connected to thousands of Midnight magiks and just what it would do to her sanity once she reached full capacity.

"Are you OK?" Sebastian asked quietly, keeping his gaze straight ahead. "You know we could just turn back."

"Is that what you've been thinking for the last two hours, Seb?" she replied, trying not to be snarly. His response was tense silence. "No, I didn't think so. My bet is that you've been playing over and over in your mind Jaeden's rescue."

He smirked wryly. "You know me so well."

"I need to get her back, Sebastian. There is no going back."

He nodded and let the silence fall between them again.

They couldn't be too far behind Lucien and the others. Caia breathed in deep relief when they found the Motel the guys had said they would crash at, and sure enough Lucien's truck sat parked outside a room further down the lot.

Caia got out of the car, her heart pounding. She could hear Sebastian's beat just as erratically as hers.

"He's going to kill us," Sebastian murmured, coming around the car to stand close by her.

"Hasn't seemed to bother you before."

They walked slowly towards the room, picking up the others' scents until they were standing immediately outside room 15. The door flew open before they could even knock and Christian stood staring at them incredulously, before ushering them in without a word.

Caia blinked in the dull darkness of the large motel room with its brown faded curtains closed across all the windows. Aidan sat on one of the twin beds with a matching look of incredulity and horror on his face. Lucien and Ryder were nowhere to be seen, and Caia couldn't smell either of them nearby.

"What in the Hades are you doing here, Caia?" Aidan jumped up, pulling her further into the room as Christian shut the door. Sebastian clung closely to her and Aidan frowned, sniffing her. His eyes widened and he spluttered at Sebastian, "You didn't dare."

Just then the door banged open nearly knocking Christian on his ass. Caia gulped as Lucien strode forward, his eyes on her, blazing with undiluted fury. Her gaze swung past them to Ryder who wore a mixed look of disappointment and sympathy.

"Are you insane?" Lucien's guttural growl was so animalistic even the other guys flinched back. And then he seemed to catch the scent of the air around him and his silver eyes darkened to almost black. Caia would always be thankful for how quickly Ryder reacted, grabbing Lucien back by the arms and enlisting Christian's help to restrain him while he writhed and spat and growled, his eyes locked on Sebastian with bloodthirsty intent.

"Why do you smell like him?" Caia flinched back from the snarl. At first she was so taken aback by how uncontrolled Lucien was, truly scared of him for the first time, that she looked around at the others in incomprehension at his question. Sebastian had paled, but stood bravely tense. Caia automatically reached out to ease him by placing a comforting hand on his shoulder. It was a bad move. Lucien struggled harder and almost freed himself before Aidan joined them to hold him back.

"Caia," Ryder groaned, struggling to hold onto his friend. "He means why do you smell of Sebastian?"

Oh dear goddess, she slumped in relief, understanding now that he had misinterpreted Sebastian's scent on her. *Oh,* she flushed, embarrassed at what they were all thinking. They thought she and Sebastian had...

Well... that isn't insulting in anyway.

"Oh, for goddess sake," she snapped stepping forward, trying to be unafraid of him. "I'm wearing Sebastian's shirt that's all."

An eruption of disjointed growling followed this.

"He's asking why?" Ryder snapped, looking truly pissed at her now.

"Because I was bare ass after running wolf-style through the woods to get to his house."

Lucien snarled some more and looked more than ready to decapitate Sebastian.

Caia threw up her hands. She knew Alpha's could get pretty protective of their mates but this was just obscene, especially considering she had told him where to stick their mating. "Oh for the love of Gaia, nothing happened!" she cried. "But thanks for the swell opinion." This was directed at them all, because they had all been thinking the same thing.

Sebastian shrugged, trying to remain cool. "She's telling the truth. I wouldn't touch her without her say so."

Oh such the wrong thing to say. Caia glared at him as Lucien struggled some more. "Sebastian, maybe you should wait outside."

He nodded and then walked past the three large males not even flinching when Lucien snapped his jaws at his ear. When Sebastian was safely outside and his scent had disappeared, Caia turned to Ryder. "Will you let him go so he and I can speak?"

"I don't know if that's..."

He trailed off as Lucien began shuddering in their arms, obviously trying to control his lykan. His breathing began to even out and his eyes became more silver, although no less angry as they glared at her.

"Leave us," he demanded.

"Lucien, you won't hurt h-"

"How could you even think I would?"

"You're just not yourself right now."

"Leave us."

The others nodded and quietly left them alone in the motel room. She flinched as Lucien strode by her and began rummaging through a holdall he had with him filled with weapons and clothes. He pulled out a black shirt and threw it at her. "Change."

His stormy scent infiltrated her olfactory senses and her stomach inappropriately clenched in desire. She blushed, turning away, hoping he couldn't sense it. Holy Artemis, how could she still want him after that he-man display of outrageousness? She shouldn't put the shirt on. How dare he tell her what to do!

As if sensing her defiance, Lucien growled and repeated the command.

Um, it may be better at this point to just humor the angry, muscular lykan. Keeping her back to him, Caia drew Sebastian's shirt over her head and heard Lucien's intake of breath. She tried not to be pleased at how she affected him, but it must have been a female thing because she couldn't help but want to wag her tail in smugness. Instead she quickly threw Lucien's black shirt on which drowned her even more than Sebastian's had. Turning back to face him, he looked somewhat appeased by her obedience, but still blazing angry.

"And why are you here?" he bit out without any 'how d'ya do's'.

She braced herself for war. "To get Jaeden back. We're coming with you."

Lucien had a hold of her so quickly he gave her whiplash. "Like Hades you are."

"You can't stop me," she replied calmly.

His face crumpled, losing all anger and filling with desperation. "Caia, I can't go into this worrying about your safety."

"You need someone, a magikal someone, in there with you. And I *need* to do this."

Lucien shook her none too gently. "It is not your fault they took her."

"Yes. It. Is."

"Caia-"

"I'm not arguing this out with you, Lucien. You either let me go with you or I'll just use my magik to keep you here and go it alone."

His eyes narrowed dangerously. "You've not got that kind of power yet."

Caia tensed at the challenge and smiled humorlessly. "You wanna bet?" And with that, she drew her focus and energy carefully into seizing a hold of Lucien. He gasped as his hands dropped from her uppers arms and he was pushed back gently with an invisible force. She smiled at his surprise which seemed to infuriate him back to his senses and he made a move towards her, only to bounce back off an invisible barrier between them.

"Caia," he growled and hit at the barrier.

Her amusement faded as he walked the length of the room trying to escape the shield she had created around him. Marion had taught her this the day she had returned from the Center, and Caia had picked it up with surprising ease. But watching Lucien growl and hiss and spit in his growing failure Caia felt terrible, caging him in. She didn't want to do this to him.

The barrier disappeared and Lucien had a hold of her again. "Don't ever do that again," his hot breath rushed across her face and she closed her eyes not wanting to see any contempt in his eyes.

"Caia look at me," he demanded.

She shook her head.

"Look at me."

Slowly her eyes fluttered open. Lucien didn't look angry at her anymore. Sad. Awed. Scared.

"You're not disgusted?" she whispered.

He shook his head. "Not happy either, though."

"I don't want to do that to you, Lucien, but I will. To protect you, to protect Jaeden, I will."

She felt him tremble and knew he was trying to remain calm. He definitely didn't like not getting his own way. He let go of her and dropped down heavily onto one of the beds, his elbows braced on his knees, his head buried in his hands. "Fine," he snapped.

Caia wanted to rejoice. She had won a battle with him. She would get to be there to see Jaeden out of the clutches of her twisted uncle. She would make sure that Lucien would get home safely, too. And then she could get on with her life. "Before we get Jaeden back, we need to talk." Quietly she settled into a threadbare armchair in the corner of the room, distancing herself physically from him.

He looked up, his eyes searching. "About what?"

"Us."

He nodded and exhaled loudly. "Is this about the Center?"

"Partly."

Unnerved, Caia waited for him to say anything, but he sat their immobile, like stone, so stoic now compared to the writhing animal he had been merely fifteen minutes before.

"I think the air should be honest and clear between us before we attempt to rescue Jaeden."

"Agreed." He shifted casually so that he lay across the bed, his back pressed against the headboard. Caia looked away, hot flashbacks scoring across her eyes and bursting into goosebumps up and down her arms. *Dammit.* It was the whole mating thing, she assured herself, the attraction between them would always be there because of that.

Caia swallowed and managed to look back up at him, annoyed by the mischievous light in his eyes that told her he knew what she was thinking.

"From the beginning, here's the truth." She breathed and tried to have the courage to maintain eye contact. "I had a crush on you almost from the start. A huge, embarrassing, adolescent crush." His lips quirked up smugly and she bristled. "Enough of that."

He chuckled and shrugged. "The attraction was mutual, believe me."

Caia didn't want to hear that. She especially didn't want to feel elated at the news.

"Anyway," she tried to sound all business, "You have to think how it was for me, Lucien. I hadn't really had anyone in my life and now here was the pack. And you. I felt safe with you."

The quiet vulnerability in her voice was obvious and Lucien shifted, sitting up straighter, more alert. "Good," was his hoarse reply.

"No. Not good-"

"But-"

"Lucien, please listen," she growled and then heaved a sigh. "It wasn't good because I was really devastated when I learned about my mother and father and the Midnights. I was torn up, and not just because of the truth… but because *you*, my safe place, hid it from me."

He swung his legs off the bed now, leaning forward, his eyes full of anguish. "You said you forgave me."

"I do." She nodded quickly. "I understand why you did it. I would have done the same thing to protect the pack. But it still doesn't change the fact that my feelings for you were no longer quite the same as before. But..." she looked away embarrassed. "I was still attracted to you, still respected you, admired you. And yes, I eventually forgave you. Learning about my powers also took my mind off it, off you, for a while. But then Jaeden was taken, and when we realized she had been taken for a long time I… you can't tell me it's not my fault."

"But it isn't," he growled as he launched himself off the bed and strode towards her. He bent down before her and grasped a hold of her hand, his silver eyes pleading with her. "You have to believe that."

"I believe that you believe that. But I will always blame myself and I can't stop that. I'm sorry."

Her Alpha cursed and then sighed, tugging on her hands. "What are you trying to tell me here?"

Caia heaved another sigh. "That night... we... well..."

"Had sex," he offered bluntly.

She nodded and continued. "Yes. It was... I was scared and sad, and you were there making me feel safe again. I wanted to be with you, I want you to know that."

She felt his hands stroke her skin softly, seductively, and had to fight herself from shivering obviously.

"I want you too," was his gravelly reply.

"Don't. That's not where I'm going with this."

"Where are you going with this?"

She decided to be just as blunt with him. "Not telling me about the mating was the last straw with you, Lucien."

He tensed instantly and she caught the angry fear in his lupine gaze. "What does that mean exactly?"

"I was a pawn for my mother, for my uncle. I'm even a pawn for the Daylights, I'm not stupid. I'm their ultimate weapon. But that night I realized I was pawn for you too-"

"Caia, no-"

"Yes. I was, Lucien!" She threw him off her, standing up and pacing away from him. "You kept everything to yourself when you had months to tell me. And you didn't even have an excuse because by then you knew me. You *knew* me. And you didn't trust me. You wanted to control me like you control the pack."

"That's not even close to the truth!" he yelled, his whole body thrumming with anger. She was pushing him to his limits.

"I don't take it personally, Lucien," she replied calmly. "It's what an Alpha does. It's who he needs to be for the good of his pack. And again... I forgive you."

The tension eased from his body. "Then you will..."

Caia shook her head. "I can't be with you like that. All my life my choices have been taken away from me. Sent away from the pack. Brought back to the pack. Hidden from the truth. I won't have that choice taken from me, too. And I won't have my choice to go to the Center taken away from me either. Even though Marita wants me for Daylight ends, I can't see the wrong in that. I can protect the pack and every other Daylight creature by going to the Center and becoming the best that I can be and taking down the bastards that have stolen all my choices from me. You got to kill Adriana and avenge your father. Well I want to avenge *my* father."

"By leaving me, by leaving the pack?"

Caia nodded. "After Jaeden is home and safe, I'm leaving with Marion."

Lucien made a choking noise, his hand clenched in his hair in frustration. "Caia, do you not know what this means? This will destroy the pack as we know it. This will lead to a Lunarmorte after my death. The pack will be in disarray."

Her heart cracked a little at his argument. "Because you can't have children with anyone but me?"
She didn't need him to answer and he didn't. What had she been expecting? Of course his family line was the most important factor here! Not declarations of love. She wasn't even sure she loved him so why should he say it to her? And would it make her stay? She didn't even want to contemplate the answering *yes* that was dying to burrow its way out of the hollowness in her chest.

"I'm sorry, Lucien," her voice cracked. "I have to put the good of the all before the pack."

He snorted. "How heroic."

"Don't."

"Don't what?" His gaze pierced her with his sorrow and disgust. "You're drunk on your power and nothing else matters."

Caia flinched. How could he think that? "I guess you don't know me very well," she whispered.

Lucien chuckled, low and incredulous, and when he looked at her again his eyes were flat and emotionless. He had never looked at her like that before. "I guess I don't. But you don't have to worry about me interfering in your plans. The pack means everything to me and I won't have anything to do with someone who puts it last. I don't want a mate like you. Not ever."

A fierce, sharp pain throbbed in her chest.

After a moment of gazing at those blank eyes, Caia numbly turned from him, pulled his shirt carefully over her head and replaced it with Sebastian's discarded *Killers* t-shirt. When she turned back, Lucien remained like stone, his eyes not even flickering over her change.

"We have one thing left in common, Lucien. And that's getting Jaeden back. Can you do this one thing with me?"

He nodded sharply, militantly, and resumed his Alpha mode. "I'll call the others in."

His heart was beating ferociously and he hoped the others couldn't hear. As they sat in the motel room going over their plans Lucien almost sweat with the exertion it took to remain cool and aloof. The others were all aware of the tension in the room, of the cool politeness he was showing Caia. He could feel Ryder's worried gaze and tried to shrug off his friend's concern.

It was over.

He couldn't believe it. For most of his life he had fought the fact that his dad had taken away his choices and given him to Caia like a toy. But then his father had died and he knew he had to protect the pack at all costs, even if that meant becoming mate to a half-lykan, half-magik young girl who had no attachments in this world.

He hadn't expected to fall in love with her.

And now he hated her for being able to walk away so easily when he felt as if his world was ending.

Lucien tried to concentrate on the plans to get Jaeden back. Jaeden who was the sweetest, kindest young female in the pack; Jaeden who loved the pack, who would do anything for the pack; who had been taken because of a young half-lykan, half-magik who would sooner have glory than give a flying fuck for the pack! Jaeden deserved his concentration. She didn't deserve to be put on the back burner while his hands still itched to claw the life out of Sebastian as he stroked Caia's arm comfortingly. Was she in love with the young lykan boy? Was that why she was leaving?

"What do you think, Lucien?"

He quickly looked up at Ryder, ashamed that he didn't know what he had said. "About what?"

Ryder sighed. "A quick bite before we go?"

Oh good, he hadn't missed anything important.

"Sure." He nodded.

Jaeden, he clenched his fists. *It's all about Jaeden.*

28 – LUNARMORTE

They decided to leave Sebastian's car at the motel and take only Lucien's truck. He drove with Ryder and Aidan up front beside him. Caia sat in the truck bed with Sebastian and Christian, enjoying the wind that tangled with her hair and beat against her face. Lucien hadn't spoken a word to her that he hadn't needed to utter. Hate she could deal with. It was an emotion. It meant he cared enough to at least do that. But the blank indifference in his gaze was like a knife cutting her into pieces. She had thought she hadn't known who she was before she came back to the pack. The pain of that was nothing compared to this new self-destruction of what could have been.

"We'll get her, Caia, don't worry." Sebastian drew her into his side, misinterpreting her silence.

She glanced up at him, and then at Christian who twirled his wedding band around and around on his finger. His face was drawn and anxious, his eyes incredibly sad. He looked so exhausted.

"If we get her back," Christian suddenly spoke quietly, "It doesn't change what's happening here. What we've decided to ignore."

"What do you mean?" Sebastian whispered in confusion.

"I mean we've been happy to hide ourselves away, protected by Marion. But while we've been doing that how many other brothers and fathers and husbands have had to hunt down their loved ones... or bury them... or die dishonored because they failed those under their protection," he choked and Caia knew he was filled with as much guilt over Jaeden's predicament as she was. He looked up at Caia now, his blue eyes, so like Jaeden's, burned with determination. The tension rioted throughout the entire truck. They were all listening to Christian's words. "This isn't just about us anymore. You're the reason we even have a lead on my sister. And if we find her, Caia, if we save her, then that's because of you. You can't just let power like that go to waste." His eyes flicked towards Lucien who had visibly tensed. Caia began to wonder if the others had been eavesdropping on her and Lucien's argument. "You have to do what you can to bring the Midnights under control and end this war. Even if it means leaving the pack." *Yes they had been eavesdropping.* "I for one wouldn't blame you."

A single tear rolled down her cold cheek. "Thank you," she whispered and he nodded before turning away, closing his eyes to the wind.

So maybe she had destroyed the person she could have been for the pack. But Christian was right. Leaving the pack wouldn't take away who she was, it would just change what she was going to be... and maybe for the better for everyone.

When the icy sensation she had now come to know as Ethan's was crawling through her skin like tiny bugs, Caia made Lucien pull over. They sat on a road that ran through woodland, and like a virtual tour in her head she could see that one mile to their left, through thick trees, past a small creek and a deer that chewed casually on foliage, was a house that was built like a large shack. The house itself was L-shaped and to the rear, where they would enter from the woods, was a small porch door guarded by an energy she could now put down to being a daemon. They would be safe from the front of the house where another daemon they would have to take care of stood. Caia concentrated and walked through the back door and into the home. It was dark, stark and dismal with the distasteful residue of Midnight magik in every corner. The sitting room with its beat up sofas and broken television was empty. Caia strolled past it, checking out the two bedrooms that were also empty. Finally she turned the corner and walked into the large kitchen. The floor in the center was completely devoid of furniture, the kitchen itself consisting of plain white cupboards and counters running the outskirts of the room. But she wasn't interested in that. She turned and walked through the pantry door and to the end of that room to pull open the door that would lead her to the basement. She inhaled and could smell Jae even on her virtual tour. To her surprise the energy she recognized as Ethan's was merely residual. He wasn't home.

Coming back to herself, Caia glanced at the males who waited expectantly by the side of the truck.
"There are two daemons." She nodded. "One at the back, one at the front. We're going to enter from the back, so the daemon there will

be the trickiest to take out without alerting the other one. Ethan's not there. But Jaeden still is."

Christian drew in a breath of relief. "So all we have to do is deal with two daemons and we have Jaeden home free."

Caia nodded. "If we move quickly. I suggest that you," she gestured to Christian, "Sebastian, Aidan and Ryder all change. Lucien and I will remain in human clothes to get Jaeden out." She glanced up at Lucien to see if he agreed.

Despite looking annoyed that she had taken control, he nodded.

"Good. Now let's talk strategy... "

Once they had formulated their plans, the four males changed and Caia and Lucien began walking into the woods. They said nothing to one another, but the tension remained thick around them. Turning, as the woods whispered behind them, Caia smiled gently at the four large lykans who padded towards her, sniffing the ground as they went. Sebastian, tawny and beautiful, padded over to her, brushing his face against her leg affectionately. She patted him and ignored the ever growing coolness emanating from Lucien.

"No heroics," he said between clenched teeth. "In and out. I mean it."

"Of course."

A quarter of a mile from the house they went into stealth mode, moving so quietly no one could hear them. Hopefully, that included the daemon that they were closing in on. Caia kept checking ahead of them to make sure there still was only the two of them. Nothing had changed.

And then they were there, hiding by the trees and peering out into the clearing where the house sat, a large daemon identical to the one she had killed stood guard at the back door. She felt a tingle across her now almost completely gone scar at the thought of that bloody fight. The taste of his disgusting blood still made her want to gag.

Poor Aidan and Ryder, she winced, thinking of the plan. And just like that, Aidan sprang from her left a few yards away, and launched through the air. He landed a mere few feet from the daemon who gaped in amazement and had little time to respond before Aidan pounced again, his jaw ripping into the daemon's jugular. His brother was seconds behind him, clawing his way up the daemon's struggling body, ripping in to any part of it he could find before sinking his own teeth into the other side of its neck. The death was quiet and sickening, neither lykan willing to stop their attack until, like Caia had done, the daemon's head rolled from its body.

She let out a breath and looked at Lucien who, to her surprise, was gazing back at her. His eyes were so unreadable. She wondered what he was thinking.

"One down," she whispered and he nodded sharply, breaking from his daze. They moved silently into the backyard to meet the brothers with their muzzles glistening gorily, their ensanguined fangs still on display.

Caia waited with Lucien while the four wolves split into two and headed to either side of the building for their next attack. And then Caia and Lucien made their move. Caia opened the back porch door with magik so that it wouldn't squeak and the two of them entered the house like professional thieves. Her heart pounded the entire time, her senses feeling constantly for any change in the air that would tell her of Ethan's presence.

They heard a whine outside and Caia flinched, her wide eyes flying to Lucien. He looked worried but shook his head at her, indicating for her to continue to lead the way. And then they were in the pantry and she was opening the door that would take her to Jaeden.

The smell of Jaeden hit like a gale force wind and Lucien's snarl erupted before he could stop it. Until then only Caia had really known the extent of Jaeden's torture but her blood was thick in the air coming up from the basement, and her fear was like the stale scent of body odor.

Feeling no one of the Midnight variety down there in the dark, Caia gave up all pretense of quiet and rushed down into the blackness. Lucien was behind her. With the flashlight.

"Oh my gods..." his voice trailed off hoarsely when the light came on.

The basement was nearly the entire size of the house, completely unfurnished except for the row of five cages that decorated the bottom end of it. In the first cage they saw Jaeden curled up on her side, recognizable for her long dark hair. And in the other four cages were the remains of other supernaturals. Caia gagged and turned into Lucien without thinking. He put a comforting hand on her shoulder and started leading her towards Jae.

Why hadn't she seen this in her dreams? she thought, trying to rid herself of the images of these poor creatures and their mangled bodies. Now she was aware of their presence, the smell of death that she had always put down to Ethan's energy, was because of them.

"Jaeden," she managed not to whimper, going down on her knees and reaching through the bars to touch her friend. She got no response. "Jaeden."

"Jaeden," Lucien was saying urgently now.

Jae whimpered.

"Jaeden!" Caia cried and shook her a little.

With that her friend whimpered but turned, still curled into herself, her naked skin covered in dirt and blood and healing scar tissue. Her dead blue eyes blinked and blinked and then widened.

"Lucien? Caia?" Her voice was hoarse and cracked as if she hadn't used it in a long time.

"Yes." Caia smiled through tears, and then looked at the cage trying to find a way in. Like the dream there was no door and no lock.

"Are you really here?"

"Yes," Lucien's chocolate warm voice would have comforted anyone. "We're here. We're going to take you home."

Jae began to cry silently.

Caia pulled back and pushed Lucien back, too. "Jae, I need you to slide to the back of the cage."

The girl complied without a word.

And with all her fury and all the impotence she felt in this disgusting situation her uncle had put the people she loved in, Caia threw out an arm of energy that twisted and bent the steel of the cage until there was enough room for Jaeden to crawl out of. Lucien took his shirt off, still wearing a t-shirt underneath it, and Caia knelt down to draw it over Jaeden's head.

"You're really here." Jae's bottom lip trembled and the blankness began to recede from her eyes. "You're really here."

Caia forgot her friend's injuries and pulled her into a tight hug, not caring that Jaeden was too dazed to return it.

"Come on." Lucien bent down now and scooped Jaeden easily into his arms.

Caia really wished she hadn't been so exultant, so cocky, as she quickly followed Lucien up the basement stairs and out into the kitchen. She was smiling, actually smiling, as he made his way to kitchen door. And then she felt it. Like ice crawling slowly through her veins, freezing her in her tracks and icing over her heart so that the next frightened beat of it shattered it and all of her hope. Caia had never felt such a malevolent trace before.

From behind her she felt the blast of power like a train chugging past her at full-speed, blowing her hair up around her shoulders and face. It knocked Jaeden out of Lucien's arms and across the room, her head slamming against a cabinet. She slumped to the ground limply. Caia whirled and stood merely a few feet from her uncle.

"My goddess, you look like Adriana," he breathed, momentarily stunned.

She was stunned too. She looked like him. Had the same blonde hair and slant to her eyes.

"Uncle," she whispered. That brought him from his lapse and his dangerous blue gaze slid past her to Lucien. Without thought Caia threw up a shield around the Alpha as he took a menacing step towards her uncle. He banged against it and growled at Caia. He wasn't in lykan form. He wouldn't stand a chance against her uncle.

"Well." Ethan smirked at her. "Seems your powers are indeed blossoming."

Caia flinched as Lucien punched at the shield. "Drop it, Caia," he snarled. "Now!"

She shook her head, refusing to look at him.

"I'll let them go." Ethan smiled evilly. "All I want is you."

"Caia, don't listen to him! Drop the shield!"

Her eyes swept past them to Jaeden who was a crumpled mess, and then back to Lucien, whose eyes blazed once more with emotion. Anger. He was furious with her. And more than that he was frightened for her.

Unflinching, she turned back to her uncle as calmly as she could, chanting at her heart to quit racing and stand strong for her.

"You'll let them go? You won't go near Lucien and the pack... if I let you..."

"Kill you without a peep." Ethan chuckled. "Of course."

"Caia, NO!" Lucien bellowed, making her wince, but she steadfastly ignored him. Ethan smiled triumphantly at Lucien and a wave of his emotions hit Caia like a battering ram to the gut. She gasped and clutched her stomach, actually staggering back from the blow.

She could feel him.

Her uncle.

Her disgusting, soulless uncle.

He never planned to let anyone go. He wanted them all here. This had been his original plan before everything had gone wrong. He wanted Lucien and the others to care about her, to care so much that they would give into their volatile natures and come crashing in like stupid, easy targets. She dropped the shield protecting Lucien and Jaeden and raised her right hand, encasing Ethan in an invisible cage that circled around him with a power that travelled in golden light, before dissipating at completion.

Lucien's sigh of relief met her ears.

"Caia," he groaned and stumbled towards her just as Ethan also moved towards her, sneering at her display of power. He wasn't sneering when he bounced back against the shield, a look of disbelief on his face when he punched it and nothing happened. Satisfied but still wary, Caia kept Lucien behind her.

"So," Ethan grumbled, gazing incredulously around him. "You really *do* have some power."

When he caught her eye and saw how carefully she watched him, he shrugged, pretending indifference. "It won't hold for long." And then he began muttering something that sounded an awful lot like a spell under his breath.

Caia turned around, grabbing onto Lucien in anger. "He planned all this! For us to come here like idiots, all guns blazing, our emotions clouding us," she hissed feeling a torturous headache coming on. "I don't know how long I can hold the shield. Get Jaeden-" she stopped abruptly, her heart slamming in her chest as she felt the tingling of another trace, their energy throbbing ten seconds away from them. "Lucien, get Jaeden quickly! There's another one coming!"

He shook his head, his face twisted in anger. "I'm not leaving you."

Caia swore. "You have to. That's what he wants, for us to be stupid and emotional!"

"Caia-"

But it was too late. The trace she had felt appeared in the kitchen in the form of a tall, rangy warlock. His wild eyes took in Ethan. "My lord..." he stumbled towards him.

"Stop them, Lars!" Ethan cried, piercing one hand through Caia's wall.

Caia looked back at Lucien in a panic. "Lucien, change!"

The bolt of white heat hit him before he even had a chance to process her words and sent him soaring with incredible force straight through the pantry door, wood splintering everywhere as he collided with the floorboards.

"Lucien!" Her eyes burned with tears as he lay unconscious.

"Don't worry, he's not dead." Ethan grunted as he punched another hand through the wall. "Yet." He grinned as if they were friends, and then turned to Lars. "What are you waiting for? Kill the girl." He pointed at Jaeden.

"No," Caia whispered, and just as she felt her own building swell of white heat spring like a root from her tingling toes up her calves and over her thighs, the kitchen window flew apart and into the room as a large lykan burst through it and lunged straight for Lars's jugular. His screamed was cut off by the sickening spurt of blood that shot up out of his neck and painted the ceiling above him.

"Ryder." Caia breathed in relief as he mauled the magik to pieces within seconds.

Enraged, her uncle broke through her shield entirely and one of his own shot up around her and himself, immediately blocking Ryder out. He growled and snarled as he bounced up against the wall of energy enclosing her with her uncle.

"Not well done at all, Caia," Ethan tutted, shaking his head and prowling around her like a tiger taunting its prey. "I must say I'm horrified to hear that you feel a Midnight's trace. That you could feel my plans for you…" He chuckled but without humor, his eyes still as soulless as ever. "In fact, you're my worst fear realized. I should make this quick." He scratched his chin as if thinking, and then stopped, his gaze drifting over her body. "But I won't."

He snapped his fingers, never taking his eyes from her, and Lucien was suddenly behind him, her Alpha's arms cuffed to chains, chains that dangled him from the ceiling like meat on a hook. Ryder growled and snapped viciously, his fur trembling visibly with the frustration of not being able to get to his friend.

Ethan laughed at the horror on her face and turned to have a look at Lucien. "You know my mother died in a similar situation."

"You touch one hair on-"

"Oh please," he scoffed, "Enough with the threats you pint-sized harpy."

Caia wanted to cry looking at Lucien. He groaned, coming to, his silver eyes finding her, eliciting an involuntary noise of pain from her. She made a move towards him only to bang up against another of Ethan's shields.

"Now, now Caia," he taunted, "Be good."

"I'll kill you."

"What did I say about the threats? Hmm? And just so you know... you won't kill me. Not even close. In fact, I'm going to kill all your friends." He flicked his hand elegantly around the room and suddenly Jaeden and Lucien's heads were snapped back by invisible hands. Jaeden cried out making Caia flinch.

"Stop it," she demanded, trying to hold onto some of her cool so her brain might function enough to come up with a plan.

Ethan shook his head. "Never. Once they're gone, you and I are going to have a little show down before I go and slaughter the rest of these mangy mutts." He sighed as if he had just eaten a very satisfying meal and turned an evil eye on her. "What is that death match you idiots have...?"

Caia shuddered in offence and rage. "Lunarmorte," she supplied regally.

He grunted at her haughtiness. "That's the one. My goddess... so uncivilized. Ripping your own people apart for a title."

She snarled at him, "Isn't that what you are doing just now?"

"No!" He spat back viciously. "You're a dog polluting the gifts of Gaia!"

"I'm your niece."

"No. Your blood is nothing like mine. Blood of low-bred, vicious animals that threaten Gaia's creation, that threaten the delicate balance of our existence with mankind, runs in your veins. Lykan... vampyre. What's the difference? You are all the same. A blight on the world and a danger to humans."

A new fury, or perhaps an ancient one, flushed across Caia's skin. "We're not a danger to humans. *We* have been civilized for centuries. It's you and your Coven who endanger the world with this continual mindless war!" She fumed, surprised by her bravery considering Lucien was dangling before her like a carcass. "And you can paint it anyway you want *Uncle*... your blood still runs in my veins."

Satisfaction spread through her as his jaw clenched, his fists curled into white knots. It seemed like forever as he glared at her in disgust. She could feel Lucien's desperation building at the same time, the burning of Lars' blast spreading up his right side. She felt Ryder's control slipping and Jaeden's numbness returning, like once more she had given up, waiting for death to finally come.

No!

"You know." Ethan drew her attention again. He looked calm again. "In a way you're right. Why don't I finish with these mongrels?" He turned on the Alpha and Lucien groaned. Caia could only watch in dread as a flame shaped like a knife burst open in front of Lucien and scored across his torso slowly and painfully.

Caia began to sob, leaning against the invisible shield and gulping for breath as the smell of burning flesh hit her nose. "Stop it," she managed to plead. He ignored her, far more interested in the lykan who refused to scream for him. Tears of agony tracked Lucien's cheeks but not a syllable was uttered from between his clenched teeth.

He shrugged and turned back to her. "If I had the time I would enjoy breaking that one. But I'm far too eager to get down to a *Lunarmorte* of our very own."

Caia tried to calm her sobbing as she met Lucien's eyes. She had done this to them all. How could he look at her like that, still fearing for her, when she had done this to them all! She couldn't even get out of this damn shield to douse whatever fire Ethan produced with her water. She searched the room, looking for anything, something to help her think… and then her eyes caught the sight of the moon through the broken window and it seemed as if a rush of wind rustled down from it and into the kitchen to carry through the shield and stroke her skin. Caia blinked.

It had come through the shield.

She closed her eyes and began pushing against the energy Ethan used with her own – gold meeting ice. Wasn't it funny, she thought distantly, that he should taste like ice when he's a fire magik and I like hot gold when I'm a water magik? She pushed. Hard. Hard enough to feel a blood vessel pop above her eye. She ignore it and continued, allowing the sounds of Ryder's clawing and snapping inside her, giving her the animalistic fury of the lykan that she needed right now.

"It's not going to work, Caia," Ethan sighed. Her eyes flew open at the sound of metal clanging and she watched in abject fear as Ethan tapped a sharp long metal spike against the wall. She had no idea where it had come from.

"You should say goodbye, Caia." He let go of the spike and it danced in the air in front of him before tilting horizontally, spike head pointing towards Lucien's heart. "Say goodbye to the dog you love… before I pierce his unworthy heart."

The spike stilled directly in front of Lucien's chest, inching slowly closer. Her breath caught, her eyes locked on his. No. No. No no no no no.

"Pity you can't say goodbye to your precious pack but that just makes this all a little sweeter."

"NO!" she screamed as he pulled the spike back as if to plunge.

He turned back to look at her, his eyebrow raised questioningly. "Something to say before the end?"

She nodded and glanced back outside, feeling that white heat in her stomach, in her chest, crawl up her throat, claw her face and blow her hair back with a force. She didn't know how she must have looked, what her uncle saw in her eyes or on her body, but his mouth gaped in disbelief and his eyes blinked in fear.

"It's a full moon."

"What?" he whispered, stumbling back, and she felt the power spark like electricity between her fingers. She looked back up at him and smiled.

She breathed, "Lunarmorte."

May the best Alpha win.

The heat exploded from her, blasting out of her seeping veins, blinding her with its deep and pure white.

Her head hit something hard.

Darkness descended.

29 – SEBASTIAN

"Caia." Someone shook her and her eyes rolled back before opening. She felt exhausted. As if someone had taken all the muscles out of her body and left her limp and useless.

"What?" she croaked and tried to open her eyes.

"Caia."

"Lucien?"

"Yeah."

She opened her eyes at the same time she tried to sit up. Lucien hissed in pain as he helped her and her eyes widened on his wounds.

Ethan!

She whipped her head around to see Lars, grotesquely dead on the floor, a naked Ryder lifting Jae into his arms. His eyes found Caia and they seemed blank with shock.

Ethan was nowhere to be seen.

Her gaze fell on the spot he had stood and felt her stomach turn at the sight. Correction. Ethan was everywhere. Literally. Pulp blood and gore lay across the floor and over the counters. He was even stuck to the walls and ceiling.

"Did I?" she whispered in disbelief, her eyes finding Lucien.

He nodded, speechless.

Alive. She cried out and pressed a hand against his cheek without thinking. He was alive, she almost laughed. They were all alive. They had done it.

"We have to go." Ryder marched by them, holding Jae as if she weighed nothing. "Sebastian's badly hurt."

And like that her joy died.

Despite his pain, Lucien helped her to her feet and out of the house. Ryder waited at the edge of the woods with Jaeden and when he was assured they were behind him he began to lead them back to the truck.

"Wait, where's Seb and Aidan and Christian?" She stumbled, clutching to Lucien.

"At the truck. I told them to go on while I made sure you guys were OK."

It seemed to take forever to get there. Lucien changed to heal himself quicker and shot off ahead of them, following the scent of the others back to his truck.

Caia couldn't speak. Ryder didn't speak. But every time Jae whimpered Caia would stroke her hair.

"We're nearly there," Ryder grunted.

Caia nodded. If she could have run she would have. To get to Sebastian.

"What happened?" she managed eventually, hoping to Artemis Sebastian wasn't nearly as badly hurt as Ryder had made out.

"The daemon was tougher. Fought back even with all four of us on him. He sliced Sebastian open pretty good. Too much damage for him to change so he could heal."

Caia gagged and tried to slow her escalating heart rate. "But he'll be OK?"

His silence was heartbreaking.

Caia began to run, stumbling and cursing at her stupid muscles that had decided to give up on her just when she needed them.

Finally she burst out of the woods and slammed against the truck.

They all turned at the whine she made when her eyes caught on Sebastian. Without thinking she jumped onto the truck bed.

"Caia." Aidan tried to hold her back but she pushed at him.

"Let her," Sebastian hissed.

His stomach was packed with as much cloth as they could find around the truck but already it was drenched in his blood. Ryder was right. His wound was far more severe than Caia's had been – it wasn't just a slash across his stomach. His stomach had been ripped open.

Sebastian coughed, drawing her attention back to his face. "Come on," he cracked wheezing and shivering. "Can't be that bad."

"Everyone into the truck," Lucien demanded, having changed. Ryder slid Jaeden into the cab while he changed and now pulled her onto his lap so Aidan could sit up front with them. Christian sat beside Sebastian on the truck bed. "We've got to get to Marion.

She'll help." Lucien nodded at Sebastian and then climbed in behind the wheel.

Caia held onto that hope and slid down beside Sebastian, shifting him as gently as possible so that his head was cushioned on her lap. The truck growled to a start and pulled away, Lucien driving as fast as he was able.

"I'm so sorry," she whispered and a warm tear trickled off her face and onto his.

Sebastian looked up at her, still shuddering in her arms. "Don't," he coughed. "Don't you do that."

"Sebastian," she moaned.

He smiled and winced at the effort it took, but his tawny eyes never left hers. "I wanted to do this. And you got Jae right. We got Jae."

"We got Jae."

"She's alright?"

"Sebastian," It was Jaeden's voice and her slender, bruised arm slid through the partition from the cab to grasp a hold of Sebastian's sleeve. He rolled his eyes enough to see the top of Jaeden's head.

"Hey beautiful," he croaked.

"Thank you," she whispered and Caia couldn't look at her for fear of falling apart at the sound of grief in Jae's voice.

No. He is going to be OK. He is going to be OK. Marion will fix this.

"No..." he shuddered hard. "No problem mi amigo."

See, he's joking and teasing even now. He is going to be OK.

She clutched him tighter.

"Cy," he whispered and her eyes got caught in his again. "I love you, Cy."

"Don't," she choked on her tears. "You're going to be OK."

He smirked. "I love you anyway."

"I love you, too," she whispered.

"That's good."

A deep silence settled on the truck and Caia began to shake with exhaustion and fear.

"Like a friend, Cy?" Sebastian whispered suddenly, and then winced.

"What?"

"Love me like a friend. You?"

She nodded, unable to lie to him even now. But his eyes never dimmed. "That's enough for me."

30 – GONE

Sebastian died in Caia's arms ten minutes later. The grief thickened the air as they drove back to the pack, Lucien staring blankly ahead at the road, while Ryder soothed a crying Jaeden, who was mourning more the loss of her friend than her innocence. Caia hummed softly, stroking Sebastian's hair, her throat thick and burning with unshed tears.

She had failed him. He loved her and she had failed him.

But she wouldn't fail the rest of the pack.

31 – THE DECISION

"They're all gone."

Sitting on her bed, Caia twisted around at Marion's words, watching as the witch walked slowly into the room. She stopped, grasping a post of the bed. Caia tucked the picture of her father beneath her bed covers so Marion wouldn't realize the full extent of her maudlin musings.

Her mentor's eyes were gentle with understanding and Caia wanted to turn away from that sympathy.

It had been a week since Sebastian's death.

With the elation of having Jaeden home came the crashing disbelief that Seb was gone.

What was worse was that no one blamed her.

She was the hero who had led them to Jaeden in the first place. Who had taken down the 'Head' of the Midnight Coven.

No one blamed her but... it seemed like it was more out of fear of her than anything else.

Lucien's home had been filled with members of the pack ever since their return and a suffocating mixture of awe and grief had wrapped around the home like a cloak. Having cried herself to sleep the night they arrived back, and then cried herself boneless the next day, Caia was numb. She had woken up every morning since, afraid to open her eyes, determined that if she lay there long enough with them closed tightly shut that it would all go away, it would all be a bad dream and that Sebastian would knock on her door any second.

But it wasn't a bad dream.

And she would never see his smile again.

Somehow she had managed to go to Sebastian's funeral but she hadn't been able to meet Isaac or Imogen's gaze... or anyone's for that matter. The only person she had even looked at was Jae, and that was only to make sure she was OK. Her friend was a former shadow of herself. Caia had never understood that expression until now. Jae stood apart from everyone, following her family a few spaces behind, despite their determination to keep her close. But she was haunted by what had happened to her and by the looks of it, that wasn't going to change any time soon.

And now everyone had gone home. Was it wrong she was relieved?

"I heard," she managed.

Marion sighed and came around the bed to sit beside her, both of them staring out the window.

"Happy Birthday."

Caia blinked. It wasn't a cause for celebration today. So what? She was a year older and one friend down. She hated to think what the next months would bring.

Marion understood her silence and changed the subject. "Marita and Vanne have been told. Their spies tell them that the Midnight Coven is in chaos."

Caia nodded numbly.

"I hate to ask but... do you feel anything?"

Every day. The hum of connection had been growing stronger and stronger, and, Caia believed, ironically, that her grief had been keeping it compressed and easy to handle.

"Yes. I already knew the Coven was in chaos. Attacks have stopped. The major players are convened at their headquarters in Moscow, trying to work out where Ethan is, if he's dead or not. A few ambitious ones are pretending that they have the trace magik."

"The headquarters are in Moscow? We thought they were in Minsk... sneaky..."

Caia smiled humorlessly.

Marion grinned back at her. "I can't believe this. I can't believe we have you. This... is the beginning of the end."

Caia didn't say anything but Marion must have detected her flinch.

"What?"

The truth was Caia was sure something was wrong with her trace. For days now she had been sensing thoughts in her trace that baffled her. It would seem there were Midnights apathetic to the war, some oblivious, some afraid, others weary, and even those who had no such hatred for other Supernaturals as she had been brought up to believe. It couldn't be right, could it?

"Caia?" Marion urged.

No, she wouldn't reveal her worries to Marion or anyone, not until she had a handle on it herself. For now, she would carry on in the capacity of advisor to the Daylights, as Marita wished.

She shrugged. "The attacks will start again. They're already panicking. Things will get out of control and I don't know if I will be able to help everyone when they do."

Marion laid a comforting hand on her shoulder. "You do what you can. That's all anyone can ask. You have it in you, Caia. For Gaia's sake, you obliterated Ethan."

Caia snorted, "Any theories on how I did that yet?"

Marion shook her head. "No, but my sister is definitely going to be taking a more avid interest in you. She feels… well… responsible for what happened. I think she was testing you… but she admits that was a mistake. Someone more experienced from the Center should have been in there with you, considering you were dealing with Ethan. She wants to make up for that error."

Silence. And then…

"I can't leave them here unprotected."

Caia knew when the magik understood what she meant because she stiffened and her hand dropped from her shoulder. "You're not leaving the pack are you? You're not coming to the Center with me."

"I can't."

"Is this because of Sebastian?"

Heaving herself off the bed, Caia approached the window and looked up at the moon. "It's about my father."

"I don't understand."

"My father did everything he could think of to protect me, and so did Lucien's. Since I came back I've caused the kidnapping and torture of one friend, the death of another, and the attack of the Pack Leader."

"None of that was your fault."

Caia shrugged, refusing to look at her. "It doesn't matter if it is or isn't. I can't turn my back on them now. They have to come first. I have to be here in case anything happens. And I can do my job for your sister just as well from here as I would have at the Center."

"But the Center will offer you training, and a chance to mingle with other supernaturals within Daylight."

"It doesn't matter. The pack matters. My father's pack matters."

"Your pack."

Caia drew in a breath and whirled around to see Lucien standing in the doorway, his silver eyes as tired as they had been all week. Tired and sad and dishonored. That's how he felt. As if he had failed in his duty somehow. She wanted to slap him across his thick head, and then hug him until he was the same old arrogant Lucien again.

Eventually Marion broke their tension-filled gaze. "Well, I can see your mind is made up. I'll leave in the morning to let Marita know of the situation."

"But you'll be back?" Caia asked softly.

Marion nodded and smiled. "Of course. I'll be your liaison."

After a nod of understanding, Marion left the room as gracefully as she had entered it. Lucien closed the door behind her and took a few more steps inside.

"So you're staying?"

"If that's OK?"

Lucien nodded. "I heard what you said. I understand it. But, Caia, Christian was right before... back in the truck... after the motel. He was right about ending this war being more important. I was wrong."

She knew it must have taken a lot for him to admit that, and she smiled gratefully. "I can still do that. From here."

He nodded again and then looked away, seeming uncomfortable. He cleared his throat before looking back up at her, his silver gaze intense and unmoving. "What I said before... I meant it. I won't interfere with your choices any longer."

"Not mates?" she breathed, hating that her heart ached at the thought.

"Not mates." He shrugged and sighed. "Maybe after I die, the pack will be ready for a change anyway. We Líder's have been hogging the title for a couple of centuries too long I think."

Caia looked away from him, not wanting him to see how upset she was. After what happened to Sebastian, she was beginning to realize she had made a mistake. Yeah, the idea of being his mate, his wife, still terrified the Hades out of her little eighteen year old ass, but they wouldn't have had to have kids right away and... Lucien could have held her every night as she tried to compress her connection to the Midnights into something manageable.

But that wasn't going to happen.

"I'll help you," Lucien suddenly said, dragging her gaze back to him. "I owe you for Jaeden and me... I want to help. Whatever I can do."

She nodded. "I'll probably be co-coordinating with the Coven to prevent any future attacks I see coming. I could use some help with that."

He smiled softly, looking a little younger than he had been these last few days. "No problem. You don't have to do this business by yourself."

She laughed hoarsely and flopped down onto the bed. "So you'll be like my business partner?"

He snorted and jammed his hands into his pockets looking like a little boy. "After what I saw you do... more like your lackey."

Caia chuckled. "I wish I could have seen it, but I can't remember."

"It was amazing," Lucien whispered reverently.

"It was revolting."

He grinned and nodded. "That too."

A howl ripped through the air.

Caia gazed out of her window. "Ella?"

"She's taking it pretty hard."

"There's more to come." Caia turned back to him and caught his gaze. "Are you ready?"

Epilogue – Jaeden

Jaeden's heart beat normally as soon as the bus pulled away from the stop. She held onto her backpack like a life jacket as the Woodrush Point gradually fell away into the distance and she could close her eyes for a moment's peace.

How had it come to this? That she, Jaeden Rodriguez, who had lived for nothing more than her pack, could only breathe again now that they were safely behind her.

Sebastian's funeral had been her final goodbye to a friend who had risked everything to get her to safety. To her it was a risk he took and lost. Because the pack hadn't rescued Jaeden Rodriguez. They had rescued Jaeden, broken and hollow, who could suddenly move things with her mind whenever she wanted to.

Two days ago when she had returned from her first run as a lykan in weeks, her emotions had been so on the surface, that before she knew what was happening, items in her room were flying all over the place. She touched her lip absently. It was split but healing. Courtesy of a book that had flown off her bookshelf.

So now she was not only broken and hollow Jaeden who didn't know how to be around the pack anymore, she was weird, tortured Jaeden who had come home less of a lykan because she had some terrible psychic abilities.

So this was better.

Some clothes, stolen money, and her Kindle were tucked into her backpack.

Leaving the pack was the right thing to do. One more agonizingly disappointed look from her father when she didn't react to one of his jokes like his pre-torture Jaeden would have, was going to send her over the edge.

Jaeden was jolted awake when the bus stopped. She yawned, looking out the windows at the city. She must have been asleep a good few hours. More passengers climbed on board and she kept her gaze locked in the opposite direction, praying someone wouldn't ask-

"Can I sit here?"

She tried not to groan, jerking her head up reluctantly. Her eyes immediately widened at the sight of the tall, pale young man that smiled down at her. His eyes were beautiful, almost black, his smile full of wickedness. He had a strong, athletic build and carried himself with a confidence beyond his years. She noted he let her see his elongated incisors. He must smell what she was.

"Sure," she said softly and the vampyre slid gracefully in beside her.

"I'm Reuben." He held out his right hand and Jaeden noted the silver thumb ring. She looked up at him as they shook, his cool skin pressed against her warmth. "What's your name lone wolf?"

Jae cracked her first real smile in a long time. "You can call me, Jae."

He nodded and looked her over like she was meal. He bit his lip ring and then sighed. "So where are you headed, Jae?"

She shrugged. "Somewhere with action."

He perked up. "Yeah? What kind of action?"

She smiled. "I don't know. Maybe you know of something." Was she flirting with the vampyre?

Reuben chuckled appreciatively. "Well, you look like someone who could use a good punch bag. I know a whole bunch of those where I'm going."

"Punch bags?"

His expression grew serious. "Predators that need to be stopped."

Jaeden's heart began to pound. This was it. This was exactly what she needed.

"You action?" His dark eyes drank her in.

She didn't need to be asked twice. "I'm action."

THE END

For more information about The Tale of Lunarmorte universe head on over to the Official Blog at
http://theworldoflunarmorte.blogspot.com

ABOUT THE AUTHOR

New York Times and USA Today bestselling author, Samantha Young, is a 26 year old writer from Stirlingshire, Scotland. After graduating from the university of Edinburgh, Samantha returned to Stirlingshire where she happily spends her days writing about people she's keen for others to meet, and worlds she's dying for them to visit. Having written over ten young adult urban fantasy novels, Samantha took the big plunge into adult contemporary romance with her novel 'On Dublin Street'. 'On Dublin Street' is a #1 National Bestseller and has been re-published by NAL(Penguin US).

For more info on Samantha's adult fiction visit
http://www.ondublinstreet.com

For info on her young adult fiction visit
www.samanthayoungbooks.com

Printed in Poland
by Amazon Fulfillment
Poland Sp. z o.o., Wrocław